Wilhelm
Das

Wilhelm Matthießen wurde 1891 in Gmünd geboren. Er studierte Philosophie und schrieb schon früh Beiträge für Zeitungen, bald Romane für Erwachsene und schließlich Kinderbücher, die schnell zu großem Erfolg führten. »Das Rote U« war neben Erich Kästners »Emil und die Detektive« die meistgelesene Detektivgeschichte der 30er Jahre. Trotz seiner umstrittenen Haltung im Nationalsozialismus sind seine Kinderbücher auch heute noch beliebt. Wilhelm Matthießen starb 1965.

Wilhelm Matthießen

Das Rote U

Eine Detektivgeschichte

Mit Illustrationen von Fritz Loehr

Deutscher Taschenbuch Verlag

Das gesamte lieferbare Programm von
dtv junior und viele andere Informationen
finden sich unter www.dtvjunior.de

»Das Rote U« erschien erstmals 1932 im
Hermann Schaffstein Verlag.
Leicht überarbeiteter Text
auf der Grundlage der Ausgabe von 1932
5. Auflage 2013
2008 Deutscher Taschenbuch Verlag GmbH & Co. KG,
München
© 1985 für die Taschenbuchausgabe:
Deutscher Taschenbuch Verlag GmbH & Co. KG, München
Umschlagkonzept: Balk & Brumshagen
Umschlagbild: Ingrid Kellner
nach einer Zeichnung von Fritz Loehr
Gesetzt aus der Baskerville 11/13·
Gesamtherstellung: CPI – Ebner & Spiegel, Ulm
Gedruckt auf säurefreiem, chlorfrei gebleichtem Papier
Printed in Germany · ISBN 978-3-423-71270-5

Inhalt

Der geheimnisvolle Brief 7

Die Villa Jück 26

Eine merkwürdige Namenstagsfeier 43

Von Kaninchenräubern und
   einer schweren Aufgabe 66

Ein sonderbares Schuljubiläum 91

Die Detektive 110

Ein Junge ist verschwunden 134

Das Rote U 165

Der geheimnisvolle Brief

Woher ich diese Geschichte oder diese Geschichten weiß? Ausgedacht habe ich sie mir gewiss nicht. Wer könnte sich überhaupt so etwas ausdenken? Nein, das alles hat mir der Herr Behrmann erzählt. Und nun wollt ihr natürlich gleich wissen, wer der Herr Behrmann ist. Aber da müsst ihr noch ein bisschen Geduld haben. Immer hübsch eines nach dem andern. Und ihr werdet den Herrn Behrmann schon kennenlernen. Vorläufig ist er ein paar Tage bei mir zu Besuch. Und manchmal kommt er dann in meine Stube, wo ich am Schreiben bin, seine kurze Pfeife qualmt und ich reiche ihm die letzten Seiten, die ich geschrieben habe.

»Hier, lies mal, Behrmann, ob da auch alles richtig ist.«

Ja, und dann nimmt Herr Behrmann die Blätter, liest und raucht dabei. Ein Blatt nach dem andern legt er wieder hin, nickt nur und sagt nichts. Das ist mir auch das Liebste. Denn dann weiß ich, dass alles seine Richtigkeit hat, was ich geschrieben habe. Aber oft sagt er auch: »Du, diese Seite schreib lieber noch einmal! Denn die Sache war doch so und so! Ich habe dir doch alles genau erzählt! Dass ihr Dichter auch immer was dazuerfinden müsst!«

Und dann erzählt er's mir noch einmal. Ja, und dann sehe ich, dass das, was der Herr Behrmann erzählt, der doch wirklich dabei gewesen ist, wirklich viel schöner ist als das, was ich dazugeschrieben habe. Ich hab es mir dann auch ganz abgewöhnt, das Drumherumerzählen. Und Herr Behrmann ist bald ganz zufrieden gewesen. Aber wie ich nun alles so genau aufgeschrieben habe, da hatte ich natürlich auch die Stadt genannt, in der die Sache geschehen ist. Aber das war nun dem Herrn Behrmann wieder nicht recht.

»Nein, das musst du auslassen«, sagte er, »denn was denkst du wohl – die Schulkinder dort würden vor Stolz ja platzen, und weiß Gott, vielleicht kämen die Leute her und machten aus der wunderbaren alten Schule ein Museum oder so was ... Jetzt aber weiß eigentlich noch kein Mensch, nur die Schulkinder und die Lehrer dort, dass es diese alte Schule überhaupt gibt, und die sagen's gewiss nicht weiter, die sind froh, dass sie diese Schule haben ...«

Ja, es stimmt schon: Das ist die schönste alte Schule, die jemals in einer großen Stadt am Rhein gewesen ist, und dazu in einer ganz neumodischen Stadt. Freilich hat die Schule in der Altstadt gelegen, und weil diese Altstadt gar nicht so berühmt war wie andere, ist auch so leicht kein Fremder hingekommen. Diese Altstadt gehörte ganz den Leuten, die dort wohnten, und den Kindern. Und die Schule war nun mal ganz und gar Eigentum der Kinder. Früher, schon länger als hundert Jahre ist es her, da war die Schule, oder wenigstens ein Teil von ihr, ein Kloster. Im Turnsaal sieht man noch heute an der Decke Bilder vom heiligen Antonius, wie er den Fischen predigt, und kletterst du an der mittleren Kletterstange bis oben hinauf, dann sperrt gerade über dir ein mächtiger Haifisch das Maul auf. Die Klosterkirche steht heute noch da, und auch die alten Klostergebäude. Aber darin wohnt jetzt der Pfarrer mit seinen Kaplänen. Man braucht nur vom Schulhof über die Mauer zu klettern, dann ist man da – in dem Gärtchen davor.

Dies Gärtchen ist ganz verwildert. Und zwischen Weißdorn und Holunderbäumen stehen, aus Stein gehauen und halb von Efeu umwuchert, riesengroße steinerne Heiligenfiguren. Und von dem wilden Gärtchen aus kann man in einen Keller hinab – die Kellertüre ist zwar längst zerbrochen, aber man findet das Loch nicht so leicht, weil es ganz mit wildem Wein bewachsen ist. Und dann geht man eine verfallene Treppe hinab und kommt durch finstere Gänge in schwarze Gewölbe; darin hausen Fledermäuse und allerlei anderes Nachtgetier und mitunter findet man sogar einen bleichen Totenschädel. Auch in der Schule selbst gab es noch alte Gänge, in denen hallte es so hohl, wenn man hindurchging; und an den gekalkten Wänden hingen die düsteren Bilder der alten Fürsten und Mönche. Hinter den Bildern aber und unter den brüchigen

Bretterfußböden raschelten die Mäuse. Auch in den Klassenzimmern piepte es, wenn die Kinder ganz still waren, manchmal unter den Dielen und oft liefen die Mäuse um das Pult und vor den Bänken herum und suchten sich die Brotkrümchen, die die Kinder übrig gelassen hatten. Erst wenn der Lehrer mit dem Zeigestock auf das Pult oder an die Tafel schlug, flitzten sie weg in ihre Löcher.

Und jetzt schlug der Lehrer auch wieder auf den schwarzen Holzdeckel, dass es nur so krachte. Denn die Zehnuhrpause war eben um, die andern Kinder saßen schon alle auf ihren Plätzen – da kamen noch, ganz zuallerletzt, eine gute Weile nach dem Lehrer, zwei Jungen hereingestolpert ins Klassenzimmer. Rasch ging ihr Atem und hochrot waren ihre Köpfe.

»Ihr Lümmel!«, rief der Lehrer, »warum kommt ihr nicht sofort, wenn es geschellt hat? Und immer sind es dieselben! Wie oft soll ich es euch noch sagen?«

»Ich habe mir noch drüben bei der Frau Schmitz einen Bleistift geholt«, sagte der eine Junge, »und es waren so viele Leute im Geschäft, da musste ich warten.«

»Zeig mal her den Bleistift!«, sagte der Lehrer.

Der Junge kramte eine Weile in allen Taschen, aber gar nicht ängstlich, vielleicht wollte er nur den Lehrer ärgern – und schließlich hielt er dann den nagelneuen Bleistift hoch.

»Schert euch auf eure Plätze!«, sagte der Lehrer,

»und wenn das noch mal vorkommt mit euch zweien, dann hat es gerappelt!«

Die Jungen drehten sich um und trampelten zwischen den Reihen der Bänke ins Klassenzimmer zurück. Der Lehrer konnte nicht sehen, wie sie alle beide verstohlen grinsten. Denn jeder hatte immer einen neuen Bleistift, einen neuen Radiergummi oder etwas Ähnliches in der Tasche – nie hätte der Lehrer sie bei einer Lüge ertappen können. Wochenlang blieben aber auch diese Bleistifte neu und spitz ... und ängstlich wurden sie geschont ... O ja, das hatte schon seine Gründe!

»Lesebücher raus!«, befahl der Lehrer.

Klappern, Seitenrascheln, Bücherblättern in der ganzen Klasse – und der Junge wollte den Bleistift gerade wieder sorgfältig einpacken –, da auf einmal ruck! – saß er ganz still und starrte mit weiten Augen in sein Lesebuch ... Was war denn das? Wer hatte den Zettel da hineingetan ... Der war doch vorher noch nicht darin gewesen! Als es schellte, zur Pause, hatten sie gerade von Karl dem Großen gelesen und der Lehrer hatte gesagt: »Nachher lesen wir weiter ...« Ja, und gerade bei Karl dem Großen lag jetzt der Zettel!

Mit dem Ellenbogen stieß der Junge leise seinen Nachbarn an – der war der andere von den Zuspätgekommenen ... »Boddas«, hauchte er, »sieh mal hier ... das war im Lesebuch ...«

Eigentlich war der Familienname des Jungen ja Boden, Wilhelm Boden, aber Wilhelm Boden, so sagte nur der Lehrer. Die anderen Jungen sagten einfach Boddas. Schon seit Jahren war das so. Der Wilhelm Boden wusste gewiss selber nicht mehr, wie er richtig hieß ...

»Boden, lies weiter!«, hörte er da wie aus weiter, weiter Ferne den Lehrer rufen.

Der Junge wusste nicht, wo und was. Er machte nur seinen Mund, der ein bisschen zu klein war, so rund wie ein Karpfen. Aber dann stotterte er:

»Als Karl der Große U von seiner ...«

»Was liest du denn da für einen Unsinn?«

Schon verbesserte sich Boddas:

»Als Karl der Große von seiner Romfahrt zurückkehrte, da befahl er seinen Räten, sich Punkt sechs Uhr in der Villa ...«

Der Lehrer schlug auf das Pult.

»Setz dich!«

Und ein anderer musste weiterlesen.

Boddas schämte sich. Sonst war er doch wirklich der Dümmste nicht. Lesen konnte er wie nur einer. Die Zeitung las er schon von oben bis unten, und wenn er einen Karl May erwischen konnte, dann las er den auch, sogar die schweren Namen konnte er lesen und Hadschi Halef Omar ben Hadschi Abul Abbas ibn Hadschi Dawuhd al Gossarah – diesen meilenlangen Namen konnte er sogar auswendig. Aber jetzt! Nein, das hätte der Lehrer ja selber nicht lesen können! Dieser Zettel im Lesebuch seines Freundes Mala hatte ihn ganz außer Rand und Band gebracht.

Mala? Ja, so hieß der Junge seit dem vorigen Jahr, wo sie in der Schule Spanien durchgenommen hatten. In Spanien gab es nämlich einen Berg, der hieß Maladetta. »Das heißt ›Die Verfluchte‹«, hatte der Lehrer erklärt. Und weil nun der Matthias Schlösser so schrecklich fluchen konnte, da riefen ihn die anderen Jungen jetzt einfach statt mit seinem ehrlichen Vornamen Matthias nur noch Mala. Und bei Mala blieb es.

»Mala, zeig mal«, flüsterte Boddas jetzt, »ich war noch nicht fertig.«

Aber Mala saß da, mit hochrotem Kopf, die Hände wie eine Mauer schützend um das Buch gelegt. Und Boddas hörte ihn tief und rasch atmen. Erst als Boddas ihn noch einmal anstieß, schaute Mala auf und seine Augen waren ganz verstört. Mit zitternden Fingern knüllte er den Zettel in seinem Buch zusammen und reichte ihn unter der Bank her verstohlen an Boddas. Der strich ihn schnell auf der Buchseite glatt – im Augenblick würde der Lehrer ihn ja doch nicht mehr aufrufen. Er brauchte also keine Angst zu haben.

Es war ein Zettel, nicht größer als eine halbe Postkarte, und Boddas fuhr mit dem Zeigefinger die engen Schreibmaschinenzeilen entlang. Und Boddas las diese Worte:

Mala, Boddas, Döll, Knöres und Silli, ihr seid erkannt! Dem großen Roten U ist es zu Ohren gekommen, dass ihr eine Bande seid und aller-

hand Streiche macht. Eigentlich sollte das Rote U euch bei der Polizei anzeigen. Aber das Rote U hat etwas anderes über euch beschlossen. Das Rote U wird jetzt euer Hauptmann sein und nicht mehr Boddas oder Mala. Nie werdet ihr das Rote U zu sehen kriegen. Ihr werdet die Befehle des Roten U stets irgendwo in euren Büchern, in euren Schultaschen, in euren Butterbrotpapieren finden. Und wehe euch, wenn ihr nicht gehorcht! Dann wird der Lehrer einen Brief von dem Roten U bekommen, in dem all eure bösen Taten stehen, dass ihr im alten Klostergarten mit eurem Luftgewehr die Karnickel schießt, dass ihr dem Hausmeister die Mäuse aus den Mausefallen laufen lasst, und einmal habt ihr dem Lehrer sogar eine Maus in das Pult getan. Aber der Lehrer hat es nicht gemerkt. Und daran, dass ich, das Rote U, es weiß, daran könnt ihr sehen, dass das Rote U alles weiß! Hütet euch vor ihm! Heute Abend, genau um sechs Uhr, habt ihr in der Villa Jück zu sein und da werdet ihr weitere Befehle von mir finden. Wie ihr da hineinkommt, das ist eure Sache!
                                                   Das Rote U

So las Boddas und seine Augen hatte er dabei aufgerissen, als schaute er in ein brennendes Haus. Dann las er den Zettel noch einmal und noch einmal und immer mehr sah er ein, dass da ganz und gar nichts zu machen war. Das Rote U hatte sie in der Gewalt.

Der Brief flimmerte Boddas bald vor den Augen, zumal das U sogar immer in roter Farbe getippt war. Rot wie Blut! Und die Us tanzten bald wie böse Flämmchen auf dem Papier herum. Da faltete er schnell den Zettel zusammen und steckte ihn in die Tasche. Und sah Mala an. Und Mala ihn. Und einer nach dem andern zuckte die Schultern.

Die Stunde ging weiter. Den beiden Jungen war es, als spräche der Lehrer durch einen Nebel, in dem lauter rote Us herumwirbelten. Noch ein paar Mal wurden sie aufgerufen, aber sie gaben wieder verwirrte und verstotterte Antworten ... Gott sei Dank nur, dass heute die Schule schon um elf Uhr aus war! Dann konnten sie endlich mit Döll, Knöres und Silli sprechen. Oh, was würden die für Augen machen! Aber vielleicht würde Silli einen Rat wissen. Silli war das einzige Mädchen in der Bande und hatte ein helles Köpfchen. Sonst wäre sie auch gar nicht aufgenommen worden, obwohl sie Boddas' Schwester war. Und es hatte Boddas auch allerlei Mühe gekostet, seine Freunde von Sillis Wert zu überzeugen. Freilich, nachher hätten sie das schlaue blonde Mädel nicht mehr missen mögen. Keiner konnte so lecker Karnickel braten wie sie, konnte so wunderbar die zerrissenen Jacken und Hosen flicken; und wenn es irgendwo keinen Ausweg mehr gab – Silli wusste gewiss den aller-, allerletzten noch zu finden.

Dabei beruhigten sich die Jungen ein wenig, und als es endlich schellte, da waren sie die Ersten, die aus dem Klassenzimmer hinausrannten, und fast hätten sie den blassen, etwas buckligen Ühl dabei umgerannt. Denn der Ühl, der Klügste in der ganzen Klasse, saß gerade neben der Türe in der hintersten Ecke. Der Lehrer konnte den armen Jungen ruhig dahinsetzen, denn er brauchte ihn wirklich nicht immer unter den Augen zu haben. Der Ühl war brav und fleißig, wusste alles am besten und darum konnten ihn die anderen Kinder auch nicht besonders gut leiden. Auf dem Schulhof stand er immer allein herum, besah sich mit seinen großen blauen Augen das fröhliche Spiel der Kameraden und selber durfte er nicht mittun. Aber der Junge beklagte sich nicht. Er war es so gewohnt. Und als ihn jetzt der Boddas beinahe über den Haufen stieß, lachte er nur und rief: »Da hätte ich dich beinahe umgerannt, Boddas!«

Aber Boddas schaute ihn nur mitleidig und verächtlich von der Seite an, stampfte mit seinen schwer genagelten Stiefeln neben Mala über den Gang, dann schwangen sich beide auf das Treppengeländer und sausten wie der Blitz in die Tiefe.

Vor der Schule warteten schon Döll und Knöres. Die waren beide ein Jahr jünger als Mala und Boddas, doch schon tüchtige Kerle. Man sah auch gleich, dass sie zu der Bande gehörten, denn die Mützen hatten sie schief auf dem Kopf sitzen, die

Hände tief in den Hosentaschen und alle Augenblicke spuckte Knöres in weitem Bogen über die halbe Straße weg wie ein alter Rheinschiffer. Döll – er war der Einzige, der wirklich so hieß –, Döll war der Größere und Stärkere von beiden. Knöres – kein Mensch wusste, weshalb er so genannt wurde – war der Kleinste von allen, aber auch der Flinkste. Augen hatte er wie ein Mäuschen, so schwarz und so rund, und auch seine Zähnchen waren so weiß und so klein und spitz. Der Döll aber, wohl zwei Hände breit größer, hatte einen dicken kantigen Kopf, raues borstiges Haar, einen breiten Mund und dicke Fäuste. Wehe dem, der ihm in die Finger geriet! Dann machte er ein paar Augen, als spritzte Feuer heraus, und mit seinen Fäusten schlug er drein wie mit Schmiedehämmern.

Aber jetzt war Silli zu ihnen getreten und sie lächelte boshaft aus den Augenwinkeln:

»Seht mal den Boddas und den Mala!«, sagte sie – die beiden kamen nämlich gerade die Schultreppe heruntergestolpert –, »die haben sicher Maikäfer in den Ohren.«

»Oder der Lehrer hat ihnen Süßholz gegeben –«, zischelte Knöres.

Das hörte Mala noch.

»Du kannst gefälligst deinen Mund halten, Knöres«, sagte er, »und jetzt kommt mal alle mit ... Es sind da Geschichten passiert ...«

Sie sahen ihn erschrocken an. Und nun nickte Boddas auch: »Fürchterliche Sachen, ja! Wir müssen sofort darüber reden. Ich denke, wir gehen an den Rhein ...«

»Ja, aber was ...«, fragte Silli.

»Willst du wohl schweigen!«, fuhr Mala sie an und böse schaute er zu dem buckligen Ühl hinüber, der eben an ihnen vorbeilief, gerade seiner Mutter in die Arme, die ihn fast jeden Morgen abholte. Eine feine Frau war sie, die Frau Landgerichtsrat Bernhard, und deshalb fanden die anderen Jungen den armen Ühl noch viel lächerlicher. Mit spitzen höhnischen Mündern machten sie's ihm immer nach: »Guten Tag, Mama.« – »Sieh da, mein lieber Junge.« Für so etwas hatten sie wirklich nur ein Lachen übrig.

»Nein«, sagte Mala jetzt, »an den Rhein, das ist auch nichts. Da könnte uns doch einer belauschen und dann wäre natürlich alles verloren! Gehen wir lieber zu Dölls ... Wie ist es, Döll, arbeitet ihr heute auf dem Speicher?«

»Ich glaube nicht«, sagte Döll, »und wenn auch mal ein Arbeiter raufklettert und einen Sack Mehl holt, dann halten wir uns einfach mucksstille und er schiebt wieder ab.«

Dölls Eltern hatten nämlich ein großes Mühlenlager und bald huschten denn auch die Kinder durch den breiten Torweg, unter den Mühlenwagen durch. Niemand bemerkte sie, sogar Dölls Mutter nicht, die gerade über den Hof kam. Döll sah sie mit einem großen Drahtkorb voll Spinat dicht neben dem Wagen hergehen, unter dem er gerade steckte, und er lachte über das ganze Gesicht. Denn Spinat mit Eiern, das war sein Lieblingsessen. Davon konnte er drei Teller voll verschlingen.

Jetzt waren sie in dem Wagenschuppen und geschwind wie Wieselchen huschten sie die mehlbestaubte Holztreppe hinauf, Döll stieß die Speicherklappe hoch, einer nach dem andern verschwand dahinter, dann machten sie die Klappe leise wieder zu, turnten über die Säcke mit Mehl, Erbsen, Mais und Hühnerfutter weg und bald hockten sie zusammen in ihrem alten Winkel unter den Dachsparren. Die Kisten und Kasten dort hatten sie wie eine Mauer herumgestellt und so konnten wirklich nur die Katzen sie hier finden.

»Hat einer seine Taschenlampe da?«, fragte Boddas, als sie so in ihrem Winkel zusammenhockten. Denn kaum ein Lichtstrahl fiel zwischen den schweren Dachpfannen durch.

»Taschenlampe? Wozu?«, fragte Silli.

»Das wirst du schon sehen!«, knurrte Mala, »Boddas, hast du den Zettel?«

Der Lichtkegel eines elektrischen Lämpchens flirrte durch die Finsternis und Millionen Mehlstäubchen tanzten in dem weißen Strahl.

»Also diesen Wisch hier, den Boddas da in den Fingern hat«, erklärte Mala jetzt, »fand ich heut nach der Zehnuhrpause in meinem Lesebuch, gerade bei Karl dem Großen. Boddas und ich und Knöres waren in der Pause ein bisschen drüben im Klostergarten, drum sind wir auch zu spät gekom-

men ... Wir konnten doch nicht zurückklettern, wo all die Lehrer noch auf dem Hof waren. Nun lies mal vor, Boddas!«

Und Boddas las, leise und doch so aufgeregt, dass Mala immer zischelte: »Schrei doch nicht so ...«

Aber schon war Boddas fertig und er knipste die Lampe aus. So konnte denn keiner die entsetzten Augen der anderen sehen. Aber sie spürten alle, wie ihre Herzen klopften.

»Was sagt ihr jetzt?«, flüsterte Mala nach einer Weile.

»Und die Us sind sämtlich rot geschrieben!«, fügte Boddas mit düsterer Stimme hinzu.

»Lass mich doch auch mal sehen!«, hauchte Silli.

Wieder flirrte das Lämpchen und über Sillis Schultern schauten Döll und Knöres in das schreckliche Blatt. Jetzt ließ das Mädchen den Zettel sinken.

»Licht aus!«, sagte sie, »wenn einer den Schein sieht, dann ist es aus mit uns!«

»Das ist es auch so!«, brummte Döll traurig.

»Was fangen wir nur an?«, fragte Mala.

»Wenn wir nur wüssten, wer das geschrieben hat«, flüsterte Knöres, »dann –«

»Was dann?«, unkte Mala.

»Dann würde ich ihm die Hucke vollhauen!«, knurrte Döll und die anderen hörten seine Zähne im Dunkel knirschen.

»Mach dich doch nicht lächerlich«, brummte Boddas, »gegen das Rote U kannst du gar nicht ankommen ...«

»Allah verdamme es in die unterste Hölle!«, fluchte Mala.

»Damit kommen wir nicht weiter«, flüsterte Silli, »sicher hat sich irgendein Verbrecher in der Pause eingeschlichen und dir den Zettel ins Buch getan und jetzt erpresst der uns für die Bande vom Roten U ... Der weiß, dass wir gut schleichen können, natürlich, und dann müssen wir des Nachts mit den Einbrechern los – wisst ihr was? Ihr gebt den Zettel bei der Polizei ab ...«

»Bist du verrückt, Silli?«, rief Knöres, »dann kommt ja alles raus von uns! Dass wir die Karnickel schießen! Dass wir dem Polizisten einen Zettel hinten an den Rock gesteckt haben – du, das gibt sicher Zuchthaus!«

Silli schüttelte den Kopf: »Und wenn wir mit dem Roten U anfangen, dann kommen wir noch viel länger ins Zuchthaus, da könnt ihr Gift drauf nehmen! Aber vielleicht sind die Polizisten froh, wenn wir ihnen die Bande vom Roten U verraten, dann kriegen wir nur eine Tracht Hiebe und davon ist noch keiner gestorben –«

»Nein, Silli«, sagte Boddas, »das nicht, aber eine Ehre ist es gerade auch nicht! Und woher willst du überhaupt wissen, was das Rote U will? Vielleicht ist es ein hochanständiger Räuber und das wäre doch was für uns!«

»Ich will euch was sagen«, flüsterte Knöres und im Schein eines winzigen Sonnenstrahls, der durch eine Lücke zwischen den Dachpfannen flirrte, sahen sie seine schwarzen Mausaugen funkeln, »die Silli hat recht und der Boddas hat auch recht. Aber es wär eine Schande für uns, wenn wir uns von dem Roten U Bange machen ließen! Nein, wir gehen einfach hin und dann sehen wir schon, was er will! Und ich glaube ja auch, dass wir für ihn einbrechen sollen. Das ist nun mal pottsicher. Und das tun wir dann einfach auch, aber vorher schreiben wir ein Briefchen an die Polizei. Hier diesen Wisch hinzuschicken hat ja gar keinen Zweck. Die lachen uns nur aus. Aber wenn wir sagen können: Herr Polizist, das Rote U will diese Nacht da und da einbrechen – am besten geht Silli mit dem Brief aufs Präsidium –, ja, dann wird der Oberpolizist sagen: Fräulein Sybilla Boden, wir bedanken uns auch recht schön für Ihre werte Nachricht und Ihr Herr Bruder Wilhelm und die anderen Herren können gleich bei uns eintreten als Detektive ... Ja, so wird es kommen! Was meint ihr dazu?«

»Der Teufel soll dich holen, Knöres«, rief Mala, »das ist mal eine Idee! Was, Boddas?«

Und er sprang auf und schlug den Freund mit der Faust auf die Schulter. Im gleichen Augenblick gab es einen Krach, als wenn der Speicher einstürzte – Mala hatte beim Aufspringen die Kistenwand aus dem Gleichgewicht gebracht und mit Donnergepolter stürzten die Nudel- und Makkaronikisten in einen wüsten Haufen zusammen. Drunter zappelten Arme und Beine und drüber stand eine Wolke von Staubqualm. Als aber der Lagerknecht hinaufkam, das elektrische Licht andrehte und umherschaute, was da geschehen wäre, da war alles schon wieder totenstill, nur in den wenigen Sonnenstrahlen über dem Kistenhaufen wirbelte noch der Staub und die große weißgelbe Katze schlich über die Dachbalken.

Die Villa Jück

Der Herbsttag war sonnig und schön gewesen, aber je weiter es auf den Abend und die Dämmerung ging, desto mehr zogen sich in dem immer stärker vom Rhein her wehenden Westwind die schwarzen Wolken zusammen, und als in der Altstadt die Laternen aufbrannten, sprühte schon ein feiner Regen über die Dächer und in die engen Straßen. Bald wurden die Tropfen dicker und dicker und schließlich regnete es in Strömen. Wie leer gefegt waren die Straßen und die wenigen Leute, die noch da und dort gingen, hielten die Regenschirme gegen den steif wehenden Wind fest in den Fäusten, dicht über den Köpfen.

»Besser konnt es ja gar nicht kommen!«, sagte Silli, »jetzt sieht uns keine Katze!«

Arm in Arm mit Mala und ihrem Bruder Boddas ging sie durch ein windiges glitschiges Gässchen dem Rhein zu. Einen Schirm hatte nicht einmal das Mädchen. Der war zu hinderlich bei dem, was sie vorhatten. Aber die Kapuzen ihrer Regenmäntel hatten sie über die Köpfe gezogen bis tief in die Gesichter hinein.

»Ob Knöres und Döll da sind?«, meinte Mala.

»Ach, die werden zu Haus schon eine Ausrede gehabt haben, genau wie wir auch.«

Wieder schwiegen sie. Und je näher sie dem Rhein kamen, desto schwerer mussten sie gegen den Wind ankämpfen. Endlich, die Uhr von Sankt Lambertus schlug halb sechs, standen sie an dem Strom und der wälzte sich düster im sprühenden Regen unter dem abenddunklen Himmel hin.

»Laderampe 87«, sagte Boddas, »man sieht ja kaum mehr die Hand vor den Augen.«

»Hier ist es«, meinte Silli.

»Nein, hier ist 92 ... ich könnte die Nummern in stockdüsterer Nacht finden.«

Silli packte plötzlich die beiden an den Armen.

»Drüben steht ein Polizist!«, flüsterte sie.

Ja, nun sahen sie es auch ganz deutlich. Gerade vor der Gasse, in der die Villa Jück lag, sahen sie die Uniformknöpfe im Schein einer Laterne blitzen.

Sie blieben stehen und sahen sich an.

»Wie sollen wir jetzt hineinkommen?«, fragte Boddas.

»Vielleicht« – Mala bekam vor Schrecken ganz große Augen –, »weiß Gott, vielleicht hat das Rote U ganz genau dasselbe getan, was wir tun wollten. Es hat der Polizei geschrieben, hat geschrieben: Heut Abend um sechs Uhr kommt die Altstadtbande in die Villa Jück – ja, und nun steht schon der Polizist da –«

Jetzt war es klar, warum das Rote U sie gerade an die berüchtigte Villa Jück bestellt hatte! Mit der Villa Jück hatte die Polizei ja schon vor zwei Jahren mal eine Geschichte gehabt. Diese »Villa« war nämlich ein uraltes Häuschen, in dem, so weit die Kinder zurückdenken konnten, nie ein Mensch gewohnt hatte. Immer waren die Fensterläden geschlossen, geschlossen die dicke eichene Türe, über der ein Esel in Stein ausgemeißelt war. Doch dann kam eine Zeit, da hörten die Nachbarn mitunter aus dem alten Hause Singen und Lachen, Gläserklirren und Musik wie von einer Mund- oder Ziehharmonika. Zuerst gaben sie nicht weiter acht darauf. Aber als sie dann immer öfter das Gejohle hörten und zwischen den Ritzen der Läden hellen Lichtschein sahen, gingen sie zur Polizei. Die beobachtete das finstere Haus eine Weile und eines Abends packte sie zu; so schnell, dass sich keiner mehr aus dem Staube machen konnte. Da kam's denn heraus: Eine ganze Bande junger Burschen hatte jede Nacht in dem öden Häuschen ihre Zusammenkünfte. Dann tranken sie den Wein und die Liköre, die sie allenthalben bei nächtlichen Ladeneinbrüchen zusammengestohlen hatten, rauchten gestohlene Zigarren und Zigaretten; mit gestohlenen Kleidern hatten sie sich fein gemacht und bald brachten sie auch Mädchen mit, unter denen verteilten sie Samt und Seide, silberne Ketten und goldene Ringe in diesen lustigen Nächten. Und eben weil's immer so lustig herging in ihrem Räuberquartier, nannten sie das leere Haus unter sich nur noch die Villa Jück ... Denn »Jux kriegen«, das heißt in jener Stadt so viel wie Freude kriegen.

Und nun hatte das Rote U sie gerade in diese unheimliche Villa Jück bestellt! Freilich, immer hatten sie schon einmal vorgehabt, dort einzusteigen. Denn so etwas Gruseliges wie dies alte Haus gab's ja in der ganzen Stadt nicht mehr! Aber damals hatte die Polizei neue Schlösser an alle Türen und eiserne Stäbe vor die Fenster machen lassen. Und Boddas und Mala hatten schon hundert Mal um das Haus geschnüffelt, aber nie ein Loch gefunden, durch das sie hätten hineinschlüpfen können. Doch vielleicht ließ sich etwas von der Hofseite her machen? Das wollten sie heute versuchen. Denn wenn das Rote U hineinkonnte, dann konnten sie's doch hundertmal!

»Jetzt sind wir bei 87«, sagte Boddas, und wirklich, kaum hatte er's ausgesprochen, da lösten sich von dem dunklen Steingeländer zwei Gestalten.

»Losung?«, rief ihnen Boddas mit unterdrückter Stimme entgegen.

»Schatten an der Kirchhofsmauer«, klang es zurück.

Denn dies Erkennungswort hatten sie am Morgen ausgemacht.

Es waren also Knöres und Döll.

»Wir wollen ganz langsam weitergehen«, zischelte Döll, »habt ihr den Polizisten gesehen?«

»Mala meint, das Rote U hätte ihn herbestellt«, sagte Silli.

Ängstlich schauten sie sich um. Aber der Polizist ging jetzt gemächlich in der entgegengesetzten Richtung.

»Ich traue ihm doch noch nicht!«, meinte der schlaue Knöres, »geht mal ruhig weiter, ich werde mich an ihn ranmachen und sage euch dann Bescheid!«

»Hier bleibst du!«, rief Mala. »Du verrätst noch die ganze Kiste!«

Aber Knöres war schon fort, verschwunden in Regen und Nacht. Die anderen drückten sich eng an einem breiten Laternenkandelaber zusammen, und als Knöres noch einmal zurückschaute auf die Rheinwerft, da sah er niemanden mehr. Aber auch der Polizist war plötzlich verschwunden. Ob er in die Straße hineingegangen war und nun an dem öden Haus auf und ab spazierte? Das wäre freilich dumm gewesen. Doch half es nichts – Knöres musste es untersuchen!

Er begann langsam zu traben. Denn das konnte am wenigsten auffallen. Der Polizist würde einfach meinen, er wäre gerade mit dem Fährboot gekommen oder über die Brücke von der anderen Seite und wollte nun eilig heim. Das würde er ihm auch sagen, wenn er ihn fragen sollte. Und er brauchte nicht einmal zu lügen. Denn diesen Nachmittag war er wirklich in Oberkassel gewesen bei seiner Großmutter.

Richtig, da kam auch schon der Polizist, und Knöres, der eben an der Villa Jück vorbeitrabte, wollte schon an ihm vorüber, da fiel ihm etwas anderes ein. Pucks!, hielt er an und sagte: »Herr Polizist, bin ich aber froh, dass ich Sie hier treffe!«

»Was gibt's denn, mein Junge?«, fragte der Polizist freundlich, »da hast du dir aber schlechtes Wetter ausgesucht!«

»Ja, ich komm gerade von meiner Großmutter auf der anderen Seite ... und hier an der Villa Jück bin ich immer ein bisschen bang ... Sie wissen ja, was damals für Kerle drin gehaust haben ... Macht es Ihnen was aus, wenn ich mit Ihnen gehe bis hinten an die Kirche?«

»Gewiss nicht, Junge – aber heute brauchst du wirklich keine Angst mehr zu haben. Die ganze Bande sitzt noch im Gefängnis. Na, dann komm nur ... Soll ich dir auch eine Hand geben?«

»Das ist nicht nötig, Herr Polizist. – Müssen Sie denn die ganze Nacht hier herumspazieren? Das ist aber wirklich kein Vergnügen!«

»Nein, nein«, sagte der Schupo, »heut hab ich keinen Nachtdienst. Du kannst ja mit mir gehen bis an den Karlsplatz, da werde ich um sechs abgelöst.«

Aber so weit mitzulaufen, daran lag dem guten Knöres im Augenblick nichts. Er wollte doch, so schnell es ging, zu seinen Leuten zurück.

»Nein, danke«, sagte er drum, »ich muss an der Kirche links herein, ich wohn in der Bergerstraße.«

Jetzt waren sie eben an dem dunklen Haus mit dem Esel vorüber. Daneben lag eine Schreinerei und im Weitergehen sah Knöres, dass das Tor zum Hof, über den es zur Werkstatt ging, halb offen stand. War einer drinnen? Knöres wusste doch ganz genau, dass nie ein Mensch in der Werkstatt arbeitete. Der Schreinermeister hatte schon vor einem Jahr sein Geschäft in eine bessere Gegend verlegt und hier verwahrte er eigentlich nur noch ein paar Stapel Bretter unter einem niedrigen Schuppen. In der Werkstatt aber regierten die Ratten.

Sollte er den Polizisten darauf aufmerksam machen? Aber sie waren schon vorbei ... Noch einmal schaute Knöres sich um ... Ja, was war das? Sein Herz tat einen gewaltigen Sprung und dann war es, als stünd es auf einmal stille ... Ganz genau hatte er es gesehen: Aus dem Tor der Schreinerei war eine Gestalt geschlüpft – er hätte darauf schwören können! Aber schon war der Schatten im Dunkel, nach dem Rhein zu, verschwunden.

›Das Rote U!‹, fuhr es dem Knöres wie ein Blitz durch den Kopf. Ja, der musste es gewesen sein! Um sechs Uhr sollten sie drinnen den Zettel finden – jetzt war es eben Viertel vor durch, gerade hatte die helle Kirchenuhr geschlagen. Und der Junge sah jetzt auch schon durch den Regen die Pfeiler des Kirchentores.

»Da sind wir an der Hafenstraße –«, sagte er und die erleuchteten Fenster der uralten Wirtschaft »Zum Schiffchen« blinkten trüb durch den nassen Abend, »jetzt kann ich allein gehen! Und ich danke Ihnen auch schön, Herr Polizist!«

»Gern geschehen, Junge«, lachte der Mann und ging mit raschen Schritten, ohne sich umzusehen, dem Karlsplatz zu.

Noch ein Weilchen blieb Knöres stehen, er wollte ganz sicher sein, dass der Polizist auch nicht umkehrte. Aber alles blieb still. Nur kamen jetzt um die Kirche herum zwei Männer in Regenmänteln und mit Schirmen, aber die gingen geradewegs auf das Wirtshaus zu und verschwanden dann in der niedrigen Tür.

Jetzt war die Stunde für Knöres gekommen. Es fiel ihm nun gar nicht mehr ein, an den Rhein zurückzulaufen und dort seine Kameraden zu holen. ›Fünf fallen mehr auf als einer‹, dachte er sich, während er weiterging, dann schaute er noch einmal nach rechts, nach links, spähte hinter sich, dann vor sich gegen den Wind, wo die geheimnisvolle Gestalt verschwunden war … aber er sah nichts, hörte nichts als den Regen rauschen. Im nächsten Augenblick war er in dem Hof der alten Schreinerei verschwunden und leise zog er das schwere, wacklige Bohlentor hinter sich zu.

Keiner konnte ihn gesehen haben und in der nächsten Minute würde auch keiner draußen des Weges kommen. Diese Zeit musste er also nutzen! Und er wusste auch schon, wie. Denn das Rote U konnte doch nicht geflogen sein, es musste Spuren gemacht haben wie jeder andere Mensch, und keine kleinen! Denn in dem alten Hof lag beinahe fußtiefer Schlamm – er wusste das genau, in der Zehnuhrpause war er ja mit Boddas und Mala und Döll oft hier gewesen und sie hatten in der alten Werkstatt die Ratten gejagt … Also Licht! Er knipste seine Taschenlampe an und leuchtete auf den Boden.

Richtig, da hatte er's schon! Hier hatte das Rote U gestanden, als er eben mit dem Polizisten vorüberging. Tief waren die Schuhe in den Schlamm eingedrückt. Diesen Spuren ging er nach. Denn es war wirklich leicht, sie zu finden. Im Dunklen hätte er sie tasten können, meinte er ... Natürlich – sie führten an der Werkstatt vorbei und dann rechts herum, auf den Bretterschuppen zu. Und dieser Bretterschuppen lag gerade an der Rückwand der Villa Jück! Da wusste Knöres, woran er war. Und er wunderte sich gar nicht, als die Spuren unter dem Schuppen plötzlich aufhörten, nicht einmal die nassen Stapfen waren in dem trockenen Staub zu sehen. ›Das Rote U ist also auf die Bretter gestiegen!‹, dachte der Junge und mit raschem Schwung war auch er droben.

Lampe an! Siehst du wohl!, grinste er – die schmierigen Stapfen waren ganz deutlich droben auf den Brettern zu sehen. Und Knöres folgte ihnen über dem zarten Lichtschein der elektrischen Birne mit seinen schlauen Mausaugen, ganz bis in die letzte Ecke des Schuppens. Da hörten sie plötzlich wieder auf. War das Rote U etwa noch höher geklettert? Knöres leuchtete hinauf. Aber nein, schon dicht über seinem Kopf war das Dach, und wenn er sich ganz aufrichtete, stieß er an staubige Spinnweben und im Strahl seiner Laterne sah er da und dort fette Spinnen in ihre Balkenwinkel flüchten.

›Also tiefer!‹, dachte er. Die letzte Spur war ja auch so merkwürdig deutlich – an der ganzen Stelle war das Brett nass und schlammig. Hier musste also das Rote U eine Weile gestanden haben. Was mochte er dort gesucht haben? Nun, die Bretter vor sich hatte er aufgehoben und zurückgelehnt! Das war doch klar. Und schon klappte der Junge das erste nach hinten, das zweite – aber er sah noch nichts. Da fühlte er hinter den Brettern her. »Holla!«, rief er leise. Er hatte den obersten Rand eines Fensters oder eines gemauerten Loches gespürt. Aber mit einem kleinen Ekelschrei zog er die Hand zurück – eine Ratte war ihm darübergehuscht mit ihren kalten Füßchen. Doch da konnte nichts helfen – hinein musste er, Ratten oder nicht. Schnell klappte er noch ein paar Bretter beiseite und nun war die Öffnung groß genug. Er sah auch: Auf diesem Brett, das nun zuunterst lag, musste der Unbekannte wieder gestanden haben. An den Abdrücken sah Knöres, dass er seine Fußspitzen nach außen gehabt hatte. Also machte er's ebenso, hielt sich an dem Brett fest und angelte sich mit den Füßen durch das finstere Fensterloch. Sand, Steinchen und Mörtel bröckelten hinter ihm hinab. Jetzt hielt er sich von außen an der Mauer und seine Beine baumelten frei innen im Haus in die Tiefe. Sollte er hinabspringen? Einen Augenblick besann er sich noch. Aber da hörte er wieder ein Steinstückchen neben sich hinabpoltern und es schlug dicht unter ihm auf den Fußboden. Er konnte es also wagen. Und er ließ sich fallen. Gleich hatte er dann auch festen Boden unter den Füßen.

Das war also geschafft! Und das Übrige bedeutete nun wirklich nur noch eine Kleinigkeit. Zuerst aber ließ Knöres einmal seine Taschenlampe aufflammen ... Sieh da! Gerade hinter ihm lag ein umgestürzter Schemel. Auf den musste der Geheimnisvolle geklettert sein, als er wieder zu dem Loch hinaussteigen wollte, und bei diesem letzten Schwung hatte er mit dem Fuß den Schemel umgestoßen. Dem Knöres war also nicht mehr bange, wie er wieder hinaufkommen sollte.

Und nun leuchtete er herum. Doch die kleine enge Stube war leer, kahl die Wände, überall kam das nackte Mauerwerk heraus und die Dielenbretter waren an vielen Stellen verfault, glitschiger Schwamm wucherte an den Bodenbalken. Knöres schüttelte sich vor Grausen und mit einem Mal wurde es ihm kalt. Überall an den Wänden rann die Feuchtigkeit dickgrün hinab und sie tropfte von den Deckenbalken. ›Jetzt schnell den Zettel gesucht und dann raus aus dem Loch!‹, dachte der Junge. Aber hier war der Befehl des Roten U nicht zu finden und Knöres ging durch die Tür, die lose in nur einer Angel hing.

In dem nächsten Zimmer sah es ein wenig besser aus. Der Fußboden war noch fast in Ordnung und in der Ecke lag ein Haufen leerer Flaschen. Hier also hatten die Verbrecher ihre Feste gefeiert! Der

Junge sah es schon daran, dass noch in manchen Flaschenhälsen Kerzenstümpfchen steckten. Er musste also nun vorsichtig sein! Denn gewiss konnte man von draußen durch die Lädenritzen sein Licht sehen! Aber auch hier war der Zettel nirgends zu finden. Also noch tiefer hinein in die grausige Höhle! Vielleicht auf die Dachkammern? Eine schmale Treppe, die eher wie eine Leiter aussah und lose an der Wand lehnte, führte hinauf. Aber der Junge sah gleich, dass die Sprossen oder Stufen mit dickem Staub bedeckt waren. Nicht eine einzige Spur konnte er darauf entdecken.

Also in den Keller! Die Falltüre, die dorthin führen musste, hatte er schon gesehen, und als er sich zu dem eisernen Ring bückte, an dem man sie hochzog, sah er gleich, dass sie erst vor kurzer Zeit offen gewesen sein musste. Leise schlug er also den Deckel zurück und leuchtete hinab in das schwarze Kellerloch. Da huschten in der Tiefe die Ratten hin und her im Lichtschein und zwei sprangen gerade vor ihm die steinerne Treppe hinab. Zugleich sah er aber auch schon an der Wand drunten etwas Weißes – das musste der Zettel sein! Rasch und doch vorsichtig stieg er hinab. Ja, da war ein rostiger Nagel in der Wand und auf den Nagel war ein frisches weißes Papier gespießt ...

Aber was war nun auf einmal das? Wie ein Seufzen klang es irgendwo, weit – war es oben, war es unten? Nein, unter ihm musste es sein. Und es war, als wenn Gewänder über eine Treppe rauschten, und dann wieder, als wenn sich der Nachhall von einem schweren Stöhnen im Düster verlöre.

Der Junge war blass geworden. Spukte es in dem alten Haus? Er riss den Zettel von dem Nagel und stürzte die Treppe hinauf. Aber da war es ja schon wieder und nun noch viel deutlicher … Seine Ohren waren auf einmal so scharf, ganz klar hörte er das seufzende Hinstreichen an hallenden Wänden, er hörte drüber das Huschen der Ratten, hörte droben den Regen dumpf an die Läden pochen.

Er hielt ein. Sollte er hinauf, die anderen rufen? Welcher Trost wäre es jetzt, den starken Döll und den langen fluchenden Mala bei sich zu haben, oder wenigstens den kleinen, zähen, hartknochigen Boddas!

Aber jedes Mal, wenn er wieder weiter hinaufwollte, hörte er von Neuem das Seufzen, immer gleich, immer dasselbe.

Er spitzte die Ohren. Nein, das konnte kein Mensch sein und auch kein Spuk. Tief beugte der Junge sich vor und plötzlich fiel es ihm ein: So, ganz genau so hatte es einst in den Nächten durch die engen Straßen geseufzt und an den Häusern vorbeigestrichen, als der Rhein so schrecklich über seine Ufer getreten war. Mit Kähnen hatten sie von Haus zu Haus gemusst, auf Kähnen waren die Lebensmittel gebracht worden, auf einem Kahn kam der Arzt zu den Kranken und vom Kahn aus stieg er gleich in das Fenster des ersten Stocks. Ja, so seufzte, so wehte, so gluckerte der Rhein in den ent-

setzlichen Nächten der Überschwemmung durch die widerhallenden Altstadtgassen. Und auch hier, unter dem öden Haus, musste also der Rhein fließen.

Knöres war wieder ganz ruhig, und wenn es ihm auch noch ein wenig schaurig um das Herz war, so stieg er doch noch einmal bis ganz in den Keller hinab und leuchtete über den Boden. Bald hatte er es denn auch gefunden: An der Seite des Kellers lag in den Ziegeln des Bodens eine große Steinplatte mit einem mächtigen Eisenring. Der Junge packte zu und zog mit seiner ganzen Kraft. Aber nur um einen Zoll hob sich die Platte. Doch dem Knöres genügte das. Der Schein seiner Lampe war in ein bodenloses senkrechtes Loch gefallen und drunten gurgelte das Wasser des Rheins.

Tief atmete er auf. Aber dann dachte er wieder mit Schauder an das Rote U. Was musste das für ein Mensch sein, dass er sie an diesen schauerlichsten Ort der ganzen Stadt lockte? Wo der Rhein durch einen schwarzen Kanal hineinstöhnte … Wie viele Menschen mochten schon dorthinab verschwunden sein!

Eisig überlief es den Jungen und so schnell er konnte, sprang er jetzt hinauf, klappte leis die Falltür hinter sich zu, dann über den Schemel in das Loch auf die Bretter, die er schnell wieder in Ordnung brachte; hinunter von dem Holz und durch den Hof. Noch eine Weile stand er von innen vor dem Tor und lauschte. Aber niemand kam. Nur der

Regen klatschte über die Straße. Im nächsten Augenblick war er draußen, eben schlug die Kirchenuhr das erste Viertel. War es Viertel nach sechs? Nach sieben? Nach acht? Der Junge meinte, mehr als eine Stunde hätte er in dem öden Haus gesteckt, und so rasch er konnte, lief er dem Rhein zu. Ja, da war die Rampe 87 und da standen auch die Kameraden.

»Wo bleibst du so lange?«, rief ihm Boddas entgegen. »Es ist schon Viertel nach sechs! Ist die Luft rein?«

Knöres winkte ab.

»Nicht mehr nötig, Leute. Hier ist der Zettel – ich war schon drin –«

»Wo drin? Doch nicht in der Villa...«

»Nennen wir sie lieber das Haus zu den hundert Morden!«, sagte Knöres großartig.

»Hast du Leichen gefunden?«, fragte Silli schaudernd.

»Nein, die hat der Rhein alle abgetrieben. Aber was will denn nun das Rote U von uns?«

Sie entfalteten den Zettel und lasen mit der Taschenlampe:

```
Heute ist Freitag. Der Schuster Derendorf in
der Kapuzinergasse hat einen ganzen Haufen
Vögel. Und die sollt ihr ihm bis morgen Abend
alle fliegen lassen.
                                    Das Rote U
```

Eine merkwürdige Namenstagsfeier

An diesem Freitagabend war die ganze Räuberbande bei Dölls Mutter eingeladen. Das war fast jeden Freitag so. Und sie freuten sich schon die ganze Woche darauf. Freilich roch in jeder Woche, die der liebe Gott werden ließ, schon seit Menschengedenken des Freitags die ganze Altstadt nach Rüböl, von vormittags bis spät in den Abend. Aber so feine Reibekuchen, wie sie die dicke Frau Döll buk, gab's auf der ganzen Welt nicht mehr. An diesen Abenden saß also die Bande friedlich um den blank gescheuerten Eichentisch in dem großen Haus, zusammen mit Vater und Mutter Döll, mit allen Angestellten, den Verkäufern, Lagerarbeitern und Fahrern. Eine Schüssel Reibekuchen nach der andern, hoch getürmt, kam auf den Tisch und im Nu waren die leckeren gelbbraunen Kuchen wieder verschwunden. Aber dann war schon wieder eine neue Schüssel da. Und so ging's wohl eine Stunde lang. Die Kinder bekamen Pflaumenkompott dazu, die Großen Schwarzbrot und schwarzen Kaffee – immer sprudelte das Wasser dafür auf dem Herd und die riesengroße Kaffeekanne wurde ein Mal ums andre aufgegossen. Großmutter Döll, die keine Reibekuchen vertragen konnte, saß dann immer in ihrem

Ohrensessel in der Ecke und mahlte unermüdlich Kaffee.

Heute schmeckte es den Gesellen vom Roten U ganz besonders gut. Denn sie waren nass und durchgefroren und unter ihren Stühlen um ihre Füße bildeten sich bald kleine schmutzige Wasserlachen. Aber davon merkten sie jetzt nichts. Die Kuchen waren so angenehm heiß, das Kompott so fein kühl, und was das Schönste war – sie wussten jetzt, dass das Rote U gar nicht so schlimm war. Keine Einbrüche, nichts Böses hatte es ja von ihnen verlangt. Nein, sie hatten jetzt wirklich eine mächtige Hochachtung vor ihm. Dem Schuster die Vögel fliegen lassen – das war die Sache! Auf diesen herrlichen Gedanken wären sie nie, nie gekommen. Das war ja sogar ein gutes Werk! Wie konnten sich die armen Zeisige, die Dompfaffen und Blaumeisen denn in der düsteren Schusterbude wohlfühlen? Nein, die armen Tierchen gehörten in den grünen Hofgarten, wofür sie der Herrgott geschaffen hatte. Wenn es noch Kanarienvögel gewesen wären – die mochten an Käfig und Zimmerluft gewöhnt sein. In das finstere Loch aber, in dem der Schuster Derendorf arbeitete, kam das ganze Jahr kein Sonnenstrahl und es roch drinnen nur nach Pech, Leder, Tabak und Schnaps.

Die Kinder waren überhaupt bange vor dem alten Schuster. Keine Frau hatte der, keinen Gesellen, keinen Lehrjungen – die paar Flickarbeiten, die ihm die Leute noch brachten, machte er allein.

Und wenn einer zu ihm kam mit Schuhen, dann sah er den gar nicht an, knurrte nur etwas in seinen zerfressenen Schnauzbart, und wer die Schuhe wieder abholte, dem warf er sie vor die Füße; aber kein Kind ließ er eher hinaus, als bis er das mitgebrachte Geld aus dem Einwickelpapier heraus Groschen für Groschen zwei- oder dreimal gezählt hatte. Es war also wirklich keine Kleinigkeit, bei diesem bösen Mann die armen Gefangenen aus dem schwarzen Gitterkäfig zu befreien.

Großmutter Döll hatte eben die Kaffeemühle hingesetzt, wohl ein Pfund hatte sie gemahlen und nun war es endlich genug. Immer öfter schob einer seinen Teller zurück, hielt sich pustend den Bauch und bat nur noch um ein Tässchen Kaffee. Auch Döll schob gerade den letzten Reibekuchen in den Mund und noch kauend stand er auf und sagte zu seiner Mutter: »Meine Sonntagsschuhe sind kaputt. Darf ich sie eben zum Schuster bringen?«

»Schon wieder mal?«, sagte Frau Döll, »euch könnte man eiserne Schuhe kaufen – die kriegtet ihr auch in drei Tagen kaputt. Bring sie aber zum Bertram in die Flingerstraße, der macht grüne Sohlen drunter, die halten länger. Und bleib nicht wieder bis in die Puppen aus. Du kannst übrigens auch für den Vater die Feldschuhe mitnehmen, da brauchen bloß ein paar Flicken drauf ... der läuft sie ja immer an derselben Stelle krumm, und nimm den Regenschirm mit.«

Döll ging und packte die Schuhe in ein Einkaufsnetz, und als er in Mütze und Regenumhang auf die Straße trat, standen die anderen Räuber auch schon da.

»Das hast du fein gemacht, Döll«, lobte Mala, »denn meine Schuhe sind zufällig mal ganz und der Bertram in der Flingerstraße ist der Onkel von Knöres, also könnte der Knöres wirklich nicht gut zu dem Derendorf gehen, und Boddas und Silli? Na, die würden schön verhauen, wenn sie zu dem schwarzen Deuwel in die Kapuzinergasse gingen ...«

»Das hab ich mir auch gedacht«, meinte Döll, »und ich muss wirklich sagen, dann ist meine Mutter eine famose Frau, alles was recht ist – eh die mich haut, beißt sie sich lieber den Daumen ab. Und mein Vater, das ist überhaupt der feinste Kerl, den es gibt. Wie es neulich rausgekommen ist, dass der Boddas und ich an der Goldenen Brücke im Hofgarten geangelt haben, und wie nachher der Polizist gelaufen kam, und der konnte kaum durch – so viele Leute standen schon um uns rum –, und da hatten wir nur einen Rollmops an der Angel und wir haben gesagt, wir wollten nur unseren Rollmops wässern, da hat mein Vater gelacht, dass die Fensterscheiben wackelten, und fünf Groschen hat er mir noch dazu geschenkt ...«

»Das hast du ja schon hundertmal erzählt!«, sagte Silli, »und für die fünf Groschen hättest du mir lieber eine Tafel Schokolade kaufen sollen – ich hatte doch gerade zwei Wochen vorher Namenstag gehabt!«

»Und eine neue Batterie? Wo hätte ich die hergekriegt? He? Eine Batterie ist nötiger als Schokolade, das kannst du dir endlich mal merken!«

Das sah Silli auch ein, wenigstens sagte sie: »Hin ist hin, darum zanken wir uns nicht mehr! Und jetzt los zum Derendorf!«

»Wir gehen natürlich alle mit rein!«, rief Boddas.

»Du bist wohl ganz verrückt?«, sagte Silli, »wir können doch die Vögel jetzt noch nicht fliegen lassen! Zuerst muss Döll einmal ausspionieren, denn wenn wir alle zusammen kommen, dann weiß der Derendorf gleich, wer's getan hat!«

Das war schlau, ohne Zweifel, und Knöres, der Kluge, klopfte dem Mädchen auf die Schulter: »Kind«, sagte er, »aus dir kann noch mal was werden.«

Da lachten sie alle. Und als sie nun weitergingen durch den Regen, malten sie sich ihr neues Abenteuer immer feiner aus – einer wusste jedes Mal noch besser als der andere, wie es werden würde. Erst als sie in die schmale Kapuzinergasse einbogen, wurden sie stiller. Und nun standen sie vor dem engen kleinen Fenster, hinter dem ein schmutziges Pappschild hing, ganz besät von Fliegendreck und so staubig, dass man nur die groß gedruckten Buchstaben lesen konnte:

KARL DERENDORF

Schuhmacher

»Die Vögel hat er nach hinten raus«, erklärte Döll, »hier vorne schläft er nur.«

»Na, dann geh mal rein«, sagte Silli, »wir spazieren langsam bis an die nächste Ecke. Er wird dich ja nicht fressen.«

Döll schaute sie verächtlich an.

»Der?« Er machte eine Faust und stemmte den Arm an. »Pack nur mal, was hier für Muskeln sitzen! Ich bin vor dem Deuwel nicht bange!«

Und er ging in den niedrigen Hausgang hinein. Kein Licht brannte und im Düstern musste Döll sich vorwärtstappen. War der Schuster nicht zu Hause? Der Junge sah nämlich, als er ein paar Schritte weiter war, auch keinen Lichtschimmer durch die gläsernen Oberlichter der Werkstatttür fallen. »Himmel, das wäre eine Gelegenheit«, dachte er, »wenn nun die Türe vielleicht offen wäre?«

Er klopfte an. Aber drinnen blieb alles still. Er hörte nur das klägliche Piepsen von Vogelstimmen.

»Herr Derendorf«, rief er und klopfte noch einmal, »ich bringe Schuhe!« Aber keine Antwort. Und nun drückte er die Klinke herunter ... Die Tür war verschlossen.

Was sollte er machen? Einfach umkehren, das fiel ihm nicht ein. Jetzt war er einmal hier und wollte fertigkriegen, was er vorhatte. Das tat Döll immer. Und wenn der Lehrer noch so eine schwere Schularbeit aufgab – der Döll setzte sich daran, knirschte mit den Zähnen, zerbiss vielleicht einen ganzen Bleistift, verschmierte ein halbes Heft, aber die Sache aufgeben, das tat er nicht. Immer wieder fing er von Neuem an, und wenn es stundenlang dauerte. Aber am Morgen in der Schule, dann stand's auch da. Zwar in Dölls dicker, klobiger Schrift, aber sauber und ordentlich, und fast immer ohne Fehler.

So war Döll. Und drum dachte er auch jetzt: ›Wenn der Derendorf Zeit hat, dann hab ich sie auch!‹ Aber so untätig warten, das wollte er nun auch nicht. Er knipste also zuerst einmal die elektrische Taschenlampe an. Zwar leuchtete auch von der Straße her die Laterne in das Flürchen, aber der fahlgrüne Strahl ging nur so ein paar Meter hinein und dann war's wieder finster.

Zuerst leuchtete der Junge einmal das Schlüsselloch ab. Es konnte ja sein, dass der Schlüssel von drinnen steckte und der Schuster schlief nur. Das kam ja oft vor, dass der Derendorf sich einen Rausch antrank, dann den halben Tag auf seinem Bett verschnarchte und seine Vögel vergaß. Jedes Kind wusste das... Aber nein, der Schlüssel war abgezogen. Döll musste also schnell bei der Hand sein, wenn er etwas ausrichten wollte, denn jeden Augenblick konnte der Schuster zurückkommen.

Er leuchtete weiter. Und der Lampenschein traf auf eine niedrige Hoftür. Richtig, da fiel es ihm ein – das einzige Fensterchen der Schusterbude ging ja nach dem Hof zu. Und wirklich, die Tür war auf. Rasch schlüpfte er hindurch – denn draußen hatte er schwere Schritte gehört. Das musste der Schuster sein. Gewiss war er nur um die Ecke in der Wirtschaft gewesen. Ja, da kam er schon. Döll war bereits im Hof, aber er erkannte ihn an der Stimme. Denn der Schuster brummte und fluchte vor sich hin, wie er es oft tat, wenn er nicht mehr ganz nüchtern war.

Jetzt hörte Döll ihn mit dem Schlüssel klappern und rasch leuchtete er noch einmal auf dem Hof herum ... Ja, das Fenster lag ziemlich hoch, aber da stand eine alte Handkarre, die schob der Junge schnell an die Mauer heran, kletterte hinauf – und richtig, es ging. Er konnte in die Schusterbude hineinschauen. Gerade ging die Tür dort auf und der kleine schwarze Kerl kam hinein und gleich darauf brannte Licht.

Der Schuster schwankte von einer Seite auf die andre. Jetzt hielt er sich an seinem runden Tischchen fest, aber schon lag es da und Nägel und Stifte, Hämmer und Feilen flogen weit auf dem Boden umher. Und drüben die Vögel in dem großen Käfig erhoben ein mörderisches Geschrei ... Döll konnte gar nicht zählen, wie viele es waren. Alle flogen sie durcheinander, krallten sich gegen die Gitterstäbe, flatterten gegen die Käfigdecke. Sie hatten wohl wieder den ganzen Tag kein Wasser und kein Körnchen Futter bekommen.

Döll kriegte eine rechte Wut auf den alten Tierfreund. Am liebsten wäre er jetzt hineingegangen, hätte den Kerl in eine Ecke geworfen und die Vögel fliegen lassen. O ja, das traute er sich zu. Aber es war ihm doch zu gefährlich. Denn das wäre ja ein richtiger Überfall gewesen. Er griff nach dem Fensterchen. Vielleicht war es offen? Er konnte ja warten, bis der Schuster einschlief, und das würde sicher nicht mehr sehr lange dauern. Dann durchs Fenster hinein, die Vögel fliegen lassen und fort. Aber so einfach würde das auch nicht sein. Der Käfig war groß und gewiss seinen halben Zentner schwer. Nur das Türchen aufmachen und das Fenster, das wäre wohl kein Kunststück gewesen. Aber hätten die Tierchen den Ausweg gefunden? Gewiss hätte der Schuster sie sich am anderen Morgen zum größten Teil wieder auf den Schränken und in den Ecken zusammenlesen können. Aber das Fenster war auch zu, wie Döll jetzt merkte. Vielleicht hatte der Schuster es jahrelang nicht offen gehabt!

Und doch – der Junge fühlte: So eine günstige Gelegenheit würde vielleicht nicht wiederkommen! Was sollte er nur anfangen? Hier länger auf der Karre stehen und den schwankenden Tänzen des Schusters zusehen, das hatte wirklich keinen Zweck. Also herunter, wieder in den Flur – angeklopft ...

Kein »Herein« wurde gerufen. Und so drückte Döll einfach die Klinke herunter und machte die Türe auf.

»'n Abend, Herr Derendorf – hier wären zwei Paar Schuh.«

»Geh zum Deuwel mit deinen Schuhen!«,

schimpfte der Mann und dann, ohne sich nach dem Jungen umzusehen, knurrte er noch vor sich hin: »Rausgeschmissen, elend rausgeschmissen! Und das gerade heut! Na warte, ich komm euch!«

Döll wusste gleich, woran er war. Den Schuster hatten sie also wieder einmal aus der Wirtschaft hinausgeworfen. Sicher hatte er längst genug gehabt. Aber was sollte das heißen: gerade heute? Was war denn heute für ein Tag? Aha, schon fiel es ihm ein: der vierte November, und heute hatten alle Namenstag, die Karl hießen, also auch der Schuster Karl Derendorf ... »Das ist aber eine Gemeinheit, Herr Derendorf«, sagte drum Döll sofort, »na, dann gratuliere jetzt wenigstens ich herzlich zum Namenstag.«

Der Schuster mit seinen kleinen verschwommenen Augen sah den Jungen von der Seite an.

»Geld hast du natürlich noch nicht mitgebracht für die Schuhe?«, fragte er lauernd und warf das Netz mit den Schuhen beiseite.

»Geld? Nein! Das gibt mir meine Mutter doch erst, wenn ich die Schuhe abhole. Das ist doch immer so.«

»Dann mach, dass du rauskommst!«, schrie der Schuster und griff nach einem Schusterhammer.

O weh, das konnte gefährlich werden – wie der Blitz war Döll zur Tür hinaus und auf der Straße.

»Na?«, fragten die Kameraden, als er wieder bei ihnen stand, »der Kerl war aber vielleicht voll!«

»Wie 'ne Unke!«, sagte Döll, »und rausgeschmissen hat er mich, weil ich das Geld für die Schuh noch nicht bei mir hatte. In der Wirtschaft haben sie ihn an die Luft gesetzt ... sicher wollte er noch Schnaps haben –«

»Und was nun? Was hast du ausspioniert?«, fragte Boddas.

Silli tanzte plötzlich von einem Bein auf das andere.

»Wer hat denn dich gebissen?«, sagte Mala.

Aber das Mädchen war schon wieder vernünftig, doch unter der Kapuze sahen die Jungen ihre Augen blitzen.

»Wer von euch kann am schnellsten fünf Mark auftreiben?«, fragte sie.

»Hm«, meinte Döll, »die bringe ich schon auf die Beine. Wozu willst du sie denn haben?«

Silli trat mit dem Fuß auf, warf den Kopf zurück, dass ihre Zöpfe, die nach vorn herunterhingen, nur so flogen.

»Mach fix«, sagte sie, »frag nicht lange. Bist du noch nicht wieder hier? Und komm mir ja nicht ohne das Geld!«

Döll trabte davon – langsam gingen die anderen ihm nach, sahen, wie er aus der engen Kapuzinergasse in die breite, helle Flingerstraße einbog. Und dann – dann verschwand er plötzlich in einer Wirtschaft ...

»Was tut der denn da?«, fragte Silli. »Ob er meint, da fänd er fünf Mark unter den Tischen?«

Aber Döll wusste ganz genau, was er tat. Heute

Abend hatten sie Reibekuchen gegessen, und Reibekuchen, das gab allemal einen höllischen Durst, besonders bei seinem Vater. Kaum dass Herr Döll freitags abends nach dem Essen einen Blick in die Zeitung getan hatte, faltete er sie auch schon zusammen und sagte: »Nein, was diese Reibekuchen einen Durst machen! Ich muss schnell einmal Reibekuchenfeuer löschen.« Sprach's, steckte die Zeitung in die Tasche, nahm Mantel und Hut und ging für ein Stündchen oder zwei in den »Kessel« an der Flingerstraße. Also würde er auch heute da sein, kalkulierte Döll und weiter kalkulierte er noch: Wenn der Vater im »Kessel« sitzt, dann ist er bestimmt gut gelaunt und die fünf Mark habe ich eigentlich schon so gut wie sicher in der Tasche.

Jetzt sah er sich in der Wirtschaft um und bald hatte er seinen Vater erspäht, der mit ein paar dicken Herren an einem runden Tisch saß und Karten spielte. Gerade warf Herr Döll die Karten hin und der Junge sah sein Gesicht strahlen: »Also, meine Herren«, sagte er, »Grand mit zweien, gespielt drei, aus der Hand vier, geschnitten fünf, angesagt sechs...«

Der Junge grinste. Besser konnte er es ja gar nicht treffen. Jetzt nur schnell an den Tisch, ehe das neue Spiel im Gange war. Denn wenn er den Vater störte, dann war's Essig mit den fünf Mark...

Und schon hörte er einen von den dicken Herren rufen: »Da kommt ja Ihr Sohn, Herr Döll. Hahaha, der alte Döll muss nach Haus kommen.«

Aber schon von Weitem winkte der Junge ab und lachend kam er näher: »Gratuliere auch zu dem feinen Grand, Vater«, sagte er, »und ob du mir nicht fünf Mark geben könntest?«

»Fünf Mark, Junge? Wofür?«

»Die will die Silli haben, Vater ... Hoppla! jetzt weiß ich es!« Er klatschte sich mit der Hand aufs Bein und tat einen Luftsprung. Ein Licht war ihm aufgegangen, aber noch ein viel helleres, als Silli in ihrem klugen Köpfchen hatte. »Ja, Vater«, bettelte er, »gib uns doch das Geld! Du sollst auch heut Abend einen Spaß haben, der mindestens einen Taler wert ist – ja, Vater? Damals hast du uns doch für den lumpigen Rollmops fünf Groschen gegeben.«

Gerade war neu verteilt worden und eben hob Herr Döll seine Karten auf: Drei Asse und zwei Buben.

»Grand«, sagte er wieder, »wer spielt auf?«

Und mit der linken Hand griff er in die Westentasche und legte ein blankes Fünfmarkstück auf die Tischkante.

»Da, Junge, nun mach, dass du rauskommst. Wer geht drüber?«

»Verlieren Sie nur Ihren Grand!«, rief der dicke Herr, der neben Herrn Döll saß.

Aber der Junge hörte das schon nicht mehr. Mit dem Geld in der Faust rannte er zur Tür hinaus, aber dann gleich rechts herum in den Flur der Wirtschaft und nun klopfte er am Schalter.

»Ich möchte für fünf Mark Schnaps für den Schuster, den Sie eben rausgeschmissen haben.«

Der Wirt besah sich das Geldstück.

»Und eben hatte der Kerl keinen Pfennig mehr!«, brummte er; dann erst schaute er durch das Fensterchen und da erkannte er den Jungen.

»Ah, du bist das, Kerlchen!«, lachte er, »nun geht mir ein Licht auf! Meinst du, ich hab es nicht gesehen, wie du dir von deinem Vater eben die fünf Mark hast geben lassen? Was schämen sollt ihr Lümmel euch! Den Kerl noch besoffener zu machen! Gehört sich denn das?«

Döll schaute den Wirt ganz erschrocken an. Oh, der würde jetzt gewiss sofort an den Skattisch gehen und sagen: »Sie, Herr Döll, Ihr Junge macht aber nette Geschichten –« Es war ja auch wirklich nicht schön von ihm – das sah er ein. Aber wie sollten sie sonst die Vögel freilassen?

Doch nein, der Wirt grinste auf einmal ganz freundlich und sagte: »Na, so schlimm wird's ja nicht sein.«

Und er machte sich am Schanktisch zu schaffen. Was er tat, konnte Döll zwar nicht sehen. Und als er ihm durch das Fensterchen eine volle Flasche reichte, wusste der Junge also auch nicht, was er hineingefüllt hatte.

»So, Junge – sag aber dem Schuster, er soll mir morgen die Flasche wiederbringen. Und die fünf Mark kannst du auch behalten ... Bestell dem Derendorf, ich ließ ihm zum Namenstag gratulieren, und wenn er wollte, schickt ich ihm gern noch so eine Flasche.«

Aber Döll war schon längst hinaus und der Wirt rieb sich die Hände. Der Junge hätte es verdient, meinte er, wenn ihm jetzt der Schuster in seiner Wut eine Tracht Prügel gäbe ...

In der Kapuzinergasse warteten schon die anderen Räuber.

»Silli«, rief Döll atemlos, »ich habe das Geld. Aber Schnaps brauchen wir gar nicht dafür zu kaufen – den hab ich nämlich auch schon! Geschenkt sogar!«

Das Mädel lachte, dass seine weißen Zähne schimmerten. »Also hast du schon kapiert, was ich wollte?«

Und dann erzählte er rasch, wie er zu dem Geld und der Flasche gekommen war.

»Bombensicher klappt die Sache!«, flüsterte er, »aber ihr müsst sofort da sein, wenn ich euch rufe! Halt, am besten geht ihr alle vier mit und versteckt euch in dem Hof.«

Schon huschten sie wie die Kobolde durch den dunklen Flurgang des Schuhmachers Karl Derendorf in den Hof. Als sie dann die Tür hinter sich zugezogen hatten, klopfte Döll herzhaft an die Werkstatt. Und ohne auf ein »Herein« zu warten, trat er auch gleich in die enge Kammer.

»Ich komme noch mal wieder, Herr Derendorf«, sagte er.

Aber der Schuster schien ihn gar nicht zu hören.

Der Mann musste doch schrecklich betrunken sein. Und die Vögelchen schrien so ... War es nicht doch eine Sünde, ihm jetzt wieder eine dicke Flasche von dem schrecklichen Zeug zu geben? Aber jetzt konnte Döll nicht mehr zurück. Er hatte einmal A gesagt und nun musste er auch B sagen. Da war nichts zu machen.

Der Schuster, der sich taumelnd an einem Schrank festhielt, hatte ihn jetzt endlich gesehen.

»Wwwas wwwillst dddu hier?«, lallte er, »raus!«

»Aber, Herr Derendorf«, sagte Döll, »ich hab Ihnen auch was mitgebracht ... Der Vater braucht nämlich die Feldschuhe morgen früh schon und da hätt ich gern drauf gewartet ... Und weil er das eigentlich nicht verlangen kann und überhaupt, weil Sie heute Namenstag haben, schickt er Ihnen hier 'ne Flasche Schnaps.«

Döll wusste selber nicht, wie ihm das alles so schnell und so sicher aus dem Munde sprudelte, als hätte er es sich lang und breit überlegt.

Der Schuster grinste mit dem ganzen Gesicht.

»Na, denn stell sie mal her, mein Söhnchen«, stotterte er und stieß an bei jedem Wort, »eigentlich wollte ich ja gerade zu Bett, aber für deinen Vater tut man schon gern etwas ...«

Döll war sehr neugierig auf diese Arbeit und nun sah er auch droben am Fensterchen Sillis und Malas Gesichter durch die schmutzige Scheibe spähen.

Der Schuster ließ sich auf den Schemel fallen –

nein, er wollte es nur, und plumps!, saß er auf der Erde, unter alten Schuhen und Handwerkszeug.

»Schadet nichts!«, sagte er, nahm von irgendwoher einen verstaubten Frauenschuh und besah die Sohle.

»Das werden wir gleich haben!«, brummte er.

»Aber das ist ja gar nicht der Schuh von meinem Vater!«, sagte Döll.

»Dddummer Junge, was verstehst denn du davon?«, knurrte der Schuster, »reich mir die Flasche her, ich muss mich mal stärken –«

Döll gab sie ihm und droben am Fenster sah er Sillis Lachen.

Jetzt setzte der Schuster die Flasche an den Mund. Gluckgluck ging es ... aber schon sprudelte er das Zeug aus dem Mund und im gleichen Augenblick flog der Schuh, den er noch in der anderen Hand hielt, hart neben Dölls Kopf vorbei krachend an die Türe. Da hatte der Junge aber auch schon begriffen, warum ihm der Wirt sein Geld zurückgegeben hatte.

In der Flasche war Wasser, sonst nichts.

Jetzt war alles verloren. ›Rette sich, wer kann!‹, dachte Döll. Und schon wieder flog ihm ein Schuh am Kopf vorbei. Wehe, wenn ihn der Schuster erwischte! Aber nein, Döll blieb in der offenen Türe stehen, sprungfertig ... doch es war nicht nötig. Der Schuster kam nicht auf. Noch einmal versuchte er's, aber dann plumpste er zurück und lag da wie ein Sack. Im gleichen Augenblick fing er auch schon zu schnarchen an, als müsste er die dickste Ulme im Hofgarten umsägen.

»Herr Derendorf, schlafen Sie?«, rief Döll.

Doch der Schuster schnarchte weiter.

»Herr Derendorf!«

Aber Herr Derendorf hörte nicht.

Nun zog der Junge ihn vorsichtig und dann kräftig am Bein. Jetzt zwickte er ihn in den Arm. Nein, der schlief wie ein Murmeltier. Und Döll wollte schon die Kameraden herbeirufen, da sah er auf dem Schrank eine Schachtel Streichhölzer liegen.

›Probieren wir das auch noch!‹, dachte er, rieb schnell ein Hölzchen an und hielt es dem schnarchenden Schuster dicht vor die Augen. Aber der muckste sich nicht.

Leise stand Döll jetzt auf, ging zur Türe und ließ die anderen ein.

»Er schläft wie ein Bock!«, sagte er, »und jetzt lassen wir mal erst die armen Vögel fliegen … Halt, vor allen Dingen kriegen sie Futter!«

Die Kinder hantierten wie Geisterchen, flink, unhörbar, und was sie sagten, das flüsterten sie kaum. Bald hatten sie auch schon in einer Schrankschublade eine Tüte mit einem Rest Vogelfutter gefunden und wie ausgehungert stürzten sich die Tierchen drüber her. Im Nu waren die Körner weggefressen.

»Jetzt herunter mit dem Käfig!«, kommandierte eines der Heinzelmännchen. Aber Döll und Boddas setzten den riesigen Käfig erst gar nicht auf die

Erde – sie trugen ihn sofort auf den Hof und nun griffen sie hinein und ließen eins der Tierchen nach dem anderen in die stille Nacht hinauffliegen.

»Das können wir ruhig tun«, meinte Silli, »die Vögel finden hier an den alten Häusern genug Ritzen und Winkel, wo sie sich bis zum Morgen verstecken können und auch nicht erfrieren.«

Aber es dauerte doch eine ganze Weile, bis das letzte Vögelchen verschwunden war.

»So«, meinte Mala, »nun hängen wir den Käfig wieder auf und gehen nach Haus. Dann kann der alte Tierquäler morgen früh ja meinen, er hätte all die Vögel im Kopf.«

»Nein«, zischelte Döll, »jetzt kommt erst meine Idee! Für die fünf Mark müssen wir meinem Vater auch etwas liefern! Das könnt ihr euch doch wohl denken!«

Sie sahen ihn an und wussten nicht, was er meinte. Es war ihnen längst unheimlich in der finsteren Bude und es grauste sie immer, wenn sie über den schlafenden Schuster hinwegsteigen mussten.

»Was willst du denn nun noch?«, fragte Silli schaudernd, »ich bin froh, wenn wir aus diesem Loch heraus sind!«

»Och, der wacht nicht auf!«, sagte Döll, aber er flüsterte trotzdem. »Und nun gebt einmal acht: Ich habe gesehen, dass man die vordere Käfigseite ganz herunterklappen kann. Jetzt stecken wir einfach den Schuster da hinein und fahren ihn auf der Schubkarre in die Wirtschaft …«

Als das die Räuber kaum halb gehört hatten, waren sie außer Rand und Band. Eins, zwei, drei schleppten sie den Vogelkäfig wieder in die Stube. Aber alle vier mussten sie anpacken, bis sie den kleinen dürren Schuster hinter den Gittern hatten. Silli hielt derweil die Zimmertüre auf, denn wenn er wirklich wach wurde, dann mussten sie fort sein wie vom Winde weggeweht.

Endlich war die schwere Arbeit getan. Nun schleppten sie schwitzend den Käfig in den Hof und schoben ihn auf die herabgelassene Karre.

»Das möcht ich nicht jeden Tag tun!«, seufzte Boddas und wischte sich mit dem Ärmel die hellen Tropfen von der Stirn.

»Es kann auch nicht jeder so viel in den Knochen haben wie ich!«, sagte Döll großartig.

»Diesmal hast du aber auch was im Kopf gehabt!«, lachte Silli und dieses Lob tat dem Jungen in der Seele wohl.

Jetzt aber schoben sie den Karren mit dem Käfig und dem Schuster durch den Hausflur, doch ehe sie auf der Straße waren, schickte die kluge Silli den Mala noch einmal zurück – eine Decke sollte er holen, um sie über den Gitterkasten zu tun. Sonst würden sie bestimmt von der Polizei angehalten ...

Als Mala mit dem Tuch zurückkam, war er blass wie eine Wand.

»Ich habe droben am Fenster, von draußen, wo wir eben gestanden haben, ein Gesicht gesehen –«, keuchte er.

Einen Augenblick standen die anderen da wie gelähmt, Boddas setzte schon den Fuß aus der Türe, um wegzurennen.

Aber da sagte Knöres: »Ich habe ja auch so eine Gestalt gesehen heute Abend. Das war das Rote U`...«

»Sehen wir doch mal nach!«, flüsterte Döll.

Aber keine Macht der Welt hätte die Kinder jetzt noch einmal in den Hof zurückgebracht. Als wäre ein Gespenst hinter ihnen, schoben sie den Karren aus dem Flur auf die Straße. Kein Mensch war dort zu sehen. Und ohne anzuhalten, fuhren sie zum »Kessel«, drückten und zogen die Karre rasch dort in den hell beleuchteten Vorraum über die Steinfliesen.

Dann klopfte Döll wieder an den Bierschalter, und als der Wirt kam, rief er hinein: »Der Herr Derendorf möchte die Flasche wiederbringen. Draußen ist er im Flur!«

Und weg war er. Im Rennen riss er noch das Tuch von dem Käfig und warf es hinter sich. Die anderen waren schon um die nächste Straßenecke und im Augenblick hatte Döll sie erreicht.

»So«, sagte Silli, »wisst ihr, was wir jetzt tun? Jetzt gehen wir zum Schuster Bertram in die Flingerstraße und tragen deine Schuhe hin. Ich habe nämlich das Netz wieder mitgebracht.«

»Du bist doch die Schlauste von uns allen, Silli!«, rief Döll bewundernd.

Und als sie wieder in die Flingerstraße einbogen,

sahen sie einen Menschenauflauf vor dem »Kessel«, hörten ein Johlen und Lachen, in das sie am liebsten eingestimmt hätten. Aber sittsam gingen sie mit ihrem Schuhnetz vorüber. Dass sie sich gegenseitig in die Arme kniffen, konnte ja keiner sehen.

Dölls Vater aber kam diesen Abend erst lange nach Mitternacht heim. Und als er am anderen Tag erzählte, wie der Schuster Derendorf mit einem Mal auf einer Karre in seinem Vogelkäfig schlafend im »Kessel« gestanden hätte, da zwinkerte er nur einmal ganz verstohlen seinem Sohn, dem Jungen Döll, zu. Aber der sah es kaum, da bückte er sich auch schon wieder tief über seine Erbsensuppe und löffelte so eifrig, als wollte er Perlen darin fischen.

Von Kaninchenräubern und einer schweren Aufgabe

Es war Samstagabend. Der Regen vom vorigen Tage hatte aufgehört und prächtig ging die Sonne hinter dem Rhein unter. Kurz nur war dann die Dämmerung und durch die alten Straßen und Gässchen kamen die Frauen, Körbchen und Taschen in der Hand, denn für den Sonntag hatten sie eingekauft und nun machten sie eilig, dass sie heimkamen, um das Abendbrot zu richten.

Auch die Frau Gebendeil aus dem alten Zollgässchen wäre an diesem Abend gern ausgegangen, um etwas Nahrhaftes für ihre vier Kinder zu besorgen. Aber das ging nun zum soundsovielten Male nicht. Ihr Mann war schon viele Monate arbeitslos und es reichte nur für das Allernötigste. Jetzt stand sie in der Küche und wusch unter der Wasserleitung einen Kessel Kartoffeln, die sie für diesen Abend kochen wollte.

Und jetzt klangen auch noch die feierlichen Glocken von Sankt Lambertus, die den Sonntag einläuteten, durch das offene Fenster. Die arme Frau konnte es kaum anhören. Sie trocknete ihre Hände an der Schürze ab und wollte das Fenster zumachen. Der Abend war ja auch zu kühl. Aber kaum hatte sie sich vom Wasserhahn umgedreht und einen Schritt ins Zimmer getan, da flog durch das

Fenster plötzlich etwas Dunkles in die Stube und fiel mit dumpfem Krach auf den Boden.

›Diese Straßenbengel!‹, dachte die Frau, ›aber das kommt davon, wenn man im Erdgeschoss wohnt! Allen Dreck schmeißen sie einem in die Küche.‹ Da, da kam schon wieder etwas geflogen, und noch einmal ... eins fiel sogar mitten auf den Tisch und im gleichen Augenblick hörte die Frau schnelle Jungenschritte draußen am Fenster vorbei die Straße hinab in Richtung Rhein eilen.

Ein paar Augenblicke später beugte sie sich zum Fenster hinaus, aber sie sah niemanden mehr. Ärgerlich ging sie in die Stube zurück, doch schon fuhr sie mit leisem Aufschrei hoch – sie hatte auf etwas Weiches getreten. Am Tisch wollte sie sich halten – aber schon wieder griff sie irgendwo hinein. Ein Fell war es, ein Tier ... Hatten ihr die Gassenbuben tote Ratten ins Fenster geworfen? Aber dafür war das Fell zu dicht ... Schnell tastete sie nach Streichhölzern und nun hatte sie das Licht an. Da sah sie es: In der Küche lagen drei Kaninchen, fette, schwere Tiere.

Ja, der neue Befehl des Roten U – diesmal hatte ihn Boddas in seinem Buch gefunden – war kurz und bündig gewesen:

```
Ihr habt heute den Gebendeils einen guten
Sonntagsbraten zu besorgen und bis in einer
Woche dem Vater Gebendeil Arbeit zu verschaf-
fen.
                                  Das Rote U
```

Ratlos hatten sich die fünfe nach der Schule angesehen. Aber weil das Rote U noch daruntergeschrieben hatte:

 Bis heute bin ich sehr zufrieden mit euch

hatten sie sich mit Feuereifer darangegeben. Die vier Gebendeil-Kinder kannten sie ja gut. Alle viere waren bei ihnen in der Schule. Nein, da hatte das Rote U ganz recht: Hier musste mal etwas getan werden! Aber woher wusste dies Rote U das alles? Die Kinder konnten es nicht begreifen und es war ihnen beinahe unheimlich.

Dann diese schwere neue Aufgabe! Sie wussten noch gar nicht, wie sie die Geschichte anpacken sollten. Mit dem Sonntagsbraten, das war allerdings nicht so besonders schwer. Aber das Rote U stellte es sich doch wohl ein bisschen zu einfach vor. Es war wirklich keine Kleinigkeit gewesen für die vier Jungen, am Samstagnachmittag, wo die Schule geschlossen war, sich in den Schulhof zu schleichen, ohne dass der Hausmeister sie erwischte, dann über die hohe Mauer zu klettern in den alten Klostergarten. Freilich, als sie einmal drüben waren, ging's schnell. Vor dem Pfarrer brauchten sie sich ja nicht besonders in Acht zu nehmen, denn der und die Kapläne waren samstagnachmittags immer in der Kirche. Und so hatten die jungen Räuber schon in zwei Stunden drei Kaninchen geschossen … Ach, die hatte Silli sonst immer gebraten, ganz wie es sich gehört, mit Estragon und Thymian. Aber heut hätte ihnen das zarte Fleisch gar nicht geschmeckt und Boddas sagte, sie müssten sich ordentlich schämen, dass sie noch nicht selbst auf den Gedanken gekommen wären. Das Rote U musste gewiss der beste von allen Menschen sein!

Ordentlich stolz waren sie, dass sie solch einen Räuberhauptmann hatten!

Aber wie sollten sie nun dem armen Mann Arbeit verschaffen? Was alles sollten sie versuchen?

»Wir müssen was rauskriegen!«, sagte Mala, als sie am Sonntag nach der Schulmesse vor der Kirche zusammenstanden, »denn das Rote U soll nachher nicht sagen, seine Räuber wären Waschlappen und Dummköpfe!«

Dann besah er sich Silli. In ihrem neuen Sonntagsmantel mit dem netten Pelzkrägelchen und dem hübschen kleinen Samtkäppchen sah sie eigentlich sehr gut aus.

»Wie so 'ne Wiener Schlittschuhläuferin«, sagte er, »die sind ja immer in der Zeitung fotografiert und sind alle sechzehn Jahre alt. Wie alt bist du eigentlich?«

»Noch nicht ganz dreizehn ... Warum fragst du so dumm?«

»Darum! Hör mal, Silli, das wäre eigentlich eine Arbeit für dich, dem Gebendeil Arbeit zu besorgen.«

Das Mädchen riss die blauen Augen auf.

»Für mich? Nun mach aber einen Punkt! Was

versteh ich von der Arbeitsucherei? Meinen Vater hab ich schon gefragt, aber der hat jetzt nur noch zwei Bauten, und außerdem ist doch der Gebendeil Schlosser ...«

»Ich meine ja nur so, Silli«, sagte der lange Mala, »was bleibt uns denn anderes übrig, als bei den dicken Fabrikers von Haus zu Haus zu laufen und zu fragen? Beim Mannesmann, beim Haniel und Lueg, beim Phönix in Oberbilk. Und was denkst du wohl, wenn da so ein Junge ankommt und sagt: ›Ich möchte gefälligst euren Direktor sprechen‹ – dann wird der achtkantig rausgeschmissen, erstens mal sowieso, und zweitens sieht man uns doch den Räuber schon von Weitem an. Kapierst du das? Na also!«

»Überhaupt, das ist gar keine räuberische Aufgabe!«, knurrte Döll.

»Das will ich nun grade nicht sagen«, meinte Boddas, »denn einer wie wir, der muss eben alles können. Und das will das Rote U gewiss mal feststellen. Meinst du, er hätte damals den Zettel, den der Knöres aus der Villa Jück holen musste, nicht geradeso gut in unser Buch legen können? Aber nein, der wollte nur sehen, ob wir die Courage hätten, in das Verbrecherhaus zu gehen. Na, und genau so ist es jetzt. Und das könnt ihr mir glauben, ich geh hundertmal lieber in die Villa Jück als zum Haniel ...«

»Alle tausend Teufel, das sage ich ja eben!«, rief Mala, »aber wenn Silli hinkommt und macht einen Knicks und so 'n Quatsch – nein, ein Fräulein an die Luft zu setzen, dafür sind sie denn doch zu anständig!«

Das Mädchen winkte ab.

»So sehe ich aus! Nein, da geht ihr mal lieber hin und schlagt ein paar Mal Rad ... Ich wollte, wir hätten wieder eine anständige Aufgabe.«

»In früheren Zeiten«, beharrte Boddas, »haben die Räuber auch immer den armen Leuten geholfen, das wisst ihr ganz genau.«

So redeten sie hin und her im Weitergehen, bis Döll sich endlich vor seiner Haustür verabschiedete.

»Sonst komm ich zu spät zum Kaffee«, sagte er, »heut haben wir nämlich Streuselkuchen.«

Dann kamen sie in Malas Straße und bei Mala gab es sicher auch etwas Gutes, denn der Junge ging von der Haustür aus keinen Schritt mehr weiter.

»Morgen ist auch noch ein Tag!«, sagte er.

Endlich war auch Knöres fort und Boddas und seine Schwester gingen das kleine Stückchen bis nach Haus allein. Eigentlich hätten sie durch die Kapuzinergasse gemusst. Aber das bisschen Umweg tat nichts. Es war wirklich nicht unbedingt nötig, dass sie an Herrn Derendorfs Flickschusterhöhle vorbeigingen ...

Der Bauunternehmer Johann Boden war mit seiner Frau heute auch ein wenig früher aufgestanden, denn gleich nach dem Kaffee wollten sie mit den beiden Kindern nach Angermund hinausfahren und dort den herrlichen Spätherbsttag verbringen. Jetzt saßen sie zusammen beim sonntäglichen Kaffeetrinken, Frau Boden schnitt gerade den Kuchen an und legte jedem der Kinder ein großes Stück auf den Teller.

»Hoffentlich ist der Kaffee ordentlich heiß«, sagte sie, »ich hab in der Kirche gefroren wie ein Schneider. Wenn ich erst an den Winter denke ... da holt man sich ja die schönste Lungenentzündung!«

»Wir fangen nächste Woche schon mit dem Einbau der Heizung an«, sagte der Bauunternehmer. Er war ja im Kirchenvorstand und musste das wissen. »Wenn nur die schrecklichen Ausschachtungsarbeiten unter dem Kirchenschiff nicht wären, dann könnte die ganze Heizung schon in drei Wochen fertig sein. Aber so!«

Boddas sah verstohlen seine Schwester an und das Stück Kuchen blieb ihm im Hals stecken. Also jetzt kamen die Arbeiter und mit dem schönen alten Klostergärtchen war es aus! Dann würde dort der Schutt aufgetürmt, die ausgeschachteten Erdmassen würden gewiss dorthin abgefahren und weiß Gott noch was!

Ja, die Kinder hassten ordentlich die neumodische Zeit mit ihren Heizungen, ihren Kanälen, Kabelanlagen, elektrischen Bahnen und Autobussen! Ein schönes Spielfleckchen nach dem andern wurde weggefressen von der Großstadt wie der Frühlingsschnee von der Aprilsonne ...

Boddas musste das morgen sofort den anderen sagen und dann wollten sie noch einmal den ganzen Tag in das Gärtchen und hinab in den Keller unter dem Pfarrhaus. In diesen alten Keller konnten doch auch die Heizungsöfen kommen, meinte er, und dann Röhrenleitungen in die Kirche. Warum wollten sie gerade unter dem Kirchenschiff ausschachten und damit das ganze Gärtchen verderben durch das Hin und Her von Arbeitern, Karren und Pferden?

Eine Schande, dass gerade in dieser Woche die Sache gemacht werden musste mit dem Gebendeil! Sie hätten so schön Zeit gehabt, von dem heimlichen Spielplatz Abschied zu nehmen! Aber da war nichts zu machen. Das Rote U hatte befohlen und damit war die Sache erledigt.

»Vater«, sagte da Silli auf einmal, »ich habe dir doch schon gestern von dem armen Schlosser Gebendeil und seinen vier oder acht Kindern erzählt; ich glaube, es sind sogar zehn oder fünfzehn ... Wenn ihr doch nun die Heizung macht unter der Kirche, dann kannst du ihm sicher Arbeit geben –«

»Das ist ja sehr schön von dir, Kind, dass du daran denkst«, meinte Herr Boden, »aber da kann ich gar nichts dran machen. Die Arbeit wird einfach in der Zeitung ausgeschrieben und die Firma, die sie kriegt, bringt ihre Arbeiter natürlich mit ... Möglich, dass sie den einen oder anderen neu einstellt. Aber dann muss sich Herr Gebendeil eben an die

Firma wenden, wenn es so weit ist. Ich will euch schon zeitig Bescheid sagen, dann könnt ihr es ihm ja bestellen lassen durch die Kinder. Vielleicht hat er Glück.«

Boddas hörte kaum hin. Er krümelte an seinem Kuchen herum, rührte mit dem Kaffeelöffel in der Tasse, dann stierte er wieder Löcher in die Luft ... Er hatte so seine Gedanken. Aber er sagte nichts.

Auch unterwegs, als sie von der Bahnstation durch die fast schon kahlen Wälder gingen, Angermund zu, war er still und ganz sonderbar in sich gekehrt. Silli merkte es wohl. Aber sie wusste, wenn irgendetwas hinter des Bruders kantiger Stirn arbeitete, dann war es nicht gut, ihn zu stören. Aber was mochte es diesmal sein? Was waren das für Linien und Figuren, die er immer, wenn sie auf einer Bank saßen, in den Sand zeichnete?

In Angermund wollten sie zu Mittag essen. Und kaum hatten sie sich an den schön und sauber gedeckten Tisch in der einsamen Wirtschaft gesetzt, da ging die Türe auf und Silli rief leise: »Da kommt der Ühl!«

Alle drehten sie sich um, und richtig – der Landgerichtsrat Bernhard, ein ernster, früh grau gewordener Mann, trat mit seiner feinen Frau und dem blassen Jungen ein. Man sah ihm an, dass er sich freute, Herrn Boden hier zu treffen. Herr Boden hatte seinerzeit das neue Haus des Richters gebaut. Auch der Junge bekam ein rotes Gesicht vor Freude, als er Silli und Boddas sah.

»Das ist aber fein!«, sagte er, »gerade ihr seid hier. Darf ich nach dem Essen vielleicht mit euch spielen?«

Boddas schaute den kleinen Jungen an, ungefähr wie ein gewaltig einhertrottender Bernhardiner ein Terrierhündchen besieht ...

»Na ja«, sagte er gutmütig, »wenn du Lust hast –«

Der Junge wurde womöglich noch röter.

»Wir wollen nämlich Kahn fahren«, sagte Boddas, »wenn du keine Angst hast.«

Herr Boden und der Richter hatten sich schon begrüßt und die Frauen schon freudig festgestellt, dass es wirklich herrliches Wetter wäre und dass man an so einem Sonntag gar nichts Besseres tun könnte, als aufs Land zu fahren, gerade hierhin, in diese Waldeinsamkeit. Frau Boden sagte das und Silli und Boddas fanden das sehr komisch. Aber es wurde doch ganz schön, das Essen schmeckte herrlich und noch feiner war die Kahnfahrt nachher auf der Anger. Der komische Ühl kreischte nicht einmal, wenn Silli im Kahn so schaukelte, dass das Wasser beinahe hineinschwappte. Selbst Boddas wurde das zu viel.

»Ich haue dir gleich mit dem Ruder auf die Finger!«, rief er seiner Schwester zu; aber als er dann seine Mutter fern am Ufer im Wirtshausgarten stehen sah, wie sie die Hände entsetzt zusammenschlug, schaukelte er selber noch kräftig mit.

Es war das erste Mal, dass die beiden Kinder mit dem blassen Jungen allein zusammen waren, und als sie nach einer Weile langsamer zurückruderten, fragte Boddas den Ühl: »Sag mal, weshalb bist du noch bei uns in der Volksschule? Dein Vater müsste dich doch eigentlich aufs Gymnasium schicken ... Bei mir ist das was anderes. Ich komme auf die Bauschule und dann geh ich gleich ins Geschäft von meinem Vater.«

Der Junge war wieder rot geworden.

»Ja«, sagte er, »du hast recht, aber meine Mutter meint, ich muss mich noch schonen – weil ich so schwach bin. Mutter will nicht, dass ich mich jetzt schon so anstrenge. Ich soll bis vierzehn Jahre in der Volksschule bleiben und dann auf eine Privatschule ... Aber wisst ihr«, Boddas sah genau, dass sein Gesicht jetzt rot wurde, nicht mehr vor Scham, sondern vor Zorn, »das meinen die nur alle! Und dabei bin ich doch wirklich nicht so schlapp ... Ob ihr mich nicht doch mal auch auf dem Schulhof mit euch spielen lassen könnt?«

»Ja, vielleicht später mal«, sagte Boddas, »muss erst mit den anderen sprechen ... Vorläufig ist natürlich noch nicht dran zu denken. Wir haben jetzt da so Sachen ... Aber darüber kann ich bei Fremden selbstverständlich nicht reden.«

Doch der Ühl war schon froh, dass Boddas nicht ganz Nein gesagt hatte. Sogar auf den Landungssteg half er ihm jetzt.

»Ich werde dich also vormerken, frag gelegentlich mal wieder nach ...«, sagte er noch. Diese

schöne Redensart hatte er natürlich von seinem Vater gelernt.

Mittlerweile war es drei Uhr geworden und sie marschierten nun alle zusammen ab nach Ratingen. Dort wollten sie Kaffee trinken und dann wieder mit der Bahn nach Hause.

Herr Boden ging mit Herrn Bernhard voran, dann kamen die Kinder und zuletzt, ein gutes Stück hinterher, Frau Boden mit der schönen Frau Bernhard. Auf einmal spitzte Silli die Ohren und dann packte sie verstohlen ihren Bruder am Arm.

»Du, hör mal«, sagte sie, »was da die Frau Bernhard sagt ...«

»Ach, das kann ich mir schon denken!«, rief der kleine Bernhard, »meine Mutter spricht beinahe den ganzen Tag nichts andres. Die hat solche Sorgen, meinem Vater könnte was passieren ... Der hat ja vor zwei Jahren die Verbrecher aus dem öden Haus da bei unserer Schule verurteilt und da haben sie ihm Rache geschworen ... Wenn sie rauskämen aus dem Gefängnis, dann machten sie ihn kalt, haben sie gesagt ... Und in ein paar Wochen ist ihre Zeit herum. Aber mein Vater macht sich nicht so viel draus.«

Silli lief es kalt den Rücken herab. Räuber spielen, das war ja wunderschön, aber richtige Verbrecher ... brr! Und sogar in der Höhle, wo diese Kerle gehaust hatten, war der Knöres schon gewesen! Wenn das der kleine blasse Ühl wüsste!

»Dein Vater soll sie doch gleich wieder verhaften lassen!«, meinte Boddas jetzt.

»Als wenn das so ginge!«, erwiderte der Sohn des Richters, »erst müssen sie sich mal neue Straftaten zuschulden kommen lassen, dann allerdings fliegen sie gleich ins Zuchthaus, als rückfällige Verbrecher.«

Ja, der Junge hatte daheim gut die Ohren aufgemacht. Und Boddas besah ihn allmählich mit etwas mehr Achtung. Schade, dass er so zart war und keine richtigen Knochen hatte! Einen, der mit wirklichen Verbrechen zu tun hatte, könnten sie sonst in ihrer Bande herrlich brauchen. Schade! – Nun, Räuber und Gendarm konnten sie ihn ja gelegentlich einmal mitspielen lassen auf dem Schulhof. Aber ihn mitnehmen über die Mauer? Herübergekonnt hätte er vielleicht ja. Denn man brauchte nur an der Schulmauer in den Holunderbaum zu klettern und von da aus rasch auf die Mauer. Aber für so feine Jüngelchen war das nichts!

Ja, da fiel Boddas wieder der verwilderte Klostergarten ein. Jetzt würde es damit ja sowieso aus sein! Er konnte es gar nicht abwarten, bis er morgen die große Neuigkeit dem Döll und dem Knöres und Mala erzählte. Und dann wollten sie wirklich jede Stunde, die sie frei hatten, noch in das Gärtchen gehen ...

Aber Mala fehlte am nächsten Tag in der Schule, er hatte Halsweh, und Knöres und Döll mussten nachmittags in die Schule. Drum blieb Boddas nichts anderes übrig, als zuerst einmal allein ihrem Garten einen Besuch zu machen. Schnell schrieb er nach dem Essen seine Schulaufgaben hin – ob er sie richtig hatte, das kümmerte ihn heute nicht – und dann nahm er sich aus dem Büro seines Vaters einen zwei Meter langen Zollstock, tat eine neue Batterie in seine Taschenlampe und machte sich mit Silli auf den Weg zur Schule.

Alles ging gut. Niemand sah sie, wie sie über den leeren Schulhof huschten und in dem Holunder verschwanden. Und nun noch schnell einmal am Pfarrhause hinaufgeschaut, ob nicht einer der Kapläne am Fenster war … aber die Luft schien rein. Rasch sprangen sie in das herbstdürre Gesträuch hinab und schon waren sie in dem niedrigen Kellerloch verschwunden. Einen Augenblick noch schauten sie durch das blätterleere Gerank des wilden Weines zurück, aber sie sahen nur ein Kaninchen flitzen. Jetzt mochte man sie suchen! – Und Boddas knipste seine Taschenlampe an, dann schritten sie vorsichtig die bröckligen und verfallenen Stufen hinab.

»Dass noch niemand diesen Keller gefunden hat!«, sagte Silli. »Da wohnen sie vielleicht schon wer weiß wie lange hier, haben ihre Kohlen und Kartoffeln im Keller und wissen nicht, dass unter ihrem Keller noch Gewölbe sind.«

»Vom Pfarrhaus kann man ja gar nicht hier hinein!«, erklärte Boddas, »das alte Türloch ist längst zugemauert und unser Gärtchen ist ihnen nicht der Mühe wert.«

»Ach, bald werden die Bauleute ja kommen und vermessen«, sagte Silli.

Boddas nahm seinen Zollstock heraus: »Zuerst mal vermesse ich, der Herr Boden!«, erklärte er.

»Du? Und was willst du messen?«

»Nun, so allerlei … Wir sind ja überhaupt noch nicht so richtig in dem Keller gewesen. Graut es dir vor den Gerippen und Totenköpfen?«

»Nein, kommt nicht infrage, Herr Boden!«, lachte Silli, »das sind keine Verbrecher!«

Nun waren sie ganz unten. Und die Lampe beschien dickes, festes Mauerwerk, mächtige Wölbungen und den mit Ziegeln sauber gemauerten Boden. Der Raum war nicht besonders groß. Über ihm hatte gerade das Pfarrhaus Platz, also das alte Klostergebäude mit seinen Kellern.

Der Junge des Baumeisters konnte sich ganz gut denken, weshalb die klugen Mönche ihren eigentlichen Keller über dem noch tieferen, dem Begräbniskeller, angelegt hatten, so hoch, dass man nur ein paar Stufen hinabzugehen hatte. Das war wegen der Rheinüberschwemmungen gewesen und die gab es früher fast in jedem Jahr, ehe der Strom allenthalben eingedämmt war, hatte der Vater gesagt. So wurde dann nur der Totenkeller, nicht aber der Weinkeller überschwemmt.

»Siehst du«, sagte Boddas zu Silli und er leuchtete umher, wo bald da, bald dort, in wirrem Durcheinander, ein Schädel oder Gebeine lagen, »hier hat das Wasser schon wer weiß wie oft alles durcheinandergeschwemmt ... Da, nimm mal mein Notizbuch und den Bleistift.«

»Was soll ich damit?«, fragte das Mädchen leise. Es war ihr doch nicht so ganz geheuer zwischen den bleichen Gebeinen.

»Das wirst du schon sehen!«

Und Boddas fing an zu messen ... »2, 4, 6, 8, 12 ... schreib: Länge 14 Meter fuffzich ... So ...«

»Breite 2, 4, 6, 8 ... genau 8 Meter ... weißt du, wo wir jetzt wahrscheinlich drunter sind? Unter der Sakristei. Aber das werden wir schon noch sehen.«

Boddas war ganz aufgeregt. Wer ihm zugesehen hätte, der würde es gemerkt haben: dass die Bodens schon von den Ururgroßvätern her Baumenschen waren. Und das steckte auch dem Jungen im Blut.

Nun visierte er über den zusammengeschobenen Zollstock.

»Der Chor der Kirche muss etwas nach rechts herüber liegen«, sagte er halb für sich und er leuchtete die Mauer ab.

»Siehst du, hier diese Mauer ist viel dicker und massiver als die an den anderen Seiten. Das sind die Grundmauern der Kirche. Und gerade da hab ich neulich was gesehen. Komm, Silli, es hilft uns nichts. Hier liegt ein Haufen Knochen, das Wasser hat sie gegen die Mauer geschwemmt. Wir müssen sie wegräumen.«

Aber das Mädchen begriff immer noch nichts.

»Die pack ich nicht an!«, rief sie.

»Dumme Gans!«, fuhr der Bruder sie an, »wenn die Toten da wüssten, weshalb ich ihre Knochen hier weghaben will, dann würden sie von selbst aus dem Weg gehen.«

Aber wie er sich nun bückte und einen Knochen nach dem anderen, einen Schädel um den andern weghob und beiseitelegte, da griff er doch so vorsichtig und behutsam zu, als wäre er bange, er möchte einem wehtun.

Doch bald war er fertig und nun nahm er Silli die Lampe, mit der sie ihm geleuchtet hatte, aus der Hand und ließ ihren Schein auf die frei gewordene Wand fallen.

»Siehst du wohl?«, triumphierte er. »Diesen Mauerbogen hatte ich schon längst gesehen –«

Ja, sie standen vor einem vermauerten Türloch.

Boddas rieb sich die Hände.

»Ich sag es ja, hier braucht nur mal so ein alter Baumeister hinzukommen. Früher habe ich nicht so drauf geachtet. Aber gestern auf dem ganzen Weg hab ich es mir überlegt ...«

»Wie du die Figuren in den Sand gezeichnet hast?«

»Merkst du das jetzt erst? Und nun raus und oben nachgemessen. Bis an die Kirche.«

Im Garten nun huschten sie flink wie die Kaninchen durch das hohe Gebüsch und das welke Gras, hinter den Heiligenfiguren herum, und bald war die ganze Seite in dem Notizbuch mit Zahlen beschrieben.

Aber Boddas sah sie sich erst genauer an, als sie wieder hinter dem wilden Wein auf der Kellertreppe saßen, und er rechnete und rechnete, verglich, zählte ab, zählte zu und schließlich sagte er: »Die zugemauerte Tür führt unter den Chor der Kirche. Wir wollen mal sehen, ob wir sie kaputtkriegen.«

Und er hob eine dicke eiserne Mauerklammer auf, über die er schon ein Dutzend Mal fast gefallen wäre. Und damit klopfte er drunten zuerst leise, dann kräftiger, erst an die Mauer, dann wieder an das Kirchenfundament, nun wieder an die Vermauerung ...

»Sie klingt heller, also ist sie nur dünn!«, stellte er fest, aber es dauerte wohl eine Stunde, bis er den ersten Stein herausgewuchtet hatte. Kurz darauf polterte schon der zweite nach innen – ein schwarzes Loch gähnte ihnen entgegen.

Tief atmete Boddas auf und warf das Eisen auf die Erde – seine Hände waren zerkratzt und blutig.

»Silli, gib mir mal dein Taschentuch!«, sagte er.

Aber schon fuhr er zurück und Silli hatte einen hellen Schrei ausgestoßen ... Mit beiden Händen klammerte sie sich an ihren Bruder ... ja, er hörte es auch ... da drinnen hinter der vermauerten Tür klang leiser, leiser Gesang. Zwar hörten die Kinder nicht die Worte, nur den Ton der düsteren Melodie, der von weit, weit her zu kommen schien ...

»Da singen die Gespenster«, hauchte das Mädchen und zitterte, als hätte es Fieber.

Aber der kleine Baumeister hatte seine Ruhe schon wieder.

»Dummes Zeug, Gespenster! Die Lampe her!«

Und er leuchtete in das Mauerloch hinein. Nicht weit fiel der schwache Strahl in die Finsternis, aber was Boddas sah, das genügte ihm: Drinnen lag Gerippe neben Gerippe in heiliger Ruhe und über die Toten hin klang wie aus der Erde heraus eine leise, traurige Melodie.

Boddas atmete auf.

»Da hast du deine Gespenster!«, sagte er, »denn das ist doch nur die Orgel aus der Kirche. Vielleicht übt der Organist gerade. Und man hört drunten ein paar Töne ... ja, ja, wir Baumeister!«

Und nun erst schaute auch das Mädchen durch die Mauerlücke ...

Eine halbe Stunde später klingelte es an der Wohnungstüre des Pfarrers. Die Haushälterin öffnete.

»Nun, Kinder, was wollt ihr?«

»Den Herrn Dechant sprechen, Frollein!«, sagte Boddas, »ich bin nämlich der Sohn von dem Herrn Kirchenvorstand Baumeister Boden.«

»Na, dann kommt mal rein, Kinderchen«, sagte die alte Frau und Boddas hätte ihr am liebsten die Augen ausgekratzt. Kinderchen! Was fiel der ein? Wer hatte noch vor einer halben Stunde zwischen

grässlichen Gerippen im Totenkeller gestanden – sie oder er und seine Schwester? Na, die dumme Person würde schon Augen machen!

Jetzt wurden sie in ein Zimmer geführt mit roten Plüschsesseln. Auch auf dem Tisch lag eine rote Plüschdecke und auf der roten Plüschdecke ein Album von Rom ... Boddas wollte es gerade aufschlagen, denn gewiss waren schöne Bauten drin zu sehen ... Aber da ging die Türe auf und der Dechant trat ein.

»Ihr wolltet zu mir, Kinder?«, fragte er, »gewiss sollt ihr von eurem lieben Vater etwas bestellen!«

Und er gab beiden die Hand, zuerst Silli und dann Boddas. Der alte Dechant war eben ein höflicher Mann.

Boddas aber nahm recht auffällig den Zollstock aus der hinteren Hosentasche und sagte: »Nein, Herr Dechant, wir kommen ganz von selber. Aber es ist wirklich etwas Wichtiges.«

Er griff nach seinem Notizbuch, leckte an den Zeigefinger, wie er es oft von seinem Vater gesehen hatte, und blätterte ein paar Seiten um, auf denen allerlei Männchen gezeichnet waren.

Der Dechant sah den Jungen groß an.

»Na, dann setzt euch mal, Kinder«, sagte er, »ich komme gleich wieder!«

Boddas sah seine Schwester an und blinzelte mit den Augen:

»Eine feine Sache wird das!«, flüsterte er.

Doch schon kam der Dechant zurück und setzte

eine bunt bemalte Blechdose mit knusprigem Gebäck vor die Kinder.

»Es schadet ja nichts, wenn ihr derweil ein bisschen hier hineingreift!«, sagte er freundlich.

»Ja ja«, nickte Boddas, »meine Schwester ist sehr für süße Sachen!«

Der Pfarrer lächelte: »Dann soll ich wohl dir lieber eine Zigarre holen?«

Der Junge wurde ein wenig rot. »Dazu ist die Sache viel zu ernst«, sagte er.

»Na, dann schieß mal los, mein Junge!«

Der Dechant lehnte sich in dem rotplüschenen Kanapee zurück und verschränkte seine weißen, dünnen Hände im Schoß.

»Die Sache ist die«, fing Boddas an, »was kriege ich, wenn ich der Kirche, sagen wir mal, 10 000 Mark erspare? Denn 10 000 Mark ist doch allerhand Geld.«

Der alte Herr riss die Augen auf.

»10 000 Mark ersparen? Der Kirche? Da musst du schon deutlicher werden!«

»Herr Dechant, es soll doch jetzt eine Heizung angelegt werden unter dem Kirchenschiff...«

»Ja, und?«

Boddas suchte nach Worten. Er hatte sich das doch alles so fein zurechtgelegt und jetzt wusste er rein gar nichts mehr!

Aber Silli konnte es schon lange nicht mehr aushalten.

»Herr Dechant«, prustete sie heraus, »Sie brauchen unter dem Schiff gar nicht erst ausschachten zu lassen. Denn gleich droben unter dem Chor ist ein altes Begräbnisgewölbe!«

Dem Pfarrer blieb für einen Augenblick die Sprache weg. Und dann fragte er noch dies und das, schließlich musste der Küster kommen, Treppenleitern wurden herbeigeschafft und bald stand der Dechant vor dem Loch, das Boddas gehackt hatte, und schaute im Strahl einer starken elektrischen Lampe in das Gewölbe der Toten.

Als er sich zurückwandte, sagte er zu dem Küster: »Bitte, telefonieren Sie gleich einmal mit dem Herrn Baumeister Boden, er möchte doch sofort herkommen!«

»Was, Herr Dechant?«, knurrte der Küster, »zuerst kriegt doch der Lausebengel mal eine gepfefferte Tracht Prügel! Was hat die Rasselbande sich hier herumzutreiben? Also komm mal mit, mein Söhnchen, in die Sakristei!«

»Herr Dechant!«, schrie Boddas.

»Keine Angst, mein Junge«, lächelte der alte Mann.

»Angst, Herr Dechant? Ich habe keine Angst! Aber von dem Küster ist es schon eine Gemeinheit! Bei mir wäre der zum letzten Mal Küster gewesen!«

Brummend war der Küster gegangen.

Und nun sagte der Pfarrer: »Sogar eine Belohnung sollt ihr haben, Kinder! Sagt mal, was wünscht ihr euch?«

»Deswegen sind wir ja eben zu Ihnen gekommen,

Herr Dechant!«, lachte Silli, »sonst hätten wir bestimmt nichts von dem Keller gesagt. Darin kann man doch so fein spielen.«

»Kind, du bist wenigstens ehrlich!«, lächelte der alte Herr. »Und was wollt ihr also haben?«

»Dass Sie den Vater von den armen Gebendeil-Kindern bei dem Heizungsbau beschäftigen und dass Sie ihn nachher als Heizer hier anstellen. Er ist doch Schlosser —«

Es dauerte eine Weile, bis der Dechant antwortete. In dem Düster konnten die Kinder sein Gesicht nicht sehen.

Und sie dachten, er besänne sich nur, ob er Ja sagen sollte oder Nein. Aber als er nun antwortete, klang seine Stimme so weich und er sagte: »Kinder, ihr könnt dem Mann gleich Bescheid sagen. Nächsten Montag fangen wir an.«

Ein sonderbares Schuljubiläum

»Das Rote U ist verrückt geworden!«
So sagte Mala.
»Vollständig verrückt!«, fügte Boddas hinzu.
»Ja, aber –«, meinte Silli, »dann zeigt doch mal her!«
Mala schüttelte den Kopf.
»Das hat gar keinen Zweck. Das Rote U ist verrückt. Basta.«
»Sollt ihr etwa die Schule in Brand stecken?«, fragte Silli.
»Würd ich dann in Dreiteufelsnamen sagen, er wäre verrückt?«, zischte Mala giftig.
»Noch was Dolleres also?«
»Ja. Wenn man die Schule anstecken will, dann braucht man nur Streichhölzer. Und wenn wir den Rhein anhalten wollen, dann haben wir weiter nichts nötig, als auf den Sankt Gotthard zu gehen und die Hand vor die Quelle zu halten. Dann haben sie hier ihren Rhein gehabt. Aber können wir mit dem Mond Fußball spielen oder die Sonne anhalten?«
»So etwas Schweres sollen wir tun?«, fragte Döll entsetzt.
»Noch etwas viel Schwereres. Die Sonne anhalten ist dagegen kinderleicht! Aber ihr könnt ja selber lesen ...«

Die fünf saßen in einer langen Reihe auf der Kaimauer am Rhein und ließen die Beine hinabbaumeln. Und nun zeigte Mala ihnen den Zettel, den er heute in seinem Rechenbuch gefunden hatte. Das Papierchen ging von Hand zu Hand ...

Lange Zeit sagte niemand etwas.

Und schließlich nickte Silli vor sich hin: »Mala hat vollständig recht!«

»Nicht wahr?«, sagte Boddas. »So ein Blödsinn. ›Ihr habt dafür zu sorgen, dass am 17. Dezember schulfrei ist.‹«

»... Dass wir die Schule nicht anstecken und die Lehrer nicht vergiften, das weiß er natürlich selbst. Wir sind doch keine Verbrecher ... Ja, wenn er geschrieben hätte, wir fünf sollten am 17. Dezember alle mal die Schule schwänzen – das wäre noch was gewesen. Aber schulfrei! Die ganze Schule frei! So was muss man sich anhören!«

»Ich pfeife überhaupt bald auf das Rote U!«, brummte Döll, »jetzt hat es beinah vierzehn Tage nichts von sich hören lassen und nun auf einmal so ein Blech!«

»Und dabei sind jetzt den ganzen Tag die Arbeiter in dem alten Garten und wir gucken in den Mond. Die Karnickel haben sie alle selbst gefressen.«

»Dann leg doch du mal einen Zettel in dein Buch, Mala«, riet jetzt Silli, »und schreib dem U klipp und klar, was er für 'n Quatschkopp ist! Vielleicht findet er deinen Brief und geht schön nach Grafenberg in die Irrenanstalt.«

»Oder er wird böse auf uns!«, sagte Knöres düster.

Ja, sie wussten nicht, was sie machen sollten. Das Rote U war doch sonst so vernünftig gewesen! Und nun diese Geschichte! »Kümmern wir uns einfach nicht darum!«, hatte Silli noch zuletzt, als sie auseinandergingen, geraten. Aber das war leichter gesagt als getan. Immerhin blieb ihnen ja noch fast ein Monat Zeit, über die Sache nachzudenken. Aber auf jeden Fall wollten Mala und Boddas einmal jeder ein Briefchen in sein Buch legen und darin dem Roten U begreiflich machen, dass es ganz etwas Unvernünftiges und Unmögliches von ihnen forderte. Es hatte ganz sicher gar keine Ahnung davon, wie es in einer Schule zugeht. Das müssten sie ihm einmal ganz genau schreiben. Ja, und dann würde es ihnen wohl eine andere Arbeit geben.

Der Einzige, der sich die Sache ernster durch den Kopf gehen ließ, war Mala. Ein schulfreier Tag, und das mitten im Jahr – war das nicht eine wunderbare Sache, für die man sich wirklich einmal anstrengen konnte? Aber wie sollte man das anfangen?

In Gedanken versunken saß der Junge mittags bei Tisch und er merkte zuerst gar nicht, dass es Rotkraut gab, was er doch nicht ausstehen konnte.

»Sag mal, Junge«, fragte sein Vater endlich, »du denkst wohl über einen Leitartikel für die Zeitung nach?«

Denn Malas Vater war der Redakteur vom Tageblatt. Und wer ihn so sprechen hörte, meinte, es gäbe nichts, was er so sehr hasste wie eben die Zeitung. Und nicht nur seine Zeitung! Er hasste sie alle. Wenigstens gab es keinen Tag, an dem er nicht über die Zeitungsschmierer, wie er sie nannte, in den kräftigsten Ausdrücken schimpfte und wetterte. Seine Hauptsorge war, dass sein Sohn nicht auch das Zeitungsschreiben anfing. Nein, der sollte gleich mit vierzehn Jahren auf das Landgut von Herrn Schlössers Bruder, der keine Kinder hatte, und ein tüchtiger Bauer werden.

»Denn den Kohl, den der Bauer zieht, kann man wenigstens essen«, sagte Doktor Schlösser immer, »von dem Zeitungskohl aber wird nicht mal ein Toter satt!«

Mala wusste das alles sehr gut, und wenn einer ihn gefragt hätte, woher er eigentlich das Fluchen gelernt hätte, dann hätte er sagen müssen: »Von meinem Vater.«

Sieh da, schon wieder stieß Herr Schlösser einen ellenlangen Fluch aus und warf die Serviette auf den Tisch. Das Telefon hatte geklingelt ...

»Nicht mal zum Mittagessen hab ich armer Zeitungsknecht Ruhe!«, schrie er.

Und als er wiederkam, sagte er zu Malas Mutter: »Man soll's nicht für möglich halten. Fragt da so ein Kamel an, ob es wahr wäre, dass morgen der Sultan hierherkäme und sich die Mannesmann-Werke besehen wollte. Ich habe natürlich gleich Ja gesagt und der König von Pamir käme übrigens auch mit ... Aber das wäre strengstes Geheimnis, keinem dürfte er es wiedersagen, und die Herrschaften kämen 10 Uhr 31 mit dem Schnellzug von Solingen, da hätten sie die Messerschmieden besichtigt.«

Frau Schlösser lachte. »Aber lieber Mann«, sagte sie, »warum regst du dich denn darüber auf?«

Und Mala rief: »Es gibt ja gar keinen Sultan mehr, der ist doch längst abgesetzt!«

»Das ist es ja eben! Die Leute glauben alles, was man ihnen sagt, und einen König von Pamir gibt es natürlich auch nicht und auch keinen Schnellzug von Solingen. Aber bitte, lauf morgen mal an den Hauptbahnhof 10 Uhr 31 ... da werden Hunderte von Menschen stehen.«

Mala sah seinen Vater an und sagte: »Dann setz doch gelegentlich mal in die Zeitung, am Soundsovielten fiele die Schule aus ...«

Herr Schlösser lachte rau: »Das könnte dir so passen, mein Söhnchen. Aber wenn ich's täte – bestimmt, kein Mensch käme in die Schule, auch die Lehrer nicht ... Doch ich werde mich hüten! Du sollst ein ordentlicher Mensch werden und kein Windbeutel! Schockschwerenotbombenelementmillionendonnerwetter noch mal!«

›Den Fluch muss ich mir merken‹, dachte Mala, ›denn den kenne ich noch nicht.‹

Und wie ganz von ferne sah er eine winzige Möglichkeit dämmern, den Willen des Roten U zu erfüllen.

Aber dass bei seinem Vater nichts zu machen war, sah er vollkommen ein. Er wusste auch ganz genau: Es gab keinen Menschen, der seine Zeitung und seinen Beruf mehr liebte als Doktor Schlösser. Dinge, über die er nicht schimpfen und krakeelen konnte, mochte er nicht. Und je mehr er über eine Sache fluchte, desto mehr lag sie ihm am Herzen. Drum wollte Mala erst gar nicht versuchen, bei seinem Vater irgendetwas auszurichten. Nein, dazu mussten andere Leute heran! Und Mala wusste auch schon, wer!

Herr Behrmann war ein Studienfreund seines Vaters gewesen, allzeit lustig und guter Dinge. Sorgen machte er sich nie, und als sein Freund Schlösser längst Herr Doktor Schlösser und Redakteur an der Zeitung war, da studierte Herr Behrmann immer noch. Das heißt, eigentlich tat er nichts als in mancherlei Büchern oberflächlich herumschnüffeln und sich, wenn es eben ging, einen guten Tag machen. Aber weil man nun doch nicht ewig studieren kann, zog er hier in die Stadt, wo Doktor Schlösser Redakteur war. Jeder Mensch muss nämlich leben und Herr Behrmann musste das auch. Drum schrieb er oft für das Tageblatt kleine und große Aufsätze über allerhand Dinge, über Altes und Neues, was ihm gerade in den Sinn kam oder was der Redakteur ihm auftrug. Das gab dann jeden Monat ungefähr so viel Geld, wie Herr Behrmann brauchte. Zudem wurde er öfter von Frau Schlösser zum Abendessen eingeladen, denn er war ein lustiger Vogel, konnte sehr schön Klavier und Geige spielen und sang mit sehnlicher Stimme alles, was man haben wollte.

Herr Behrmann also war Malas Mann. Und Mala wusste auch, wo er wohnte. Denn oft hatte er ihm von seinem Vater ein Buch oder Theaterkarten bringen müssen und über das Buch oder das Theaterstück musste dann Herr Behrmann ein paar gescheite Worte für die Zeitung schreiben.

Aber Mala bedachte sich doch noch ein paar Tage. Erst als eine Woche seit dem sonderbaren Befehl des Roten U herum war, klopfte er des Abends an Herrn Behrmanns Stübchen, vier Treppen hoch, in der Bolkerstraße.

Gleich hörte das feine, leise Violinspiel drinnen auf und Herr Behrmann stand in der Türe, die Geige noch in der Hand. Trotz der tiefen Dämmerung erkannte er Mala gleich.

»Ah, der junge Herr Schlösser!«, rief er, »komm herein, mein Sohn, und sag, was du Gutes bringst! Warte, ich mache Licht!«

»Nicht nötig, Herr Behrmann«, sagte Mala, »was ich mit Ihnen besprechen wollte, kann ich gerade im Dunkeln am besten sagen ...«

»Dann schieß los, mein Sohn!«

Mala setzte sich also auf das Bett und Herr Behrmann schwang sich auf den Tisch am Fenster. Nur ganz dunkel sah der Junge seine Umrisse gegen das dämmerige Fenster.

»Die Sache ist so«, fing Mala an, »wir möchten am 17. Dezember gern schulfrei haben.«

»Na, dann schwänzt doch einfach.«

»Nein, nein, das geht nicht! Das geht ganz und gar nicht! Die ganze Schule soll frei haben – das ist es!«

»Mein Sohn, du bist verrückt! Und kann ich denn daran etwas machen?«

»Ja, Herr Behrmann, das können Sie! Aber zuerst müssen Sie mir schwören, dass Sie mich nicht verraten! Hören Sie?«

»Wo denkst du hin?«

Und feierlich hielt er die Hand hoch: »Ich schweige wie ein Rheinkiesel!«

Nun erzählte Mala das mit dem Sultan und dem König von Pamir und der Vater hätte gesagt, die Menschen glaubten alles, was man ihnen sagte ...

Herr Behrmann lachte, dass es in seiner Geige widerhallte.

»Da hat dein Vater ganz recht, da hat er wirklich und tausendmal recht – aber wie ich euch damit schulfrei verschaffen soll, das begreife ich immer noch nicht. Und dann gerade am 17. Dezember! Wie kommst du auf den Tag?«

»Auf den haben wir uns nun mal geeinigt«, erwiderte Mala kleinlaut, »da ist nichts mehr dran zu ändern. Herr Behrmann, können Sie nicht in die Zeitung setzen, Sie hätten gehört, der König von Pamir oder der Dalai Lama käme an diesem Tage hierher? Geht das nicht?«

»Nein, mein Sohn, das geht wirklich nicht«, lachte der ewige Student, »aber sonst – das würde ja ein himmlischer Spaß werden, ein himmlischer Spaß!«

Er sprang von seinem Tisch und fing an, in der engen Stube auf und ab zu spazieren.

»Nein, das müsste man wahrhaftig probieren ... ist ja egal, was es ist ... aber den Leuten mal zeigen, wie dumm sie sind. Wo hast du eigentlich die Idee her, Junge?«

»Och, die haben wir uns so ausgedacht«, grinste Mala.

Aber Herr Behrmann hörte schon nicht mehr hin und fing wieder an, im Zimmer herumzuwandern. Und schließlich sagte er: »Du bist vor die richtige Schmiede gekommen, mein Sohn! Wenn es sich um einen tollen Spaß handelt, dann ist der Onkel Behrmann immer zu haben. Nun lass ihn mal nachdenken ...«

Er setzte sich wieder ans Fenster und Mala sah ihn kaum noch, so dunkel war es mittlerweile geworden. Er sah nur, wie Behrmann die Geige hob – und nun fing sie auch schon an, ins Dunkel hinauszusingen, zuerst ganz leise, dann heller und geschwinder, wie die Vögel singen um Ostern, und dann wieder ganz leise ... oh, es war so schön und Mala meinte, er sähe von den mächtigen Bäumen der alten Seufzerallee die welken Blätter fallen. Ja, Mala hatte die Musik gern. Und Herr Behrmann hätte seinetwegen bis in die Nacht weiterspielen können.

Aber plötzlich setzte er die Geige ab und sagte: »Jetzt hab ich es, mein Sohn! Wollen sehen, ob es glückt! Schau also, sagen wir mal von Samstag an, jeden Morgen in die Zeitung. Und – halte den Mund!«

»Gerade ich werde doch nicht schwätzen!«, lachte Mala, gab Herrn Behrmann die Hand und polterte die steile Treppe hinunter.

In den nächsten Tagen aber dachten sie alle nicht mehr viel an das Rote U und an Herrn Behrmann. Denn ein sehr früher Winter hatte plötzlich eingesetzt, mit Eis und Schnee, und keiner von ihnen hatte nun etwas anderes mehr im Sinne, als auf dem Rodelschlitten in sausender Fahrt den Napoleonsberg im Hofgarten hinunterzujagen. Als dann nach wenigen Tagen auch noch die Weiher in den Anlagen vereist waren, rannten sie, kaum dass sie sich nach dem Essen den Mund abgewischt hatten, auf den Speeschen Graben hinaus und fuhren Schlittschuh.

Wie eine Bombe schlug es drum ein, als Mala eines Mittags kam, in der einen Hand seine Schlittschuhe, in der anderen ein Zeitungsblatt schwenkte und schrie: »Am 17. Dezember ist schulfrei!«

Es dauerte keine Minute, da standen zwanzig, fünfzig, hundert Jungen und Mädchen um ihn herum.

»Hier steht's in der Zeitung!«, rief er. »Am 17. Dezember hat unsere Schule ihr dreihundertjähriges

Jubiläum! Und extra steht dabei ...« Er las vor: »Hoffentlich hat die Schulbehörde so viel Einsehen und gibt den Kindern an diesem Ehrentag ihrer Schule frei!«

Jubelnd rannte die ganze Schar fort über das blaublanke Eis. Nur Silli, Boddas, Döll und Knöres blieben bei Mala stehen.

»Das ist ja unheimlich«, sagte Silli, »wie hast du das nur fertiggebracht?«

»Na ja, amtlich ist es natürlich noch nicht«, lachte Mala, »aber der Herr Behrmann hat wirklich das Menschenmögliche getan ...«

Und nun steckten sie die Köpfe über dem Zeitungsblatt zusammen, alle fünf, und stotterten langsam, Zeile für Zeile, den Aufsatz Behrmanns herunter.

So fing er an:

»Unsere altehrwürdige Schule an der Zitadellstraße begeht am 17. Dezember dieses Jahres einen seltenen Tag, den Tag ihres dreihundertjährigen Bestehens. Ausdrücklich gibt die Gründungsurkunde des Fürsten, der damals unsere Stadt zu seiner Residenz erkor und den Grundstein zu ihrer Blüte legte, als Tag der Schulgenehmigung den 17. Dezember des Jahres des Heiles 1630 an ...«

Und so ging's dann weiter. Es wurden noch allerlei wissenswerte Dinge von der alten Schule erzählt, wie zuerst die frommen Mönche dort die Jugend der Stadt erzogen hätten und den Kindern die Anfänge der menschlichen und göttlichen Wissen-

schaft beigebracht ... Oh, es war sehr schön zu lesen. Nur verstanden Silli und die Jungen nicht allzu viel davon. Ganze Abschnitte mit Jahreszahlen und Namen überschlugen sie und lasen nur noch den Schluss:

»Der Turnsaal der Schule, den heute noch die uralten Deckengemälde zieren – war er doch einst der Kapitelsaal der Mönche –, dieser in seiner Art einzige Turnsaal wäre so recht wie geschaffen für die Festfeier am Jubiläumstag. Wir weisen die verehrte Lehrerschaft sowie auch die maßgebenden Stellen der städtischen Behörden jetzt schon auf alles das hin, denn dieser große Tag darf nie und nimmer vergessen werden und er soll auch den Kindern der ehrwürdigen Schule in ewiger Erinnerung bleiben.«

»Darauf kann Herr Behrmann sich verlassen«, sagte Silli, »aber wissen möcht ich doch, ob das mit dem Jubiläum auch stimmt?«

»Ob es stimmt oder nicht«, lachte Mala, »danach fragt doch keiner, oder meinst du, die Leute würden jetzt noch lang und breit nachforschen, wo es doch in der Zeitung steht?«

Aber Silli war schon wieder weg. Kaum sah man, wie sie lief. Ihr rotes Mützchen leuchtete, ihr Mäntelchen und die Enden des Schales flogen hinter ihr her – wie ein buntes Vögelchen war sie mit rotem Kopf. Und lachend rannten die Jungen hinter ihr drein.

Aber als es auf den Abend zuging, klopfte Mala

doch wieder bei Herrn Behrmann. Der saß heute aber nicht mit seiner Violine da, sondern im behaglichen Schein der elektrischen Tischlampe tippte er emsig auf seiner Schreibmaschine.

»Solche Musik muss auch sein!«, sagte er zu dem Jungen.

»Was schreiben Sie denn da, Herr Behrmann? Vielleicht wieder etwas vom Schuljubiläum?«

»Hahaha!«, lachte der alte Student und seine goldene Brille funkelte nur so, »das war ein feiner Spaß, nicht wahr?«

»Aber stimmt es denn nicht?«

»I wo! Natürlich – eure Schule, die ist alt, sogar sehr alt. Aber dass sie gerade an diesem 17. Dezember 300 Jahre alt wird, ist bestimmt falsch ... Das hat der Onkel Behrmann nur mal so geschrieben.«

»Und das mit den Mönchen früher? Und all die Fürsten und Herzöge? Und die Jahreszahlen?«

»Begreifst du das denn nicht, Junge? Natürlich ist das alles richtig! Siehst du, das ist wie in einer Erbsensuppe ... wenn die anderen Erbsen alle gut sind, dann merkt es kein Mensch, wenn auch mal zufällig eine schlechte drunter ist.«

»Und fallen sie drauf rein?«

Behrmann hielt sich an den Stuhllehnen fest, so lachte er.

»Und wie!«, rief er, »hat dein Vater nichts davon gesagt?«

Nein, Malas Vater war diesen Mittag nicht zum Essen heimgekommen.

»Na also! Dann konnte er dir auch nicht erzählen, wie den ganzen Morgen bei der Zeitung das Telefon geklingelt hat. Alle wollten sie wissen, wie und was, und wie wir das rausgekriegt hätten. Auf den Gedanken, dass der Onkel Behrmann und also die Zeitung nur ein bisschen geschwindelt hat, ist kein Mensch gekommen.«

»Auch mein Vater nicht?«, fragte Mala kleinlaut.

»Nein, der natürlich auch nicht. Der glaubt jetzt auch an den Sultan und an den König von Pamir... Wehe dir, wenn du ihm auch ein Wörtchen nur sagst!«

Als Mala die Treppe hinabstieg, hatte er nun doch ein schlechtes Gewissen. Jetzt war sein Vater, der sich jeden Tag von Neuem so ärgerte, wenn die Leute alles glaubten, was sie in der Zeitung lasen, jetzt war der Vater selber ganz genauso hereingefallen. Und er konnte ihm doch nichts sagen. Denn dann war erstens der freie Tag hin und zweitens – was würde Herrn Behrmann passieren? Der Vater würde sicher nichts mehr von ihm in der Zeitung drucken und dann konnte der arme Herr Behrmann nicht mehr die Miete bezahlen, keine Kohlen mehr kaufen und musste überhaupt hungern... Nein, das ging nicht!

Aber bald hatte Mala es ganz vergessen. Er sah, wie in der Schule der Rektor und die Lehrer ihre Köpfe zusammensteckten, und dann wurde in den Geschichtsstunden immer viel erzählt von der alten Schule, wie es früher gewesen wäre, und das mussten sich die Kinder dann aufschreiben und am anderen Tag mussten sie es auswendig wissen ...

Nein, das war wirklich nicht sehr angenehm. Dann konnten sie den Herzog Johann Wilhelm und den Jan Wellem nicht auseinanderhalten und von jedem Herzog sollten sie wissen, was er für Gebäude und Straßen hatte anlegen lassen ... Nein, es war schon ein Kreuz! Außerdem durften sie nicht mehr in den Turnsaal. Denn es waren Anstreicher gekommen, die mussten die Wände neu weißen, den Boden lackieren, und ein richtiger Maler besserte sogar die Gemälde an der Decke aus – alles für die Jubiläumsfeier!

Bis dahin waren es noch vierzehn Tage. Und sie hörten in der ganzen Zeit nicht ein Wort vom Roten U. Es war ihnen auch ganz recht, denn das Winterwetter hielt an, immer fester froren die Gräben und Weiher im Hofgarten und an der Königsallee zu und auf dem Rhein trieben jeden Tag mächtigere Eisschollen.

Da hatten die Kinder genug zu tun. Aber eins hätten sie doch gar zu gern gewusst: Weshalb sollten sie gerade am 17. Dezember frei haben?

Hatte das Rote U an diesem Tage etwas Besonderes vor?

Immer wieder bedachten und besprachen sie sich, wenn sie zum Eis gingen, wenn sie abends vom Eis nach Hause liefen. Aber sie konnten und konnten nichts finden ...

Es war gerade ein Sonntag. Herr Behrmann war bei Doktor Schlösser zum Mittagessen eingeladen. Ein vergnügtes Essen war das. Und Mala hatte gar keine Lust, diesen Nachmittag, wenigstens solange Herr Behrmann noch da war, zum Eislaufen zu gehen. Denn der alte Student erzählte so schön und lustig und nach dem Essen spielte die Mutter Klavier und Behrmann die Geige dazu. Nein, Mala beschloss, diesen Nachmittag zu Hause zu bleiben. Sein Vater hätte ihn vielleicht weggeschickt, aber er merkte ja kaum, dass der Junge da war. Denn Mala saß still in einer Ecke und las Karl May oder er tat nur so. Er horchte auf die Musik und auf Herrn Behrmanns Geschichten.

Auf einmal klingelte das Telefon. Doktor Schlösser ging selber an den Apparat. Und als er wiederkam, sagte er: »Nun hören Sie aber mal, Behrmann, da haben Sie ja ein nettes Zeug geschrieben von dem Schuljubiläum ...«

Mala zuckte zusammen. Oh, jetzt würde alles herauskommen ... Er fing zu zittern an. Vielleicht hatte das Rote U selber angerufen?

Herr Behrmann drehte sich vom Notenpult ein wenig um, schaute den Redakteur über seine goldene Brille hin an und sagte: »Nanu?«

»Ja, nanu!«, polterte Malas Vater, »der Schulrektor hat selber angerufen. Das muss ich sagen, schöne Geschichten sind das, schöne Geschichten ...«

»Na, und?«, fragte Herr Behrmann seelenruhig.

»Na, und – der Lehrer Longerich, der alte Herr –

Sie kennen ihn ja wohl –, also der hat mal seine Nase ein bisschen genauer als Sie, Sie leichtsinniges Huhn, in die alten Bücher und Urkunden gesteckt.«

»Hätt er sie gleich drin stecken lassen«, lachte Herr Behrmann gemütlich.

»Machen Sie nicht auch noch Witze! Also das Schuljubiläum ist ja erst am 28. Dezember, und dazu nicht das Dreihundertjährige, sondern erst das Zweihundertjährige …«

»Mein Gott, man kann sich auch mal verschreiben!«, brummte Herr Behrmann und er schüttelte den Kopf. »Komisch, komisch«, sagte er so vor sich hin.

»Was ist da komisch?«, brauste der Redakteur auf.

Aber Behrmann gab keine Antwort. Er konnte dem Doktor Schlösser doch nicht gut sagen, dass es wirklich ein komischer Zufall war, so hart an der Wahrheit vorbeizulügen. Denn auch von einem zweihundertjährigen Jubiläum hatte er keine Ahnung gehabt.

»Na, und nun sagte mir der Rektor, ich soll es morgen in die Zeitung setzen lassen. Denn die Jubiläumsfeier findet doch am 17. Dezember statt – am 28. sind ja schon Weihnachtsferien und auf ein paar Tage käm's auch nicht an.«

»Das hab ich ja gleich gedacht«, lachte Behrmann.

Immer mehr rutschte Mala auf seinem Stühlchen heran.

»Ja, und dann: Sie wollen jetzt alle zehn Jahre am letzten Sonntag vor den Weihnachtsferien so eine kleine Schulfeier veranstalten. Alle fünfzig Jahre eine große und alle hundert Jahre eine ganz große.«

»Donnerwetter, denken die weit!«, rief Behrmann.

»Ja, es passte ganz gut«, meinte der Rektor, »der 17. Dezember fiele ja dieses Jahr sowieso auf einen Sonntag!«

Bums! Mala war von seinem Stuhl heruntergefallen.

Und Doktor Schlösser wusste gar nicht, weshalb Herr Behrmann auf einmal so furchtbar lachen musste.

Die Detektive

Der 17. Dezember war da. Und es war den Kindern ganz recht, dass sie nicht viel davon merkten. Dass sie gerade sonntags noch zu einer Schulfeier mussten, hatte sie mächtig geärgert. War doch des Sonntags das Eis noch schöner, noch heller schien die Wintersonne und herrlicher als am schönsten Werktag leuchtete der Schnee. Gewiss hatte der Schulrektor das auch eingesehen. Denn schon vor neun Uhr war die Feier aus. Gleich von der Schulmesse her waren die Kinder hinübergelaufen, hatten ihre Gedichte aufgesagt, die Rede vom Herrn Rektor angehört und ihre Lieder gesungen. Nun gingen sie eilig nach Haus, denn sie hatten gewaltigen Kaffeehunger und alle Stuben daheim rochen schon nach Äpfeln, Kuchen, Marzipan und Weihnachtsbaum.

»Au!«, rief Silli auf einmal, »wie kommt denn die Nadel in meine Tasche?«

Sieh da, sogar am Taschentuch steckte sie fest... Nein, und dies Taschentuch gehörte ja gar nicht ihr. Noch am Morgen hatte die Mutter ihr ein sauberes in die Manteltasche getan. Aber dieses war arg schmutzig, ganz wie Jungentaschentücher...

»Hat das einer von euch da hineingetan?«, fragte sie die Kameraden, »denn ihr putzt euch mit euren

Taschentüchern ja immer die Schlittschuhe ab. Und grade so sieht es aus!«

Silli hielt es an einem Zipfel hin. Aber die Jungen schüttelten die Köpfe.

»Wirf es weg«, sagte Knöres, »wer weiß, was da dran ist.«

Und schon flog das schmutzige Ding im Winde dahin. Aber im gleichen Augenblick rannten ihm alle fünfe nach ... Es war ein Zettel darin! Mit einer Stecknadel daran festgemacht.

›Das Rote U!‹, ging es ihnen allen zugleich durch die Köpfe.

Ein paar Augenblicke später standen sie in einem Hauseingang und Silli las mit flüsternder Stimme den Zettel vor:

Das Rote U hat selber nicht daran gedacht, dass der 17. Dezember ein Sonntag war. Aber das ist egal. Ihr habt wieder einmal gezeigt, was ihr könnt! Jetzt kommt aber eine schwerere Aufgabe: Heute, Punkt elf Uhr, werden drei Verbrecher aus dem Gefängnis entlassen. Ihr sollt sehen, wo sie hingehen! Und schreibt es sofort

An das Rote U. Hier.
Hauptpostlagernd

Und daran erkennt ihr die Verbrecher: Dem einen fehlen zwei Finger an der linken Hand. Macht eure Sache gut!

                                  Das Rote U

Sie sahen sich an.

»Das ist eine ganz verdammt große Sache«, meinte Mala und spuckte aus dem Hausgang bis auf den Fahrweg hin.

»Aber dass er sich grad diesmal hinter ein Mädchen steckt, gefällt mir eigentlich nicht an ihm – das ist feig!«, sagte Boddas.

»Das Rote U hält mich wohl für schlauer als euch alle zusammen, das ist doch klar!«, rief Silli schnippisch.

»Gib doch nicht so an!«, knurrte Boddas, »was hast denn du mit den Roten-U-Sachen bisher zu tun gehabt? Genau gar nichts! Alles haben wir Männer fertiggekriegt!«

»So ein Quatsch, jetzt zu streiten«, schimpfte Knöres, »schon neun Uhr ist es durch und beinah eine ganze Stunde haben wir zu laufen bis zum Gefängnis. Wisst ihr überhaupt, wo die Ulmer Höhe ist? Na also! Ich weiß es aber! Jetzt gehen wir Kaffee trinken und Punkt zehn Uhr treffen wir uns an der Normaluhr am Corneliusplatz ... einverstanden?«

Frau Döll schüttelte den Kopf. Sonst saß ihr Junge des Sonntags immer eine geschlagene Stunde am Kaffeetisch, doch heute war er nach fünf Minuten schon fertig gewesen. Und dabei hatte er doppelt so viel Kuchen und Butterbrote gegessen ... ›Nein, dafür kann man schon nicht mehr gut essen sagen‹, dachte sie ... ›doppelt, nein dreimal so viel als sonst in der sechsfachen Zeit. Aber das ist eben dieses ewige Eislaufen!‹, meinte sie. Doch wie sie nun in die Küche kam, da lagen Dölls Schlittschuhe friedlich auf dem Schrank ...

Genauso wunderten sich die anderen Eltern. Überall waren die Schlittschuhe daheim geblieben und seit drei Wochen beinahe waren sie doch nicht mehr kalt geworden. Frau Schlösser hatte es ja schon oft zu ihrem Jungen gesagt: »Ihr lauft ja eure Schlittschuh glühend.«

Indes marschierten die fünf in langer Reihe durch den Hofgarten, dann durch viele hässliche breite Straßen, die nur der Knöres kannte, denn Knöres' alter Onkel wohnte in diesem Viertel, in dem die elektrischen Bahnen den ganzen Tag rasselten, die Autos flitzten, die Menschen hasteten. Arg ungemütlich war es der kleinen Gesellschaft. Alles schien ihnen hier so kalt, so fremd, alles so gleichgültig und gar böse. Und das Rote U bekam dann auch für sie, je näher sie der sogenannten Ulmer Höhe kamen, ein ganz anderes Gesicht, ein viel ernsteres und gefährlicheres als in den vertrauten Winkeln der Altstadt.

»Ob wir diesen Mittag überhaupt nach Haus können?«, sagte Boddas, »denn der Himmel weiß, wo die Kerle hingehen. Und vielleicht müssen wir stundenlang vor irgendeiner dreckigen Wirtschaft warten.«

»Dann lösen wir uns natürlich ab, das ist doch klar« – Silli hatte gleich einen Ausweg gefunden –, »und die anderen gehen dann schnell essen.«

»Ja, meinst du denn, die drei bleiben den ganzen Tag zusammen?«

»Und wir sind zu fünfen, da kann uns keiner durch die Lappen gehen. Und zwei haben doch noch immer Zeit, schnell nach Hause zu rennen.«

Die Gegend wurde ihnen mit jedem Schritt fremder. Jetzt mussten sie gar einen Feldweg entlang, über den eisig der Nordwind strich, und sie waren froh, als sie wieder in eine Straße einbogen. Zuerst kamen ja nur hässliche Bauplätze mit Haufen von Schutt und altem Baugerümpel, dann aber fingen die Häuser an, schmutzige, abscheuliche Häuser, und die noch abscheulicheren Stuckverzierungen waren oft schon heruntergebröckelt. Die Kinder wussten gar nicht, dass es solche Straßen in ihrer schönen Stadt gab.

»Ulmenstraße!«, las jetzt Mala auf einem Schild, »ist es hier, Knöres?«

»Ich glaube wohl.«

»Wo sind denn die Ulmen?«, fragte Silli.

»Du bist aber blöd!«, rief Knöres, »sind denn in der Kapuzinergasse vielleicht Kapuziner? Und ist in der Poststraße etwa eine Post? Vielleicht vor tausend Jahren einmal ... Du, Silli, wie spät haben wir?«

Ja, Silli hatte des Sonntags immer ihr Armbandührchen an.

»Zwanzig nach acht ... was ist denn damit los?«

»Die Zwiebel geht ja nicht. Damit hat dich deine Tante schön angeschmiert«, lachte Döll, »geradeso gut hätte sie dir eine Kartoffel schenken können!«

Es war das erste Mal, dass sie auf dem langen Wege wieder einmal lachten, und es tat ihnen gut, ohne dass sie es wussten.

Glücklicherweise war an dem Gefängnis eine Uhr ... Es grauste sie, als sie den riesigen schmutzig roten Ziegelbau sahen mit seiner dreifach mannshohen Mauer. Und sie waren froh, dass die Uhr schon fünf Minuten vor elf zeigte. Sie brauchten also wenigstens nicht lange zu warten.

»Wo wollen wir uns nun aufpflanzen?«, fragte Mala.

Aber da hatte Knöres schon einen langen Eisstreifen am Rande des Gehweges entdeckt, und als die Uhr mit raschen hellen Schlägen elf schlug, waren sie alle zusammen einig beim Rutschen. Ein paar Kinder aus der Straße hatten sich auch schon herbeigefunden und so konnten die Kerle, die gleich kommen würden, wirklich keinen Verdacht haben.

Aber es dauerte doch noch fast zehn Minuten, ehe das kleine eiserne Pförtchen neben dem Haupttor sich öffnete und hintereinander drei junge Kerle von etwa zweiundzwanzig oder dreiundzwanzig Jahren herauskamen.

»Das sind sie!«, sagte Silli sofort, »wir brauchen gar nicht erst nach der kaputten linken Hand zu suchen ... Holla, pass auf, Döll, sonst renn ich dich um.«

Sie flog hinter dem Jungen dahin über die blanke Bahn und nun lief sie noch ihre paar

Schrittchen über das Ende weiter, drehte sich um und rief laut: »Jetzt müssen wir nach Haus. Um zwölf Uhr wird gegessen, das wisst ihr doch!«

Die drei ging eben an ihnen vorüber und sahen überhaupt nicht hin. Erst als sie ein gutes Stück weiter waren, machten sich die Spione des Roten U hinter ihnen her auf den Weg, aber vorher besprachen sie noch schnell, dass sie so tun wollten, als gehörten sie nicht alle zusammen; und Mala und Boddas schlenderten nun ein wenig hinter den anderen und auf der gegenüberliegenden Straßenseite.

Doch all diese Vorsicht war nicht nötig – die drei Burschen schauten sich gar nicht um, geradewegs gingen sie, fast dieselben Straßen, die der kleine Klub vom Roten U eben gekommen war, der Altstadt zu. Und bald, als sie in das Menschengetriebe der großen Straßen kamen, waren die Verfolger dicht hinter ihnen. Sonst hätte es leicht geschehen können, dass sie die Kerle aus den Augen verloren.

»Ob das die sind, die den Richter Bernhard kaltmachen wollten?«, flüsterte Mala. »Sperr doch mal deine Ohren auf, Silli, denn du hörst doch sonst die Fliegen an der Wand krabbeln.«

Aber die Straße war zu laut, auf und ab rasselten die Straßenbahnen mit einem oder gar zwei Anhängern vorbei, unzählige Autos mit puckernden Motoren jagten vorüber, und kaum dass die drei Kerle mit den Verfolgern hinter ihnen in eine stillere Straße der Altstadt eingebogen waren, verschwanden sie auch schon in der Wirtschaft »Zum Bären«.

»Na, da hätten wir sie mal glücklich!«, sagte Boddas, »und sicher bleiben sie eine gute Weile hocken ... Drei von uns können also nach Haus rennen und essen. Wer hat den größten Hunger?«

Aber keiner wollte gehen. Schrecklich, wenn die Verbrecher inzwischen herausgekommen wären! Und jeder wollte doch selber gern der Detektiv sein, der sie verfolgte!

»Macht keinen langen Quatsch«, sagte Silli endlich, »essen müssen wir doch, schon dass sie zu Haus keine Angst kriegen. Ich und mein Bruder, wir gehen zuerst, und Döll auch – der wohnt ja gleich hier um die Ecke.«

»Natürlich«, brummte Knöres, »und wenn der Mala und ich nachher gerade beim Essen sind, dann seid ihr fein heraus und könnt sie allein verfolgen!«

Aber Silli kümmerte sich gar nicht um ihn. Wenn sie einmal etwas gesagt hatte, blieb es auch dabei.

»Komm, Döll!«, sagte sie und griff den großen Mühlenjungen am Arm.

»Ein freches Aas!«, knurrte Mala, als sie weg waren. »Na, wir rächen uns! Das kann ich dir sagen!«

»Sollen wir mal sehen, was die da drinnen anfangen?«, fragte Knöres und zwinkerte mit den schlauen Augen.

»Ja, fein!«, rief Mala, »hast du Geld bei dir?«

Sie suchten in ihren Taschen und jeder nahm sich einen Groschen, für den er sich drinnen Schokolade kaufen wollte.

»Aber mach es nicht zu auffällig!«, sagte Knöres noch. »Nicht dass du sie dir besiehst, als wolltest du ihnen einen Anzug machen.«

»Keine Angst, Kleiner!«

Aber als sie drinnen an der Schenke standen, den Groschen in der Faust, pufte Knöres den Mala verstohlen in die Seite. Gerade neben ihm lehnte einer von den dreien über dem Schanktisch, und als der Mann nun sein Glas Bier hob, sahen's die Jungen: Es fehlten ihm an der linken Hand der kleine und der vierte Finger ... Ein Glück war es, dass der Kerl nicht merkte, wie sie ihn anstarrten. Aber nun fragte auch schon der Wirt: »Na, und ihr zwei da?«

»Eine Tafel Schokolade für 'n Groschen.«

»Mir auch eine!«, sagte Knöres.

Aber erst kramte der Wirt noch in seiner Ladenkasse herum: »Tut mir leid«, sagte er dann zu dem Mann mit der verstümmelten Hand, »Briefmarken hab ich keine.«

»Na, dann nicht«, brummte der Fremde, »dann müssen wir noch zur Post gehen.«

»Ich kann Ihnen ja eine am Automaten ziehen!«, rief Knöres auf einmal.

Der Kerl lachte böse: »Das könnte dir so passen, du Bengel, da kämst du mal leicht zu einem Groschen! Durchbrennen tätst du damit. Hahaha, ich hätt es ja als Junge auch nicht anders gemacht.«

›Als Junge?‹, dachte Knöres, ›so machst du's ja heute noch ...‹ Aber er grinste nur freundlich und sagte: »Ich habe selber noch einen Groschen! Was krieg ich, wenn ich Ihnen die Freimarke hole?«

»Eine Zehner brauch ich. Dann geb ich dir nachher einen Groschen extra.«

»Schön, Herr, machen wir. In zehn Minuten bin ich wieder da.«

Dann nahmen die Jungen ihre Schokolade und stürmten hinaus.

»Das hast du verflucht fein gemacht, Knöres«, sagte Mala, »vielleicht hören wir nachher was. Ob sie uns zu einem Glas Bier einladen?«

»Das wäre famos! Dann tun wir so, als wenn wir tränken, und schütten es heimlich unter den Tisch. Und dann spielen wir die Besoffenen und die Kerle meinen, wir wären am Schlafen, und dann fangen sie an zu quatschen.«

Knöres blieb auf einmal stehen.

»Du willst doch nicht etwa mitgehen an die Post?«, fragte er.

»Natürlich – denn in der Zeit gehen sie bestimmt nicht fort! Die warten doch auf die Briefmarke.«

»Den Brief hast du deshalb aber noch lange nicht!«, rief Knöres, »wenn sie nun die Marke inzwischen anderswo auftreiben? Es sind doch genug Leute in der Wirtschaft! Oder sie wollen uns bloß weghaben – vielleicht haben sie was gemerkt –, das kann man alles nicht wissen … Übrigens gehe ich gar nicht an die Post. Ich laufe nur um die Ecke zu Dölls, die haben immer Marken, und vielleicht nimmt Frau Döll den Groschen von mir gar nicht

an und dann hab ich zehn Pfennig verdient ... Also warte nur schön, bis ich wiederkomme!«

Und weg war er. Mala wurde die Zeit doch lang, bis er zurückkam; dann gingen sie wieder zusammen in die Wirtschaft. Aber der Kerl stand jetzt nicht mehr an der Schenke und die Jungen mussten eine ganze Welle suchen, bis sie ihre Leute endlich in der hintersten Ecke fanden. Da saßen sie an einem Tisch für sich und eben brachte ihnen der Kellner das Essen. Feines Essen, stellten die Jungen sofort fest, denn vor jeden wurde eine mächtige Kalbshaxe hingestellt mit Erbsen, Kartoffeln und Kompott. Das Wasser lief den hungrigen Jungen im Munde zusammen ... Mussten diese Kerle ein Geld haben!

Zwei von ihnen zogen nun auch gleich die Schüsseln zu sich heran, der Dritte aber, der mit den fehlenden Fingern, saß über einen Briefbogen gebeugt, den hatte er mit einem kleinen Bleistiftstümpfchen schon beinahe vollgeschrieben. Die Jungen hätten beinahe laut gelacht. Buchstaben malte der, Buchstaben! Es sah aus, als wären Hühner oder Enten über das Papier gelaufen. So etwas hätten einmal sie in der Schule machen sollen! Der Lehrer hätte ihnen was erzählt!

»Hier ist die Briefmarke«, sagte Knöres jetzt.

»Her damit«, rief der Briefschreiber, »und damit du siehst, dass wir ehrliche Leute sind, hier hast du zwei Groschen.«

›Hat sich was mit ehrlich!‹, dachten die Jungen

und schon wollten sie wieder gehen, zwischen ein paar Tischen waren sie schon durch, da rief der Kerl noch einmal: »He, ihr zwei, kommt noch mal her! Ihr könnt euch noch einen Groschen verdienen. Wartet einen Augenblick, ich bin jetzt fertig. So.«

Er steckte den Brief in einen Umschlag und klebte ihn zu. Die Adresse hatte er schon geschrieben.

»Den steckt ihr mir in den Briefkasten, aber gleich in den nächsten, sonst vergesst ihr es noch ... Und dann kommt ihr noch mal herein und sagt, ob es auch richtig besorgt ist.«

»Aber den Groschen wollen wir gleich jetzt haben!«, sagte Mala, »eben haben Sie uns nicht getraut und nun trauen wir Ihnen nicht. So ist das!«

Die Kerle lachten alle drei.

»Das geschieht dir gerade recht«, rief der eine von ihnen dem Briefschreiber zu, »da, Jungens, habt ihr von mir auch einen Groschen!«

Und strahlend zogen sie mit dem Brief und zwei Groschen in der Tasche ab. Und außerdem hatte Frau Döll dem Knöres die Freimarke geschenkt.

Als sie auf die Straße kamen, waren Boddas und Silli schon wieder da.

»Ich dachte schon, sie wären fort«, flüsterte Silli, »und ihr hinterher ... Was habt ihr da drin gemacht?«

»Detektivarbeit«, sagte Knöres wichtig, »und auf die Idee bin ich gekommen. Und vier Groschen verdient.«

»Schnell, raus mit dem Brief!«, drängte Mala, »wir müssen doch verflucht wissen, was drin steht! Und jetzt ist der Leim noch nass und wir kriegen ihn vielleicht noch auf.«

Boddas und Silli machten große Augen und Silli sagte schließlich: »Das hätt ich von euch denn doch nicht gedacht. Ihr seid wirklich nicht so dumm, wie ihr ausseht!«

Gleich neben der Wirtschaft war ein Haus mit einem großen Torweg und das Tor war immer offen. Das wussten sie natürlich. Und im nächsten Augenblick waren sie dahinter verschwunden.

»Gib mal den Brief her«, sagte Silli, »ihr habt alle so ungeschickte Finger.«

Ja, es dauerte zwar lange, aber es ging noch, und nun hielt Silli den kleinen schmierigen Bogen in der Hand, der war noch ganz voll Bierflecken, und leise las sie vor:

»Lieber Aujust!

Indem das wir wissen, das du des sonntag immer nicht da bist, und kellnern gest, schreiben wir dir und es bleibt dabei wie wir uns Ausgemacht haben. Denn heute sind wir aus dem Knast gekommen, und du sollst morgen wenn es dunkel ist mit dem Faltboot da sein, du weist ja wo, du kannst noch immer rein. Das Eis am Rhein macht ja nicht viel. Köbes und Peter grüßen auch.

                Dein dich libender Bätes«

»Was soll das nun wieder heißen?«, meinte Boddas. Aber alle zuckten sie die Achseln.

»Fehler sind ja genug drin!«, sagte Silli, »aber damit kann man nichts anfangen. Was wollen die Kerle denn mit dem Faltboot machen? Das versteh ich nicht. Vielleicht ist es ganz harmlos?«

»Wisst ihr was?«, zischelte Knöres, »wir schicken den Brief einfach dem Roten U, wenn wir ihm heute Abend schreiben. Das Rote U wird schon wissen, wo der Hund begraben ist!«

»Du bist wohl nicht ganz gescheit?«, rief Silli, »den Brief müssen wir richtig abschicken! Sonst merken die Kerle doch gleich, dass wer hinter ihnen her ist. Nein, dieser August muss den Brief auch bekommen!«

»Dann schreiben wir ihn schnell ab«, riet Boddas, »das ist ja geradeso gut! Hat einer Bleistift und Papier?«

Nein – sie hatten ja ihre Sonntagsanzüge an. In den Werktagshosen allerdings, da war immer alles drin, Bleistift, Kordel, Nagel, Messer, Streichhölzer, Knetgummi, Süßholz und Bonbons. Aber heute hatten sie nicht einmal ihre Taschenlampen eingesteckt.

»Also los, Knöres, zu Dölls!«, kommandierte Silli.

In ein paar Minuten schon kam Knöres zurück und den Döll brachte er gleich mit. Dann hielt Mala das Papier gegen die Innenseite des Tores und Silli diktierte ihm.

»Lieber Aujust! Aujust mit j ... In dem das ... das

mit einfachem ... die Fehler müssen wir natürlich mitschreiben ...«

Rasch waren sie fertig, dann steckten sie den richtigen Brief wieder in den Umschlag, klebten ihn zu und schon wollte Knöres damit weg, da rief ihm Boddas noch nach: »Halt! Die Hauptsache haben wir ja vergessen! Die Adresse!«

Und sie notierten:

»Herrn Aujust Liebenbein, Gerresheimstraße 307, 3. Stock links.«

Jetzt erst konnten Knöres und Mala den Brief wegtragen, aber als sie dann in die Wirtschaft zurückkamen und ausrichteten, dass sie die Sache richtig erledigt hätten, hörten die drei Kerle kaum hin, so eifrig tuschelten sie miteinander. Die Jungen trotteten also zwischen den Tischen zurück. Aber sie waren noch nicht an der Tür, da kam ihnen schon der eine, der mit den fehlenden Fingern, nach und hielt sie an.

»Hört mal, Jungens, ihr seid doch sicher in der Schule an der Zitadellstraße ... Na also ... Da war ich nämlich auch mal darin ... Lebt eigentlich der alte Lehrer Longerich noch? Wir haben gerade davon gesprochen und wollten das mal gern wissen.«

»Ja, der lebt noch«, sagte Mala und schaute den Fremden ganz erstaunt an.

Was wollte der mit dem Lehrer Longerich? Vielleicht den auch kaltmachen? Aber da würden sie wohl schlecht ankommen. Denn gestern war der alte Mann auf der glatten Straße gefallen, und so unglücklich, dass er das Bein gebrochen hatte. Jetzt lag er im Krankenhaus. Und Mala erzählte das auch dem Kerl.

»Das tut mir aber leid«, sagte der, »aber dann habt ihr jetzt sicher oft eine Stunde frei?«

»Nein, wir haben den Lehrer Longerich gar nicht.«

»Müsst ihr denn jeden Nachmittag in die Schule?«

»Nein, nicht immer, nur montags, dienstags und donnerstags.«

»Na, dann grüßt den Lehrer Longerich auch schön, wenn er wiederkommt. Sagt nur: vom Köbes, dann weiß er schon Bescheid.«

Als sie den Kameraden von dieser dummen Fragerei erzählten, schüttelten sie den Kopf. Sie begriffen die Kerle immer weniger und schließlich sagte Mala: »Das müssen wir natürlich auch dem Roten U schreiben.«

Ja gewiss, das sahen sie ein, vielleicht war es sehr wichtig! Man konnte nicht wissen!

Aber als sie nun langsam vor der Wirtschaft auf und ab gingen, meinte Silli: »Nur eins ist dumm dabei! Jetzt können Knöres und Mala nachher nicht mit, wenn wir die Kerle verfolgen. Weil sie euch ja kennen...«

»Ach was«, sagte Knöres, »nachher ist es dunkel ... es geht ja jetzt schon auf zwei Uhr zu. Und wir wollen uns schon im Hintergrund halten! Die merken nichts ...«

Aber den jungen Aufpassern wurde die Zeit doch lang. Die drei kamen und kamen nicht aus der Wirtschaft und es war, als schlügen die Viertelstunden an der Kirchenuhr in immer längeren Zwischenräumen. Und allmählich fing es auch zu dämmern an. Immer mehr spürten die Leute vom Roten U einen tüchtigen Kaffeehunger. Aber das half nichts. Das Abendessen sollte dann umso besser schmecken.

Endlich schlug die Uhr Viertel vor fünf. Es war schon ganz dunkel. Mit Nachlaufen hatten die Aufpasser sich manchmal die Zeit vertrieben, die Zeit und die bittere Kälte ... Jetzt aber, als sie wohl zum hundertsten Male die Türe der Wirtschaft aufgehen sahen, jetzt waren's endlich die drei ...

»Hoffentlich laufen sie nicht zu weit!«, flüsterte Döll, »es wäre wirklich nicht nett von ihnen, wenn sie uns durch die halbe Stadt schleppten.«

»Und in ganz fremde Stadtteile«, fügte Silli hinzu.

Aber nein, jetzt sahen sie die Kerle schon links um die Ecke biegen, tiefer in die Altstadt hinein. Und ganz nüchtern waren sie auch nicht mehr, das sah man an ihrem Gang.

Die Spione, die nun wieder zu zweien und dreien gingen, blieben immer hinter ihnen, immer so weit, dass die Verfolgten sie nicht hören und nicht sehen konnten. Auf einmal schauten sie sich alle an ...

»Merkt ihr was?«, sagte Boddas.

»Ja, sie gehen zur Villa Jück.«

»Jedenfalls in diese Gegend. Aber gleich werden wir es ja wissen.«

Noch eine Ecke ... da, nun waren sie an ihrer alten Kirche und hinter den Säulen des Eingangs versteckt spähten sie den Verbrechern nach. Die gingen jetzt wirklich das enge Gässchen zum Rhein hinab, wo das öde Haus stand, dasselbe Haus, in dem sie damals verhaftet worden waren.

Und richtig, nun hielten sie an und im nächsten Augenblick waren sie verschwunden ...

»Aha«, sagte Knöres, »jetzt sind sie durch das Tor nebenan gegangen, wo die Schreinerei ist.«

»Ob sie drin bleiben?«

Sie liefen eilig die menschenleere Straße hinab und schauten vorsichtig um die Ecke. Es war so dunkel, dass sie gewiss nichts hätten sehen können, wenn nicht der helle Schnee gewesen wäre. Denn keine Laterne brannte in dem Gässchen und finster lag das alte Haus da, nur über sein Dach schien der bleiche Mond. Aber auch der verschwand immer wieder hinter dicken Wolken und bald war denn auch der ganze Himmel bedeckt.

Da, jetzt kamen sie wieder heraus ...

»Sie haben nachgesehen«, erklärte Knöres sofort, »ob das Loch an der Schuppenmauer noch da ist.«

Und gerade wollten die fünfe ihnen nachschleichen, da blieben sie wie angewurzelt stehen: Einer von den Kerlen hatte gerade gegenüber von der Villa Jück an einem Haus geklingelt. Sie hörten die altmodische Schelle deutlich über die Straße durch die kalte Winterluft tönen. Und nun wurde an dem Hause ein Fenster aufgemacht.

»Wer ist da?«, rief die Stimme einer Frau hinab.

»Wir!«, rief der Kerl zurück, »können wir vielleicht für eine Woche bei Ihnen Zimmer haben? Wir sind zu dreien – bezahlen tun wir im Voraus.«

»Is gut«, sagte die Frau, »ich komm schon und mach auf.«

Dann wurde das Fenster zugeklirrt und bald rasselte ein Schlüssel in der Haustür.

Die drei gingen hinein.

Die Leute vom Roten U atmeten auf.

»Erledigt!«, rief Silli.

Denn das Haus kannten sie gut. Fast alle Tage kamen sie ja daran vorbei. Sie wussten, darin wohnte die alte Frau Schmitz, die aussah wie eine böse Hexe, und die Frau Schmitz vermietete Zimmer. Immer hing ein schmutziges Schild am Fenster und darauf stand:

LOGIS

Zimmer für Tage und Wochen

Also dort wollten die Verbrecher wohnen. Nun, da gehörten sie auch hin. Die Kinder wussten keinen, der besser zu ihnen gepasst hätte als die schlampige Frau. Alle Schulkinder machten einen Bogen um sie. Denn sie roch immer furchtbar nach Knoblauch.

Schon ein paar Minuten später saßen sie auf Dölls kleinem Zimmer und nun schrieben sie den Brief an das Rote U zuerst einmal mit Bleistift vor. Immer wusste der eine noch bessere Sätze als der andere.

Schreiben musste natürlich Mala, denn Malas Vater war Redakteur.

Und so war der Brief, den sie dann sofort in den Kasten steckten:

Hochgeehrtes Rotes U!

Wir wollen Ihnen schreiben. Denn wir haben es richtig fertiggekriegt. Es hat sehr viel Mühe gekostet, das können Sie sich denken. Aber, geehrtes Rotes U, wir sind für Sie gerade die Richtigen. Die drei Kerle wohnen nämlich bei der Frau Schmitz im Fährgässchen. Die Kerle haben den Knöres gefragt, ob der Lehrer Longerich noch lebt. Schicken Sie zu der Frau Schmitz mal die Polizei. Die mögen wir alle nicht leiden. Sie stinkt nach Knoblauch. Wir haben auch einen Brief von den Verbrechern. Den sollten wir in den Kasten schmeißen. Aber den haben wir aufgebrochen. Und haben ihn abgeschrieben. Und dann haben wir ihn doch in den Kasten geschmissen. Denn der Aujust hätte das gemerkt. Können Sie was mit ihm anfangen? Wir nicht. Wir tun ihn in diesen Brief.

Mit herzlichen Grüßen ...

Und dann unterschrieben sie alle: Silli, Boddas, Mala, Knöres und Döll.

Nie aber hat ihnen der Kaffee so gut geschmeckt wie an diesem späten Nachmittag.

Ein Junge ist verschwunden

Am Montag konnten Mala und Boddas kaum das Ende der Zehnuhrpause erwarten. Denn gewiss würde das Rote U wieder seine Zettel in ihr Buch gelegt haben. Am Sonntag hatten sie doch viel mehr geleistet, als ihr unsichtbarer Hauptmann von ihnen verlangte, und wenn er ein anständiger Kerl war, dann musste er ihnen auch ein ganz gehöriges Lob geben. Außerdem aber erwarteten sie neue Befehle für den Montag. Oder würde das Rote U alles andere allein erledigen?

Aber sosehr sie auch blätterten – sie fanden nichts. Doch konnten ja auch die anderen heute einmal den Zettel bekommen haben. Die zwei Stunden bis zwölf Uhr wurden ihnen entsetzlich lang. Endlich, endlich klingelte es doch und wie die Wilden rannten sie hinab auf die Straße.

»Habt ihr was gefunden?«, fragte Knöres sofort.

Und bei ihm standen Silli und Döll und schauten sie mit großen erwartungsvollen Augen an. Da wussten sie es: Das Rote U hatte heute nicht geschrieben. Vielleicht hatte es sich ihren Brief von der Post noch nicht abgeholt?

Nun, heute Nachmittag würden sie es ja sehen.

Und sie freuten sich zum ersten Mal, dass sie des Nachmittags in die Schule mussten.

Aber auch jetzt fanden sie nichts. Was half es ihnen, dass sie auf dem Nachhauseweg alle Taschen umkehrten in Rock, Hose und Mantel? Sogar in ihrer Kapuze schaute Silli nach ...

Was mochte mit dem Roten U geschehen sein? Sie rieten hin und her, aber sie konnten sich nichts denken. Silli meinte sogar, sie sollten einmal an der Post fragen, ob der Brief noch da läge. Aber das ging doch nicht. Was würde der Schaltermann von ihnen denken? Vielleicht ließe er sie glatt verhaften.

Aber wie sie daheim ankamen, hofften sie schon allesamt wieder auf morgen.

Als sie am Dienstag aufstanden, war in der Nacht neuer Schnee gefallen. Und noch immer schneite es in dicken Flocken. Da vergaßen sie fast das Rote U und sie dachten nur noch daran, dass in wenigen Tagen Weihnachten wäre.

Schon lange hatte es zur ersten Stunde geschellt, aber der Lehrer war noch immer nicht in der Klasse. Eine Viertelstunde verging, noch eine, und die Kinder machten einen Lärm wie eine ganze Bande Menschenfresser. Auf einmal wurde die Tür aufgerissen und der Lehrer stand darin.

»Ruhe!«, befahl er.

Du lieber Himmel – der Rektor war ja bei dem Lehrer und in der Klasse war es auf einmal so still wie in einem Grab ... Da – sie spürten plötzlich ihr Herz kaum noch – neben dem Rektor ging noch einer ... Oh, sie kannten ihn alle – das war der Mann, den sie am meisten in der ganzen Welt und in Himmel und Hölle fürchteten – das war der Kommissar Rademacher ...

Eine ganze Menge von Kindern war bleich geworden. Sie erinnerten sich plötzlich an all ihre Untaten aus dem letzten halben Jahr: Äpfel gemopst, Laternen ausgeworfen, aufs Eis gegangen, wie's noch verboten war, auf treibende Eisschollen gesprungen, dem Wachtmeister Zirkenfeld die Zunge herausgestreckt ... Mit einem Schlag war ihre ganze Weihnachtsfreude dahin.

Da, nun ging's auch schon los. Der Kommissar mit dem Rektor und dem Lehrer kam in die Klasse. Sie hatten furchtbar ernste Gesichter. Die Kinder meinten, sie hörten Ketten in der Tasche des Kommissars rasseln ... Wen würde er alles gefesselt abführen nachher? Mit weit aufgerissenen Augen starrten die Kinder hin ... Und nun fing der Rektor zu sprechen an.

»Jungen«, sagte er, »es ist ein schreckliches Unglück passiert. Gestern Nachmittag nach der Schule ist der kleine Bernhard nicht mehr nach Hause gekommen. Die armen Eltern haben gewartet – eine Stunde lang, und dann haben sie mit mir telefoniert. Und ich bin gleich zu eurem Lehrer gelaufen. Ich habe gedacht, vielleicht hat der Junge Nachsitzen. Aber nein, er war wie ihr alle um vier Uhr gegangen, als es gerade dunkel wurde. Und dann haben wir die Polizei alarmiert.«

Den Kindern lief es kalt über den Rücken, wie sie das fremde, aufregende Wort »alarmieren« hörten.

»Und nun bin ich selber mitgekommen«, fing der Herr Rademacher, der Kommissar, an, »und muss jetzt fragen, vielleicht wissen die Jungen was. Sagt mal, wer von euch ist gestern Nachmittag mit dem kleinen Bernhard gegangen?«

»Ich, ich!«, meldeten sich gleich zwei Kinder.

»Rauskommen – wie heißt ihr?«

»Das ist der Fritz Weber und der Peter Kuhlenbeck«, sagte der Lehrer.

Der Kommissar nahm sein Notizbuch.

»Mal aufschreiben.«

Er notierte die Namen.

»Wo wohnt ihr?«

Die beiden stotterten es heraus – der eine wohnte am Wallgraben, der andere in der Burgstraße.

»Sehen Sie, Herr Kommissar«, sagte der Lehrer, »die beiden hatten also mit dem kleinen Bernhard ein Stück Weg gemeinsam.«

»Wie weit seid ihr also mitgegangen?«, fragte der Kommissar.

»Bis an unsere Haustür«, sagte Peter.

»Ich auch bis an unsere Haustür«, rief Fritz.

»Und von da aus hatte der Bernhard also noch ungefähr so zehn Minuten. Habt ihr denn gar nichts Verdächtiges gesehen? Sind Leute hinter euch hergegangen?«

Die Kinder schüttelten die Köpfe. Nein, nichts, gar nichts war ihnen aufgefallen. Sie hatten auch auf die Leute gar nicht geachtet. Denn sie hatten

von Weihnachten gesprochen. Und der blasse Junge hatte noch erzählt, er hätte sich eine Indianerausrüstung gewünscht, aber wenn er sie kriegte, dann spielte er doch nur zu Hause damit, weil ihn sonst sicher alle auslachen. Und da hatten sie ihn noch gefragt, ob sie dann nicht einmal zu ihm kommen dürften. Sie lachten ihn nicht aus, nein, sie nicht. Ja, und dann hatten sie ihn noch gefragt, warum ihn denn heute seine Mutter nicht abgeholt hätte ... Die müsste jetzt immer dem Christkind helfen, hatte er gesagt, und dann hatte er ihnen noch versprochen, dass sie kommen dürften, und nun war der Peter gegangen und nach einer Minute auch der Fritz.

Der Kommissar klappte sein Notizbuch zu.

»Also wieder mal nichts«, sagte er. »Wohnen noch mehr Kinder Ihrer Schule da in der Gegend?«, fragte er den Rektor.

»Da müssen wir schon in den einzelnen Klassen nachforschen«, meinte der, »auswendig weiß ich das nicht.«

»Na, dann los – vielleicht hat ihn doch später noch einer gesehen.«

Sie gingen wieder, alle drei. Und in der Klasse fing zuerst da und dort ein Flüstern an, dann ein Summen, und nun war's ein aufgeregtes Geschrei, das wie ein Brand über die Bänke flatterte.

Nur Boddas und Mala waren still. Und endlich schaute einer den anderen an. »Was meinst du – ob wir es hätten sagen müssen?«, fragte Boddas.

»Was? Das mit den drei Kerlen?«

»Ja, sicher. Das Rote U hat Bescheid gewusst. Da kannst du Gift drauf nehmen.«

»Wir wissen ja überhaupt nicht, ob sie es waren!«, flüsterte Mala. »Es kommen doch jeden Tag Kerle aus dem Gefängnis.«

»Und wir, wir kommen hinein, wenn wir die Geschichte mit dem Roten U erzählen; wir können doch nicht einfach sagen, da bei der Frau Schmitz sind am Sonntag drei Kerle eingezogen, die sind grad von der Ulmer Höh gekommen und die haben es gemacht ... Dann wollen sie doch auch wissen, woher wir das haben und warum wir denen so nachspioniert haben ... Nein, das geht nicht. Hoffentlich schwätzen die anderen nichts heraus.«

Aber niemand hatte auch nur ein Wort gesagt. Zwar erzählte Silli in der Zehnuhrpause, sie hätte sich beinahe die Zunge abgebissen ...

»Ich habe so im Gefühl, dass da was nicht stimmt«, meinte sie.

»Und das mit dem Faltboot, das der August aus der Gerresheimer Straße besorgen sollte«, sagte Döll, »wer weiß, vielleicht haben sie den Ühl Rhein herunter nach Holland gefahren und verkaufen ihn als Sklaven.«

»Den Rhein herunter! Du bist ja verrückt!«, rief Knöres, »bei dem Eisgang ... die Fähre nach Oberkassel geht ja schon vierzehn Tage nicht mehr. Nein, damit hat das Faltboot bestimmt nichts zu tun und auch unsere Verbrecher nicht ... Was sollen die mit dem armseligen Ühl anfangen? Sie können ihn doch nicht fressen!«

Silli schüttelte sich vor Grausen.

»Vielleicht haben sie ihn umgebracht, um sich an dem Landrichter Bernhard zu rächen.«

Als Silli das sagte, war es ihnen, als hätten sie einen elektrischen Schlag bekommen. Ja, sie musste recht haben. Das war es. Oder doch nicht?

»Ausgeschlossen, Silli«, sagte Boddas, »meinst du vielleicht, das Rote U hätte das dann nicht gewusst? Bestimmt hätt es geschrieben, wir sollten auf den kleinen Bernhard aufpassen.«

»Vielleicht finden wir nach der Pause doch wieder einen Zettel?«

Ja, daran hatten sie gar nicht mehr gedacht. Und sie atmeten ein wenig auf. Jetzt konnte ja noch alles gut werden. Bestimmt würde gleich der Zettel da sein und das Rote U würde sie auf die Spur der Verbrecher setzen. Und dann brauchten Bernhards sich nicht mehr zu sorgen. Die Leute vom Roten U würden die Sache schon machen!

Aber kein Zettel war da. Noch genauer als gestern suchten die fünfe. Jede Seite in ihren Büchern blätterten sie um. Hinter die Umschläge schauten sie, aber nichts, nichts!

Sie waren wie vor den Kopf geschlagen, als sie heimgingen. Und auch zu Hause erfuhren sie nichts Neues. Nur Malas Vater, der Redakteur, konnte einiges erzählen und so kam es, dass Mala an diesem Tage sein Kompott stehen ließ und spornstreichs hinausrannte zu den Kameraden. Die warteten schon an der Kirche auf ihn.

»Die drei Kerle bei der Frau Schmitz sind schon verhaftet worden!«, rief er ihnen entgegen.

»Woher weißt du das?«, fragten alle wie aus einem Munde.

»Natürlich von meinem Vater. Heute Mittag um elf Uhr schon – alle drei, es sind wirklich die gewesen, die gesagt hatten, sie wollen den Landrichter kaltmachen.«

»Woher wusste denn die Polizei, wo sie wohnten?«

»Na, ihr seid mir aber schöne Esel!«, rief Mala, »das ist doch klar: vom Roten U!«

»Hat das dein Vater gesagt?«

»Nein, aber das kann man sich denken. Man ist doch nicht auf den Kopf gefallen! Nur hätten die Kerle mit der ganzen Sache nichts zu tun, sie würden sicher heute schon wieder entlassen. Mein Vater wusste das schon.«

»Na, die würde ich aber festhalten, wenn ich der Rademacher wäre!«, sagte Döll. »Die setzt ich so lange auf einen glühenden Herd, bis ich alles raus hätte, das tät ich.«

»Und ich würd ihnen Stückchen für Stückchen die Ohren abschneiden und dann die Nasen und dann die Finger... Dann täten sie schon den Mund auf«, knurrte Boddas grimmig.

»Skalpieren, das wäre auch eine gute Sache«, meinte Knöres.

Aber Silli schüttelte ärgerlich das blonde Köpfchen.

»Das ist ja alles Unsinn«, sagte sie, »was stehen wir überhaupt hier so dämlich herum? Ich meine, wir könnten auch was tun! Irgendwas! Man fliegt ja in die Luft!«

»Wenn nur das Rote U uns schreiben wollte!«, seufzte Döll.

»Ach was, jetzt sind wir eben selber das Rote U!«, rief Silli und sie trat mit dem Fuß auf. »Der arme Kerl muss gefunden werden, muss!«

Ja, bisher hatten sie ihn kaum beachtet und nun drehte sich auf einmal die ganze Welt um ihn. Und jeder von den Jungen spürte plötzlich sein schlechtes Gewissen. Hätten sie ihn doch wenigstens öfter einmal mitspielen lassen, ihm ab und zu einmal ein gutes Wort gesagt. Aber nein, gestoßen hatten sie ihn, ausgelacht, verspottet ... oh, das spürten sie jetzt bitter. Wie wollten sie zu ihm sein, wenn er wiederkäme! Jeden Tag dürfte er mitspielen und niemals mehr würden sie ihn auf der Treppe oder in den Gängen umrennen, und wenn die Mutter ihn nicht abholte, dann würden ihn jedes Mal die Leute vom Roten U selber nach Hause bringen.

Aber vielleicht war es nun zu spät, für immer zu spät ... Langsam gingen sie durch das Fährgässchen, tappten durch den tiefen Schnee. Der war um Mittag noch beiseitegekehrt worden und nun ging er ihnen schon wieder fast bis über die

Schuhe. Dabei schneite es noch immer und die Luft war so still – sie konnten das knirschende Geschiebe der Eisschollen vom Rhein her hören.

Nun kamen sie an dem hässlichen und schmutzigen Logishaus vorbei. Aber nichts regte sich drinnen, böse und stumpf schauten die halb blinden Fenster.

Es fiel ihnen gar nicht ein, dass sie ja diesen Nachmittag in die Schule mussten. Erst als es zu spät war, dachten sie daran. Und Boddas sagte gleich: »Morgen schwänzen wir auch. Und übermorgen kriegen wir ja sowieso Ferien … Was meint ihr – sollen wir hier an dem Haus noch aufpassen?«

»Silli, was denkst du?«, fragte Mala.

»Ja gewiss«, sagte das Mädchen, »aber sie werden wohl jetzt noch nicht zurück sein. Vielleicht werden sie von der Polizei erst heute Abend entlassen oder morgen früh. Aufpassen müssen wir natürlich schon. Und wenn sie kommen, dann sind wir immer hinter ihnen her. Es bleiben also drei von uns jetzt hier, die anderen zwei gehen sofort an die Post und fragen nach dem Brief für das Rote U. Wir müssen endlich wissen, ob es ihn abgeholt hat oder nicht.«

»Du tust ja grad, als hättest du jetzt über uns das Kommando!«, rief Boddas.

Das Mädchen nickte:

»Das hab ich auch! Ihr wisst ja alle keinen Rat, und weil ich einen weiß, darum hab ich jetzt auch zu kommandieren! Also los, Mala, du bist der Größte, und weil dein Vater Redakteur ist, verstehst du auch was von schriftlichen Sachen und so. Mein Bruder geht mit dir, die anderen bleiben bei mir. Wir treffen uns nachher hier in der Gegend. Ihr seht uns schon oder wir sehen euch. Und wenn ihr dann einen neuen Rat wisst, könnt ja meinetwegen ihr wieder kommandieren.«

Es war ein weiter Weg zum Hauptpostamt. Das lag am Bahnhof und sie mussten ein großes Stück durch die Stadt. Aber je näher die beiden Jungen ihrem Ziel kamen, desto langsamer gingen sie. Keiner wollte es dem anderen sagen – aber sie hatten beide eine Heidenangst. Und erst als sie in das Postgebäude gingen! Aber nun atmeten sie auf.

Von 13–15 Uhr geschlossen

stand da auf einem Plakat.

Sie hatten also noch eine halbe Stunde Zeit. Erst in einer halben Stunde würden sie vor dem schrecklichen Schalter stehen und fragen: »Haben Sie keinen Brief für das Rote U?« – Ja, und dann würde der Schaltermann sie von unten herauf schrecklich ansehen und sicher sofort den Telefonhörer aufnehmen und hineinrufen: »Herr Rademacher, kommen Sie doch mal schnell mit dem Überfallkommando an die Post!« Und dann?

Sie standen an einem Fenster und schauten trübsinnig hinaus in das Schneetreiben. Noch nicht drei Uhr war es und schon sah es aus, als finge es zu dämmern an. Es kam ihnen vor, als wäre Weihnachten in Nebel und Nacht versunken, als würde nun nie, nie mehr das schöne Fest kommen.

Mala stieß einen kleinen Schrei aus und fuhr totenblass herum. Es hatte ihm einer auf die Schulter getippt... »Herr Behrmann?«, rief er dann ganz erleichtert. »Ich dachte schon.«

»Na, was denn? Du machst ja ein Gesicht wie 'ne Katze, wenn's donnert. Was ist denn los mit euch? Und was treibt ihr hier an der Post?«

Mala sah Boddas an und Boddas nickte...

»Hören Sie mal, Herr Behrmann«, sagte Mala jetzt, »haben Sie eine halbe Stunde Zeit für uns? Ich möchte Ihnen was erzählen. Etwas sehr Wichtiges...«

»Dann schieß los, Junge«, ermunterte ihn der ewige Student, »wir haben ja sowieso gewisse kleine Heimlichkeiten zusammen...«

Mala nickte eifrig.

»Ja, das Schuljubiläum, das hat auch damit zu tun. Aber sagen Sie auch nichts weiter?«

»Hab ich vielleicht damals geschwätzt?«

Herr Behrmann lachte jetzt nicht. Die Jungen kannten ihn kaum wieder. So ernst war er auf einmal.

Ja, er hatte gemerkt, ganz plötzlich, dass es etwas Furchtbares war, was die Jungen bedrückte...

»Was wolltet ihr hier an der Post?«, fragte er, »das

müsst ihr mir zuerst mal sagen. Aber nicht wahr, ihr verkohlt mich nicht?«

»Sie werden es ja doch nicht verstehen, wenn wir es sagen«, meinte Boddas, »wir wollten nach einem Brief fragen, den haben wir vorgestern an das Rote U geschickt, und nun wollen wir wissen, ob das Rote U ihn auch abgeholt hat!«

»Nu schlägt's aber dreizehn!«, rief Herr Behrmann und er sah einem nach dem andern tief in die ängstlichen Augen ... Nein, die logen nicht.

»Ich will euch was sagen«, meinte er dann, »wartet, ich werfe hier eben den Brief in den Kasten. Dazu bin ich ja gerade hergekommen. Denn der Brief soll noch zeitig zur Bahn. Also ihr geht jetzt mit mir. Hier um die Ecke ist ein kleines Café, da stört uns niemand. Ich stifte euch eine Tasse Schokolade und ein paar Kaffeeteilchen und dann könnt ihr mir erzählen!«

Bald saßen sie dann in dem kleinen Stübchen, niemand außer ihnen war da und die Wirtin saß hinten in einer Ecke und strickte.

»Also nun los, Mala, ich kann dich ja jetzt auch so nennen. Ich gehöre ja nun zu euch ... Mala, wie ist das mit dem Roten U? Wer ist das Rote U?«

»Ja, wenn wir das wüssten! Wir haben keine Ahnung ... Seit Sonntag haben wir ja nichts mehr von ihm gehört und Sonntag haben wir ihm geschrieben ... Jetzt wollten wir sehen, ob es den Brief abgeholt hat ... Wir haben ja solche Sorge um den kleinen Bernhard!«

»Hat der mit dem Roten U zu tun?«

»Aber, Herr Behrmann! Der und das Rote U!«

Und nun erzählte Mala, von Anfang bis zu Ende. Ab und zu fragte Herr Behrmann etwas dazwischen und immer mehr erstaunte er. Manchmal lachte er hell auf, und als Mala erst von dem Schuster Derendorf erzählte, wieherte er beinahe und die Tränen liefen ihm die Backen hinunter. Dann kam das mit dem schulfreien Tag, und weil diese Geschichte Herr Behrmann schon beinahe kannte, hatte er endlich Zeit, einmal von dem Lachen auszuruhen und sich eine Zigarre anzustecken.

In der Zeit schlang Mala schnell ein Kaffeeteilchen herunter – Boddas, der nicht zu erzählen brauchte, hatte schon drei gegessen ...

»Weiter!«, sagte Herr Behrmann dann.

Und nun erzählte Mala das letzte Abenteuer. Dem Herrn Behrmann ging dabei die Zigarre wieder aus, und als Mala fertig war, rief er sofort die Wirtin, bezahlte und dann ging's in raschen Schritten zum Postamt hinüber.

»Ich möchte drauf schwören, dass der Brief noch da liegt«, sagte er, »denn euer Rotes U – na, ich will nichts gesagt haben ...«

Nun riss er an dem »Schalter für postlagernde Sendungen« einen Zettel von dem Papierblöckchen, das dort hing, und schrieb mit Bleistift darauf:

Rotes U

»Bitte, sehen Sie doch mal nach«, sagte er zu dem Schalterbeamten und hielt ihm den Zettel hin.

Der Mann in der Postuniform schüttelte den Kopf. So eine komische Adresse war ihm denn doch noch nie vorgekommen. Aber er sagte nichts, nahm einen Packen Briefe aus dem Fach und fing an nachzublättern. Da – die Jungen, die mit den Köpfen über das Schalterbrett schauten, kannten ihren Brief schon, den gelben Umschlag, mit dem Stempel links in der Ecke, Hermann Döll, Mühlenfabrikate ...

»Danke«, sagte Herr Behrmann, nahm seinen Brief und ging mit den beiden an ein Fenster. Gleich riss er den Umschlag auf und nun las er. Zuerst den Brief, den die Jungen geschrieben hatten, und dabei lachte er immer wieder schallend heraus ... Nun den anderen Brief – aber jetzt wurde Herr Behrmann ernster und schließlich schaute er ein paar Augenblicke in das Dämmern und den Schnee hinaus, dann sagte er: »Kommt, jetzt geht unsere Arbeit los ... Aber zuerst wollen wir den Herrn ›Aujust‹ mal ein bisschen verhaften lassen. Wollen mal eben telefonieren!«

Die beiden Jungen baten und bettelten so lange, bis sie sich mit in die Telefonzelle quetschen durften. Und nun hörten sie, wie Herr Behrmann das Polizeipräsidium anrief.

»Bitte Herrn Kommissar Rademacher!«, sagte er und dann dauerte es ein Weilchen. Endlich hörte man eine Stimme im Apparat schnurren und nun

nannte Herr Behrmann seinen Namen ... »Ja, ganz richtig, Herr Kommissar – Behrmann, vom Tageblatt ... Und nun notieren Sie sich, bitte, folgenden Namen: August Liebenbein, Gerresheimer Straße 307, 3. Stock links. Ich habe erfahren, dass die drei Kerle, die Sie heute Morgen im Fährgässchen festgenommen haben, vorgestern an den Mann einen Brief schrieben ... Warten Sie, ich lese ihn vor – ich habe eine Abschrift da.«

Und nun las Behrmann langsam, Wort für Wort. Die Polizei am anderen Ende der Leitung schrieb sicher mit. Und als er fertig war, da sagte Behrmann noch: »Jetzt dürfen Sie die drei natürlich nicht entlassen. Danke schön, Herr Kommissar! Ich komme heute Abend noch mal herüber zum Präsidium!«

Das Schneetreiben hatte aufgehört und der klare Mond glitzerte nun über dem Rhein.

Silli und die beiden Jungen, Knöres und Döll, stampften auf und ab an der Rheinpromenade, immer gerade gegenüber dem Fährgässchen. Es war ihnen zu gefährlich, selbst zwischen den dunklen Häusern herumzuspionieren. Wie leicht hätte das einem auffallen können! Und von hier aus sahen sie ja in dem hellen Mond und dem Schneelicht auch jeden, der hindurchkam.

Wenn nur Boddas und Mala da wären! Sie hatten ihnen so Wichtiges zu erzählen ... Aber kamen sie da nicht? Nein, das war nur ein kleiner, dicker

Mann mit zwei Jungen ... Und sie waren es doch! Aber der Mann bei ihnen? Wer konnte das sein?

Knöres wusste es schon. Er sah Silli und Döll an und flüsterte beinahe andächtig: »Das Rote U!«

Vielleicht hatten sie es gerade an der Post getroffen, als es den Brief abholen wollte ...

Die drei wagten gar nicht, ihnen entgegenzusehen. Sie waren ganz voll von Ehrfurcht. Doch der fremde Mann gab ihnen schon die Hand.

»Na, da seid ihr ja. Und nun wird euch der Onkel Behrmann mal ein bisschen helfen.«

Ganz enttäuscht waren sie. Also Herr Behrmann war das nur, der Mann mit dem Schuljubiläum. Aber vielleicht war Herr Behrmann das Rote U? Man konnte es doch nicht wissen.

Und Silli sagte: »Wenn Sie das Rote U sind, Herr Behrmann, dann will ich es Ihnen gleich erzählen: Vor einer Stunde, wie es gerade dunkel wurde, ist ein Kerl in die alte Schreinerei neben der Villa Jück gegangen, und erst als es halb fünf schlug, ist er wieder herausgekommen ... Man kann die Spuren im Schnee jetzt noch sehen. In einer halben Stunde sind sie wieder verschneit!«

»Nanu?«, rief Herr Behrmann, »habt ihr das ganz genau gesehen?«

»Ganz genau ...«

»Aber die drei Kerle sind doch noch eingesperrt!«

»Dann war's eben der ›Aujust‹«, rief Knöres sofort.

»Natürlich, der August Liebenbein. Wir haben eben den Brief an ihn wieder abgeholt. Das Rote U ist noch nicht an der Post gewesen. Ihr seid dem Kerl natürlich nachgegangen?«

»Ja, ein Stückchen«, sagte Silli kleinlaut, »aber es war so furchtbar am Schneien auf einmal – da haben wir ihn aus den Augen verloren ... Hinten an der Hafenstraße ging er um die Ecke und auf einmal war er fort ... Es kam auch grad eine Straßenbahn, die fuhr ganz langsam, und vielleicht ist er da hinaufgesprungen.«

»Na, dann wird ihn die Polizei ja verfolgen ... Und jetzt, jetzt gehn wir natürlich mal in der Villa Jück nachsehen.«

»Das wollten wir auch schon tun«, sagte Knöres, »aber wir hatten Angst, einer von den Kerlen käme zurück.«

»Das war klug von euch«, lobte Herr Behrmann, »denn ihr konntet ja nicht wissen, dass ich die Polizei wegen des Augusts angerufen hatte. Also los! Ich werde ja hoffentlich nicht zu dick sein für das Mauerloch im Schuppen.«

Aber sie hatten noch kaum ein paar Schritte vom Rhein weg getan, da sahen sie drüben an der Kirche ein Auto mit hellen Scheinwerfern um die Ecke flitzen ... Da, nun hielt es und von Weitem konnten sie genau sehen: Es stieg einer aus, gab dem Taxifahrer Geld und ging dann eilig auf die Fährgasse zu.

»Verstecken!«, rief Herr Behrmann.

Aber als er sich umsah, war schon keiner von den Roten-U-Leuten mehr da. Fort waren sie wie ausgeblasene Lichter.

»Die sind fixer als ich!«, dachte Herr Behrmann und langsam ging er in die Gasse hinein, wie wenn er einen Spaziergang an den Rhein gemacht hätte und nun, froh über den schönen Winterabend, nach Hause bummelte.

Der Fremde musste also an ihm vorüber. Vielleicht war er ein harmloser Mann, der sich hier nur bis in die Nähe seiner Wohnung hatte fahren lassen. Doch man konnte nicht wissen. Stehen bleiben und ihm nachschauen, das ging aber nicht. Herr Behrmann spazierte also mit brennender Zigarre an ihm vorüber ... Ja, der Mann musste Eile haben und vielleicht auch kein gutes Gewissen. Denn er hatte den Mantelkragen hochgeschlagen und die Sportmütze tief in das Gesicht hinabgezogen. Man konnte wirklich nur seine Nasenspitze sehen. Aber schon war er vorbeigehastet und Herr Behrmann bog um die nächste Ecke. Er hatte keine Sorge. Fünf Paar junge Augen folgten jetzt dem Fremden und diese Augen waren scharf wie die Augen der Adler.

Richtig, er war noch nicht weit gegangen, da knirschte es hinter ihm im Schnee und wie aus der Erde gewachsen stand Knöres da.

»Herr Behrmann«, stieß der Junge ganz außer Atem hervor, »der Lump ist durch den Torweg in die Schreinerei gegangen ... Ganz lange Schritte hat er gemacht, dass man nicht so viele Spuren sehen sollte.«

Herr Behrmann begriff sofort: Der Mann war eben mit der Straßenbahn nach Hause gefahren und vielleicht hatte er gerade die Polizei, die ihn verhaften wollte, hineingehen sehen. Da hatte er natürlich sofort kehrtgemacht, sich ins nächste Taxi gesetzt und war wieder hierhergeeilt.

»Jetzt versteckt er sich vor der Polizei in der Villa Jück!«, sagte Knöres.

Aber Herr Behrmann schien das besser zu wissen.

Er hatte auf einmal eine Eile, als ginge es um Tod und Leben.

»Junge«, sagte er, »du rennst jetzt, so schnell wie du kannst, drüben in die Wirtschaft und sagst dem Wirt, er soll sofort das Überfallkommando nach der Villa Jück bestellen ... Schnell, schnell!«

Im nächsten Augenblick war der Knöres weg und der Schnee sprühte hinter ihm hoch.

Aber auch Herr Behrmann rannte jetzt. Obwohl er ein bisschen dick war. Rannte an dem öden Haus vorbei ... da, nun war die Gasse zu Ende ... Wo waren nur die Kinder? Aha, da aus einem Hauseingang sah er Sillis rote Wollmütze spitzen.

»Wo sind die anderen, Silli?«

Aber da kamen sie schon.

»Habt ihr Courage, Jungens?«

»Sie fragen aber blöd!«, sagte Boddas.

»Dann hinein in die Villa Jück! Der Kerl ist bestimmt schon im Keller. Silli, du bleibst hier und wartest auf das Polizeiauto ... Sagst, wir wären schon drin.«

Schon stand das Mädchen allein da und ängstlich schaute es sich um. Es wusste kaum, wie das so schnell alles geschehen war. Aber da kam auch schon Knöres aus der Wirtschaft gerannt und hinter ihm drein all die Leute, die darin gesessen hatten. Da war das Überfallkommando gerufen worden und das wollten sie natürlich sehen ...

»Was ist denn los? Was ist passiert?«

Alle fragten sie durcheinander.

Aber Silli und Knöres gaben keine Antwort. Sie zitterten nur so vor Aufregung.

Gott sei Dank – da kam das Polizeiauto und fünf, sechs, sieben Polizisten sprangen ab, an ihrer Spitze der Herr Kommissar Rademacher. Knöres erkannte ihn sofort. »Da drin, Herr Kommissar, da drin sind sie!«, rief er.

»Wer denn? Nun rede doch, Junge!«

»Wer denn? Der Herr Behrmann natürlich, und die anderen vom Roten U – die sind hinter dem Kerl her, der hat sich drinnen versteckt!«

»Dann los, wir haben ja den Schlüssel!«

Und schon knirschte der gewaltige Schlüssel im Schloss, aber es wollte nicht nachgeben.

»Man kann auch hinten herum, durch das Mauerloch!«, rief Knöres hastig.

Aber da stöhnte die alte Tür in ihren Angeln und schwarz starrte ihnen der Eingang entgegen.

Zuerst sahen sie nichts, hörten nichts. Aber dann schwankte auf einmal der Lichtschein einer elektrischen Taschenlampe die Kellertreppe hinauf.

»Hände hoch!«, wollte gerade der Polizist rufen und seinen Revolver hatte er in der Faust – aber da erkannte er Herrn Behrmann und Herr Behrmann hatte den Finger auf den Mund gelegt.

»Kommen Sie ein Stückchen mit, Herr Kommissar, etwas weiter vom Kellerloch ab ... Drunten halten meine Jungen Wache ... und auf die können wir uns verlassen.«

»Warum denn auf einmal so leise? Was ist los?«

»Wir sind nun doch zu spät gekommen, Herr Kommissar«, sagte Behrmann, »der Kerl, dieser August Liebenbein nämlich, war schon unten und jetzt ist er in den Kellerschacht geklettert ... Da können wir ihn nicht herausholen. Drunten muss er den vermissten Jungen haben, wahrscheinlich in einem Faltboot! Denken Sie an den Brief. Da hatten ihm die drei ja geschrieben, er sollte mit dem Faltboot zur Stelle sein ... Der Schacht geht nämlich gerade hinab in den Rhein.«

»Unsinn!«, brummte der Kommissar, »wird wohl ein Brunnen sein!«

»Und was soll der Mann in einem Brunnen machen?«

»Ja, da müsste der Schacht doch in einen Stollen führen und der Stollen in den Rhein. So was gibt's aber gar nicht. Nur ein einziger Kanal, der Abfluss von unseren Teichen hier, führt in den Rhein.«

»Da haben wir's ja und der Stollen geht eben irgendwo in diesen Kanal ... Wie stellen Sie sich das nun vor? Sollen wir hinter ihm dreinschwimmen?«

Der Kommissar dachte eine Weile nach.

»Hat er Sie und die Jungen gehört?«, fragte er dann.

»Nein, ich glaube nicht!«, erwiderte Behrmann, »und wenn er wüsste, dass wir hinter ihm her sind, dann wirft er den Jungen womöglich ins Wasser. Drum sagte ich Ihnen auch, Sie sollten leise machen.«

Der Kommissar winkte einem Polizisten: »Gehen Sie mal rüber zur Feuerwehr, das ist ja nur drei Minuten weit – sie soll sofort an den Kanalausgang kommen, aber bitte ohne den üblichen Feuerwehrspektakel ... und irgendwo einen Kahn auftreiben.«

Knöres und Silli hatten alles mit angehört und schon waren sie fort. Sie wussten ja ganz genau, wo der alte Kanal in den Rhein ging, und gewiss waren sie eher da als Feuerwehr und Polizei.

Schon sprangen sie die Basalttreppe zum Kai hinab und vor sich sahen sie den weiten Strom, auf dem in unendlichem Zuge die Schollen hinabrauschten.

»Da, da!«, stieß Knöres auf einmal hervor, zeigte hinab auf das Ufer und packte Sillis Arm.

Nun sah das Mädchen es auch. Gerade da, wo das schwarze Kanalloch unter der Mauer war, sprang eine dunkle Gestalt; ein großes Bündel trug sie schwer auf der Schulter und nun stolperte sie über den hart gefrorenen Flussrand hinab dem knirschenden Strom zu.

Wollte der Mann von Scholle zu Scholle springen und dann auf die andere Seite? Ja, gewiss, schon hatte er die erste Scholle erreicht, deutlich sahen die Kinder, wie sie schwankte, als er daraufsprang. Nun die zweite ... ja, er würde hinüberkommen. Denn nicht einmal in der Rheinmitte war eine Wasserrinne mehr frei. Oh, wenn doch die Polizei nur käme! Wie die Schollen schwankten! Und jetzt war der Mann mit seinem Bündel schon ein Stück abwärtsgetrieben ... Nun springt er wieder ... nein, er macht nur einen längeren Schritt. Zu springen braucht er ja gar nicht. Dafür schwimmen die Schollen zu nah beieinander.

Am liebsten möchte sich Silli die Hände vor die Augen halten. Und hell schreit sie plötzlich auf – der Mann ist ausgerutscht, aber nun hat er sein Bündel wieder gepackt und will weiter. Doch bei Sillis Schrei schaut er um. Und wieder schreit das Mädchen, noch viel schrecklicher, noch viel gellender ... Der Mann ist beim Umschauen fehlgetreten, schwer nach der Seite schwankt die Scholle und er ist verschwunden. Das Bündel aber liegt am Rand auf dem kreisenden Eisinselchen. Die eine Seite taucht ein ganzes Stück tiefer hinab. Wird sie halten? Und wenn sie weiter hinabtreibt – wer wird dann den armen Jungen noch finden können in den Millionen Schollen bis hinab nach Wesel und

Emmerich? Und wenn's dazu diese Nacht noch schneit? Schon jetzt fallen wieder da und dort dicke Flocken ...

Wie diese Gedanken alle so schnell durch Sillis Köpfchen gingen, wusste sie später selber nicht mehr. Aber Knöres hörte fast noch ihren Schrei, als er sie auch schon die Treppe hinabrasen und wie eine Feder von Scholle zu Scholle springen sah.

Oh, Silli hatte keine Angst, sie könnte untergehen, nur entsetzlich fürchtete sie sich, jeden Augenblick würde neben ihr der Kerl auftauchen und sie in die Tiefe reißen. Aber sie sah sich gar nicht um. Hielt den Blick nur starr auf die Scholle mit dem Bündel. Immer näher kam sie ihm, immer näher. Und nun hatte sie's erreicht. Ein leichter Sprung, und sie stand neben dem Bündel. Wie die Scholle schwankte! Und fast schwindelig wurde es ihr, mitten in all diesem kreiselnden Eis. Vorsichtig ließ sie sich auf die Knie nieder und dann zog sie das stille Bündel mit allen Kräften etwas mehr vom Rande ab. Ja, nun schwamm das Eisstück wieder waagerecht und das Mädchen konnte aufatmen.

Aber sie war auf einmal so müde. Um sich her hörte sie nichts als das ungeheure Singen und Mahlen der Schollen. Wohl kein Wort hätte sie mehr vom Ufer her verstehen können. Und es war ein grauenvoller, entsetzlicher Gesang, ein Gesang nicht wie ein Lied. Nein, alle Stimmen der Welt waren in diesem Getön. Das war ein Knirschen und Stöhnen, ein Pfeifen und Ächzen, ein Brüllen wie von weit her und wie aus der Tiefe, und dazu die stille Nacht rundum, in der alles hundertfach laut ineinander tönte.

Kaum wagte Silli, sich umzusehen, vor Angst, sie würde schwindlig. Aber nun musste sie es doch. Irgendwo mussten sie geschrien haben – ja, da liefen sie schon. War's die Feuerwehr? Die Polizei? Sie konnte es nicht mehr erkennen. Alles flimmerte ihr vor den Augen. Aber noch einmal lächelte sie froh und glücklich. Denn sie sah, wie das Bündel vor ihr sich bewegte. Und sie schlug ein wenig die alte Decke zurück ... ja, da sah sie das todbleiche Gesicht des kleinen Ulrich Bernhard. Und die Augen hatte er aufgeschlagen.

»Silli, liebe Silli!«, hörte sie ihn noch sagen. Und dann sah und hörte sie nichts mehr.

Als sie wieder zu sich kam, schaute sie verwirrt um sich. Und schnell richtete sie sich auf. Sie saß auf einem schwarzen Ledersofa in einem kleinen Zimmer. Dann bullerte ein dicker alter Ofen, der glühte, als wenn er alles um sich her fressen wollte, und um sie herum standen viele Polizisten und ein paar Feuerwehrmänner. Und neben ihr, ja, da lag der kleine Bernhard und schlief.

»Na, Kleine, wieder munter?«, sagte der Herr Kommissar Rademacher.

Sie schaute mit scheuen Augen um sich.

»Das war ja famos, was du da gemacht hast. Wir hätten den Jungen ohne dich nie mehr gefunden. Es schneit schon wieder in dicken Flocken.«

»Nicht wahr, Herr Kommissar«, sagte sie, »der Herr Behrmann ist doch das Rote U?«

Der Polizist schüttelte den Kopf.

»Ich weiß gar nicht, was ihr immer von dem Roten U daherredet«, sagte er.

Also der wusste noch nichts! Umso besser!

»Wo sind denn die anderen?«, fragte sie, »mein Bruder und der Knöres und der Döll und der Mala?«

Ja, die waren alle zum Herrn Landgerichtsrat Bernhard gelaufen und jeden Augenblick mussten sie zurückkommen.

Silli sprang auf.

»Ich laufe ihnen entgegen!«

Und hinaus war sie.

Mit langen Schritten ging der Richter neben Herrn Behrmann her. Der arme Herr Behrmann konnte kaum Schritt halten. Und die vier Jungen marschierten mit ernsten, wichtigen Gesichtern drum herum und unterhielten sich flüsternd über das Rote U.

»Ja, Herr Landgerichtsrat, da können Sie von Glück sagen. Ohne die tüchtigen Jungen hätten Sie Ihren Kleinen wohl so leicht nicht wiedergesehen ... Wissen Sie eigentlich, wer das Rote U ist?«

Der Richter hatte keine Ahnung.

Und nun sagte ihm Herr Behrmann etwas ins Ohr.

»Sind Sie des Teufels, Herr Behrmann?« Der Richter war ordentlich zusammengezuckt.

»Herr Landgerichtsrat, es ist so, wie ich sage! Und wäre dies Rote U nicht auf dem Posten gewesen und hätte aufgepasst – weiß Gott, was passiert wäre! Das Rote U hat durch die Jungen die drei Verbrecher beobachten lassen von dem Augenblick an, wo sie aus dem Gefängnis kamen. Das Rote U hat geahnt, dass sie was im Schilde führten. Und hätte das Rote U den Brief, den ihm die Jungen am Sonntag schickten, gleich am Montag abholen können, dann wäre Ihr Junge von den Kerlen gar nicht verschleppt worden. Aber als wenn es das Rote U geahnt hätte – schon vor zwei Monaten hat es von den Jungen die sogenannte Villa Jück untersuchen lassen, bis tief in den Keller hinab. Das Rote U hat gedacht: Die Lumpen kommen sicher dorthin zurück! Und das ist unser, ist Ihr Glück gewesen.«

»Ja, und dann die Silli!«, rief der Richter.

»Das ist nämlich meine Schwester!«, sagte Boddas.

»Ja, deine Schwester, das ist ein Mädchen! Was meinen Sie, Herr Behrmann, weshalb wollte der Vierte von den Kerlen mit dem Jungen über den Rhein?«

»Oh, auf der anderen Seite hätte ihn vorläufig so leicht keiner gesucht! Und nach ein paar Wochen hätte er Ihnen vielleicht aus Holland geschrieben, wenn Sie ihm nicht dreißig- oder fünfzigtausend Mark schickten, dann sähen Sie den Kleinen nicht wieder. Und hätten Sie dann die Polizei angerufen, dann wär's um ihn geschehen gewesen.«

Das Rote U

Es war Weihnachtsabend. Sonst wurde überall, bei Bodens, bei Schlössers, bei Dölls und bei den Eltern von Knöres immer schon am Heiligen Abend beschert. Aber diesmal sollte der Baum erst des Morgens, nach der Christmesse, angesteckt werden. Und als nun um sechs Uhr abends die Weihnachtsglocken läuteten, ging bei Bodens, ging bei Dölls, ging bei Knöres und Schlössers die Haustür auf und die Kinder kamen heraus. Alle liefen sie der alten Kirche zu. Denn dort wollten sie sich treffen.

Richtig, als Boddas und Silli kamen, denn die hatten den weitesten Weg, waren die anderen schon da. Und nun gingen sie mit raschen Schritten über den funkelnden Schnee dem Berger-Ufer zu, wo Bernhards wohnten. Und zu Bernhards sollten sie am Heiligen Abend kommen.

Schnell waren sie in der kleinen stillen Straße und da war auch schon das Haus. Ja, der Lichterschein des Baumes strahlte schon durch das hohe Fenster. Aber wenn sie gedacht hatten, ihr neuer Freund wäre ihnen entgegengesprungen, als sie geklingelt hatten, so waren sie im Irrtum. Ein feines Dienstmädchen öffnete und führte sie nach oben. Und droben nahm sie die Frau Bernhard in

Empfang ... Oh, die war ja ganz greis geworden. Silli sah es sofort. Und vor ein paar Tagen war sie noch blond gewesen. Aber sehr glücklich sah sie aus.

»Da seid ihr ja!«, rief sie. »Nun zieht eure Mäntel aus und kommt! Das Christkind ist schon da gewesen!«

Aber als nun die fünf vor dem strahlenden Weihnachtsbaum standen, da schauten sie gar nicht so recht hin. Wo steckte denn nur der kleine Bernhard? Nirgends war er zu sehen! Ob er krank war?

Aber sie hatten gar keine Zeit zum Fragen. Schon führten der Richter und die Frau Bernhard sie an einen kleinen Tisch, der ganz beladen war mit Geschenken. Da gab's für jeden ein paar wunderbare verchromte Schlittschuhe, dann für Silli eine goldene Armbanduhr, prachtvolle Taschenlampen für die Jungen, und noch vieles, vieles andere. Dazu bekam jeder einen Teller mit den feinsten Esssachen – Printen, Spekulatius, Marzipan –, aber sie schauten doch immer von den Herrlichkeiten weg. Vielleicht entdeckten sie den blassen Jungen irgendwo in einer Ecke, wo er sich gewiss versteckt hatte. Und Silli hob sogar verstohlen den schweren Vorhang beiseite. Aber niemand war dahinter. Die Frau Bernhard hatte das wohl gesehen. Und nun lächelte sie ganz vergnügt und sagte: »Ja, Kinder, das war nun der erste Teil. Jetzt will ich euch mal etwas anderes zeigen. Oder nein, ich zeig es euch nicht ... geht nur selber hinein.«

Sie zeigte auf die Nebentüre und der Landgerichtsrat steckte sich schmunzelnd eine Zigarre an.

Silli klopfte.

»Meine weißen Brüder mögen eintreten!«, rief eine Stimme von drinnen.

Zögernd machte das Mädchen die Türe auf. Und da standen sie nun.

›Den Kopf könnt man mir abschlagen‹, dachte Boddas, ›hier sag ich nun gar nichts mehr.‹

Denn nur ein Teppich lag in dem großen Zimmer und darauf waren fünf mächtige Indianerzelte aufgebaut, in jeder Ecke eines und eines in der Mitte. Und vor dem mittleren stand in feierlicher Haltung ein kleiner Indianerhäuptling in vollem Kriegsschmuck. Rot war sein Gesichtchen bemalt, den Medizinbeutel und die Friedenspfeife hatte er umhängen, im Gürtel Messer und Tomahawk ... In der Hand hielt er seinen Schild, einen schwarzen Schild.

Und auf den schwarzen Schild war ein riesiges rotes U gemalt.

Und nun nahm das Rote U die Friedenspfeife und winkte die fünf näher zu sich heran.

Aber keiner rührte sich ...

Also der Ühl, der arme kleine Bernhard-Junge, war das Rote U gewesen! Das Rote U, das nun in seiner ganzen Pracht und Herrlichkeit vor ihnen stand! Kaum wagten sie, ihn recht anzusehen. Denn sie schämten sich plötzlich alle ein bisschen, und vielleicht am meisten darüber, dass sie die Sache nicht schon längst gemerkt hatten.

Waren die Zettel des Roten U nicht meistens in ihren Büchern gewesen? Und dahinein konnte sie der Lehrer doch nicht gut gelegt haben! Und wussten sie nicht ganz genau, dass die Entschuldigungen für den kleinen Ulrich – denn der schwächliche Junge hatte oft in der Schule gefehlt – immer mit der Schreibmaschine getippt waren? Und wer von ihren Eltern hatte eine Schreibmaschine? Doch nur der Baumeister Boden und dann – der Landgerichtsrat Bernhard!

Da fiel dem Boddas denn auch sofort der Sonntagsausflug nach Angermund ein. Der Ulrich hatte damals von den Verbrechern aus der Villa Jück erzählt, und als dann der neue Befehl des Roten U kam – da hatten sie wieder nichts gemerkt! Und sie waren doch sonst so schlau! Und überhaupt: Mit welchem Buchstaben fing der Name Ulrich an? ... Da hatten sie also einmal eine schöne Lehre bekommen!

Und nun sprach das Rote U. Sie hörten es zuerst wie aus weiter Ferne, aber gleich horchten sie auf: »Meine liebe weiße Schwester, die Blume der Prärie, und meine berühmten weißen Brüder mögen näher treten! Denn das Rote U hat Verlangen danach, mit ihnen die Pfeife des Friedens zu rauchen!«

Ganz scheu sahen sie den kleinen Kameraden an. Konnte der sprechen! Das war ja der richtige Winnetou!

Und noch viel mehr sagte das Rote U zu seinen

neuen Freunden, aber diese berühmten Bleichgesichter hatten bald alles vergessen. Und gar nicht lange dauerte es, da war eines der Zelte in der behaglich durchwärmten Diele aufgeschlagen, ein anderes auf dem Speicher, das dritte im Fremdenzimmer und in der Wäschestube das vierte. Nur der Wigwam des Roten U war an dem alten Ort geblieben. Und treppauf, treppab schlichen verwegene Späher, die Kriegsbeile in der Faust. Dann tobten sie wieder in wilder Horde das Stiegenhaus donnernd hinab und das sonst so stille Haus hallte wider von schauerlichem Angriffs- oder Siegesgeheul.

Doch Ulrichs Eltern ließen die Kinder gewähren. Erst als sich ein Lasso in dem Kronleuchter verfing und zugleich dem Dienstmädchen ein Pfeil in dem dichten braunen Haar stecken blieb, mussten die Friedenspfeifen geraucht werden. Eigentlich waren es ja Friedenszigarren und die Zigarren waren sogar aus Schokolade. Aber das machte nichts. Sie schmeckten doch.

Und erst recht schmeckte dann die Weihnachtsgans. Doch sie war noch nicht gegessen, da hatten sich die fünf bereits mit ihrem Häuptling, dem Roten U, für den nächsten Nachmittag wieder verabredet zu neuem Spiel.

Und nun stampften sie durch den knirschenden Schnee, beladen mit ihren Geschenken und auf den Schultern die zusammengerollten schweren Zelte, durch die stille Weihnachtsnacht heim.

»Ich habe schon Angst gehabt«, sagte Silli, »dass

einer von euch wieder der Räuberhauptmann und der oberste Häuptling sein wollte.«

Mala schaute sie groß an.

»Wieso? Die ganze Zeit ist das Rote U unser Hauptmann gewesen und wir haben keine Ahnung davon gehabt – und nun kann er es erst recht bleiben! Das ist doch klar wie Buttermilch! Howgh!«

»Überhaupt auf diese Idee zu kommen!«, sagte Boddas. »Das soll ihm mal einer nachmachen! Nein, dem haben wir schwer unrecht getan ... So 'n Kerlchen, wer hätte das gedacht!«

»Da könnt ihr langen Laster alle nicht gegen an!«, lachte Silli, »sieht aus so schwach und krank, dass man meint, man könnt ihn umpusten! Und in dem armseligen Laternchen so ein Licht!«

»Da haben wir mal wieder was gelernt«, brummte Knöres, »so viel – wahrhaftig, dafür könnten wir ein ganzes Jahr die Schule schwänzen!«

»Und mit unserem Roten U auf Abenteuer ausziehen!«, sagte Boddas.

»Ob es denn jetzt auch so weitergeht?«, meinte Döll.

»Aber klar!«, rief Silli, »mir hat er es doch gesagt! Jetzt, das sollten ja nur so Probestückchen sein ... Er hätte doch schon immer so gern mit uns gespielt. Aber er hätte es gar nicht gewagt, es euch zu sagen. Kleiner Körper, kleine Seele, hättet ihr gedacht ... Na, und da wäre er denn gleich mit Taten gekommen. Und jetzt würden wir's aber noch viel toller treiben.«

Da schwang Boddas seinen Tomahawk, dass die Silberschneide im Mondlicht funkelte, und rief über die stille weihnachtliche Straße hin: »Das Rote U, es lebe ...«

»Hoch, hoch, hoch!«, schrien sie alle zusammen.

Sie merkten gar nicht, dass an dem Haus, an dem sie eben vorüberkamen, droben im vierten Stock ein Fenster aufging, und ganz erschrocken waren sie, als eine laute Männerstimme hinabrief. »Ja, es lebe hoch! Hoch! Hoch!«

Das war der Herr Behrmann.

Sie hatten gar nicht daran gedacht, dass er hier wohnte.

dtv junior KLASSIKER

Heiß geliebt von Jung und Alt: dtv junior Klassiker

71267-5 Ab 8

71269-9 Ab 8

71268-2 Ab 6

71270-5 Ab 10

71271-2 Ab 8

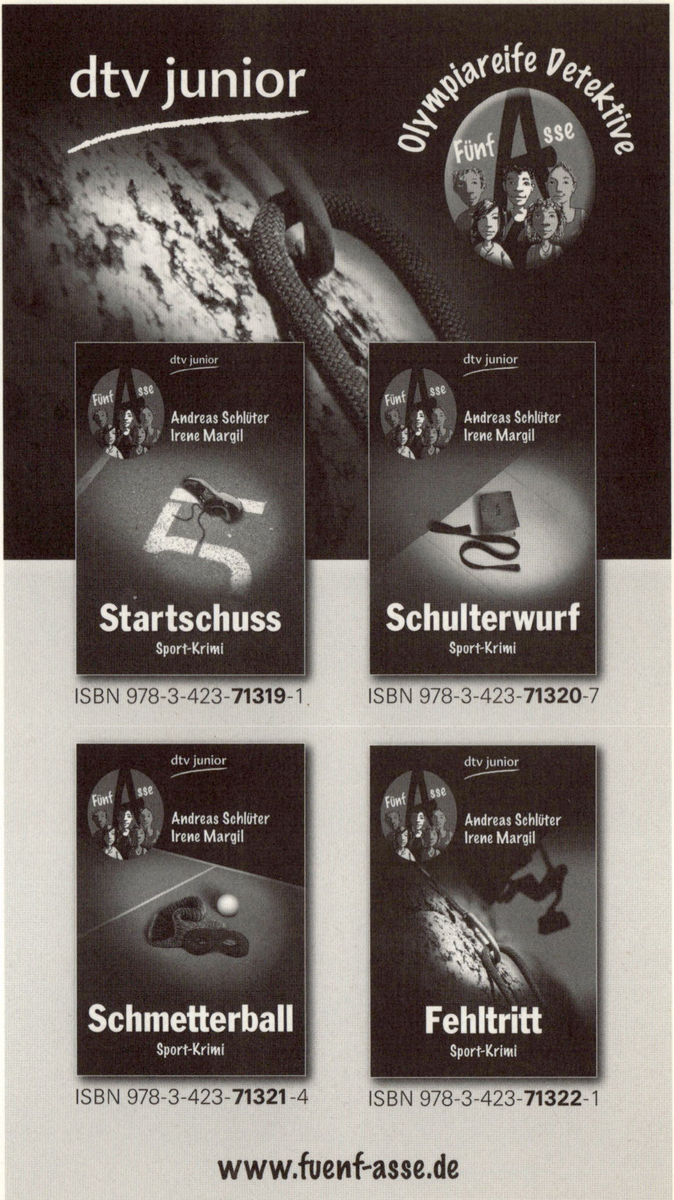
dtv junior
Olympiareife Detektive
Fünf Asse
dtv junior
Fünf Asse
Andreas Schlüter
Irene Margil
Startschuss
Sport-Krimi
ISBN 978-3-423-71319-1
dtv junior
Fünf Asse
Andreas Schlüter
Irene Margil
Schulterwurf
Sport-Krimi
ISBN 978-3-423-71320-7
dtv junior
Fünf Asse
Andreas Schlüter
Irene Margil
Schmetterball
Sport-Krimi
ISBN 978-3-423-71321-4
dtv junior
Fünf Asse
Andreas Schlüter
Irene Margil
Fehltritt
Sport-Krimi
ISBN 978-3-423-71322-1
www.fuenf-asse.de

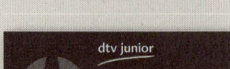

Printed in Great Britain
by Amazon

finger. "Cameron, I swear to God. You better stop right now -"

Before I can finish, Cameron reels me in for one of her knee-knocking kisses, and we stumble inside. It's ridiculous how quickly I can forgive her.

As she closes the door behind us, I still have to pinch myself because, somehow, we got here. Since I've known Cameron, we've always existed in a world of two. Now it's a family of four, I couldn't be happier, and I know in my soul of souls that I'm finally *home*.

ceiling, and I think they always will now. In her arms, I also feel something new. I feel safe.

Perhaps this was written in the stars before we even met. Like it was meant to be. Childhood friends, adult lovers.

We stay locked in a tight embrace, and there's nowhere I'd rather be. Cameron kisses the top of my head, while I inhale the warmth of her. We really are together. I am hesitant to move, feeling the strength in this woman who somehow means more and more to me with each day that passes.

"Chloe," she eventually murmurs.

"Mmm."

"I can't feel my butt."

I burst out a laugh. "Okay." Slowly, we detangle, and Cameron helps me to my feet. "Ever the romantic," I tut with a light tap on her behind.

"Wh-... I am! I swear..." Cameron protests, and I giggle into her shoulder. Pinching my sides, she whispers, "I'll show you just how romantic I am... inside."

In a grand gesture, she even opens the door for me. And they say you can't teach an old dog new tricks.

But then Cameron drags her thumb down my arm and says, "You know, I would've been prepared to do long distance. All that pining for each other, the kinky hot phone sex to look forward to..." She winks with a huge grin, and I slap her hand away, then hold up my on a local boat for sale. You know, for some more high-sea adventures. Obviously, it's far more sturdy. Fibreglass, not wood. Comes with fancy life jackets for when things get hairy."

"Cameron!" I lean into her neck, giggling.

"Oh, and a first aid kit for sandfly bites," she adds with a smirk.

"It was a freaking jellyfish!" I protest.

Cameron chuckles. "We'll always have two different versions of your brush with mortality."

Suddenly, the door rips open to a galloping Willow and equally frenetic Frankie. Oh, my heart.

"Double locks, too! Really?" Cameron huffs.

"Hi, Willow and Frankie!" I beam, but bending over is not the smartest idea because Willow is now the size of a small pony. "Oh my God. What have you been feeding -" My words cut short as I'm knocked off balance, and the pair of them shower me with slobbery kisses. "Help!" I laugh-cry as their wagging tails drum against the wooden deck.

But instead of helping, Cameron collapses to the ground, wrapping us all in a warm embrace. "We're not letting you go anywhere, Chloe," she promises.

Gigantic pink hearts fly around my head.

Ah, and there you have it.

Finally, I have all the love in the world with a family of my own. When I look up to the sky, the stars shine far brighter than they ever did on my bedroom location like that, it wouldn't be too hard to turn that business around. It has a lot of potential."

"Wow. All these big moves." I shake my head in amazement. Her face so genuinely happy, I almost crumble to dust. "When did you get so brave?"

"When you barged your way back into my life," she says cheekily.

"Hey!" I smack her chest.

Cameron beams. "The café will need a new chef. Not to mention some amazing cookies."

"Oh, I see..." I say, my cheeks start hurting from smiling so much. I loop my arms around her waist, losing myself in those blue ocean eyes. This was all planned with me in my mind. "The possibilities seem endless now."

"Uh-huh. Anything is possible with you by my side," Cameron says, holding my gaze. "I don't want to lose you again, Chloe."

"That makes two of us. Let's take it slow but I like everything I'm hearing. Please just promise me one thing. Don't lie to me again. I want to know – good or bad. I need to know that we are in this *together*."

"I know, Chloe. And I promise. No more secrets," she assures me.

We grin stupidly at each other. I could never have imagined that Cameron would want me the way I want her. But she does. And wow, does it feel amazing.

"So... I guess if we're not doing secrets, then I should tell you that the brave new me also has an eye

Alice wanted to retire years ago but stayed because she thought I needed her."

"You do need her. She's family to you."

"She is, but it doesn't mean we have to live in each other's pockets. I've been holding her back, and also impacting her social life. She's sick of hanging out with gnomes."

I start to laugh.

Cameron rubs her forehead and chuckles. "Straight out of her mouth, I swear. She's already found a place in Hammond Bay. It's about five miles from here, so, you know, she can still keep tabs on me."

"Good idea, given your tendency to flout local laws. You know, stealing boats, bikes, rabbits," I tease, blowing out a breath. "Someone needs to bail you out."

Cameron rolls her eyes. "Pretty sure I had an enthusiastic and skilled accomplice."

I can't help but laugh. "Okay, well... If you're not going to be a thief, then what are you going to do here? Not really a business hub."

She shrugs. "I've got plenty of work to keep me busy."

"Don't think Bianca will enjoy the extra hour drive."

"I let her go. The relationship had run its course."

A smile spreads across my face. "Oh... not saying a word."

"I actually thought about putting in an offer for that café. You know, the one with no service. With a

Another firework explodes, but I'm lost in her eyes tracing the burst of light.

She meets my gaze, and we smile.

I hear a mariachi band start up in the distance. "Is that -" I turn, flummoxed, but am unable to pinpoint where the music is coming from. "What is going on tonight?"

Cameron begins laughing. "The sleepy hamlet isn't so sleepy after all. Appears you've brought the festivities along with you. The light does always seem to follow you, Chloe."

I try not to blush, but it's impossible. Nothing about this feels cliché because it's all so real: fireworks, music floating around my head. I feel every bit of it.

My heart still pounding, I grab her face and capture her lips in another kiss, feeling the warmth of her smile against mine.

Her hands move to my hair, brushing it back gently. "You know, I'm buying this place off Alice."

I pull away, shocked. "What? Really?" I ask because I wasn't expecting that.

Cameron has lived in the same house all her life. She hates change, or at least she used to.

"Yes. Really. Alice and I had a bit of a heart-to-heart, and after a bit of gentle prodding, she told me she's ready to retire, move to a seaside apartment. So, I thought that instead of investing in a moat, well, maybe I should finally get a place of my own. Apparently, was excited to see you, excited to get to know you again. The stupidest thing I've ever done in my life was to let you go. Every day has been horrible without you. I'm crap at texting -"

"Well, I'm crap at phone sex," I mutter under my breath. This is despite some very, very good lessons.

She looks perplexed. "What?"

"Nothing."

Cameron takes my cold hands in her warm ones. Looking into my eyes, she says, "I love you, Chloe, and I never thought I'd say this, but I really want to try this thing called a family with you."

I can't stop the giddy smile spreading across my face. Taking her face in my hands, I crash our mouths together. Without thought, without question.

Her hands slide up my back, bringing me in tight and reclaiming my lips. She kisses me with a passion that still manages to catch me off-guard. Now, *this* is a kiss that tastes of love, I know it in my heart.

The way she holds me, the way her mouth possesses mine. It's addictive, and I want it forever.

Suddenly, fireworks burst overhead, and we jump apart, breathless.

Geez, timing.

Cameron laughs and points to the sky, but her eyes never leave mine. "You're not behind?"

"No. Far too elaborate. Would need a few more days to organize that."

"I know. It's taken me a while to realize that, but I do now. I need to confront issues rather than just run away, which brings me to the next part." I inhale deeply because here goes nothing. "Cameron... I'm not like the other women in your world. I have a crappy car, no grand plan to be loaded or leave a dynasty. I'm simple, some would say too chaotic, too chatty. Sure, I could get you two for one bras, but -"

Cameron widens her eyes. "You know, you're really selling yourself here. Plus, endless bras -"

I swat her arm and give a half-laugh. "Obviously, not great at this kind of thing." But when she tenderly sweeps a curl out of my eye and tucks it behind one ear, the lump in my throat seems to melt. The truth slipping out of me before I can stop it. "I'm in love with you, Cameron..." All my anxiety seems to float away. I exhale loudly. "There, I've said it. I love you so much it's terrifying, and sometimes I can't breathe or want to throw up, or both. But..." I give a strained laugh. "I really, *really* want to try if you do?" Because this is where I belong. This is where I fit. A second passes, then another. I watch the woman like a hawk for something, anything. Come on, Cameron. Seriously? She's going to clam up on me now? "Not that you need to say it back, but..."

Cameron lets out a soft chuckle. "Chloe, I never thought I could feel this way, but I do. I've completely fallen for you because you are you and no one else. I'd choose you every single time." My smile starts growing by the second. "I've barely slept since you got here. I

underworld and met one of them on my way to New York -"

"Cameron, are you fucking crazy! That's so dangerous."

"Well, how else would I know that you would be okay?" she retorts.

I blink because I think she just told me how much she cares about me. In a Cameron sort of way.

She smiles sheepishly. "Anyway, that lot won't be hassling you again, at least. And Chloe, I only met your mom the day I said my computer wasn't working. You know, the day you left. She rang me in the morning, wanting to drop by the house. I panicked and told her to meet me at my office. I think Bianca overheard because she was hovering by the door when I hung up. I didn't confide in her. And for the record, I told your mom she wouldn't be getting a penny from me. She threatened to go to the papers, and I told her to do it. I don't care about any of that. I care about you."

"I know..." I sniff. "Can you believe my mom actually came to my work, too? Only the second time she's ever bothered to visit, but of course, it was only to talk about money. Threatening me, you... I've actually sought legal advice, and I'm getting a restraining order against her just to end this cycle of behavior."

Because everything inside me has shifted, and I feel stronger now. I need to let go, focus on the future.

"You need to look after yourself," Cameron says, her expression softening.

about me. I was already freaking out because I was due back at work and knew my stay was coming to an end. When Bianca told me that my mom visited you, about the affair. Well, it gave me an excuse to run away before you did. All my own insecurities. That I'm not good enough for you. That you would disappear again like you did when I was ten."

"You realize I have the same insecurities?" she says gently.

I offer a small smile and nod.

Cameron palms my cheek, forcing me to meet her gaze, and I swear all the air is sucked right out of the universe. Because that's all it takes, one look from her, and tears fill my eyes. "Sorry, Chloe. I should've told you about the affair. I only found out a few days before you."

"Was that why you were a bit weird?" I ask, cocking my head slightly. "Normally, you're throwing me into the library, stealing my underwear. You know, trying to have your way with me any chance you get..."

Cameron rolls her eyes and smiles. "Yeah, I wanted to tell you, I just didn't know how. Guess I was in shock, too. Anyway, I thought I was protecting you in some stupid way. I was still on edge from the Mafia's involvement -"

"Mafia?" I echo.

"Yes, the loan sharks. The threats were more serious than I thought. For the first time ever, my father was actually useful. I used his connections with the

My heart surges, but I can't appear to speak.

"Trying to train Frankie to wear glasses is proving nearly impossible, though. She buried them in a dune yesterday. Took borrowing a metal detector from Bobbie, and two painful hours to excavate them."

I scrunch my forehead. "Frankie has glasses?"

"Uh-huh. Visited a renowned specialist in Cedar Creek. We've been trialing a high-tech pair from South Korea," Cameron explains. "They're strapped to her head during the day, but she seems to hate me a bit for it."

"She's giving you the cold shoulder."

"Or maybe she's sad," Cameron suggests with a shrug. "You know, because you're not here."

My throat tightens. "Cameron, I want to apologize. I know you didn't deserve what I said. Your mom also paid me a visit and -"

"My mom?" she interrupts, eyebrows shooting up.

"Sorry, that slipped out," I wince, then say, "Don't be mad at her. She loves you. She was just trying to keep your family together."

Cameron sighs, nodding. "Chloe, you and I were just kids. We had nothing to do with any of that."

I lower my gaze. "I know."

"As for seeing your mom, honestly, yeah, I was in two minds about telling you. I didn't want to hurt you anymore. You've been through so much..."

"Cameron, I know you were just looking out for me," I admit softly. "I'm sorry I just left. I was thinking

She half-laughs. "I haven't caught one since school, but some things are worth the sacrifice."

Tentatively, I climb the porch steps with my hands still in the air.

There's some hysterical barking from inside.

I shift on my feet. "You're not alone?"

Cameron shakes her head. "No-..." she sighs. "Chloe, you can put your arms down."

"Oh, right." I kind of snort, and they drop to the side.

Cameron places her wrench on the small table. "Hardly alone. Dogs are running amuck. Had to install some double locks. Crafty things kept opening the doors and running to the beach. I suspect Willow has been giving Frankie some training."

I feel a tug in my chest, an irresistible force pulling me to her. Slowly, I move closer. A breeze dances across the porch, and each step sends a shiver through the aging wooden deck, and me. "Dogs as in our dogs? You kept them?"

"Of course."

I stop a few feet short of Cameron. "But wasn't that a temporary arrangement?"

"Temporary until it wasn't."

So, temporary *can* become permanent after all.

This time, Cameron takes a small step closer. "You see, I've come to love them, and now, well, I'm just waiting to make it official." Then she adds, "Going to adopt them."

I'm shivering, but I'm not cold. I'm nervous. Eventually, I compose myself and clear my throat. "A wrench again, really?"

Even dangerously armed, she's so beautiful it aches in my chest.

Cameron shrugs and says quietly, "Wasn't expecting a visitor at eleven o'clock at night... And this." She waves the wrench around. "Appears to be my weapon of choice. Perhaps I should've been armed with a fifty-ton bag."

Still has jokes, I see.

I press my lips together, fighting back a smile. "Sorry, I know it's late. There were a few outfit changes, had to borrow a reliable car, watch out for animals, trees on the road. You know, the usual." Oh, get to the point. "Anyway, I popped by your house first, so obviously, that added extra time. Alice said you broke down -"

"I was coming to see you, but I didn't make it out of the dirt road."

I nod. "Saw your car."

"Did you know that Bill is farming llamas now?"

"What?"

"Yeah, well, I threw my wrench when I busted the nut on the wheel, and it almost smacked a llama in the head. Then, it took a massive dump -" Cameron stops. "Doesn't matter. I was going to catch a bus tomorrow."

I gasp. "Cameron Maxwell on a public bus?"

CHAPTER TWENTY-EIGHT

Chloe

"Stop right there! Hands where I can see them!"

I pause mid-step, pulse thundering in my ears, and hoist my hands in the air. The outdoor light flickers to life, drawing a trail of moths. Floorboards groan beneath footsteps, then fall silent.

The voice softens. "Chloe? Is that you?"

My stomach flips over, and I spin around.

There's Cameron on the back deck, looking like she's seen a ghost, clutching that stupid tire wrench. Her profile edged in the luminous white of the moon.

Hell, I've missed her.

My heart thumps against my ribcage. Night shrinks around us, and my body seizes up under her gaze.

I want to do everything at once: run over, fling my arms around her, and say I've missed you! Please kiss me! But just as my heart catches at the sight of her, my words stick in my throat. I stand there like an idiot, managing nothing more than a breathy "Cameron."

Chloe

"Oh, yay!" yells Lexi. "Hang on, it's six o'clock at night!"

"This can't wait!"

"No, you're right. Go!" Lexi blows me a kiss, and I spin around, bursting out the door.

Shit.

I dash back in, trying to avoid the eye of the furious instructor. "Can I borrow your car by any chance? I'm not sure mine will make it."

"Sure!" Lexi tosses me her keys with a wink. "Don't mess it up this time!"

Whatever this is, whatever this could be, there's only one way to find out.

"So, you're still going to drive down to see Cameron tomorrow, right?" Lexi asks, her breath so even it's like she's just moseying through Zara.

"Yeah," I pant, wiping my brow. "I already have a speech worked out in my head."

"Can the Chatty Cathy's in the back row please stop talking!" barks the instructor.

Lexi whispers behind her hand. "I don't think you'll need to convince her."

My phone buzzes, and I nearly fly off my bike when I see that it's from Cameron.

No text, just a picture of us baking cookies. Just me and her floury, ghost-like face, both of us beaming, while I have a tear running down my cheek. I'd never been happier.

I feel a surge of pain, and my eyes well up. The happiness in that photo such a stark contrast to my current reality.

Okay, that's it. My resolve snaps in an instant.

I leap off the bike with more energy than I've had all session. I curse my stupid pride. What am I waiting for? I need to see Cameron now.

Lexi startles. "Where are you going?"

I hold up the photo. "To see the woman who can't cook her way out of a paper bag. Oh, and to tell her that I love her."

There's a collective "Shhh!" and the instructor cranks up the music to deafening levels.

what I'm trying to say is, please don't be angry at her when you should be angry with me."

My chest tight, I clear my throat before I speak and set down my mug. "You were only trying to keep your family together." Part of me wants to tell her that she kind of ruined two girls' lives, but there's no need to rub more salt into her wounds. The lack of a close relationship with her daughter probably serves as a daily reminder. I glance down at my watch. "Sorry, Leanne, but I really do have to get back to work."

"Yes, of course. I apologize for holding you up," Leanne replies, pushing out of her chair, and once we settle the check, we walk outside. "It was really nice seeing you again, Chloe. Please don't be a stranger."

"You too," I say with a smile, and Leanne surprises me with an uncharacteristic hug. I hug her back because this visit, well, it does actually mean something.

Not surprisingly, I feel a bit lighter, like I'm finally able to let go of some of my resentment.

As for my mom, that's another story, but the meeting with her has finally given me some clarity, and when I finish work, I get in touch with a local lawyer to discuss my options. It's time to regain control of my life, even if it involves making some uncomfortable decisions.

In the evening, I meet Lexi at our local Soul Cycle. Despite Lexi nursing a hangover from a bottomless brunch with clients, I'm the one hanging off the side of the stationary bike, practically dying.

Brad brings over our coffees, and I offer a quick thanks before taking a sip.

Leanne nurses her mug. "I was young, naïve, and not very wise, Chloe. I wanted to keep my family together, protect my child. I wanted to get a grip on the situation. Not knowing what else to do, I separated you and Cameron."

I fill in the blanks. "That's why she didn't come to my birthday."

"Yes. Rather than tell her the truth, I made sure she never had time to see you by moving her into extracurricular activities she really didn't care for. Ballet lessons, French tutoring. I saw how sad she was, but I turned a blind eye to it.

Neither of you deserved it, and I am so genuinely sorry. I have continued to make a mess of things throughout our adult relationship rather than just listening to what she wanted. I've made it my purpose to meddle in her personal life and set her up with women she had no interest in because I thought that's what she needed to be successful in life.

But when I saw you two together, well, everything seemed to click into place. For the first time, I saw real happiness in my daughter. And you were the one to bring it to her." She blows her nose with a handkerchief. "Cameron didn't send me here. In fact, she would kill me. I only told her about the affair recently. Obviously, she was shocked, but more than anything else, she seemed worried about how you would take it. I guess

I glance around for my mom, but she's nowhere in sight. "Sure."

We head back into the same sandwich shop. The server, Brad, does a double take. I open my mouth before he does. "Table for two, please? I'll have a cappuccino with extra cream, and?"

"One americano, no sugar, thank you," Leanne adds. We sit at a free table close to the front counter. "Sorry, Chloe. I don't want to waste your time," she says, fiddling with her hands.

"I can't be long. I'm actually due back at work."

Leanne nods. "I know. First of all, how are you?"

Such a loaded question.

I plaster on a smile. "Fine, thanks. Enjoying being back in New York," I lie because, for some reason, I feel the need to put on a front.

"I see," Leanne sighs, her voice softens. "Look, being a mom never came naturally to me. I had Cameron a few years after school, and let's just say Carter and I weren't exactly in love. Marriage was just expected back in those days. Still, we tried to make it work. I first became aware of his philandering ways when I saw monthly payments to your mom, and when I confronted him, he told me they had an affair. Only happened a few times, apparently, which was supposed to make me happy. According to Carter, your mom threatened to go to the papers unless he paid her, so he did. He promised me the affair was a one-off, and stupidly, I believed him."

help, but you really do need to look after yourself at some point.

I push myself up with a white-knuckled grip, chair scraping the concrete floor. "I can't do this again with you. Enjoy your lunch, Mom. I really hope you get some help one day."

Dropping a ten-dollar bill and some coins on the table to cover the check, I walk away with my stomach in knots. When I look back through the window, perhaps in the hope that I may share one final moment with my mom, I see her hand scrambling to pocket some of the loose change.

"Chloe!"

Oh my God. Is this take two?

I whirl around, just steps away from my building, and hell, if I'm not popular with the moms today!

"Mrs Maxwell?" I exclaim, eyebrows reaching for the sky because what on earth is she doing here?

Draped in a vibrant red coat over a long floral dress, her hair catches the light like polished steel as she moves toward me. "Leanne, please," she corrects.

Is it my imagination, or does she seem a little nervous?

Well, I'm glad I'm not the only one.

"Got time for a coffee?" Leanne asks, brushing my arm.

because I have a very hard time cutting off my mom, and if she senses any weakness, she'll pounce.

She takes a bite of her roll, crumbs tumbling onto her cardigan, and studies me shrewdly. "Okay, but your girlfriend, Cameron. She's rich, and she can afford it."

I feel like I've been punched in the chest. "God, back to this, Mom. The world doesn't work that way."

She rolls her eyes, her broken acrylic nails tapping an impatient rhythm on the table. "Oh, God. You've always been so dramatic. I'm the one on the streets!"

"Yeah, by choice," I snap back, slapping the table, and the utensils rattle. She recoils, wide-eyed, and I see my reflection in them, but I refuse to back down. "No, this time, I mean it. I'm not giving you any more money."

My mom calmly places her roll to one side, dabbing her mouth with a paper napkin. Her expression darkens, her voice turning to steel within seconds. "Chloe. I don't think the papers would like to know that your mom was sleeping in a tent. The Maxwell reputation will be torn to shreds." She frames the scandalous headlines with her hands. "*Socialite Cameron Maxwell sleeps in a luxurious mansion while her girlfriend's mom is slumming it on the streets...* And, oh, if the affair gets out," she says with a shrill laugh.

My mom is unreachable. No matter what I try, I can never peel back the cover. Anger starts raging inside me, and it takes everything not to react with a venomous spray. It's devastating knowing you can't

I run my hand over my hair, exasperated. "Lunch now, or nothing."

We go to a sandwich shop and order two pizza rolls, but my appetite evaporates as soon as we sit down. Her cold, dry hands slip over mine, and I gaze at them, observing how unnatural they look and feel. I can't ever remember them feeling right or mom-like.

"How have you been keeping?" Mom asks, although I know she doesn't care about the answer, so I keep my response brief and without detail. "Yeah, good. Working a lot."

"Good. Good." She taps my hand, and a weird shiver runs through my veins.

I pick at my roll, then eye her warily. "Mom. Why are you here?"

"Can't I just drop by to see my daughter?" Her lipstick bleeds into tiny lines around her mouth. When I don't respond, she says, "Your settlement must be due soon. A small payment would help, you know, keep me off the streets."

And there you go.

I snatch my hand away.

"Mom. We've been over this. You refuse to go into rehab, and I can't keep enabling an addict. Last time was it. You're not getting a dime from me anymore. I'm swimming in debt because of you. I've had to hold down two jobs, had no life."

My words come out heavy, clouded with years of pent-up anger and resentment. I clench my teeth going. We walk along the sidewalk as she points to *that* photo of Cameron and me at the mental health charity night. Wow, it's certainly doing the rounds.

My mom drags her thoroughly-chewed fingernail across the page, ink smearing our faces. "So, you've reunited with your old friend, Cameron Maxwell? Don't you two look cozy -" she starts.

"How do you know where I work?" I interject. I've never disclosed that information, fearing moments exactly like this.

She brushes off my question. "Took a Greyhound here, you know. Even managed a bit of sleep." I feel her eyes burning into my temple. "So, you two are dating?" When I stay silent, she persists, "Swung by our old neighbor's, thought I'd say hello. Cameron is such a lovely woman," she says with mock sweetness, and I immediately feel ill because I wonder how much money Mom managed to extort from her.

Suddenly, I'm walking a bit faster. "I'm not discussing Cameron -"

"You hit the jackpot dating that one." Her voice floats around me like a toxic cloud. "Actually, I was thinking -"

"Have you had lunch?" I interrupt, stopping abruptly in the middle of the sidewalk.

She waves me off. "I don't want to intrude on your busy life. I'm not really hungry anyway." But her bony structure suggests otherwise. "You could just give me some money instead, and I'll grab something later," she says, swiping at mascara smeared under her eyes.

CHAPTER TWENTY-SEVEN

Chloe

I'm just heading down to the mall on my lunch break and literally have one foot out of my office building when I hear, "Chloe?"

My body freezes.

"Chloe, it's me."

I turn very slowly, and there she is. "Mom?... Jesus. What are you doing here? I was just getting some lunch."

"Hi, honey." Mom looks at me with dull and lifeless eyes, and I see nothing of her in me. Her mauve cardigan is inside out and hanging loosely over an athletic grey t-shirt dress.

My heart squeezes for someone who is supposed to mean something in my life but chooses to play no part. Inside those eyes, there's a stranger. One that I don't even like.

I move away from the entrance of the building, and my mom follows me. She pulls out a newspaper from her tattered handbag, and I sigh internally because I already know where this conversation is

gurgle sound and then a high-pitched squeak underneath my ass.

I hear her chuckle, followed by the click of the door.

Hell, if I was going to be heartbroken, I may as well be devouring gin and cheese with my bestie while getting a crash course on how to talk sexy.

Because who needs tissues when you can have tears of laughter.

out with stars in her eyes! What women wouldn't give for someone to look at them like that," Lexi winks, and a watery giggle escapes me. She says softly, "You know, from where I've been sitting, I've only seen Cameron go out of her way to help you. If she was keeping things from you, maybe she figured you'd been through enough."

Like so often, I feel her words catch me as I fall.

A tiny voice inside my head also reaffirms the fact that Cameron is *not* Erin. Yeah, she should've told me about the affair and my mom, but she never betrayed me, not really.

My heart sinks. "Stop being so wise, Lexi," I sigh.

Lexi taps her thigh and then stands. "Now, miss, I think you should get out of the tub. I'm going to make fondue, pour us some artisan gin. I've got a few things up my sleeve to spice up your phone sex technique. We're going to make a foul-mouthed tramp out of you yet!"

I snort a laugh, and we share a grin. Appears resistance is futile. "Alright, I'll be out in a second," I say.

Lexi pauses in the doorway. I know that look a mile away.

"I'm not going to drown myself, Lexi!" I pull out the plug and hold it up in the air. "See?"

Lexi laughs. "Okay, okay... I'm going." She turns to leave, but not before the water makes an unflattering

"So, feeling any better now that you're back at work?" Lexi asks.

"Not really. Thought a bath might help, but all I can think about is her."

Lexi chews her lip. "Hmm. I guess you're probably still processing the whole affair thing."

"Yeah, it was definitely a shock, but I think it was more that Cameron kept it from me." I swirl my hands through the water. "Doesn't really matter anyway, she doesn't do commitment, remember?"

"Chloe." Lexi touches my arm gently. "Do you really think if Cameron falls for someone, she won't give them her heart?"

"Yes…"

But for some reason, that feels like a lie. I bury my head between my knees and groan.

"She's probably as confused as you are, and maybe you were looking for an excuse to run?" Lexi offers, and I lift my eyes to hers.

Mascara trails down my cheeks in tracks. "Lexi, I just want someone who cares as much about me as I do about them," I blubber. "I've never had that before. It's always been freaking one-sided."

"Are you sure about that?" Lexi throws me a doubtful look, then disappears into the steam, reappearing with a newspaper clipping from that awful charity night. "Now, look at the state of you - passed out, ice cream slopped through your hair, mouth open like a small bird. And there's Cameron, carrying you head to the duck, I whisper, "And just between you and me, I'm absolutely shit at phone sex -"

"Really?" a voice interrupts, and I startle, sending a tsunami of water over the rubber duck and flipping him upside down.

"God, Lexi!" I scramble to scoop up the duck.

Smiling from ear to ear, Lexi waltzes in through the steam, Arnold cradled under her arm. Arnold opens one sea-green eye, decides it's all too boring for him, and then goes back to sleep.

"Sorry, the door was open, and I couldn't help overhearing. I'm equally fascinated and appalled," Lexi says, perching on the edge of the bath. "Just how bad are we talking? Want to try your material on me?"

"Oh, ha-ha." I squeeze the rubber duck, water spurting out of his mouth and onto Lexi's shirt. Arnold growls and launches from her grasp, disappearing into the hallway.

"Hey! Just trying to help!" Lexi flicks bubbles at me, and we dissolve into giggles. "Talking through your problems with a toy duck always works."

I dip my shoulders beneath the soapy water. "Well, you weren't here, so..."

"Next best option, I see." Lexi plucks her ruby-red thong from my hair and shoves it deep into her pocket. "Sorry, that accessory really wasn't working for you." She takes a sniff of my tea, then gags. "Ew, gross!"

I manage a half-hearted chuckle.

CHAPTER TWENTY-SIX

Chloe

I'm hugging my knees in a piping hot bath, a washing line of Lexi's premium Bra Bar underwear dipping down on my head. Melancholy clings to me like a second skin, my heart a kaleidoscope of glass shards.

The mirror on the back of the door confirms how I feel. My pasty face stares back at me with red-rimmed eyes, blotchy skin, and a shiny new zit on top of my nose. I miss *her*. It hits me hard in the pit of my stomach.

I slap the water beside me and take a swig of my foul-tasting herbal tea. Calming, my ass. The radio silence from Cameron has been deafening. Honestly, I don't know why I'm finding it so difficult to accept that it's over. I've had almost twenty years to accept that I wasn't good enough for Cameron Maxwell.

"Better to rip the bandaid off now, right?" I comment to the yellow rubber duck floating beside me, but he doesn't have much to say. "I mean, long distance never works anyway. Starts out with good intentions, alternate visits, but then it just fizzles out." Bowing my

"Oh, for fuck's-... Really!" I huff, throwing my hands wide, and it turns away, showing me its ass.

Goddamn, stupid llama.

I slap my thighs in frustration. What the hell am I going to do now? The closest real town might as well be on Mars. Maybe Bill can help if he's not stoned out of his mind, but when I glance at his house, I notice the lights are off, and I groan out loud.

So, I do what any sensible person would do: I kick the tire as hard as I can, almost breaking my foot in the process. Feeling marginally better, I grab Willow and Frankie and limp back to the beach house.

Guess it's time to work out a new plan.

CHAPTER TWENTY-FIVE

Cameron

But there's no hope for my car.

"Fuck you, you fucking piece of shit!" I yell as a nut tumbles off the wheel, broken, and hurl the tire wrench into her neighbor's field, narrowly missing a llama.

Yes, that's right. Not only is new neighbor, Bill, growing weed next to Alice's beach house, but now he's farming llamas.

I've only driven out here because Alice said she needed a few things and, well, it's on the way to Chloe's, so I offered. Obviously, I'm useless at texting. I thought I could express myself better if I saw Chloe in person, but I didn't even make it out of the dirt road when I got a flat tire. I've wasted two hours trying to remove the damn thing, only to pull my shoulder and break a stupid nut. Looks like my visit to Chloe is screwed.

When I look at the llama, it spits at me, and I almost back into the ditch. "Hey, sorry. I'm having a rough time of things," I say, rubbing my muscles, but the llama gives me a filthy look and then drops a steaming shit right on top of my wrench.

Our eyes meet. This time, we *both* smile.

Perhaps there's hope for Mom and me after all.

"Maybe you two can catch up over a coffee, then? I mean, that's if she decides to ever see me again," I say with a frown.

Mom gives me a reassuring smile. "I'm sure she feels the same way as you. I'd also really like a better relationship with my daughter. Do you think we could try?"

"Sure." I massage my temples. "But some topics are still off limits."

There's a brief silence, then, "Do you talk to Alice about your sex -"

"What? No!"

"I thought that maybe I could buy some cordless blackout shades -"

"Mom!"

She's freaking relentless.

Mom starts laughing again, finding this all very amusing. Sometimes, you forget that your aging parents still have young hearts inside and that they find similar things funny. "Okay, okay.... Just let me into your world a little bit, then?"

I let out a dramatic sigh, resigning myself to a lifetime of embarrassment.

"Cameron. I really think it's time we work on us. I can't do it all alone -"

Reaching across, I cover her hand, and she glances at it, surprised. Maybe I've had my walls up for far too long. "Mom. I'd like that too," I say.

Her eyes go wide. "What? Don't get mad. I was picking flowers from the garden. Your curtains were open." Oh my God, I want to crawl into a hole. Even a very small one will do. My brain finding it near impossible to process this information. "Anyway, I want you to have a virile sex life. Maybe that would've helped me and your father, but there was none of that. You should be careful with your back on the wooden desk, though, Cameron -"

"Oh, God. Mom!" I leap up from the couch, ready to fling myself out the very same horrible window where she witnessed Chloe's mouth on my...

This cannot be happening!

Mom pulls me back down. "Darling, a healthy sex life is important. Especially with someone you care for. I want all of that for you!"

"Mom!" I snap even louder this time. "You and I can't have this conversation!"

She chuckles while I contemplate the logistics of relocating to a remote island. "Okay, I'll stop now. What I'm trying to say in a roundabout way is that if Chloe makes you happy, then I'm happy. I'd like to get the chance to know Chloe better, too. You realize I've only seen her twice recently, and she hasn't been clothed either time."

There's a moment when we just look at each other.

Her mouth twitches, and I can't help but snort a laugh myself because it is true. God, Chloe can never know of this conversation.

Mom gives a short laugh. "Yes, well, who knew I liked dogs?"

"I mean -"

"I know what you mean," she interrupts, smiling weakly. "Speaking of dogs, I take it you're still in the doghouse with Chloe?"

I nod.

Mom sighs heavily. "Look, I never thought Chloe wasn't good enough for you, Cameron. I know I suck at being a mom, but I've always wanted the best for you, whether you believe me or not. I married your father at nineteen, not out of love, but because I had you and wanted security for us both. He never let me work, so I was dependent on him financially." She wrinkles her forehead. "I wasn't expecting to uncover a mountain of debt when he passed."

"Mom, my business is doing well, and I've almost paid off the mortgage. I don't need a rich partner to be okay. I want to be happy. And Chloe makes me happy."

She closes her eyes briefly. "Yes, I know, Cameron. I know... Look, I knew something was going on between the pair of you when my friends told me you carried her out of the gala. I saw the photo in the paper, and you might as well have had 'smitten' stamped on your forehead. Plus, there was obviously the time when I spotted you getting up to mischief in your home office, looking like a pair of love-struck -"

My head snaps around.

What did she just say?

Reluctantly, I lead her to the couch. We never do this. Mom looks as uncomfortable as I feel. We sit there for a few seconds in awkward silence while the clock in a glass crystal dome with a metronomic swinging device tick-tocks, sending us into an almost hypnotic state.

To my surprise, Mom breaks the silence and points to the bottle of whiskey. "Do you mind if I?"

"Uh... Sure," I stammer, then fetch a glass from the cupboard, picking mine up along the way. Whatever it is, I'm going to need one, too. I pour each of us a generous portion and hand her a glass, settling back into the cushions.

Mom taps the crystal rim, and little Frankie pushes through the door. She spots my mom, waddles over, and leaps onto her lap, giving a squeaky yawn. I wait for Mom to push her off, but instead, she lets out a resigned sigh.

"I think I was always jealous of the relationship you had with your father, even Alice," Mom confesses, her voice tinged with vulnerability. "I just struggled for a connection, to understand you. Instead of accepting you for who you are, I tried to change you, to mold you into someone you're not. I started meddling in your life, trying to set you up with the wrong women. In my own silly way, I thought I was helping. It also gave me an excuse to talk to you because..." She shrugs, patting Frankie, who snuggles deeper into her lap. "I don't know how to otherwise."

"This is a start," I say quietly.

but how does she feel about me? The longer you leave something unresolved, the more your thoughts start resembling a tangled slinky. Suddenly, I'm questioning everything.

The slam of a car door snaps me out of my reverie, my heart instantaneously lodging in my throat.

Chloe.

I drop my glass abruptly and rush over, straightening my top and patting down my hair. A timid knock follows.

Please, God. Please let it be her.

Thinking I look presentable, I swing the door open, only to find my mom standing there.

I frown.

"Honestly, you could try to hide your disappointment, Cameron," Mom remarks, her gaze flicking to the open bottle of whiskey, and I feel her judgment.

"It's been a rough week," I add quickly.

Mom nods. "Yes. Can we talk?"

I clench my teeth because I don't have many pleasant words for my mom right now. It doesn't take a genius to work out that she told Bianca about my dad's affair. Something that she had chosen to hide from me for a very long time. But is my anger misdirected? Is any of this really her fault? She didn't have the affair. She didn't try to maim Chloe with this information.

I also thought I could just switch off my feelings like I've done so easily in the past, but that's bitten me in the ass, hasn't it?

Yet, despite feeling like my heart's been crushed in a vice, this whole thing might prove cathartic. Because who knew that I'd ever consider having a family? Spending time with Chloe has changed me, and for the first time ever, I know what I want to be happy. I want a home by the ocean, some crappy supermarket herbs on the windowsill. Sure, throw in some kitsch framed prints, but most of all, I want to have someone I really love. Someone I love like Chloe.

I pick up the phone and tap out a message:

Hey. Just wanted to see if you're okay? Also, need to clarify a few things and was hoping we could meet to discuss.

I stare at the text for a bit. Do I have feelings for her, or am I her lawyer?

God, I'm definitely not Max. Frustrated, I toss my phone away. I'm so crap at this. This is her first week back at work, I don't want to mess that up and give her another reason to hate me.

Padding over to the liquor trolley, I pour myself a shot of whiskey, but a sideways glance at the clock confirms it's still morning, so I scarf down an almond coconut protein bar. I can't destroy myself completely. Soon, the whiskey burns a trail down my throat, and I stare out the window at the darkening sky as though it knows the answers. It's clear how I feel about Chloe,

Frankie's passed out.

Unbelievable.

Pressing my head back into the pillow, I exhale loudly, but how can I possibly be mad with these two?

They say pets are like little emotional sponges, soaking up all your feelings and giving back love, even when they are blue themselves. I lift my compressed big toe to scratch Willow's underbelly and rub Frankie behind the ears. Still, as I relish in their warmth, I know that Frankie's tiny frame isn't the cause of the heaviness weighing on my chest. I sigh wearily, wondering how life can be so beautiful and horrible at the same time.

Slowly but surely, my anxiety ebbs away in their silent companionship, and my eyes become too heavy to keep open.

My furry bedmates and I stay in this exact position the entire night.

Despite waking with a crick in my neck, I find a renewed sense of purpose the next morning and dive straight into work. But it doesn't take long until I'm back to thinking about Chloe.

I was angry when she first left, angry at her words. Now, however, guilt washes over me because I certainly don't want to be the source of her pain. She was betrayed in her closest relationships with her mom, her ex. And while I didn't cheat, I kept things from her, important things.

to the present. I flick on the reading lamp to find Willow sitting beside me, her sad puppy eyes searching mine.

"I'm okay. I know you miss Chloe too," I whisper and pat the bed. She leaps up, settling by my feet. Correction – settles *on* my feet, practically crushing them in the process. But that's okay, I'm enjoying the affection.

Not one to be left out, Frankie also springs up onto the mattress and waddles over to my face, inspecting me.

"Oh, hi. I didn't see you there," I say, smiling.

She's so close, I'm going cross-eyed. Frankie doesn't know the meaning of personal space, but she should because she's just feasted on that rank, smelly fish from the Farmer's Market. I try not to heave. Apparently, it'll give her a shiny coat, for whatever that's worth. Not content with being an inch from my face, she licks it.

"Frankie!" I pull away, squeamish from her breath, but still manage a giggle. She catches me off-guard with another sneaky lick to the chin and then spins around in a tight circle, wrapping around my neck like a scarf. "Right, okay, that's a bit too close, Frankie," I gasp, trying to breathe. "Um, Frankie?"

There's a little contented snort, followed by immediate heavy breathing.

I lift my head a mere ten degrees because that's all I can without squashing her, and angle my eyes downward. "Oh my God, are you sleeping? Already?"

CHAPTER TWENTY-FOUR

Cameron

Despite Alice's valiant efforts to keep me occupied all day, nightfall brings another staring contest with the ceiling.

Silence seems to expand at night, filling the crevices of the house with more emptiness. Lying in bed, memories of Chloe start whirling in my brain like confetti. From our cozy cuddles in front of the TV to our strolls with the dogs, and even sharing chaotic scenes in the kitchen.

In all honesty, I knew Chloe had me when we went shopping for colorful chopping boards. One for fruit, one for meat, etc. I mean, who needs rainbow-colored cutting surfaces! I definitely don't.

But whatever we were, I *liked* it.

And when I get a flashback of her playfully swatting my behind with the green chopping board (vegetables), I finally break down in tears. This time, I don't fight them, I let them fall. It's only when I feel a wet, slobbery tongue on my hand that I'm pulled back

Alice's gaze softens. "Then it's her loss. You don't want to look back and think, what if? Trust me." Leaning across, she kisses the top of my head, and I stare at her, wondering what I would regret at her age. "Okay, grumblebum. I need your help assembling an IKEA bookcase," she says, rising from her seat.

I groan inwardly. "Isn't that what you have Gus for?"

"Yes, but we're both visually challenged, so we need help *reading* the manual!" Alice holds out her hand. "Now, ready?"

steaming cup of coffee. "I know what you're thinking," I say.

Alice holds her hands up in the air. "What? I'm just an exhausted bystander in all of this," she protests.

I chuckle.

She hands me a sandwich. "Turkey and provolone. Your favorite. Not from a can. Eat."

I give her a side smile. "Thanks," I say, taking a bite because I'm starving.

Alice puts her arm around my shoulder. "Go see her, Cameron. Make it right. Sort it out. Far too easy to just get on Grindr these days."

I feel my mouth twitch. "Grindr?"

"Look, my relationship with Gus isn't smooth sailing all the time. Do you know how much I hate him binge-watching General Hospital?" she huffs, and I watch her fists clench so tightly that her veins bulge. Okay, so a lot. "Drives me bananas. You don't see me quitting and getting on Grindr, though, do you?"

I cough to cover my laugh. I think Alice may have confused her dating apps, but I just can't bring myself to tell her that Grindr is for gay males.

"Relationships take work, Cameron. Nothing worth having was ever easy," Alice says with a knowing smile.

Wiping the crumbs from my lips, I sip my coffee. "What if Chloe doesn't want the same?" I say, voicing the fear that has plagued my thoughts.

Frankie emerges from under the bed, equally traumatized, then shoots between Alice's legs and out the door on her stumpy little legs.

"You're not the only one," I say, and then point to the accordion. "Now, can you please throw that damn thing away?"

Alice feigns deafness, cupping her hand to her ear. "What?" she grins.

FFS.

She is testing me.

Ignoring my irritation, Alice winks. "I'll brew some coffee, and we'll sit out on the back porch, shall we?"

I nod but don't say anything.

Alice disappears out the door and starts whistling down the hallway. I roll my eyes. Honestly, I'm going to bury that accordion under the same bush I was going to bury Chloe.

Oh, Chloe.

Why do even horrible, horrible thoughts lead back to her?

"Is that spaghetti sauce?" Alice asks, eyeing the stain on my sweater.

"Huh?" I glance down. "Apparently, so. It's very hard to eat out of a can in a pitch-black room," I sigh and sit beside her on a wicker chair. She hands me a

My face whips around, and Alice is standing in the doorway with that hideous instrument from next door looped around her neck. She starts moving her arms in and out, squeezing the bellows until tortured wails fill my room.

What the fuck is Alice doing?

"Alice!" I yell and wince at the assault on my senses.

But she just keeps playing with even more ferocity, fingers dancing messily over the buttons. Oh, God. Every howling sound more treacherous than the last.

"Would you -" I hurl a pillow in her direction, but Alice does a quick sidestep.

This is like a nightmare. I have history with that accordion. I've wanted to blow it up with dynamite since day dot. Nothing has changed.

"Alliiccee!" I pull the duvet over my face and scream even louder.

A minute later, I throw back the covers because I can't last. No way. I leap out of bed, holding up my hands in defeat. "Okay! Okay, you win! I'm getting up! And dressed!"

Alice stops immediately. "Good because this wretched thing is aggravating my sciatica." She removes the shoulder strap and places the accordion on the floor. "I think I might also be partially deaf."

Three days later

"Wakey, wakey. Rise and shine!" yells Alice, ripping open my curtains and ambushing me with unwanted sun rays.

I squint against the brightness. "Ah, Alice! Not today!"

Alice casts a disapproving look around my room. "You've been hiding away in here for days, not working, not eating properly. How much longer do you plan to stay cooped up like this?"

I groan, burying my head deeper into my pillow. "As long as it takes for this hideous feeling to go away. Can you actually die from this -"

"Oh, for God's -" Alice rolls her eyes. "Would you just get up?"

"No. I'm quite comfortable here," I mumble defiantly.

Alice tugs at my duvet.

Is she serious?

I tug back, lifting my head. "Alice! What are you -"

Alice lets go of the duvet, and I flop back onto the bed. Good, peace at last.

"Okay, you leave me no choice," her voice holds a note of exasperation.

I hear some shuffling and huffing, then the god-awful moans of an accordion.

Next day

Oh God, I feel horrible.

I don't answer because I know it's a trick question. Alice has been outsmarting me since I was seven.

"Family. That's right. And haven't you always told me that you are not your parents? So, why do you think it's doomed to work out?" Alice steps forward, grabbing me by the arms. "You and Chloe have something your parents never did... Love."

"You want us together?" I scrunch my face, only to be interrupted by Alice's emphatic declaration, "You want the two of you together! I've never seen you so gaga over someone."

"Ga -" I start to protest, but Alice isn't having any of it.

"Yes! Gaga!" she affirms.

My stomach churns, and I stare wordlessly across the kitchen.

"Think about it, okay?" Alice says, trailing off into a loaded silence.

That's all I do.

In my office. On my bed. Tripping over all the dog toys.

I really am gaga!

But hey, don't worry, tough times don't last, tough people do. Tomorrow is another day, and I'll be better in the morning. One hundred percent, back to my normal non-gaga self.

This can't go on forever.

"Cameron! You're scaring the dogs," Alice chides, nodding to Willow and Frankie, who bolt outside with their tails between their legs.

When will life go back to normal? When will I stop feeling as if my radar has been taken hostage by an invisible magnetic force?

Alice tugs at her apron and lets out a long exhale. "I've left you alone for the weekend to process all that has happened, but maybe it's time you talk to me?"

I open the fridge. Close the fridge. Open the fridge. "Goddammit!"

Alice comes up behind me. "What are you looking for?"

I don't know.

Answers, maybe. Or a portal to a dimension where my life makes sense.

I slam the fridge close.

"You've lost weight. Here, eat this," Alice commands, shoving a ham and cheddar bagel into my mouth.

"Thanks," I garble and then sigh. "You know, it's for the best, Alice. Chloe thinks I'm a liar... Plus, she wants a family, and I don't want to get in her way. Anyway, it was good while it lasted, I guess. Now, it's time to move on."

"Would you just -" Alice starts, shaking her head in exasperation. "And what are you and me, Cameron?" she challenges.

CHAPTER TWENTY-THREE

Cameron

Chloe unpinned and lobbed a grenade into my life, only scattering before the smoke cleared.

Obviously, I'm still in disbelief over the affair, but nothing compares to the anguish I'm feeling now that Chloe has left. My anxiety has reared its ugly head, and while I throw everything at it - running, meditation, the dogs - it waits for me when I wake. Like a bully waiting for you in the corridor in junior high, ready to pounce. Tight fists in my stomach, heavy boots pressing my chest. It's there. The quiet in the house is also driving me batty, and I'm wearing misery like a mask. Even Willow and Frankie are avoiding me.

I was in love once when I was twenty with a girl called Dani, but the relationship just ran its course, and we went our separate ways. Sure, I was sad, but life moved on. I thought I'd feel that way again. Instead, my heart feels like it's been ripped out with a pair of rusty pliers and then tossed under the wheels of a garbage truck.

"Cookies are officially banned from this household!" I proclaim as I enter the kitchen, all spiky-haired and bad mood.

Chloe

Images start flashing through my brain like a cheesy slideshow. The way we shared silly moments, the laughter. The way she kissed me. Her horrible yet endearing attempts in the kitchen.

"No. Just stop," I scold them.

I knew this thing had an expiration date, but I still blew it up in my head. Looks like I'm back to my old pattern of hanging onto relationships that have run their course. But why did this time feel different?

A voice of reason interrupts my pity party. *You needed to come back to New York anyway. You'll be getting money from the settlement in a few weeks. You don't have to run yourself ragged anymore.*

Here's to self-care and a fresh start.

I nod at my reflection and take a deep breath, then pick up my phone for step one of operation 'sort your shit out.'

"Hi, Guiseppe. Have you got a minute?... No, I can't take Aurelio for a foot spa. Actually, I just want to resign... When? Well, now would be good."

CHAPTER TWENTY-TWO

Chloe

For the first time ever, being back in New York feels like wearing a pair of shoes that just don't fit right.

I hate the noise bouncing off my windows at all hours. I hate the icy grip of my sheets. I hate being a million miles from Cameron.

Last week, my world was painted in vibrant hues, but now it's as if someone drained the palette, leaving only shades of gray.

Why would she keep things from me? The affair, my mom's surprise visit. And why would she confide in Bianca, of all people?

I open my window, the cool breeze blowing the smell of a dumpster and dollar-slice pizza from the new place across the road into my room. I slam it shut and then glance at my duffel bag, which I have refused to unpack for sentimental reasons. Unpacking would really mean it was over. Honestly, what am I waiting for?

Frowning, I wander over and slowly unzip the bag. Only when it's empty do I start to cry.

Heart pumping, I swivel around and wrench the door open in one movement. Forget the lift; I need the stairs. I run as fast as my legs will take me and burst onto the cold, damp pavement outside with winded gasps.

And just like that, my stay with Cameron has come to an abrupt and unceremonious end.

The whole time? Who the hell are you even?" God, I feel crazed, but I can't stop. Words snapping from my mouth, far harsher than I intend. "Money fixes everything, right, Cameron? Too bad about the people that get crushed along the way."

Cameron throws me a glare, her blue eyes turning arctic. Full of contempt and things she won't say, but I hear them, loud and clear.

You will never be good enough for me.

And suddenly, I'm back to being ten years old again, and Cameron no longer my friend. Maybe that's exactly what I want. Cameron at a distance, safer that way.

There's a hesitant knock, and the receptionist whispers through the gap in the door, "Your midday appointment is here, Cameron."

"Okay." Cameron nods tersely, then glaring at me, she grits her teeth. "Talk about this later at home, Chloe."

I glare back.

A few feet and an ocean of doubt now between us. The tension in the air is unbearable.

"No." I struggle for air and choke out my words, heavy with resignation. "I'm going home, Cameron. My home... What's the point of hanging around a few extra days, right? You'll just lie to my face anyway."

I can't bear to look at her for a second longer. I need to escape right now.

It actually hurts to look at her. "Bianca couldn't wait to tell me. Mom wanted money from you. Why did I have to hear it from her? I wanted this all to end, and now you've started it again. She will never stop -"

"Hang on a second..."

But I'm so raw that words spill out of my mouth like hot lava. "Because that's what your family does, isn't it? Just throws money at problems to make them go away. Like father, like daughter."

Cameron stumbles back like she's been hit, and it feels like a million miles.

Drawing breath, I continue. "All those years ago, your father did the same thing to my mother after they had an affair. I always wondered how she funded her addiction since my father didn't give her any money. And it was *your* family, Cameron. Your family. I checked some bank statements that were in storage. Payment after payment. Hush money, right?"

We stand there locked in a bizarre vortex, staring, silent as my words land in the space between us.

Cameron frowns, but she doesn't reply. Wow, and as if that isn't confirmation. All of it's true.

I hate how I wear my feelings on my face. I hate how whatever we shared meant more to me than to her. All of this while my mom still has a chokehold on my life. The noose getting tighter and tighter.

Questions spin around in my mind. I grab one of them, the most important to me. "How long have you known?" I probe, my gaze boring into hers. "A week?

By the time I arrive, I'm so riled up that I practically launch head-first into her office.

The stick-thin receptionist startles, shooting up behind a glossy desk. "Oh no, you can't go in -"

I'm already slamming the door shut.

Cameron jumps at the noise, a stack of files tumbling from her grasp. "Chloe? What are you -" She bends down to collect them, but her eyes never leave mine. "Wait. What's wrong?"

My feet rooted to the floor, a heavy weight pressing on my chest.

Nothing. Everything.

"I won't be long," I stammer.

Cameron rushes forward. "Hang on, you've been crying," she says, grabbing my arm, and I fling it away.

"Don't," I snap.

Her voice is soft, filled with concern. "Chloe..."

Tears blur my vision, but I don't let them fall. "Tell me. Are you just a liar?" I ask, my voice trembling.

Cameron straightens, stunned. "What?"

The air crackles between us, just like it always does.

Arm crossed defensively, I confront her. "Why didn't you tell me my mom visited you?"

Cameron's expression falters, a flicker of guilt crossing her features. Pulling on the back of her neck, she sighs. "How do you..."

But Bianca isn't done. "I don't know how Cameron let you stay in this house, knowing your mom was a homewrecker. I certainly wouldn't."

Wait, Cameron knew and didn't tell me? I was right. She has been hiding things from me, and confiding in Bianca? That thought alone makes me feel sick, but there's no disputing the gleam in Bianca's eye. She's basking in my humiliation.

"I guess you were the last to know. Oops, sorry to be the bearer of bad news," Bianca says insincerely, then flashes her bleached teeth in a venomous grin before sauntering off. "Don't let the door hit you on the way out!" she yells over her shoulder.

Tears prickle my eyelashes, and I blink back furiously as I try to process everything I just heard. For all her bitchiness, I don't think Bianca is lying. My father must've known, too. That's why he kept those bank statements as records. Maybe that's also why he was so disengaged with our family, with me.

Why the hell didn't Cameron tell me? Was she sleeping with me and keeping secrets at the same time?

I race to find those bank statements, but they only confirm my worst fears. Mom even had her own account. Why didn't I look closely at these before?

Snatching my jacket from the back of the chair, I call a taxi and head straight to Cameron's office, Bianca's taunts echoing in my ears like a never-ending loop. She couldn't contain her glee at having something over me.

"You heard me," Bianca taunts. "Cameron met up with her. Probably wanted money, the little gold digger." Her disdainful gaze roams my body. "Well, the apple doesn't fall far from the tree, does it?"

She must see my face turn gray. The buzz of the refrigerator suddenly roars in my ears like a swarm of mosquitos. Cameron saw my mom? When? Why didn't she tell me?

"Know your secret, honey," Bianca chuckles darkly, relishing my discomfort. "And so does this family. Your 'thing' will never be more than a charade, so why don't you pop back to your trailer park where you belong..."

My fingers curl into angry fists, and it takes every ounce of willpower not to respond.

"You know, I can't believe your mom had an affair with Cameron's dad, too," Bianca says casually. "How Cameron let you stay here -" She locks eyes with mine. "Oh, you didn't know?" she coos, clasping her hands in feigned sympathy.

My mom and Cameron's dad? Okay, what the heck is she talking about now?

"Cameron's dad gave her money. And all these years later, you're here. Leeching off Cameron. How fitting," Bianca snorts derisively, and my mind starts reeling.

Suddenly, I recall the bank statements I found in storage, those highlighted monthly transactions, and all I can do is latch onto the counter.

Not knowing what else to do, I sigh and make my way to my safe space, the kitchen. Nothing like being elbow-deep in pots and pans to –

My step falters.

Bianca looms before me, all five foot ten of her, hair slicked back, clad in a relaxed luxe suit and designer kicks. "Call you back," she dismisses whoever's on the call, her crazed eyes zeroing in on mine.

Oh, God.

She's still pissed about the gala.

"Why haven't you left yet?" she sneers, and I make a beeline toward the pantry.

"Because Cameron asked me to stay," I retort, grabbing ingredients for a cinnamon tea cake.

There's a momentary pause before she unleashes, "Do you honestly think Cameron will fall for someone like you? Tongues are already wagging down at the Country Club after your little stunt at the charity event. I can't imagine she'll let *this* go on for much longer. Far too damaging for the family's reputation."

Okay, that's it.

Just as I spin around to defend myself or maybe even dump a bag of flour on her head, she smirks, her tone dripping with malice. "And how's your mom, Sherie? Still chasing her next fix?"

Caught off-guard, I can only blink. "What did you say?"

I sit up, the weight of unease settling like a heavy stone. I look at my phone, no message. Cameron never leaves without a word, especially not without saying goodbye.

Glancing around, I bite my fingernail. Once thoroughly chewed, I move on to the next, then chastise myself for overthinking things. With a heavy groan, I slip out of bed and shower and change, but when I pad around the house, Cameron is still nowhere to be found.

"Morning, Alice," I say, entering the living area, and Alice greets me with a smile. She's unwrapping a garden gnome from glittery paper. "Morning, Chloe. Gus and his presents," she says with a giggle. "I don't have the heart to tell him that I don't really like them. This is number fourteen. When will it ever stop?"

I laugh and squeeze her shoulder. "Oh, Alice. It's sweet. Must be his way of telling you that you're always on his mind."

"He could just stop being a man and tell me?"

I just smile. "Hey, do you know where Cameron is?"

"She's working from her office in town today. Something about her computer acting up," she says, and not that I don't believe her, but something niggles at me.

On my way back to my room, I slip into Cameron's home office, move the mouse, and her computer flicks to life. My shoulders slump because what the hell? Is Cameron avoiding me all of a sudden?

in fits of giggles and sharing chocolatey kisses, but beneath the surface, there's an undeniable tension, like we're both tiptoeing around the elephant in the room.

In the quiet lull after the TV fades to black, things stay pretty PG. I lie in her arms with her warm skin pressed against mine. Her hand traces lazy patterns across my lower back and up my spine, but neither of us speaks, preferring to marinate in our own thoughts.

I find myself grappling with the depth of my emotions, the lingering uncertainty of how I'll handle life post-Cameron. I know it's just a fling, and it will end when I head back to New York. I thought I could live in the moment, but I guess that's not me. I can't just turn off my feelings like that. I wonder how Cameron can. Maybe some part of me believed she may grow to care about me as much as I do about her. That's the problem with hope. A little goes a long way.

As if sensing my sadness, her arm tightens around me, and I blink away unshed tears.

Saying goodbye is going to be hard.

As morning sunlight filters through the curtains, I stretch out my hand, expecting to find Cameron's warm body beside me. But instead, there's nothing but empty space, cold and unfamiliar.

My eyes snap open. "Cameron?"

The room echoes with the sound of my own voice.

Silence.

was living and growing up without her. Hell, this living slash dating arrangement is temporary.

I frown, scratching behind Frankie's ear.

"Thought she might make you happy," says Cameron softly, and not that her heart isn't in the right place, but why does Frankie feel like a bit of a token effort?

"She does," I sigh.

All of a sudden, I catch Cameron's eyes roaming my face like she wants to tell me something, but she's searching for the words. She parts her lips, and I zero in on them, waiting. But in the end, she just offers a tentative smile before averting her eyes.

My stomach lurches, and not in a good way. I keep my stare trained on her.

Cameron, what exactly aren't you telling me?

Later that night when Cameron joins me in bed, she doesn't hold my gaze - although she does get brownie points for bringing a pint of mint choc ice cream and an extra spoon.

Staring at her gorgeous face while she wrestles open the lid, I wonder why I don't just ask her again and get to the bottom of it, but I can't because there's an even bigger part of me that wants to savor every fleeting moment we share.

So, I shove that unsettling feeling aside as we watch an old rerun of Friends. Soon enough, we're lost and perfectly spotty. There is a skittering sound on the floorboards as Willow hurtles in to sniff the newcomer. Cameron holds the dog in the air, and I immediately notice the smattering of brown fuzz on her black shirt.

"I went to get medication for Willow's wonky eyes, and well, this little one was hovering out front. I couldn't just leave her there, especially after she rammed into my leg," Cameron explains, blinking, and I rush over. "I can't believe someone dumped her. Do you know how cold it is out there now?"

My heart swells at her indignation.

"I think Frankie suits her, don't you?" Cameron says, and Frankie licks her hand as though she is saying thank you.

Grinning, I pat her head. "Uh-huh. She's completely adorable. How old is she?"

"According to her teeth, only three," Cameron replies.

Frankie turns to me, and I gasp, "Oh my God! She's wearing an eyepatch!"

Cameron nods. "Exactly. She has one eye!"

"Wait. So, now we have two dogs?" I narrow my eyes. "What has happened to you?"

"Nothing. It's just temporary until they find a good home," Cameron assures me.

Temporary.

My heart sinks. There's something about that word that I don't like. I've heard it my whole life. Mom's addiction was supposed to be temporary. As

CHAPTER TWENTY-ONE

Chloe

My sixth sense says that something is wrong.

It wasn't Cameron's reaction to the sale of my family home but the elusive shadow flickering in her eyes, a shadow I can't quite decipher. Whatever it is, it has her pulling her back.

Sure, she's still being affectionate, just not wanting to rip off my clothes. I don't mind because I'll take any time I can have with her, but it's impossible to shake this weird feeling. Is that why she's acting this way because I'm about to leave? I was under the impression Cameron wanted to make the most of our time together. I hate the feeling of her slipping away. The sensation gnaws at me, a hollow ache in my chest.

"Chloe?"

I hear her voice in the foyer and drop the dishtowel on the counter as I walk out of the kitchen. "Yeah, just tidying up -"

I stop dead.

Cameron is standing by the front door, and in her arms, a scruffy dog the size of a toaster oven. It's tan

"Just a tough day at work," I reply as normally as I can, trying to mask the whirlwind inside. "But this is about you. Honestly, I'm really happy for you, Chloe."

And I am.

Another beautiful smile explodes across her face. "Thanks. You know, I even bought a half-decent bottle of champagne. I thought we could celebrate?" Chloe lifts an eyebrow, and I manage to summon a smile of my own. "Sure. Sounds good," I say weakly.

Okay, so I'm not going to ruin her shining moment. I'll keep this to myself for now and share it with her at another, more appropriate time. That's better, right? I groan inwardly because when will ever be the right time?

Point is, I don't want to hurt Chloe or see her upset - not now, not *ever*.

hates me for it? She's been happy here, I'm sure of it. I can see it in her face. Do I potentially ruin our last few days together?

My stomach sinks, but my mind won't stop seesawing back and forth.

"Hey," says a familiar voice, and I swing around to see Chloe walking in. She's beaming.

"Hi," I reply, swallowing a knot of guilt.

"I have great news!" Chloe stops in front of me, her face a picture of happiness. Pressing her hands together, she wriggles her fingers. "Just got off the phone with Bill after crunching some numbers... And I'm going to accept his offer!"

I reach out and squeeze her arms. "Chloe, that's amazing. I'm so happy for you."

"Max is drafting up the contract now."

This elicits a grunt from me. "Still dealing with that halfwit?"

"Cameron, she's just finalizing the contract, and that's it.... Then I'll find a new lawyer," Chloe says softly, and I smile. "You know, Bill said we could just do a private sale and save money. His son's itching to move back to the area with his family. Obviously, going to completely remodel the place -" She stops, catching the sudden shift in my demeanor. "Wait. What's wrong?"

"Nothing," I lie, but I'm back thinking about the affair.

Chloe gives me a searching look.

Cameron

"Oh, I know. Do you have any idea how crushed I was not being able to see her anymore? She was my only real friend," I reply. My relationship with my mom is so complex and bound up in regret and anger that communicating with her is difficult. Perhaps that's why I've never confronted her about Chloe until now.

"Cameron..."

"Chloe isn't fake and pretentious like all those women you're hell-bent on setting me up with. She is completely real. Maybe if you took the time to know her, you'd see that she's warm and funny and kind, and exactly the sort of woman I should be hanging around."

Mom shoots me a stern look. "Alright, Cameron Elise. It's time you and I had a chat. Now, sit down, young lady," she orders, pointing to the couch.

Elise? She only used my middle name when things were serious.

Why do I get the feeling this will be an uncomfortable conversation?

Her mom and my dad?

An affair?

Mom sure knows how to bring my world crashing down. My chest tightens with anger, and the weight of all the lies surges up from my gut. Another posthumous reason to hate my father that little bit more.

Honestly, I don't know what to do. Do I lump Chloe with this horrible bit of information? What if she

They say it's the big things that grab your attention when you're single, but for me, it's the almost inconspicuous things. The way she recognized the SOS in my eyes when Bianca brought up the ball, how she rescued Dad's Queen piece from the garden and slipped it back onto the chessboard when I wasn't around. And the batch of her famous cookies that mysteriously found their way into my packed lunch for my NYC trip.

"She's pretty amazing, isn't she?" I say, almost goggle-eyed at the photo of Chloe in my arms as I carried her out, and Mom spins around so fast that she almost burns a hole in the carpet. "Cameron -"

Before she can finish, the door slams open, and in bounds Willow looking like she's been rolling in mud. She does a manic lap of the room, sending Mom stumbling over a trashcan, then flies out the door.

"Honestly, this place has gone to the dogs! Quite literally!" she yelps.

I burst out a laugh.

"Cameron! I'm being serious. Ever since Chloe came along -"

My mood shifts in an instant. "What? I've been happy? Yes, I know you like to see me miserable, Mom. Mixing with people who I couldn't care less about. You never thought Chloe was good enough for me. Just like you did all those years ago when you didn't give me the invitation to her party?"

Mom turns to me, aghast.

press a soft kiss to her temple, and soon, I'm drifting off to sleep, too.

The next morning, the taste of her lips still lingers on mine, even halfway through a punishing five-mile run. My legs hammer out a relentless rhythm, but it doesn't stop my smile.

I know I'm walking on a dangerous tightrope because she's leaving soon, but how can I possibly stop when it feels so good?

I guess I'll deal with that part later.

"Oh God, the tabloids are having a field day with this." Mom theatrically tosses the newspaper onto my desk and strides toward the window.

I glance at the headline, *"On like Donkey Kong at the Benefit Gala!"* and start to laugh. "Oh, come on, that's a reach. Hardly worth the write-up, but we did raise a record amount of money because of the coverage. That's the important thing, isn't it?"

Mom ignores me, having done a wonderful job of developing selective hearing over the years. "Suppose I'll have to donate more now to smooth things over with the committee," she muses.

I roll my eyes. Mom is still tutting disapprovingly, but my mind drifts to Chloe. She's charismatic, sexy, and, if I'm honest, always the most mesmerizing person in the room – even when she wipes out on an ice cream sundae.

CHAPTER TWENTY

Cameron

We lie on our sides facing one another, naked and exhausted.

The glow of moonlight casts a silvery sheen over our entwined bodies.

Chloe stares at me with those beautiful dark eyes, but they're not just eyes, they soothe the soul. "Penny for your thoughts?" she murmurs, her voice a soft caress against the silence. I take a piece of her hair, twirling it around my finger absentmindedly. "You're perfect. Every inch of you," I whisper, and Chloe smiles with the light of a thousand suns, then nuzzles into the crook of my shoulder, her warmth seeping into my skin.

I give a contented sigh. Honestly, I love being her pillow as much as everything else. Her gentle breathing is like a rhythmic lullaby, calming my anxious soul. I don't need my nightly meditation when I can listen to this. How can one woman hold so much power?

It doesn't take long until Chloe drifts off to sleep, her chest rising and falling against mine. Smiling, I delicately run my fingers through her tousled hair and

Chloe

"Playing chess," I deadpan, deliberately tugging down the hem of my dress. "Goodbye, Miss Maxwell," I say, unable to hide my smug smile.

"Goodbye, Miss Bentley."

Bianca turns a glorious shade of green as I sweep past her sour face and quickly moves to close the door.

"Keep it open," says Cameron, and I smile even wider, practically floating all the way to my room.

I throw myself onto my bed, screaming into my pillow, and only now does it dawn on me that something is not quite as it should be. Oh, right, I'm thong-less. It's still in Cameron's pocket. I giggle to myself, then flip onto my back and sigh.

Honestly, I can't help but feel this is it. I've found *her*. Everything I've ever wanted in a woman is right here in my hometown.

When I think of leaving, I still with an ache in my chest and wonder how I can possibly leave now.

How can I when I've been falling in love with Cameron since that night she gave me a ride?

When Cameron stills, she rests her forehead against mine and tries to slow her breathing. She almost looks embarrassed by our lack of control, and I gently withdraw my fingers, and then press my mouth against her ear, grinning. "I *really* like your office."

Cameron smirks as I lift her into my arms. I brush the hair from her face where it's stuck to her damp skin, and we kiss. Lips still melded, we move around the office, reaching down periodically to pick up items of clothing.

Finally breaking apart, I cup her cheek with my palm. Both smiling, Cameron dresses, and I fix myself and try to tame my bedhead hair, but our eyes never leave one another. Not for a second.

There's another irritating knock on the door. "Um, Cameron?"

"I'm going to go," I whisper, kissing the scar above her brow. But when I go to move, my feet appear to be glued in place, and I just stare like a zombie.

Cameron stifles a laugh, smacking me on the butt before spinning me around and gently nudging me forward.

Grinning, I walk away, and I don't need to turn around to know that Cameron's still watching me. Taking a deep breath, I swing open the door. "Hello..."

"Oh, it's you." Bianca's frown deepens as she peers over my shoulder. "What are you two doing?"

gripping the desk, one hand gripping my head forward, Cameron's moans fill the office. Her back starts to bow as my tongue swirls faster and faster.

"Chloe..." she breathes my name, and I hear her tremble.

Knock, knock.

Are you fucking joking?

Cameron yanks me up, my fingers still deep within her. "Don't you dare stop," she whispers against my lips.

Is she crazy?

Never going to happen.

She's rocking her hips for more friction; I work her harder.

"Cameron?" Bianca's voice invades the room. Oh, no way. Not today, Satan! And definitely *not* when Cameron's writhing over the desk, naked.

"We have a Zoom meeting at 2pm?" says the annoying voice. I glance at the clock – 1:47pm - nice try. She doesn't get to ruin this.

Cameron whimpers again. Suddenly, her body jerks, her legs shuddering under my touch. She rips her mouth from mine, breathless. "Coming!"

And she sure *is*.

I recapture her lips in a kiss, and Cameron squeezes, tight, around my fingers, moaning into my mouth while her body shakes around me.

my blush taking over my face, but I barely catch my breath because there are more voices from the hallway.

Cameron goes rigid, but her eyes remain dark, full of heat. "Should we -"

I don't let her finish. Fisting my hand in her hair, I lift her to her feet and seize her mouth with my own because we're finishing this.

Pushing Cameron backward, I strip off her pants. "I can't be the only one half-naked," I murmur, and her mouth curves into a grin. She helps remove her shirt, flinging it somewhere far away, and kicks off her heels.

With a flick of the wrist, I unfasten her bra, and her breasts spring free. I squeeze one in my hand while my mouth swoops down, sucking the other taut nipple until she's grinding against my thigh.

"Mmm," Cameron moans, tipping her head back, nails sinking into my shoulder muscles.

My hands slide up her thighs, I tug her panties to one side. She's warmer than the sun, the heat of her dangerous. I circle her entrance with the tips of my fingers, and she stumbles, letting out a loud gasp of pleasure. "Oh, God."

Propping her on the edge of her desk, I nudge her thighs open with my knees. Before she can stop me, my head is there, and my mouth is on her clit. Cameron leans back, her breath ragged, palms pressing down on the desk. My tongue dances over her skin, flicking lightly over her sensitive flesh.

"So good," she whimpers, her walls snapping around my slick fingers as they slip inside. One hand my soaking core. I spread my thighs even wider. Sucking my clit into her hot mouth, I throw my head back with a moan. She tortures me for a while with her tongue until I'm begging, "Cameron, please...More."

Honestly, her touch turns me into someone I don't recognize.

When she pushes her fingers inside, snug against her tongue, my breath hitches. I squeeze around her as heat courses through my veins.

Her fingers move faster. Her tongue presses harder.

"Oh, fuck," I whimper and drop my hips grinding down on her, the door creaking on its hinges.

God, she feels so good.

I claw at her back, waves of pleasure rolling through me, and she gives me what I need. I rock my hips until stars flicker behind my eyelids, drawing out a primal cry as an orgasm burns through every cell like wildfire. Suddenly, I don't care if the whole Bridge Club hears.

Cameron doesn't stop, however, wrapping her arms around the back of my thighs to pull me closer. It doesn't take long until I feel a familiar warmth building again in my stomach. Thank God Cameron holds me in place as the tremors ripple through my body, or I might fall over.

She places a soft kiss *there*, then looks up, her lips swollen and glistening. When we share a smile, I feel with a look that makes my legs tremble. Stopping at a safe distance, she licks her lips. Pent-up arousal pulses through me, but we just stand there, locked in a silent exchange.

Okay, seriously, what the hell are we doing?

Then it happens.

Cameron slams me against the door, kissing me with so much fire, my skin burns from the heat. Loosening the strap of my dress, it falls to my stomach and exposes my breasts to her. She palms them with her hands, squeezing, and traces her tongue over my nipple.

I whimper at the contact.

Shameless and needy and desperate.

When did I turn into this person? Desperate for anything she offers me. I hook one leg around her waist because I want her on me, her fingers inside me. My body screaming for her to touch those places only she can reach.

Dragging one finger through my wetness, Cameron stifles a groan, but I hear it. "I fucking need to taste you," she says, popping a nipple from her mouth, and I shiver at her words. Dropping to her knees, I meet her gaze, wild and hungry, and then I feel her breath, impossibly warm. She presses her tongue flat against me, but when she licks the length of my slit, my knees all but buckle.

I reach for her hair, curling my fingers into her dark waves as long, languid strokes of her tongue lash

Cameron glances at the lace number looped through her fingers, then she's giggling, too.

The voices get louder: "There are even more gnomes than last time", "Someone needs to have a stern word to Gus", and now there are footsteps.

I freeze. Cameron groans.

We're both facing the door. She quickly stuffs my thong into her pocket.

"Beautiful day outside," says someone in a sing-song voice.

I turn my head an inch to Marlene and Betty, who are walking this way, arm in arm.

"Uh-huh. Stunning," says Cameron, eyes fixed on the door. Laughter bubbles up inside of me as I clock her pants hanging off her hips.

"Just gorgeous," I add with a smile.

"*Do* make sure you go outside," says Marlene, and I really hope I'm mistaken, but I think Betty waggles her almost-white eyebrows at us.

Oh God, I don't know where to look.

The second they're gone, Cameron swipes her keys from the carpet and almost breaks down the door, slamming it shut behind us. I quickly flick the lock, and my shoulders begin to shake with laughter.

Cameron drags her hand over her face. "I've lost my fucking mind."

"And almost your pants," I gurgle, and her gaze drops like a boulder. Cameron gives a pained laugh, then points accusingly. "You..." She takes a few steps

She peels my thong down over my legs, then hikes up the hem of my dress until it bunches around my hips, giving her access to whatever the hell she wants. I feel her hot breath, and oh my God –

Bang!

A door slams, and Cameron leaps up like a startled gazelle, head swiveling left and right like she's just realized we're in the library. We stare at each other, hearts racing.

"Come on," Cameron says, grabbing my hand.

Thankfully, she adjusts my dress before we sprint to her office because I'm on another planet. My legs wobbling like Jell-O all the way down the hall.

Cameron, in her fluster, drops a set of keys outside her door.

"What? Why's it locked?" I ask.

"Willow's been tearing up my pillows," Cameron says, and I roll my eyes.

We hear some muted voices.

Oh, crap.

Cameron gestures to the floor. "Quick. Pick them up!" she whisper-hisses.

"No!" I start to giggle.

Her head snaps to mine. "What? My pants are undone."

"And you have my thong in your hand!" I half-shriek.

Not long after, Cameron throws down her napkin. "Sorry, I have a meeting. Chloe, should we -"

"Yes." I stand so abruptly the chair scrapes. I'm pretty sure Max mouths call me when Cameron turns, but as if that's going to happen.

I spot Alice in the kitchen organizing a tray of cupcakes as we shoot past, and when she glances over, I get the double thumbs up.

Cameron stops dead. "Did Alice just -"

"No!" I push her ass forward. "Keep moving."

Alice totally gave us her blessing, but I don't want her to get in Cameron's pretty little head. Our legs getting faster and faster as we walk-run to her office. I almost start gurgling. God, this is going to be so good.

When I round the last corner, Cameron is nowhere to be seen. Hang on, where did she go?

Suddenly, a hand yanks me into the library, and her mouth claims mine, hot and demanding, in a clash of lips and tongues. She pushes me up against shelves stacked with leather-bound books. I pull her hair, fingernails scraping over her shirt, fighting to get her closer. Closer to where I need her to be. A book tumbles to the floor.

I unbutton her pants, lower her zipper. Cameron slips her hand between my thighs, brushing her fingertips right over the damp patch on my crotch. "Chloe," she groans, and I start squirming like it's the first time I've been touched.

have eyes for her. "I don't know.... Move to another planet?" Cameron mutters.

"Now, now, ladies." Alice sweeps into the room with a large assortment of perfectly sliced sandwiches. "I've put a bit of effort into this high tea, and I'd appreciate it if you could both mind your manners. There's ham and mustard, cucumber with mint cream cheese, smoked salmon and lemon butter, and roast beef with horseradish. Please help yourselves. Dessert is on the table in the corner."

So, our lunch kicks off with a bang, but twenty minutes in, it feels like the Max show. No one can get a word in edgewise, and I stuff myself with too many sandwiches. How did I not see this before? Rather than feel drawn to Max, I feel repelled. She is nothing like the woman beside me.

"No sandwiches, Cameron?" asks Alice, licking her fingers clean.

"Just dessert for me, thanks Alice." Cameron spoons some cake into her mouth while dragging a fingertip across my thigh.

Fuckity fuck.

What is it about her? Every touch is magnified. I start wondering what it would feel like to kiss her right now, if I'd still be able to taste the buttercream on her lips. I wonder how it would feel to kiss her whenever I wanted to.

Oh, shut up, Chloe. Stop building this up in your head.

"I know. Me too," I say softly. "Can we just go in there and get this over with? Won't be for too long, I promise."

Her head drops, and she nips at my bare shoulder. "We need to build a moat."

I giggle. "Cameron, please? For me?"

She sighs loudly, then tucks in her shirt and motions with her hand. "Okay... lead the way."

On shaky legs, I push through the door, but I'm desperate to finish what we started.

"Can you believe that, Alice?" Max snorts, but the laughter dies in her throat when she sees us. "Cameron. You're back."

"Max... Disappointed?" Cameron retorts.

She gives a bark of laughter. "It's your house, I suppose."

"Well, I *suppose* you're leaving then?" Cameron says abruptly, and Betty snickers while Marlene splutters into her cup of tea.

"Chloe asked me to stay for lunch," replies Max nonchalantly. "And well, I was thinking of asking her out on a date. Actually, you might be useful. What's my best angle?"

What the hell is she doing?

I'm standing right here!

A nerve flinches in Cameron's cheek, and I subtly squeeze her side, hopefully letting her know that I only body ignites. Memories of her writhing beneath me flood back like a tidal wave.

Her eyes glint with mischief. "It's not what I need."

I tilt my head to the side. "Oh, and what do you need?"

"I think you know," Cameron says, stepping forward, and I feel the brush of her lips. I open my mouth. An invitation. She meets it with fervor in a kiss that steals my breath.

Her mouth, her body. *Her.*

I've missed this.

I arch my back, pushing my curves against her body, wanting more. She pinches my nipple through my dress, and I gasp sharply, yanking her shirt free. When my hand moves underneath it, a loud groan emanates from her throat, her fingers already slipping inside the waistband of my thong.

Suddenly, Cameron breaks our kiss with a shuddering exhale. "Chloe, we need to stop. Or I won't be able to."

"Shit," I stammer and glance around, having completely lost my bearings. If Cameron's mom sees me like this –

No, I can't even.

Cameron's thumb drags across my lower lip, possessive and demanding. It's a massive turn-on. Foreheads pressed together, she murmurs, "I need more."

"I've been thinking about kissing you all day." Cameron tilts my face toward hers, and my entire being liquifies. Closing my eyes, I part my lips and -

There's a sudden howl of laughter.

Cameron drops me to the floor. "Who's the banshee?"

Hmm, how to explain this?

I start fiddling with the strap of my dress. "Ah, we have some visitors. Alice's friends from Bridge Club, Marlene and Betty. Alice made some lunch, her take on high tea, spent all morning in the kitchen -"

"Chloe..." She narrows her eyes in suspicion. I don't blame her; I'm rambling again.

"That was Max," I say with a heavy sigh.

Cameron's eyes turn into dinner plates. "Max? Why is she here!"

"Max got an offer from Bill, the estate agent, on my home and wanted to tell me the good news," I explain quickly. "She's been, you know, helpful."

"Oh, I bet. She couldn't be professional and just email you?" Cameron peeks through the gap in the door, then gasps, "She's sitting in my chair!" I have to cover my laugh at her outrage. "And what is she wearing! You can see everything," she hisses.

"Would you stop..." I bite the inside of my cheek to hide my smile. So, she might be a bit jealous. "We need to at least go in and have a sandwich."

But just as I am about to slip past her, her hand lightly skims my hip, stopping me, and every cell in my

"Hey, Alice!" Max hollers. "What are you baking? I haven't eaten since sparrow o'clock. Extra seat for one?"

Dear God.

And just like that, Max Farrow has invited herself to lunch.

I almost combust when I see her slip into Cameron's seat, but that's all forgotten when I hear a car in the driveway.

Cameron.

Dropping a pot of English Breakfast tea on the table, I rush to the front door and whip it open before Cameron can even turn her key. She gives me a panty-dropping grin when she sees me - startled but pleased - and my stomach swoops, just like it always does.

Today, she's wearing high-waisted black trousers with a crisp navy shirt tucked inside. Her hair is pulled back in a ponytail, while her lips are painted with cherry red lipstick that I think I want all over me.

Oh God, will I ever be immune to her gorgeousness?

Her eyes hold mine, and the air swirls between us.

"Hey," I smile.

"Hey, yourself. You look gorgeous..." Cameron smiles back. Her gaze drifts over my outfit, and I turn beet red, then she surprises me by sweeping me into her arms, lifting me off the ground. "I'm back early," she whispers, and my breath catches in my throat.

"Do I need a reason?" Max teases, fixing me with an unyielding gaze.

"Um... Well -"

"Just joking!" Max trills. I think she gets off on making me squirm. "Actually, I wanted to share some news. Bill has made an offer on your home. It's just below your asking price, but I'm confident we can nudge him higher."

I almost scream. "Oh, Max! That's amazing!" And it really is because I need that financial freedom desperately. "I don't know what to say. That happened so quickly."

"Well, it's not a done deal yet. Bill still needs to sign the contract, and you'll have to agree on a settlement date, but let's squeeze him for a few more dollars."

"Okay, whatever you think. Thanks so much."

"Can I get a hug?"

"Oh, yeah. Sure," I laugh because it catches me off guard, but as I reach forward, Max grips me in position and slides her hand to my lower back. More than a few seconds pass. Crap. Is she going to let me go? What's proper etiquette in ending a hug? All I can think to do is lamely pat her shoulder. "Okay, well. Thanks for that," I say casually as I crouch down like some weirdo to slink free and quickly move toward the door to usher her out. But Max takes a sneaky side-step that I don't count on.

What is she -

I visibly recoil at the mention of her mom, given our last encounter, but thankfully, Alice is too busy fussing over a bunch of sunflowers.

"How did you go with Bill, the estate agent, today?" she asks, arranging the flowers in a vase.

"Well, I walked him through the house, and he asked lots of questions, took photos. His son wants to move back to the area, so fingers crossed I get an offer because I don't think there'll be many. I've done as much as I can to the place."

"I'm crossing everything for you," Alice says sweetly, then hands me the vase. "Now, be a good girl and place this on the table for me."

Just after midday, Marlene and Betty arrive. But what I'm not expecting is for Max Farrow to come striding in behind them in a pair of tight charcoal-coated jeans and a barely-there floral satin camisole with spaghetti straps. Half her face obscured by giant tortoiseshell shades.

"Chloe! So good to see you," Max exclaims, extending her arms and kissing me on both cheeks.

"Hey, Max." I smile.

Max whisks off her shades. "Hope you don't mind? I followed the ladies' Mini and the gate was open, so I thought, why not?" she grins.

I don't mind, but Cameron sure might. I need to get rid of her quickly. "Is there something you wanted to see me about?"

Chloe

"Willow! It's me!" I crouch down, holding my hand out in front of her, and she takes a hesitant sniff, which gives way to major tail thumping.

Alice's smiling head pops up from behind the kitchen counter. "Well, don't you look nice? Expecting someone important?"

"I don't know what you're talking about, Alice," I retort in a breezy tone as I stand. "Your friends from Bridge Club are coming over for lunch, so I thought I'd make the effort." I realize I'm standing on the rug we *you know* and a myriad of images fly through my head. I promptly jump off it.

"You make a terrible liar, Chloe," Alice says, stirring a bowl. We share a conspiratorial smile before bursting into laughter.

Giving my dress a twirl, I ask, "Is it that obvious?"

"Uh-huh. We're only having sandwiches."

I laugh. And dessert, if I have my way. Why else do I have a ridiculously annoying thong riding halfway up my butt? "Do you need a hand in the kitchen?" I ask her.

"No, thank you, darling. I just finished the cucumber sandwiches, and the vanilla sponge cake is browning in the oven. About to get started on the buttercream filling and lemon glacé. Leanne, Cameron's mom, is coming in the afternoon, and she has a bit of a sweet tooth like her daughter."

CHAPTER NINETEEN

Chloe

Cameron's been away for a mere two days, and I'm as skittish as a cat on a hot tin roof.

So, when I get a text announcing her afternoon return, it sends me into a tailspin. Opting for an extra-long shower, I moisturize everywhere, dabble with some makeup, and straighten my hair with the flat iron, which inevitably means I burn my fingers.

Realizing none of my clothes are up to par, I raid Cameron's wardrobe, and after trying four outfits, I settle on a slinky, midnight blue dress with a touch of glitz along the neckline. *Perfect.* I pair the dress with my white sneakers and then run my tongue over my teeth, wiping off a lipstick stain while glued to my reflection in the mirror. Plucked, preened, and primed to go.

God, I haven't gone to so much effort since I don't know when.

Point proven when I mosey into the kitchen, and Willow charges in from the yard, barking at me as if I'm a complete stranger.

the engine roars to life, I floor the accelerator, leaving skid marks on the asphalt like a signature. I speed through the parking lot, get air over a couple of speed humps, and even manage to swipe a side-view mirror of a sleek black Mercedes S-Class.

Shit.

I hope it wasn't Vladimir's, or he really will feed me to the sharks.

As I fishtail out of the driveway and onto the road, hysterical, unbridled laughter spills out of me until I'm gasping for breath.

"Holy fuck," I wheeze between laughs.

I think I might've just pulled off the impossible.

nothing will happen, but that's up to you, isn't it, Vladimir? The ball's in your court."

I don't miss the twitch in his right eyelid, his brow pulling into a deep scowl.

Please, *please*, just say yes. I have no more lies left to give.

Vladimir pauses and then taps his nicotine-colored finger against the grey scruff of his chin. All of a sudden, he howls with laughter. It's only broken by a hacking smoker's cough. "Bravo. Impressive. You have bigger kahunas than most men that I know..." He arches a shrewd eyebrow. "Want to work for me?"

"No," I croak. The word echoes around the room, bouncing off the walls. "Do we have a deal?"

Vladimir lets out a disdainful snort, hand running over his jaw. He gives me a single nod. "Now get the fuck out of here before I mess with your pretty face!"

He doesn't have to tell me twice because I stand and shoot out the door before him, and his merry band of henchmen can bundle me up in black plastic and dump my body deep in the Atlantic.

A vicious wind whistles around my head as I burst outside, my hand already scrabbling for my keys. I sprint to my getaway vehicle, casting nervous glances over my shoulder because I'm half-expecting a sniper to turn me into a perforated pincushion, and practically dive into my car.

I'm shaking like a leaf and don't even bother with my seatbelt, fumbling with my key in the ignition. As

Vladimir gives a shrill laugh and turns to his henchman, nostrils flaring. "Can you believe this broad?" He rubs his tongue across his false teeth, then narrows his eyes at me. It's obvious he doesn't like to be challenged. Smirking, he says, "The police will bury it."

"Well, that's why I'd send it to the press first," I reply, unfazed, and my mind drifts back to the charity night with Chloe's ex. "I have very good connections at NPC -"

Vladimir stands so abruptly that his chair somersaults backward. He's literally vibrating with anger. "What the fuck are you playing at here!" He roars, slamming his fist on the desk with such force, papers scatter like leaves in a storm. Every cell in my body is trembling with fear. "Do you know who I am? I could make you disappear very easily. Cement blocks around your dainty little feet, or perhaps a tub of acid to melt away your soul. What would be your pleasure?" he snarls.

To kick you in the nutsack.

I think Chloe's violent tendencies are rubbing off on me.

Despite shitting my pants, I try to put on a brave front. "Really? I've made sure the right people know where I am, and the recording is stashed in a place where if something happens to me, it'll become public knowledge. Obviously, there's a lot more dirt on you. This is just the tip of the iceberg. You've been a busy man. Of course, if you let it slide, we forget all of it, and

The fact that it looks like it might be held in a safe deposit box gives me a slither of hope that it's legitimate.

Vladimir bristles. He blinks once. Twice. "You're bluffing."

"Unfortunately, I'm not. Imagine your name being dropped into the investigation. Even worse, a phone recording with you and Franco Biordi confessing to the murder." My eyes widen theatrically. "I mean, I don't practice law anymore, but I'm pretty sure that's life, no parole."

Something dark crosses his face, and his eyes burn an imaginary hole all the way to the back of my skull. "Let me get this straight. You came here to blackmail *me*?" he grinds out his words with such ferocity that dentures launch out of his mouth and splat on the carpet.

To be honest, it takes a bit of the sting out of his delivery.

His henchman dives to the ground, scrambling to pick them up, and Vladimir shoves the wayward teeth straight into his mouth, carpet fuzz and all.

God, gross.

He stubs his cigarette out in an overflowing ashtray, swiftly lighting another, and looks even more pissed off than before.

I need to keep talking before he wipes the floor with me. "I'm only asking you to forgo a very, very small debt. Oh, and to never bother the daughter again."

robbed me blind. Answer is no." He stares right down my eyes, trying to unnerve me. Luckily, I've met thugs like him before, and I'm not easily intimidated. "Right, well..." Pushing his feet off the desk, the chair swivels across the carpet. Vladimir rips open the door. "Get out."

He's all charm.

I turn my face to him. "Just like that?"

"Just like that." Vladimir grins darkly and then barks, "Out!"

Obviously, he didn't like my request, but I don't like his answer.

I remain in my chair and swallow down the knot in my throat because it's time to drop a bomb. "Well, you're right on one count," I say, casually inspecting my nails before lifting my head to meet his gaze. "My father was as crooked as you. You know, he even kept a little book of dirty secrets, and apparently, you killed Irish mobster, Paddy O'Lonergan, at Murphy's Pier back in 2020. I hear the NYPD are looking at reopening the case."

I have absolutely no idea what the fuck I am talking about, but I'm praying that, for once in my life, my father doesn't let me down. All I gathered from his notes on Vladimir was a name, a cross, Murphy's Pier, and a mysterious reference to a phone recording on 03/20/2020 with Franco Biordi held at Capital One Bank.

God, I hope I've joined the dots correctly, or I'm cactus. Who knows what's actually on this recording?

loosely on his wiry frame, ketchup, no probably blood, smeared over his front pocket. There's a three-inch diagonal tear on his left shoulder. Honestly, it looks like he got into a fight with a trashcan, and the trashcan won.

"Vladimir, I'm assuming," I say, slapping on a smile.

He nods. "Cameron."

Okay, I think that's our introduction done.

Vladimir lights his cigarette and takes a deep drag, swinging his feet onto his desk. Smoke furls around him like a sinister cloak. "You look nothing like your father."

"Well, thank God for that."

He erupts into a raspy, phlegm-filled laugh, the cherry of his cigarette ending up on the carpet.

Clearing my throat, I cut through the mirth. "There's a debt for a Sherie Bentley. I want you to forget it."

Vladimir scoffs. "Forget? Might've snorted a tonne up my nose, but my memory is sharp as a tack. I don't forget anything." He pulls out a battered book and flicks through it with grimy fingers. "Oh, she's a junkie. Never pays her bills. It's peanuts, really, but needs a lesson regardless."

"I'm hoping you can waive it. Being my father's friend and all."

He snorts, ashing on the carpet. "We weren't friends. Did a good job. I stayed out of prison, but he then grunts, and I think that means to follow him, so I do, down a grotty hallway and through some cavernous space, dimly lit by flickering overhead lights that cast long shadows across stacks of wooden crates and barrels. Pallets loaded with mysterious cargo line the walls, shrouded in tattered tarps, while rust-colored chains hang from the rafters, and I try not to imagine myself hanging from one of those.

Of course, that's exactly what I do!

I swallow hard as we abruptly veer left down another passage to what appears to be a makeshift office.

The henchman knocks on the corrugated iron door. "Oi. Boss," he grumbles.

Heart in my throat, I peer tentatively around the door.

I'm expecting someone impressive. He's a kingpin, after all, but rather than a large looming presence, I spot a frail, hunched-over man, perhaps in his sixties, sitting behind a broad, chaotic desk.

Thin lips fixed in a snarl, he waves me in wordlessly like I'm a no-one and then points to a chair. Communication clearly not their strong suit.

I take a seat and try not to breathe in the stench that appears to emanate from his pores. Instead, I assess him. Curly ashen hair springs up in every direction from his scalp like snakes while hollowed-out bags border slate-colored eyes. He has the kind of unhealthy pallor you'd expect from someone who's just done a long stint in prison. His beige shirt hangs

CHAPTER EIGHTEEN

Cameron

I'm outside an abandoned warehouse freaking out. Seriously what the fuck am I doing here?

Oh yeah, I'm meeting a career criminal and asking him a favor.

This ranks as one of the dumber things I've done in my life, even if it's one of the most important.

It was impossible to leave Chloe, and I even entertained her offer of chaining me to the bed. Thank God logic prevailed because, with the due date of her mom's debt fast approaching, I need to know she is safe.

"Hi. I'm um… here to see Vl- Vladimir," I stammer to a gigantic block-like man clad in black who's standing fifteen feet away by the rusted metal door of a nondescript building. There's a dragon tattoo on his neck, orange flames licking his windpipe. Blood starts thundering through my ears, and I tell myself to get it together.

The man motions me over with his finger, and I waddle to him, legs stiff as boards. He pats me down,

"Chloe. I really need to go."

"I really need you to come."

Cameron laughs. "Again? God, you're a nympho."

I nod, unable to deny it.

Wasn't before I met you.

"I'm a freaking mess," Cameron sighs.

My fingers slip between her legs. "I'm going to have to agree," I grin, and Cameron flings my hand away like it's a ticking bomb. "You're not helping," she says with a laugh-groan.

And I'm really not. But how do you stop when you're freaking borderline obsessed?

I slap my hands over my eyes. "Go. Before I chain you to the bed," I grunt as my face falls against the bed, and there's a chuckle, followed by the rustle of sheets and a thud on the floor.

When I finally turn my head, her eyes are fixed on mine, and I wonder if she can feel this, too? Whatever this is.

I think that's why I feel so crazed around her. Because I know in my heart that it *has* to be something special. Or at least, it could be.

corner of my mouth twitch. Only when her face breaks out into a smile do I let myself giggle.

"You don't need to apologize." I reach for my fork, but Cameron swiftly whisks my plate away.

"No. Chloe. I'll put on some toast," she says, already near the trashcan. "I don't want to take you to the ER."

"Oh, that's sweet -"

"The hospital is more than an hour's drive," she replies with a gleam in her eye. "I have a busy schedule today."

"And you were doing so well." I pick up the dishtowel and throw it at her stupid, smiling face.

Cameron chuckles, snatching it in the air in one hand.

Still hungry, I push off my stool and move over to the toaster.

It can't be two seconds, and a pair of warm arms wrap around my waist. I feel the heat of her body against my back. The feel of her breath against my ear. The slide of her hand over my hip.

"Cameron..."

"Chloe..."

And just like that, the no-touching rule is out the window.

Turns out Cameron makes up for her lack of cooking skills in other departments.

I poke out my tongue, and she laughs.

Even though it's apparent that Cameron isn't a good cook, I indulge her by watching her flit around the kitchen half-naked with a look of absolute concentration. She drowns the eggs in half a gallon of milk, and most of the shells end up swimming around inside the pan, not out of it.

It's hard not to smile, but it doesn't take long until a grumpy crease settles across her forehead. Cameron throws me a look. "I can feel you staring. What? Am I doing something wrong?"

I shake my head, still smiling. "No. Nothing."

She's completely adorable.

Even more so when she tries to fluff up the eggs with a fork, and they refuse to oblige, but I don't have the heart to step in. Soon, she's frying the mixture in a pan and standing there with her hands on her hips, scowling. "I don't understand. I followed the recipe to the tee -"

I have my doubts. "I'm sure it's fine. Come sit," I say, tapping the seat beside me.

Cameron hesitantly places a plate of what looks like baby poo in front of me. "Um."

I force enthusiasm into my voice. "Looks... I mean, smells great!"

Cameron groans, covering her face. "I'm sorry. I've been coddled my whole life. I wasn't even allowed to butter my croissants until I was twelve. I'm completely useless in the kitchen." She glances at me, and I feel the

That's me told.

I chuckle, slipping onto a bar stool by the kitchen island. "Better?"

Cameron turns and then nods slowly, staring at me, and oh my God, I want to rip that sweatshirt off her and pin her to the counter. "Okay, you can't look at me like that either," she says, spinning back around.

This time, I laugh, but I get it because everything feels so charged between the two of us. I silently scream into my hands, then continue to ogle her.

"You know, I think I've got this," she says with a quick glance over her shoulder. "I mean, how hard can it be?"

I'm not saying a word.

Although Cameron doesn't want to relish control, she lets me set the table and pour some fresh orange juice. "So why are you going to New York?" I ask, closing the fridge.

"Purchasing a small ad agency and a start-up IT company. Thought I could combine their resources for the digital space, but convincing one of the owners is proving difficult. He hates women and hates lesbians. Basically, he's an asshole. So, I might have to stay a few days to close the deal."

Something yuck settles in the pit of my stomach because, right now, even ten feet away, Cameron isn't close enough. Instead, I say, "I'm sure they'll be dazzled by your charm, and you'll be back before you know it."

Cameron's head swings around. "Like you were?"

"Uh-huh," I murmur, biting her neck, my hand venturing where it shouldn't. I know I should be sated, but I'm not, and Cameron responds with a low groan. "Maybe we should take the bed with us. Apparently, multitasking is all the rage right now," I suggest.

Cameron throws her head back, laughing. "Chloe!"

But I'm thoroughly enjoying our banter. Propping herself on one elbow, she kisses the inside of my palm. "Let me make it up to you. I know… How about I cook you breakfast?" she offers.

Oh no, it appears our baking session has given Cameron newfound confidence in the kitchen, but the second her blues meet my browns, I just nod and stroke her face. "Yeah, that would be really nice."

Grinning, Cameron leaps out of bed.

Although I'm still wearing a goofy smile of my own, I get up with far less enthusiasm and make my way out to the kitchen, where I find Cameron hunched over the counter, googling recipes on her phone.

She's wearing my sweatshirt from last night and nothing else. Why does everything look so much better on her? I sneak up behind her, giving her a little squeeze on the butt, letting my hand linger. "Need help?" My lips dust the shell of her ear.

Cameron freezes. "Chloe, I swear if you touch me *anywhere*, this breakfast will be a disaster. Other side of the kitchen, please."

I grin because hearing Cameron scream my name has to be one of the highlights of my life, and I pepper her neck with tiny kisses. "Thanks. You're not too bad yourself. So, are you working today... or calling in sick?" I smile against her skin.

Cameron gives a groan. "Unfortunately, I need to go to New York. Actually, I should've left by now. You appear to have derailed my plans."

"Hey, it takes two to tango," I giggle as my head drops back onto my pillow, but I'm sad she's going away because every moment feels precious. Lost in the golden flecks of her eyes, I gently trace the faint scar above her brow. "I'm sorry for this, by the way."

Is it weird that I feel rather proud that I left my mark on her for all these years?

Cameron regards me steadily. "Are you now? Some twenty years later?"

"Better late than never."

"Uh-huh."

"At least you'd never forget me."

"I don't need a scar to remember you," Cameron says softly, staring at me with her beautiful blue eyes. She places my hand on her heart, and I'm practically melting into the mattress. Then we kiss and kiss, and just when I think we'll be in this bed forever, an alarm starts shrieking.

Cameron smacks it quiet. "Sorry, I really do need to get up," she sighs heavily. "You must be hungry?"

Cameron's fingernails dig into my skin. "Chloe..." There's that stern voice again, which I secretly love. She lifts her hips up from the bed, but I press down in a circular motion even harder. Not only can I feel how wet she is, I can also hear it.

I thread my fingers through her hair. "Yes?" I reply, and Cameron brings her mouth to mine, close but not quite touching, whispering, "You shouldn't do that. Or I'll..."

Does she not know who I am?

I rise to the challenge and flick my tongue at hers while still moving back and forth between her legs, smirking, "Or you'll -"

Cameron flips me over with a wicked grin, and I laugh-scream as she crushes her mouth against mine in a searing kiss. When she sinks two fingers deep inside me, I'm all but whimpering with shameless need.

Suddenly, I don't want to play games anymore.

"You've ruined me," Cameron gasps, collapsing beside me.

I bite her shoulder. "Good. You deserve it," I tease, my mouth curving into a broad smile. "Don't play naked games with me at eight in the morning."

Cameron laughs, rolling onto her side to face me. Her finger traces a path along my cheek. "Like I had a choice... You're far too hot, you know," she says, her voice so smooth it washes over me and settles in my bones.

Sighing, I trace the curve of her breast. She's beautiful, I just can't get enough, and no matter how much time I spend with her, I still want more.

As though she can hear my thoughts, her eyes flick open, and she stretches into a smile. "Hey, you..."

"Hi..." I whisper, placing a warm kiss on her lips.

"Mmm, and I thought you weren't a morning person."

I rub her nose with mine. "I'm not... but apparently, I don't always need an alarm."

Cameron trails her fingers across the top of my shoulder and down between my breasts. It has me shivering. "Guess the fact that you're naked, I'm naked, might be a little distracting."

"I guess," I say with a smile as heat pools in my core. One touch, and I'm gone. Pathetic, really.

Cameron pulls me on top of her, hands on my ass. I lose my breath. My clit starts to throb, I can barely keep it together. "So, what's the plan for today?" she asks with a flicker of amusement while angling me to her groin.

Eight in the morning, and she wants to do this, then ask me silly questions!

I lift an eyebrow while thrusting my hips into her, and she groans. "Oh, I don't know. Nothing really tickles my fancy." I try to sound very blasé, but my breath hitches with every searing brush of her skin as slick, wet heat burns between my thighs.

CHAPTER SEVENTEEN

Chloe

I wake up with a smile on my face.

Of course I do.

Sunlight streams in through the window, bathing us in a soft, yellow light. Cameron is rolled on her side, long, thick lashes fluttering on her cheek, with one arm draped over me. Her breath soft and even. Her flawless skin practically glowing. Everything perfect. Everything except her hair, which is an utter mess. I reach up to my head. Yep, mine is exactly the same. It's to be expected. Sex in the living area was followed by sex in the shower and chasing each other around her king-size bed throughout the night.

I can already feel how much I'll crave her when I'm gone. The idea that I could just get her out of my system with one night feels so silly now. I know the noises she makes, how her hands move over my skin, the casual confidence with which she drives me crazy.

Getting into bed with Cameron was easy, getting out of it... not so much.

"Chloe..." Cameron breathes, hips arching into my touch. I can't get enough. I want everything from her. She's clawing at my skin for release, while those soft moans and her ragged breathing turn me inside out.

When I curl my fingers, hitting the spot, Cameron's legs shoot out, and her eyes spring open. She fists the rug, perhaps a mountain top or two, until, finally, a moan rips from her throat, her back bowing in pleasure, and she climaxes against my tongue.

As her shudders subside, I kiss my way up her body, the taste of her still on my lips. Something shifts within my DNA, a longing that I've searched for but never found. I also can't help wondering what happens now? This is not familiar territory for me.

But I don't have to wait too long because Cameron swoops down and kisses me, her tongue sliding over mine, knocking the breath out of me once again.

Oh, God. I don't know if I'm coming or going.

All of a sudden, Cameron draws away from my lips and lifts me to my feet. "Come on," she says with half-hooded eyes.

"Huh? Where are we going?" I breathe heavily, still dazed, because I'm quite comfortable on this rug.

"To bed. For real, this time. I'm nowhere near done with you."

Okay, that will work, too.

Gasping for breath, my eyes strain to focus on her face before I finally surrender, dropping my head onto her shoulder.

I don't know how long we stay like this, but the second Cameron kisses my collarbone, neck, every fiber of my being tingles with energy. Because all I feel is *her*, everything else falls away in the periphery.

The fullness of her lips.

The demand of her mouth.

I want all of her.

Grabbing her face, I slide my mouth over hers. Cameron deepens our kiss, consuming me like a fire does oxygen, and I cup her breasts, savoring the contrast of her soft skin and hard nipples.

Cameron moans softly as my hand slips inside her panties. "Can you feel how much I want you?" she asks huskily.

I give a satisfied groan. She's like hot, liquid silk.

My fingers make contact with her clit, feeling her pulsate beneath me. Then I'm tearing off her underwear because, suddenly, I want to burn myself in her brain like she is in mine. My lips trace the curves of her entire body, kissing and sucking every inch of skin I can reach while I rub circles around her wet center.

Cameron starts writhing against me. Sinking my fingers inside her, I drop between her legs. I kiss her inner thigh and then run my tongue through her core before swirling it over her clit.

She pushes a finger inside me, and my walls clench around her.

"Oh, God," I breathe, my knuckles turning white as I grip the rug.

When Cameron adds another finger, I hear the sound of my arousal on her as she drives in and out of me. The pressure builds in my core and rolls through my thighs, and I start writhing around, moaning, and completely ruining this rug, but I don't seem to give a flying fuck about this x-rated spectacle in my neighbor's kitchen.

Apparently, I like to be naked in this house.

"Cameron..." I grab her neck, clinging to it as I drag my lips over her skin, feeling every vibration of her muscles while she's grinding the heel of her palm against my clit. Warm waves of electric heat pulse through me, and my breath quickens. "Oh, fuck," I whimper in her ear as Cameron groans in mine.

I'm close, *so* damn close.

I fist her hair, my moans growing frantic. When my hips start to jerk, Cameron holds my chin in place, so our eyes remain fixed as I start to lose control.

"Come, Chloe," Cameron whispers, and with that command, I fall apart around her, an orgasm shredding me to pieces and tearing into my limbs like tiny starbursts igniting every cell. She wraps an arm around my waist, massaging my inner walls as my body continues to shudder around her.

Cameron's hand slips between us, and honestly, she shouldn't be surprised by what she finds, but she is. "Chloe. God..."

What? Hardly my fault.

Cameron slides a finger through my wet folds, and shockwaves of pleasure pulse through me.

"F-fuck," I stammer.

Her eyes blaze with fire as I push into her palm, and she grinds into my leg. I rock harder against her, hard enough that she groans, so I do it again, showing her what I want.

Without warning, Cameron lifts me up and spins around. "Bedroom," she orders, but we crash back onto the floor, and I'm splayed across a plush rug with what I think is an imprint of the Norwegian Mountains on it, naked, and at her complete mercy.

A shiver runs down my spine, and my heart beats wildly as she stares at me. So open and exposed and vulnerable. Call it women's intuition, but that look in her eye tells me I won't be making it to her room; I'll be lucky to make it out alive.

I go to move, and Cameron lunges forward, pinning me down. She sucks a nipple into her hot mouth, flicking the stiff peak with her tongue, and I gasp. When the pads of her fingers find and circle my swollen clit with the perfect amount of pressure, my eyes damn near roll back into my head.

"So wet," Cameron hisses.

Embarrassingly so.

realized I'm not wearing any underwear. "Also, on purpose?"

"Perhaps," I smirk.

Definitely.

"Fuck." Cameron crushes me against her, sucking and searing my skin with hot kisses.

I think I hear myself rasp, "I like you."

"I like you too..." Cameron twirls my hair with her finger and then pulls, whispering, her breath hot on my ear, "But you better fuck me, Chloe, or I swear to God..."

A loud moan emanates from my throat.

I lose all my faculties, slamming her up against the counter, feeling crazed like a caged animal. Because I have been caged, day in day out, with this woman and my thoughts. Not anymore.

Tongues tangle, and then I bite, hard, on her lower lip, leaving my imprint.

Cameron mutters something, but whatever it is, it has her ripping off my sweatshirt. When her mouth finds mine, I smile against her lips because, wow, do I fucking love seeing Cameron Maxwell unhinged.

Her fingers glide over my back, running over every inch of skin. She pushes my head down to her breasts (like I need an invitation), and I take a perfect nipple in my mouth.

Rolling, teasing, tugging.

Until I feel it pebble in my mouth.

I feel stuttering in her breath, the heat in her body. I brush my chest against hers, and that's it, that's *it*. I know I'm not going back. I'm taking what I want, what I need.

And I do.

My mouth crashes over hers like a thunderstorm, shattering the fine line that has been drawn. Cameron moans into my mouth and kisses me back just as hard. I grab her face with both hands, desperate to get closer and try to communicate everything in this kiss. My frustration, lust, perhaps even how much I care. Her lips are heaven, soft and full, but my thoughts - anything but angelic.

Teeth smash, tongues lash.

It's fierce, messy, and *everything*.

My breath is knocked out of me, as is my footing, but Cameron grips me by the neck and yanks me into another breathtaking kiss. She tastes like raspberries and mint, laced with an undercurrent of something dangerous.

Her robe slips off one shoulder, and I lift the remaining fabric with my finger until it cascades onto the floor. Tearing my lips away from hers, I almost pant for air. My eyes rake over her perfect, bare breasts and across her toned stomach. She's so ridiculously hot, I can't stand it.

Cameron is licking a path up my neck; I'm clawing at her back with my nails, breathing her in until she is everywhere. Her hand moves to my thigh, dragging it across to my hip. She pauses like she might've just

I clear my throat. "It was in one of the drawers. Hope you don't mind?" Cameron doesn't say anything, so I continue. "It's soft, comfortable. Anyway, I won't be sleeping in it."

A flicker of something passes over her face.

Yes, Cameron. I'll be naked.

Like the splits, *naked*.

Cameron gulps down. "Why couldn't you sleep?" she asks.

"Don't know," I shrug, then I take an uneven breath and stare at her as the walls close in around me. I'm actually shaking, like full body rattle.

You know that feeling when you're about to do something unwise, but you think, what the hell, and just do it anyway?

That's me right now. I know I'm all about commitment, but one night. I just want one night with her. Is that so bad?

We're not touching, but I still feel her all over me. My body quivers with electric anticipation, every cell vibrating with sexual energy.

A tiny voice says don't do it, but I ignore it and step forward, taking one more risk. "Maybe I heard you and came out on purpose," I say.

Cameron steps back, and something tells me I'm playing with fire. Her eyes drop to my lips. "Chloe..."

"Mmm," I reply and close the space, making sure there's only a whisper between us.

CHAPTER SIXTEEN

Chloe

Close to midnight, I pad out to the kitchen, hungry. Cameron's there, too, and my heart seizes in my chest. Because I'm not hungry for food, I'm hungry for *her*.

When she meets my gaze, sparks fly between us. It's hard to breathe. Barefoot, she's wearing a robe with a slit high on her thigh. Her hair wet and tousled. But it's her eyes, dark and stormy like the Atlantic Ocean, that I can't stop staring at. There's just something wild in her eyes.

"Couldn't sleep," Cameron says, her voice instantly sending a shudder up my spine. She starts playing with her hair like she's not in complete control of herself, and what I'm seeing makes my skin tingle.

"Me neither," I reply, transfixed. With baby steps, I start edging closer. "You had a shower?"

Of course, she has! Look at her!

"Uh-huh." Cameron's gaze dips to my chest. "You're wearing my sweatshirt?"

And not much else. Thank God, it's oversized.

"No, too messy."

"Cameron, she doesn't even like chess! She threw your Queen out the window!"

She gasps. "You're right! We have absolutely nothing in common! I'm so glad you pointed that out. I no longer have to spend endless nights pondering what could have been. Thank you, Chloe," she replies mock-seriously while her eyes glimmer with amusement.

And just like that, I'm back to smiling.

For some reason, Cameron can always pull me out of my dark cloud.

So, *so* happy that she could finally see the light. Now that's off my chest, I shuffle onto my side and settle into her incredibly comfortable lap for the rest of the ride.

It's amazing how much better I feel.

and am always honest when someone gives me too much change. Why is the universe testing me!

Okay, I'm not really complaining.

Cameron sits back up with her phone in one hand.

Obviously flustered, I suddenly blurt out, "Even though she's hot, I don't think you're compatible with Bianca."

I also think she has the emotional intelligence of a walnut, but I omit that bit.

"Bianca?... Oh, I don't know," Cameron muses and then looks out the window. "We have interesting chats."

"Like about her bra size?" I screech. "She practically had her boobs jammed in your throat."

"She has boobs? I didn't notice."

"Cameron!" I snuffle a laugh against her wrist.

She tries to hide her grin, but I see it.

"Anyway, you were saying about our lack of compatibility?" Cameron glances down at me, but I'm distracted by those eyes. I also see sunshine and rainbows. Wait, maybe that's concussion.

"I, um..."

Keep your cool, woman.

"Yes?" she prompts.

I shake my head. "Well... One. She doesn't like cookies," I say, counting off the reasons on my fingers.

"No, too much sugar."

"Two. She doesn't like dogs."

Cameron chuckles. "The charities do, but not these people. I actually can't believe how composed you were. You were *this* close to the dessert station; I thought you might return fire with a slab of tiramisu. God knows the pair of them deserved it."

A half-giggle slash sob escapes me. I'm not capable of finding anything funny right now, so I file it away for later. "Well, I did entertain that thought for a second, but I didn't want to stoop down to their level."

Cameron smiles, gently stroking my hair. "No, Chloe... You are nothing like them." Then she shakes her head. "Daria was like some sort of possessed doll."

I hiccup a laugh. "She was trashed. Courtesy of Moet and Chandon."

"Wait. Isn't she Erin's boss?"

"Yeah. She hates me, but I don't know why."

"You're a threat," Cameron says, and all I can do is shrug. "I wouldn't be surprised if Daria is let go. Her studio was the main sponsor."

I snort inelegantly. "Couldn't happen to a nicer person."

Cameron laughs.

I like making her laugh.

All of a sudden, there's a thud as Cameron drops her phone. "Shit. Sorry," she says, bending forward, and even though I turn my head, I'm immediately aware of her breasts squished against my face. This is so unfair. I am a nice person. I help the elderly cross the street

Chloe

My ex. Her fiancé.

Something hitting the back of my head.

Cameron rests her arm across my chest. "You slipped on the ice cream sundae that Daria aimed at your head, and I kind of carried you out. Now, Gus is driving us home," she adds, filling in the blanks.

Oh, my -

Just when I thought it couldn't get any worse. Cameron must think my life is a trashcan fire!

I make a strange noise, kind of like a dying seal.

"Ssh, you're safe now," Cameron says softly.

More weird noises come from my body.

"How are you feeling? Are you in pain?" Cameron inquires as it starts to rain and drum on the car roof. "Chloe?" she asks again.

I shake my head, but I am numb, numb beyond words. "I'm fine... Lexi?" I mumble.

"I've texted Lexi to let her know you're okay," Cameron says. "She was helping organizers mop up."

My hand flies over my eyes, trying to block out the visuals, and I groan, "This is beyond mortifying."

Cameron gives a tired laugh. "Quite the night. Don't worry, Bianca trumped you all when she slipped on the same puddle of ice cream, and her ass collected the champagne tower."

I remove my hand from my eyes, groaning some more, "Oh, God. I'm so sorry, Cameron. I know it means a lot to you."

"Come on, guys. We've got better things to do than hang with these dropkicks." Lexi swipes a panna cotta parfait, and we start to walk away. Did I mention that Lexi has always been my safe harbor in rough waters?

Suddenly, something hits me in the back of the head, halting me in my tracks.

It's running down my neck just like ice cream would.

No freaking way.

I spin around to shocked silence, heads swiveling everywhere, but there's no mistaking Daria's maniacal eyes and Cheshire-like grin while Erin just stands there with a look of abject horror.

Rage simmers beneath my skin, my hands ball into fists. It's high time I stick up for myself. "Daria. Think you and I need to have a little chat," I assert, taking a determined stride forward, and -

Unfortunately, that's when everything goes black.

I hear voices before I see shapes.

Cameron is chatting to someone when I gasp loudly, "What did I do!"

From the pitched angle, I am most definitely lying on Cameron's lap.

She brushes some hair out of my face. "Chloe, it's okay. You had a little tumble and hit your head."

"Little tumble?" I squeeze my eyes shut. "Oh my God."

Cameron cuts her off without offering her hand. "Can't say I do. Always skip the weather report. You know, it's well so... *boring*. And full of fluff. Prefer to just glance at my phone for a second to get an update. Or even ask Siri. Much more efficient."

Erin's whole face spasms in shock, and laughter swells up inside me. I desperately try to contain it.

Suddenly, a tiny blonde in a figure-hugging grape-colored dress appears. It's her fiance, Daria. She's lathered in so much fake tan, she looks like a Cheetos. Her eyes are red and struggling to stay open as she sways from side to side. Oh my God, she's drunk! She drapes an arm around Erin. "How's life treating you, Chloe? Still broke and single?" she slurs.

The jibe so unexpected that I just stand there, carp-mouthed.

I never even met Daria, apart from vicious texts she sent post-breakup. Honestly, why does she hate me so much? I'm not pining for Erin, nor do I want her back. Deep down, I know Erin did me a favor. I also don't know why I've suddenly lost my voice, forgotten how to act.

As though she can sense my anxiety, Cameron suddenly slides her arm around my waist. And Lexi, well, my comrade-in-arms, she just can't help herself. "They're dating!" she yells.

Erin gives an incredulous laugh, and Daria snorts. "But Chloe works at The Bra Bar," she says acidly.

I feel my cheeks blaze. What's that supposed to mean?

She's all flicky auburn hair, tight emerald-green dress, and tanned bare shoulders. Unfortunately, Erin is still attractive.

"We used to date," Erin says to Cameron. "Casually -"

"Such an asshole." My fuming, protective friend pops up from behind. "You were in a relationship until you got caught fucking around."

"Oh, Lexi," Erin chuckles. "Still eloquent, I see."

"And you're still a loser," Lexi fires back, unimpressed.

Erin mock toasts her, but she just rolls her eyes. Unfortunately, Erin turns her attention to me. "Chloe. This lighting is really working for you -"

"She's beautiful, isn't she?" Cameron interrupts.

I spin around and, for a moment, I forget all about my ex being there. Cameron's eyes linger on my face, and it sends my stomach into freefall. Those soul-rendering eyes. That smile. It's there again between us: the electric current. One look, and I'm lost. I also can't remember the last time anyone told me I was beautiful. I mean, apart from my aunt and Lexi. As Erin so kindly pointed out, I looked good under lighting.

I blush, suddenly shy, and say quietly to Cameron, "Thank you."

"Wait. You're Cameron Maxwell. Thought I'd recognized you from somewhere," Erin purrs. She holds out her hand. "I'm Erin Daly. You'd know me as the weather gal from NPC -"

Chloe

"I thought you knew. It's all over social media."

"Like I have time to stalk my ex anymore."

Suddenly, a pair of shapely legs appear next to us. I recognize them straight away.

Cameron crouches over. "What's so interesting down here?" she asks, then says to Lexi, "Hi, I'm Cameron."

"Hey, I'm Lexi. Chloe's flatmate and best friend in the universe."

"Oh, right. Nice to meet you," smiles Cameron.

Lexi grins. "You, too. My company is sponsoring this event... Also, Chloe's buffoon ex is over there."

I whack her arm.

"Ah, so we're hiding behind the dessert station. Makes sense. Plan on staying here all night, then?" Cameron glances between Lexi and me, and I mentally beg for an escape.

"Could think of worse places to hide, plus they've just restocked," Lexi replies, and her hand reaches up, latching onto a maple pecan brioche roll. "I haven't eaten since noon."

"Chloe, is that you?" asks a very familiar female voice.

Here we go.

The sound is jarring. I haven't seen Erin since she called me boring and ended things. Old feelings of hurt and rejection come at me from all angles. I swallow several times, feeling hot all over, and slowly stand. "Hi, Erin."

away, staying in her house.... And what's not to like?" She fans herself, grinning. "Her ass is perfect."

I snort into a laugh. "Pervert."

For a moment, we both just stare.

"Bianca's a total vulture," Lexi comments.

"I know."

Bianca laughs out loud, and this time, I imagine shoving her head in the punch bowl.

I frown. "But I shouldn't like her, Lexi."

"Cameron?"

"Mmm," I mumble.

"Yeah. She's beautiful and charming and, by the looks of it, pretty funny." Lexi pretends to consider this. "All terrible traits, I might add. God, how do you cope?"

I elbow her, and she grins. "I shouldn't want to spend all this time with her, but hell do I want to," I admit with a sigh. "I want to talk to her right now, and it's shit -"

"Not really. Not when compared to queen douchebag." Lexi tilts her head to a woman taking selfies by the ice sculpture.

"Erin!" I gasp, and it's like she hears me because her head whips around, her eyes like pinwheels when she sees me.

I immediately yank Lexi to the floor.

"Chloe! What on -"

I grip Lexi by the shoulders, panicked. "What the heck is she doing here! Why didn't you tell me!"

Chloe

I grab her by the arms. "Lexi! What the hell are you doing here?"

Lexi points to the sign. "Amadeus is one of the sponsors of the event, and as marketing coordinator, I'm obliged to attend. What are you doing here, more importantly?"

"I'm here with Cameron."

"Hang on. Cameron Maxwell?" Lexi asks with a lifted brow. She spins around, searching for her in the crowd. "Oh my God, how did I not recognize her in the photo you sent! Oh, wait, she looked like a drowned rat in a safari suit." She stares at me, bugged-eyed. "Chloe... You did the naked splits in front of her!" she shrieks.

FFS.

"No shit, Sherlock!" I whisper-hiss. "Now, do you understand my trauma?"

Lexi nods slowly, glancing over at Cameron, and fiddles with her silver drop earring. "I can see why you're freaking cuckoo over her."

"I'm not cuckoo!" I huff, but Lexi throws me a look, and I say, "Okay. Just a bit."

Lexi giggles, then gestures in Cameron's direction. "And who's that with her now?"

"Bianca," I huff, and Lexi pulls a face.

Cameron and Bianca chat for a bit, but soon Bianca laughs like the attention seeker she is. I groan into my champagne flute.

"Ugh," Lexi exhales. "You know, it was always going to happen, especially after your cozy weekend

Cameron shoots me a look, and I say, "You go. I'm fine here," then point to the dessert station right beside me. Her face creases into a smile. If that smile doesn't shoot right between my legs.

Goddammit.

As I wriggle around, I scoop up a coral-colored macaron and sip my champagne. I watch Cameron cross the floor and watch people, watch her. Cameron can be reserved, serious, and brooding. But the rules are different when you look like her. Men and women fall over each other to decipher your complexities.

A possessive, prickly feeling starts to rise up within me again, and I tell it to rack off.

However, if Cameron notices the staring, she doesn't let on, the attention all but bouncing off her demeanor.

I'm so entranced that when my phone buzzes in my bag, I literally jump two feet in the air.

Argh.

I pull it out and read the message.

LEXI: *Your underwear is tucked into your dress.*

My hand shoots to my butt, and I swivel on the spot, looking around. "What the -"

"Surprise!" Lexi screeches. She's all jazz hands and wearing a celestial silver dress with a fitted bodice full of tiny, sparkling sequins that are so shiny she could be seen from the moon.

"Cameron," coos a voice from behind.

We turn to a glamazon of a woman in a velvet noir cocktail dress with long coffee-hued hair pulled back in a French twist, and I immediately feel very small. She has eyes the color of whiskey, slightly slanted, and a massive pair of chandelier earrings. Fluttering her eyelashes at Cameron, she completely sidelines me.

"Ashley. Nice to see you again. This is Chloe." Cameron places a hand on the small of my back, and it sends a zing straight up my spine.

I flash her a polite smile only to get a fake one back.

Ashley brushes Cameron's arm. "Time we caught up again. I haven't seen you since..." she smirks.

Great. She's seen her naked, and I immediately stiffen.

Ashley glances at me with curiosity. "Is she your new assistant?"

"Chloe?" Cameron moves her arm around my waist. "No. She's my date," she adds, and goosebumps break out over my skin.

Her forehead wrinkles into a frown. "Oh."

I force a smile. Take that, Miss Photoshop. And thankfully, we say our goodbyes.

A second later, a short, paunchy man in a midnight plum shirt pulls Cameron to one side, telling her in hushed tones that he wants to introduce her to some congresswoman.

of her gaze. *I'm so doomed.* Offering her arm, she says, "Shall we, Miss Bentley?"

Sighing inwardly, I loop my arm through hers. We shuffle past doormen in black suits and then down a long corridor. While Cameron is a picture of poise, I'm just trying not to trip over my own feet. Thankfully, it's only a short walk, and waiters reward us with trays of champagne flutes once we step inside the gorgeous ballroom. As if I'm going to say no.

My eyes flit around the space as guests mill around in dinner jackets and posh dresses. I spot at least four people who are famous and watch Bianca arm herself with two fancy cocktails, one for each of her personalities. Then she's off flouncing around as though she's at New York Fashion Week. "Good God. Please stay far away," I say to myself.

Cameron chuckles.

Did I say that out loud?

"Come on," she says, and we move across the floor. People nod at Cameron, and she nods back. We stop by a group of executives, exchanging small talk. It can't be a minute, and Cameron suggests we move on. I laugh inwardly. She really *doesn't* like these things.

Cameron whispers behind her hand, "Sorry, this just isn't me."

"You don't say."

Her eyes go wide. "Honestly, I'd rather be in the kitchen with you."

It's hard not to laugh, but then again, so would I.

Cameron is looking straight ahead, but she is one hundred percent, copping an absolute eyeful. As is Gus, who quickly averts his eyes every time he glances into the rearview mirror. It's impossible not to. It's also impossible not to notice how handsy Bianca is around Cameron. Every time she talks, she touches Cameron. Her arm, her leg. She's also moving closer and closer. Any closer, and she'd be on her lap!

Could she be any more obvious?

"Fuck off," I mouth out my window.

After what feels like forever, the car finally screeches to a halt, and Gus says, "We're here, ladies!"

Oh, thank God for that.

I tuck my clutch under my arm and fling myself onto the sidewalk before Gus can even open the door. Panic washes over me at the sight of these glamorous people, and I quickly smooth out the silky fabric of my dress as we join a snaking queue. Thankfully, motormouth Bianca takes a phone call.

"You, okay?" asks Cameron, but I only glance at her briefly because, honestly, it's hard to look at her.

She's intimidatingly beautiful. Her off-the-shoulder onyx bandage dress has a cinched waist, and her heels could double as weapons. While Cameron is all class, I feel completely out of my element.

Cameron must sense my apprehension because she leans in and says, "I hate these things, too. All the mindless babble, boring people -" I look up, and Cameron smiles. I feel myself shiver under the strength

CHAPTER FIFTEEN

Chloe

Kill me now.

I'm in the ride from hell with Bianca and Cameron, heading into town for the fundraising event. All three of us squeezed in like proverbial sardines in the backseat of the car because, apparently, Bianca needed to chat with Cameron.

Well, she hasn't shut up.

It doesn't take long for poor old chauffeur Gus to start speeding and weaving through traffic. He wants to get there as quickly as I do.

Honestly, it couldn't be more uncomfortable. The fact that I'm wearing one of Cameron's black sheath dresses doesn't help either because it's hard to breathe. Alice even had to help shoehorn me into it. The sizing is too tight around my waist, but given my solid A cups, it's probably roomier than it should be at the top.

Meanwhile, Bianca is all boobs and flawless makeup. I know it's not right to compare, but how can I not when her breasts are spilling out of her bronze mermaid dress like toothpaste bursting from a tube.

Why is she looking at me?

That's a hard no. I wash windows, remember?

Cameron lifts Bianca to her feet, winking a smile over her shoulder, and my stomach flops around the floor like a fish out of water. My brain mightn't know what it wants, but my body sure does.

Maybe this ball won't be so bad after all.

"I am?" I kind of squawk, but when I catch the desperation in Cameron's eyes, I nod slowly and stutter, "Y-Yes, I am." Well, I certainly owe her a favor or two.

Bianca's face looks like a popped balloon. "But your mom insisted I go. She even gave me a ticket."

I bet she did.

Cameron gives a strained smile, clapping her on the back. "Great! Well, it's for a good cause. Looks like all three of us are going, then!"

Bianca is a picture of mortification, and laughter swells inside me. That is until I start to actually *think* about très amigas. Oh, and my outfit. I don't have any dresses! What am I supposed to wear!

Just as I begin to panic, Willow bursts in and lines Bianca up.

"Willow... No!" she warns, wagging a finger, but no way Willow is taking orders from someone like her.

I settle against the doorjamb, suddenly more relaxed as Willow barrels toward Bianca, who crashes back onto the chessboard, pieces scattering like startled birds, her bony ass hitting the floor with a thud.

"Idiotic dog. Ow!" Bianca yelps as Willow's enormous tail thumps her face. "Get off me!" She shoves Willow away and plucks the Queen piece from under her butt cheek, tossing it over her shoulder. Unfortunately, the window is open. I see Cameron's whole face flinch. "I freaking hate chess," Bianca hisses and flaps her arms in the air. "Argh, help! Will someone help me up!"

"Chloe's the old neighbor that I told you about," says Cameron, smiling. "Can you believe it's been almost twenty years since we've seen each other?"

"Mmm. So cute," Bianca replies in a saccharine voice. "Hi, Chloe."

"Nice to meet you," I say to her with a broad smile, but I definitely do not mean it. Especially given she was Cameron's part-time lover or whatever you want to call it.

Bianca doesn't extend any more niceties; her eyes are pinned on Cameron. A smile flashes across her perfect pouty lips. "I've been looking for you all morning!" she says in a whiny voice, strutting over in her aerobic wear. "Honestly, Cameron. You shouldn't eat so much sugar."

Cameron quickly swallows the rest of the cookie just as Bianca tries to swipe it from her mouth.

Oh my God, what kind of evil monster *is* she?

"Sorry, I was on a conference call," says Cameron.

"That's okay. I'm here now," Bianca purrs, placing a possessive hand on her shoulder, and a thread of something green starts to unravel in the pit of my stomach. "What time are we leaving for the ball?"

I see Cameron flinch. She's completely forgotten. "The ball for mental health? That's tonight?"

Bianca nods, smiling. "Yes."

"Oh, Chloe is coming with me," Cameron blurts out, and Bianca's smile slams into a brick wall.

wavy ash blonde hair hovering over me with boobs so large it looks like she's smuggling two bald men into the house under her hot-pink tank top.

She glares at me with cat amber eyes. "This office is off-limits. Not a good look sleeping on the job," she scolds, shoving my feet from the armrest. "Well, off!"

"Hang on. Wash the -" I frown, then swing my body upright and stand. "No, I'm Chloe."

Her face contorts. "The neighbor with an aversion for clothes?" she snips.

I have no choice but to nod. Okay, so she's pals with Cameron's mom.

Her eyes narrow in deep suspicion. "Looks like you've made yourself at home. Living in the guest quarters, slothing around, bringing in the pound."

Oh, wow. She's as friendly as a crocodile.

Only fair I return serve, I guess. "Now that you mention it, I am very comfortable. I'm even wearing Cameron's shirt. Oops. How did that happen?" I ask, and the busty woman barely disguises her horror.

Enter Cameron.

Even better than that, Cameron with one of my cookies hanging out of her mouth. My heart swoons.

"Oh, have you two met?" she mumbles, wiping crumbs from her shirt. "Bianca meet Chloe. Chloe, Bianca."

Right, so *this* is Bianca. Her assistant. Her one-time fling. Suddenly, my jeans feel very mom-like.

Chloe

When I knock, Cameron startles. "What? She was having nightmares."

"Uh-huh." I bite the inside of my cheek to stop my smile.

As I turn around to leave the two running buddies to bond, I pause long enough to see Cameron reach across with one hand and scratch Willow's belly.

I smile goofily, feeling an overwhelming affection for this woman who can't see what I see, and suddenly, I feel like I'm in on the world's biggest secret.

The woman with the beautiful eyes also has a beautiful, beautiful heart.

I'm comfortably stretched out on Cameron's couch when my phone pings.

It's Lexi.

She's sent me a photo of a gymnast doing the splits, and I gasp and giggle at the same time. This is what happens when you tell your friend about the most humiliating experience in your life. She makes fun of you day in and day out! Okay, well, I'd do the same.

"What are you doing lying on the sofa?" snaps a female voice all of a sudden, and I startle, dropping my phone like a hot potato. "Aren't you here to wash the windows?"

Jesus Christ.

I scramble for my phone, fumbling with the screen lock, and then tilt my head to an attractive woman with

CHAPTER FOURTEEN

Chloe

The next morning when I hear the click of the front door, I leap out of bed and rush to the window.

My stomach lurches because I didn't see Cameron when she came in last night, and I missed her. She can't be leaving again?

But rather than seeing her race off in her car, I spot her fastening a leash onto Willow's collar, and a smile explodes across my face. The pair quickly launch into a run under an overcast sky, and I stare, transfixed, at her flying hair and the dark soles of her sneakers as they vanish into the woods. Even with rain looming, I feel nothing but warmth.

When Willow disappears after lunch, I search everywhere. She's not out the back terrorizing the geese or in the living area destroying her squishy toys. A nagging suspicion gradually takes root, and I head straight to Cameron's office, where I find her absorbed in something on her laptop, sipping a cup of tea. And low and behold, right next to her is Willow, belly up and snoring, in a massive bed with her tongue lolling to one side. A bowl of food and water sits beside her.

My gaze darts to the clock. "Oh, crap. I need to leave." I rush to the cupboard. "God, where is it? I just had it a minute ago?"

Alice rolls her eyes. "You might have to be a bit more specific."

"My coat, Alice! I need my coat."

When I spin around, she gives me an odd look, then points. "Um, you're wearing it."

I glance down. "Yes, yes, I am."

This is *exactly* what I mean.

Apparently, I don't even know what clothes I'm wearing.

I'm simply frustrated because I want Chloe. I want her. She's not only set up home here but a home in my head, too, where she invades my thoughts. The look of her. The smell of her. The everything of her.

I just don't know what to do about it.

around the kitchen when she cooks, bakes, experiments. For the first time ever, the house feels like a home. There's laughter, chatter. Chloe and Alice are always curled over in stitches about something. A complete contrast to my childhood, where stoney silence and heated yelling reigned supreme.

Willow bowls Chloe over, and all I see is a jumble of hands and feet, and then her breathtaking smile. She's the most beautiful woman on planet Earth. I groan out loud.

"What? You want to get rid of Willow?" asks Alice.

Hardly, especially seeing how Chloe lights up around her.

"No," I reply with a sigh, and motion dramatically out the window to the woman, ass-up on the ground, covered in leaves and twigs with her hair everywhere. Can't she see? "The issue I have is far, *far* more serious, Alice."

Because, suddenly, Chloe isn't just my neighbor. She's an attractive female who lives with me and is on my mind 24/7. She's constantly wearing a smile that could blow up the world or interrupting me with strange little requests. *Cameron, where's the vegetable spiralizer?* Or, just ten minutes ago, *Cameron, can you please hold Willow in your arms while I clip her nails? Stroke her back so she stays calm.*

Honestly, what has happened to me?

"Oh... I see," Alice says with a slow grin while I have Chloe's little voice in my head over and over. It's driving me to absolute distraction.

CHAPTER THIRTEEN

Cameron

"Well, she didn't do that, did she?" I remark to Alice as we linger by the window. "The freaking dog levered the door open to the bathroom and watched me shower. Didn't budge until I turned off the faucet."

Alice lets out a giggle. "Oh, really? Maybe she was worried about you. How adorable!"

"Hardly going to drown in there. It's completely intrusive," I grunt.

She stifles a chuckle behind her hand. "Well, it's certainly more lively around here."

My eyes widen. "You think?"

Still, as we watch Chloe play fetch with Willow in the yard, every muscle in my body softens. She's always been a kind and caring person. Far nicer than me.

"You can act all grumpy about it, but deep down, I think inviting Chloe to stay here was one of your better ideas," Alice says, and it's true. Despite my whining, I don't seem to mind the chaos. Even the splatter all

only a puppy and could've been hit by a car! It's just for a little while, I promise. Gus and I are going to ask around the neighborhood tomorrow."

"I see." Cameron sighs and then looks at Willow, perplexed. "Is there something wrong with her? She looks cross-eyed."

"Oh, that's why she was disorientated," I say. "She has Strabismus -"

"What?"

"An inner ear infection," I clarify. "Maggie, the vet, said it can cause vestibular problems, and she gave us some antibiotics. Should clear up in no time."

Cameron pushes out of her chair and walks toward the door. "Right. Well, hopefully, you can find her owner tomorrow... Goddammit!" Stopping mid-stride, she stoops down, pulling a knotted bone from under her foot before flinging it to one side. "Worse than freaking Lego."

I cover my laugh with my hand, scuttling across the carpet to pick up dog toys I bought from Bill's dollar store.

Cameron hobbles past me with Willow right behind. "Well, you need to keep your eye on her, Chloe," she says over her shoulder, even though Willow appears to have lost all interest in me. "I've got a meeting with a client in town."

I crawl to my feet. "Oh, sure, no problem. I can do that."

And the two of them disappear out the door.

on Cameron's shoulder. I guess that's what happens when you're far too comfortable in someone's space. You bring in a dog.

While I just stand there agog, Cameron's voice goes up a few bars, "So, I give you a cookbook and you give me a dog? Are we doing reciprocal presents all of a sudden?"

"Ah ha-ha..." I laugh-groan. Oh, God. How do I get out of this? "Um, not exactly. You see, the dog was kind of loitering near the house?"

"Near the house?"

"Okay, near the street."

Cameron angles me a look.

I let out a huff. "A few blocks down and maybe two streets over. And before you say anything, yes, Gus was with me. Alice said he needs to lose a few pounds. She's dramatically cut his hours of watching General Hospital on the sofa. Anyway, I was taking him for a walk. Gus, not the dog. Can you believe his blood pressure is one forty over ninety? He's also pre-diabetic, so..."

Cameron tilts her head back, exhaling loudly, and her eyes skim the ceiling.

I try to resume the conversation. "Um, Willow -"

Her eyes snap to mine. "Willow?"

"Well, she looks like a Willow, don't you think?" Her tail starts to wag, and I point excitedly. "See! She likes the name. Anyway, it was cold, and she was all alone, stumbling and looking a bit off-balance. She's

CHAPTER TWELVE

Chloe

It's amazing how well Cameron and I have been getting along away since our weekend getaway.

Yesterday, she helped me deep clean the grimy bathrooms in my family home, and I almost fell over when she asked if I wanted to go shopping for cooking utensils.

Yet despite this positive momentum, I may have miscalculated one *tiny* move because en route to her office, my eyes slam shut when I hear, "Would you just quit it? I'm not giving you a scratch."

When I peek into her office, I recoil at the scene. Oh, God. Best to keep walking in these situations -

"Chloe!"

I freeze.

Shit.

"Um, yes?" I reply, still in half a mind to run.

"Why is there a fucking massive dog in my office?" asks Cameron, incredulous.

I turn ever so slowly to a young Labrador mix, balanced on its hind legs with one paw casually placed

Chloe bursts out a laugh. "True..." She waves the book in front of her. "Well, this is a first. No one has ever written a recipe book for me or named one in my honor." She pauses in thought, gently dabbing one eye, then the other, with the sleeve of her sweater.

I think she might have pretzel dust in her eyes again.

My stomach swoops because I'm having one of *those* moments.

Chloe reads the cover, her eyes widening. "Chloe's Amazing Recipe Book?"

"Yeah, I was twelve, so don't hold the incredibly creative title against me. I kind of collated all the recipes of the meals you made with Alice."

Her head snaps up. Her eyes pierce me. Those eyes, those *damn* eyes. "So, wait... you made this for me when we were kids?" she asks.

I nod. "I was going to give it to you for your birthday, but -"

"You never got my invitation," Chloe finishes. She blinks slowly, then scrunches her forehead. "And you didn't throw it out? You hate clutter."

I shrug. "Must've slipped through my cleanup because it would've *definitely* been the first thing to go," I reply with a wry smile.

Her mouth twitches as she starts flicking through the pages in bewilderment. "But how? How did you remember them all?"

"Well, like you pointed out, I was just standing there in the background, not doing much so..."

She wriggles her cute nose. "You were recording all the details in that big brain of yours and taking notes," she says, staring at me, and I feel my face glow.

I shuffle from one foot to the other. "I ate most of the meals, too, so that also helped with memory recall."

high-performance superglue, so that presented all sorts of problems. My fingers stuck together, then there was the carpet always attaching itself. Even our Miniature Schnauzer, Henry, unwittingly became part of the project when he sat on top of the book. I had to cut his fur with nail scissors to remove the cover from his behind.

Tracing each letter with my finger, I remember how much grief this damn book caused me. It took three painstaking months to collate, and I never even had the chance to give it to her. Well, now's my opportunity.

With a heavy sigh, I tuck the book under my arm and weave my way back into the kitchen, where I find Chloe humming, head buried deep in the pantry.

"Hey, Chloe?" I call out.

Chloe jumps in a mid-air pirouette. "Holy crap. You scared me." She clutches her hand to her chest, and I cross the oak floor in a few long strides. "Sorry, this is like some freaking treasure trove. You know how I get around premium ingredients," she says with a shining smile.

I snort, stopping in front of her. "Yeah, I remember... Um, when I was clearing out the house, I stumbled across this. Anyway, I think you should have it." Suddenly shy, I hand her my gift and watch her closely.

You know when something is blurry and comes into focus?

"What the hell?" I splutter, coughing out flour, and Chloe is in hysterics. "Cameron!" she manages between fits of giggles.

I also accidentally turn on the mixer, but that just spins her into more peals of laughter.

Ugh.

Red-faced, I flick off the switch. Chloe laughs and laughs and laughs, and then finally, I do, too.

Laughter rings throughout the kitchen, and even with flour shooting out unflatteringly from my nose, I know I'm happier than I have been in a long time.

Fresh from our culinary adventure, I appear to be riding a wave of nostalgia because suddenly, I remember something I had long forgotten and rush out to the garage, yanking open a cupboard full of clutter.

My fingers dance across the front of the cardboard boxes. "No, no, no... Come on, where are you?" I huff impatiently when a black-and-white pattern catches my eye. I yank a box from the depths of the cupboard and rifle through it.

There it is!

I pull out a book, blowing off dust so thick I feel like I'm part of an archaeological dig, and grin when I see the cover: "Chloe's Amazing Recipes!"

I'd cut out random colored letters from some of my mom's Woman's Weekly magazines and fixed them to the front, but I didn't have glue like a normal kid, only

Chloe falls about laughing.

Oh, God. I stare straight into the bowl, my cheeks glowing. College-educated and can't even mix butter.

She pulls herself up on the granite counter and sits beside me. Ah, go away. I hate that she's watching. Cooking does not come naturally to me. I must look so incongruous. My competitive nature means I don't give up, though, and her laughter eventually dies down as the butter starts to cream.

"There you go. That's it," Chloe grins, and I bite back a smile of my own. She hands me a cup of sugar. "Now, add," she says, and I do, still mixing. Then come the eggs, the vanilla extract. I start to relax because I think I'm getting the hang of it.

A timer goes off, and Chloe swipes a mitt and leaps off the counter, opening the oven. She pulls out a tray, shakes her head, and then slides it back.

Glancing over my shoulder, she says, "Yep. Good," and takes the bowl from me, pointing to another bowl with dry ingredients. "Now you're going to mix the flour into the batter you just mixed. I'll hold the batter, and you just use the hand mixer."

"Okay," I say hesitantly, then I pick up the bowl with dry ingredients, tilting it toward her batter, but it gets stuck, so I give it a tap. Nothing happens. I tap it again. Hard. Suddenly, all the flour falls out, and a big cloud of flour puffs out from the bowl. All over my face, and me.

bowl and hands me the hand mixer. "Beat it," she orders.

I wipe my lips. "How?"

"What do you mean how?"

"You guys never let me touch any electrical appliances," I reply as if that should answer the question.

"And you've never ever touched one since? In TWENTY YEARS?" Chloe almost shrieks.

"Of course not," I reply smugly. "I do as I'm told."

Chloe rolls her eyes. "Wow... Look, I'll show you." She comes up behind me, covering her hand over mine on the mixer, and a billion volts shoot through me. "Like that," she instructs, moving the appliance in a smooth, circular motion, her breath tickling my ear.

Obviously, I completely lose my train of thought. All I can think about is how good her body feels and then her doing the splits. Seriously, that's it! I'm going to burn down that damn bathroom! One less, who cares!

There's something very wrong with me.

I frown into the bowl. Sure, I've known gorgeous women before, but none have corrupted my mind like she has.

All of a sudden, Chloe flicks a switch, and the mixer smacks into the side of the bowl.

Butter flies everywhere, and I use both hands to get the mixer under control.

"I've tweaked the recipe over the years. I use white Belgian chocolate now and have added cornflour to make the dough softer. Oh, and the raspberries at the end give it that extra special kick of flavor," Chloe says, and I peer at the golf ball-sized balls in the oven, nodding. "So, you're telling me that they're even better than they used to be?" I ask, almost salivating.

"Don't tell Alice, but I think so..."

I let out a low whistle, still staring into the yellow glow of the oven.

Chloe grabs my arm. "Come on, you can help. I'm making another batch."

"Oh, I need to work," I reply and reach across to a tray of cookies.

She slaps my hand away. "Cameron Maxwell. I know most of them will end up in your belly, so you're helping."

She is *not* wrong.

I glance at the cookies again, and she rolls her eyes. "Go on, then. You'll burn your tongue, though."

Grinning, I swipe one before she changes her mind, almost inhaling it whole.

I burn my tongue, my throat, and every other internal passage. My eyes water as I wolf it down, and I avert my gaze, but not before I catch a smile on Chloe's face.

God, I'm such a moron.

Now, standing beside her and feeling three inches smaller, I watch as Chloe throws a stick of butter into a bags. She's wearing a knitted sweater and ballooning linen pants.

Alice clocks us both, then grins. "Oh, hello..."

"Hey, Alice," beams Chloe, and I say hi too. "Join us for some cookies?"

"Well, I would love to -" Alice bursts forward but then stops, her eyes tick-tocking between Chloe and me. She holds up a solitary hand. "No, I've just remembered. Book club is calling! Meeting with Delilah to discuss... books! I'll see you girls later." She dumps her bags in the corner and then shoots in reverse, yelling, "Don't have too much fun without me! Bye!"

I snort a laugh. Could she be more obvious?

Chloe scrunches her forehead. "Hmm. Is it me, or was that a bit weird?"

I shrug. "That's just Alice." My nose starts to twitch, and I start sniffing like a bloodhound. "Hang on. Are you making those special -"

"Yes."

Suddenly, I'm transported back to being twelve years old and don't give a flying fig about cleanliness. "Oh my God!" I yelp, then trip on the Tundra-inspired mid-century rug in my rush to reach her.

Alice and Chloe's special white chocolate and macadamia cookies.

Deliciously nutty and chocolatey with a chewy, buttery center and crisp edges, I used to dream about these cookies. They are to die for.

I roll my eyes, relenting. "Thursday, then? I'm in Diamond Hill, but I'll drive up to see you."

"Fine. 3pm. I'll text you the address. Don't bring anyone, or there'll be trouble," he warns ominously.

"Okay, see -"

The line clicks dead.

Shit.

What have I just done?

Close to midday, I'm drawn to the kitchen in an almost trance-like state by the aroma of warm cookie dough.

Cookies straight out of the oven have always been my downfall. But it's not Alice, it's her prodigy, Chloe, that I find in there.

Barefoot in her jeans with most of her hair tucked into her sweater, she's rummaging through the fridge as the TV blares with the news headlines.

"Morning!" Chloe whirls around with a flour-dusted nose, grinning. "Back in my happy place."

"Hi..." I murmur as I survey the chaotic scene. "I can see that."

Oh, boy, the kitchen looks like a hurricane ripped through it. Every inch of the countertop covered in ingredients, bowls, and *mess*. She certainly hasn't learned to clean up after herself.

I'm still frowning when Alice staggers into the kitchen under the weight of four massive shopping

Not long after, her hand wraps over mine and my stomach almost floats out of my body at the contact. The press of her palm is warm, soft, female.

And it's completely perfect.

I hardly sleep that night.

I'm worried that Chloe is in danger. I think I've worked out what my dad had over his client, Vladimir, so the next morning, when I'm in the office, I punch in a number on my phone. "Vladimir, this is Cameron Maxwell. Carter Maxwell's daughter?"

There's a palpable pause before his gravelly voice cuts through the line, sharp and suspicious. "And what the hell do you want? How did you get my number?"

I tap my desk with my pen. "I'm calling to ask you a favor."

"Favor? I don't do favors."

"For my father then. I have a debt that -"

He coughs into the phone. "All debts have to be paid."

"I was hoping to negotiate," I press.

Come on, don't make this hard.

"Well, you'll need to come and see me."

"I was really hoping to sort -"

"No. I'm old school. You have to meet me in person."

traitorous brain flashes a frame-by-frame visual of Chloe doing the splits in the bathroom, and I shoo it away. Not now!

Instead, I try to focus on the canopy of stars above like Chloe would've all those years ago, and suddenly, I feel awash with sadness for the little girl I once knew as I imagine her here in the darkness. She watched her mom spiral, all alone, and the only thing I ever gave her was a crappy neon cardboard moon.

Thinking of her like that feels like tiny sharp knives digging into my chest. I want to hug her, brush my hand over her hair, and make the past better, but I can't, so I stay still and silent just like we did when we gazed at reams of stars, thick and vivid like spilled glitter, from the floor of my treehouse.

"You're right. The moon is on its last legs," I say eventually.

We watch as a star peels off the ceiling and gently drifts down onto my leg.

Chloe nods slowly. "The whole solar system has had it."

We share a giggle.

Suddenly, I feel compelled to say, "Chloe... I'm here if you ever need me."

Something I should've said all those years ago. I knew the first day I met her, looked into her eyes. I knew she was special, and nothing has changed.

Chloe stops in front of a mountain of paper on the floor, separated into different piles. "Just going through Dad's paperwork. Gus and I cleared out the storage unit in town, but I thought I should have a quick look before I discard it all," she explains.

I nod and glance around. "Your room still looks the same."

"I used to stand here and spy on you," she says, smirking by the window, and it's impossible not to smile.

"Yeah, I know. I saw you on my telescope. You weren't the only spy," I reply.

"Tele-... Of course, you need to one-up me."

My mouth starts to twitch. "Your curtains are sheer, too, by the way. Totally see-through. What did you think of my underwear the other night? Probably not as nice as you can get at The Bra Bar, but not bad, right?"

Chloe inhales sharply.

"What? I don't wiggle my butt for just anyone."

"That's it. I officially hate you," she says.

Her cheeks might also go a bit pink, and I start to chuckle.

Chloe flops back onto her bed, tapping the space beside her. "Room for two."

After a moment of hesitation, I walk over and lie down. Hardly room for two. Our bodies are pressed against one another, and I feel the heat radiating from her body. Lust hitting me at the worst possible time. My

"Maybe not today. Thanks," I mumble, and for a moment, I just stand there rigid as a plank, like I was the one that was naked in the bathroom.

"Do you want to come in?" asks Chloe, far calmer than me.

"Yes," says the man, pushing up his glasses.

"I mean her." Chloe points to me, and he looks so disheartened.

Poor guy, I almost want to invite him in. Almost.

As I dust off my butt, Chloe stares at me, so I quip, "That fence is a hazard."

"We should cut a gate in to prevent further injury." Chloe places a hand on my shoulder and my whole body electrifies.

I swat her hand away. "This will be the last time I ever visit."

"Promises, promises," Chloe snickers, her eyes full of mischief, but then she catches sight of the scratch on the back of my arm and frowns. "Hey, you're hurt."

"It's nothing," I assure her, but a flicker of concern crosses her face. "Really."

Chloe hesitates, then smooths out her expression. "Okay, if you say so... Come on in."

We move toward the door, and I'm expecting to stay downstairs, but Chloe immediately starts walking up the carpeted, creaky staircase. I close the door behind me and shuffle upstairs to what appears to be my second visit ever to her bedroom.

My heart hammers in my chest. Barefooted, I rush out the door and almost t-bone Alice in the hallway as she enters from the living area. I latch onto her apron strings to steady her. "Where's Gus!"

She straightens the rollers in her hair. "He had to pee -"

Is she serious!

"Not allowed!" I yell as I sidestep her and fling open the door, then barrel across the lawn, only to step on multiple spiky burrs. "Ow, shit!" I curse, hop on one leg, then the other, and pluck the prickles from my feet without stopping, only to hit another vicious patch. "Fucking hell!" I rip them out before running some more. Huffing and puffing, I scramble over the fence and jump, scraping my arm before crashing down on my ass.

Chloe spots me, and it's obvious from her expression she heard my carry-on.

Pink-faced, I stand and straighten, fixing my hair, while she looks picture-perfect in leggings and a long-sleeved sweater that slightly hangs off one shoulder. Great, she's not wearing a bra. I'll just add that to my torment, shall I?

Chloe folds her arms across her chest. "Cameron, relax. It's just a Jehovah's Witness."

A pint-sized, balding man in a brown suit and rimless glasses holds up his bible. "Jesus can save you!"

Cameron

The next morning, I'm back in my office when I hear banging next door and notice a Carpet World truck parked in her drive.

She must be having her carpet installed.

Good, Gus is there. Even if he is slouched by the curb, reading a goddamn soap opera magazine and grinning. Boy, he's changed. Gnomes, daily soap operas. Alice is making him softer than a cinnamon roll.

Shaking my head, I start flipping through my diary, periodically checking the security footage on the camera. We haven't seen that man with a limp again, but that doesn't mean we won't.

I rub my face and take a gulp of coffee, only to realize it's the wrong cup – a stone-cold one from the evening. God, gross. I almost spit it out when suddenly, an image pops up in my peripheral vision, and my head snaps toward the screen.

I hit the zoom button.

A man is trudging up her front path, holding something bulky in his right arm, but my vision is obscured by his jacket.

Dammit. Where the heck is Gus?

I pan the camera three sixty degrees, however I can't see the gentle giant anywhere.

Shit.

"I'll keep an ear out for any other information, Cameron." Gus walks toward the door, turning his head as he leaves, and my smile is tight.

Why couldn't it be simple?

This problem isn't just going to go away, which means Chloe will be in danger. I drum my fingers on my desk. Mafia. Mobsters. I glare at the chessboard. My father would know what to do.

I go to the safe in the cupboard, typing in the combination. The door pops open, and I pull out a small brown leather notebook that I stumbled upon in a wall cavity after my father's passing. I never knew if it would come in handy, but the fact that it was hidden made me conclude it was valuable. Maybe it will help now. I flick through his scribbled notes on customers, information he could use against them if they ever threatened him, and wince. His penmanship worse than a doctor.

I sink into my couch, looking for only one name - Vladimir Ivanovic.

Later that night, I gravitate toward Chloe's room. Yeah, like I have a choice. I'm a masochist. Those invisible cords are practically strangling my common sense.

The door is slightly ajar, and Chloe is asleep on the bed. Her socks are missing, and thankfully, the only skin I see is the powder-white soles of her feet. She's curled on her side with her hands pillowing her cheek. I sigh inwardly and gently close her door.

I won't always be here to protect her.

Ah, and I'm back to thinking about Chloe.

Turning the final corner, I notice the same white Nissan van I saw yesterday parked down the street. When the driver sees me, he pulls away so quickly that I'm unable to make out the plates. Are those creeps watching Chloe?

Racing home, my legs sluggish beneath me, I shower, then work through the rest of the afternoon with my door closed, but I can't stop thinking about the van.

That evening, there's a knock on my door, and I bristle. *This is Chloe Bentley, your childhood friend. You do not think about her like that.*

"Come in," I half-stutter and breathe a sigh of relief when I see a hairy face peek around the door. "Gus, hey. What's up?"

"Just wanted to give you an update on the guy that was snooping around last week." Gus hands me a sheet of paper. "His name is Roman Hartof. He's one of Vladimir Ivanovic's cronies."

I blink, immediately recognizing the name. "One of my father's clients? Runs his operations from Long Island?"

"That's right. Apparently, the market is pretty tight now, so they're hiring henchmen like Roman and rounding up all their debts along the entire East Coast."

I frown, and my stomach knots. "Oh, I see. Thanks, Gus."

throat, but you must never give in to it. Anxiety. So, I do what I always do. I go to the cupboard, slip on my activewear and sneakers, and leave out the back door.

I glance up at the sunny blue skies and curse the deity that would ever do this to me. How will I ever erase that image of Chloe? And sharing that moment with my mom, of all people! There are simply no words.

Funny, they say you can't outrun your problems, but it works for me. Well, it used to. I race past Sir Lancelot and his army of geese, then leap over a pond, across the field, up the grassy hill, and toward the woods. I love it amongst the scented pine. It's easy to find calm in a place that outdates you by a country mile. A thick canopy of trees soon brings shadows, and I concentrate on the sound of the steady beat on the ground and the feel of the stretch of my legs. Almost immediately, my anxiety cedes. Thank God for that.

After years of therapy that really didn't help, I found a natural alternative in college. Running. I'm almost positive that's what got me across the line with my final exams. I'm not a pretty runner. I have a shoddy technique and go bright red, but I try to squeeze in a run every day, even in inclement weather, for my mental health. I've recently added transcendental meditation to my arsenal, and naked surprises aside, I feel in control of my anxiety, not the other way around.

I pick up my pace and follow a small river out of the woods, passing the local elementary school and mechanic, where I see Ted's wiry body peering out from underneath Chloe's wreck of a car.

"Well, thank God, she has clothes on now," chides Mom. "Take it you're one of Cameron's exes?"

The woman is a liability.

I scrunch my brow. "No, Mom. She's our old neighbor."

"Oh?..." The penny drops because her eyebrows disappear into her hairline. "Oh!"

"As in Chloe Bentley."

"Yes."

"That's me!" Choe says. "Hi."

"Hello..." Mom replies as if humoring her, then stares at her like she's an exhibit at the museum. "You're all grown up now."

"Yes."

I pinch the bridge of my nose and try to think of something to say to break this bizarre interlude, but I've got nothing except, "You know, I think I'm starting to get a migraine."

"Well, I'm going shopping!" trills Mom like I knew she would.

Even Chloe is predictable. "I need to get started on cooking that soufflé."

And that, ladies and gentlemen, is how you clear a room.

Obviously, the first thing I do after they leave is pop two Advils. But then a familiar pressure starts in my chest, a rising panic that I try to shove away as I double over. A nameless terror that grips you by the

CHAPTER ELEVEN

Cameron

Good move, Cameron. Excellent decision getting Chloe to stay here!

Not only is sharing a house starting to short-circuit my brain, but it's also starting to feel... intimate.

Frowning, I turn my attention to my mom, who has one foot in the room and one hand on the doorknob, while Chloe appears besotted with the fabric of the curtains at the far end.

Obviously, this is not how I was hoping their introduction would go.

There is no way this won't be awkward. I'm just hoping my mom doesn't make it unbearable.

I rub my forehead, sighing. "Chloe... this is my mom, Leanne."

Chloe wheels around slowly, her face the color of baked lobster. "Yes, hi!" she chokes out with a wobbly smile.

My eyes dart to Mom.

Please don't mention her naked. Please don't mention her naked.

Her mom saw me naked.

How did I not see the similarity? Sure, her hair is styled differently, no longer a deep chocolate, now gunmetal grey, but they have the same intense blue eyes, full mouth!

I stumble back and latch onto the curtain, trapped in a silent scream.

This cannot be happening.

Panic gripping my chest, I loom over her, an inch from her face. No, no, no! Suddenly, her eyes snap open.

We both scream.

"Oh my fucking God! Chloe!" Cameron leaps up from the couch at the same time as I fall backward onto my ass. "What are you doing!"

"I thought you were dead!" I yelp and scramble to my feet. "You weren't moving or responding! Why didn't you answer me!"

Cameron pulls out her earbuds. "I was trying to freaking meditate!"

"Medi – But why?"

I already know the answer.

Because Cameron Maxwell saw me naked.

She frowns at me. "I just started practicing Transcendental Meditation. It's supposed to help calm the mind!"

"Er... Did it work?"

"How would I know! You interrupted me as I entered the hypnotic phase!"

"What on earth is going on -" A woman flies through the door, and I freeze. It's her. The woman from the bathroom. Except this time, she's looking at my face. "You. Again!"

"Mom," Cameron sighs wearily.

My eyes almost pop out of my head.

Mom? That's her mom!

Oh my fucking God!

I must be suffering from some sort of PTSD because I swing between bouts of hysterical gurgling, and folding over and cursing. Now I'm staring at water flowing down the drain, much like my dignity just did. Why? Why did that have to happen? Who was that other woman?

Wait till Lexi hears about this.

Oh my God. And Cameron's face!

I slap the wall at my idiocy, then at my panicked, addled brain. Now, I have to see her and all she's going to see is my...

God, it's too much to bear. I cover my eyes.

In fact, I'm so dreading our encounter that I almost skip it and go straight to bed. But it's not even midday, so that would be a bit weird. After some stern internal dialogue, I bite the bullet. Obviously, I let a decent amount of time pass before I reemerge. For everyone's sake, but mostly mine.

Forcing myself to take some deep breaths, I walk to her office. Hmm, she's not in her chair. I stick my head in through the door, eyes swiveling left then right, and notice a human lump on the couch. Is she sleeping?

I knock gently. No movement.

"Cameron?" I try again, but there's still no response. I shuffle over to her side. "Cameron?" I repeat.

Dropping to my knees, I try to listen to her breathing. I can't hear anything. She's like a dead body. Oh my God, I killed her with my splits. I'm a murderer!

Cameron stops dead as the other woman hurtles out the door. "What on -"

"Cameron!" I shriek.

However, she just stands there like a statue, eyes wide, and seems to age about ten years in a minute. Luckily, we are both female, and there's nothing new to see. But I know - the mirrors, angles, *this* precarious position.

Her hand flies over her eyes, too. "Why on earth are you here, Chloe! Trying out all the bathrooms!"

"The shower in the en suite hardly came with a manual. It has more buttons than a space station! Nothing worked!"

Now Cameron's shoving fists into her sockets. "God, help me!"

"I'm the one that needs help. Please, Cameron!"

There's an audible groan, then she throws out her arm, and I latch on. With one swift pull, I slam into her chest. Naked.

For a moment, neither of us speaks. We're aligned. I feel her breath on my lips. I feel everything.

Mother of God, this is not what Cameron signed up for.

"Chloe?" Her voice tight.

"Sorry!" I jump back, and with her eyes pinned to the ceiling, she swivels and swiftly exits.

It's practically impossible to shower after that scene.

happens. I try an absurd number of combinations. Still, nothing! This is unbelievable. "Stupid space-age shower," I mutter. "Well, I need to find another one."

I pad along one of the many hallways until I stumble upon a bathroom. *Yep, this will do.* Grinning, I happily twist the faucet on and off, then shed my clothes, flinging them onto a chair along with my underwear, and rush to the shower.

Unfortunately, fate seems to have other plans because I go for a slide on the slippery black marble tiles, my left leg lunging forward until I am in a very, *very* uncomfortable position.

Holy shit.

I'm doing the splits!

Well, almost. I'm hovering a couple inches from the floor.

Age is supposed to betray me because I haven't even attempted one since the third grade. I think I'm kind of amazed by my achievement. Oh, why am I floundering? Just get up -

Suddenly, the door whips open, and I'm feeling a breeze in all the wrong places.

An older woman with a slash of scarlet lipstick and a curtain of steel-colored hair stands there with her mouth open. Eyes so stunned, I have to wonder if she can see me. But then she screams, slaps her hands over her eyes, and turns, only to bounce off something. *Someone.*

"He's very handy. And given his size, you won't need to cart around a ladder."

I stifle a laugh. "True."

A crease appears between her eyebrows. "Chloe. I think it's safer if you stay here. I know you haven't heard from those loan sharks, but they *are* dangerous."

My stomach sinks because I don't have long until D-Day, and I still haven't come up with the money or a way out of it. I nod because I know I'm protected here. "Thank you, Cameron."

Honestly, what would I have done without her these past few days? She has made me feel safe. I can count on my fingers the number of people who make me feel that way.

Shuffling over to the window, I peer outside to a grassy but empty backyard. "Hey, did you move your treehouse? I can't see it."

"Sold it too, unfortunately, to pay off Dad's debt."

I feel a visceral pang of sadness. "Oh, no."

The phone rings. "Sorry, Chloe, I have to get this call. I've been chasing this CEO for weeks."

I smile, retreating to my room, but not before catching a glimpse of Alice and Gus canoodling in the kitchen. I giggle to myself. Blushing, Alice shoos me away with her hand while Gus just beams at her, completely oblivious to anything around them.

With not much else to do but relax, I opt for a lavish shower in my en suite using Cameron's fancy gels and cremes. I press a few buttons, but nothing

I smile. "Like a diva who needs to sleep on her own sheets?"

She rolls her eyes. "Just like a diva. As for the photo, we were happy in that moment. Unfortunately, marriage isn't a snapshot. It's a journey."

So, anti-romance warrior Cameron has a point.

All of a sudden, there's a downward weary cast to her forehead, to her eyes. "You know, sometimes I feel guilty for missing my dad given that he was such a... you know."

"Cameron. He was your father. You never have to feel guilty. You loved him, and he loved you."

She flashes me a semi-smile. "Yeah."

Cameron's a good egg, I find myself thinking.

I fidget with my hands. "Look, Cameron. I'll be getting out of your hair and going back to mine tomorrow morning. Thank you -"

"Why?"

Why indeed? She's been very hospitable.

We stare at each other for a few seconds before I shift uncomfortably. "Well, this isn't my house, and yes, you have been a gracious host, but I don't want to overstay my welcome. I don't have any way to repay you."

"Stay," she says simply. "Gus can help you with whatever needs fixing."

"But -"

my stomach bottoms out at the innocent gesture. Ugh, this is not good.

Cameron says into the phone, "Absolutely, Ray. No problem at all," while pulling a face. We share a smile, and she ends the call. "Any news on the car?"

"Yeah, Ted said it might take up to ten days to source the parts. The alternator blew, and something else beginning with S. Not sure," I say, glancing at black and white prints of African wildlife on her wall.

Cameron snorts a laugh. "Right. Well, you're keeping him busy."

"Mmm." I point to a lioness with two cubs. She has her front paw draped over the smallest one. "These are beautiful."

"Thanks. I took them in 2016 on a trip to Tanzania."

"You took them? Wait. The same person that took those blurry shots on the beach? Can't be," I tease, then look over my shoulder and grin.

Cameron shakes her head at me. "Yeah. I like taking photos. Captures things that words can't always express."

I pick up a lone photo of Cameron and her mom and dad on the mantel. She's sitting on the fence in a pink frilly tutu. "You look happy in this photo, Miss Ballerina."

Cameron gives me a cute side-eye expression. "I did ballet for one day only and threw out my tutu in a massive tantrum."

even a fancy Japanese heated toilet seat. God, I could quite happily spend the rest of the afternoon in here.

"Please feel free to use anything you need. If there's anything else -"

"Fire up the satellite communication?" I grin.

Her mouth twitches, and she starts to walk away.

"What? This place is ginormous." I turn to her. "Cameron?"

Cameron glances over her shoulder. "Yes?"

"Thank you," I say as she leaves, then nosedive onto the bed with a huge smile fixed on my face, thrashing my arms and legs about. This is heaven! I'm going to have the best sleep ever!

I flip over onto my back and stare at the ceiling, giving a dreamy sigh when I take a call from my now best friend, Ted. Propping myself up on the lush pillows, he tells me that he's gone into the workshop on his day off to give me an update on my car, and it may take up to ten days to repair because he has to wait for parts. I send a couple of rapid-fire texts and Gerry is cool with it, but Guiseppe will probably want to cook me in that heavy cast iron pan I wanted to throttle him with.

Regardless, I push Guiseppe's angry Italian face out of my mind and set about to find Cameron. It's not long until I hear her voice on the phone and pause outside her office door. She's seated behind a large desk covered in important-looking paperwork. When she glances up, I mouth sorry, but she waves me inside, and

"Even when it comes to furniture, it seems."

Cameron sighs. "When my mom moved to Paris, I did a big cleanup. What she didn't take, I sold or gave to charity. Mainly to cover debt, but I also don't like clutter. Clutters the mind and all that," she says, still walking, and then points to the corner table in her home office. "Dad's prized chess set was about the only thing I kept. We used to play a lot as a kid. It was our thing."

"Yeah, I remember," I say with a smile.

After navigating a few turns, Cameron pauses by some double doors and then opens them. "So, this is your room."

I step inside and take in the gigantic bed draped in the softest-looking white linens, two bedside tables, a walk-in wardrobe, and a monster balcony. There's also a separate nook with a flat-screen TV, coffee table, and a freaking three-seater leather couch.

"My room?" I gurgle.

This space is bigger than my entire apartment.

"Yes," Cameron nods. "I hope it's okay?"

"Horrible."

Her face actually sinks.

"I'm joking. It's lovely," I smile.

"Good." Cameron opens another door. "Oh, there's an en suite here too."

I peek inside, and it's also massive. There's a mound of fluffy white towels, a claw-foot bath, and

"This car is a catastrophe," Cameron mutters. She pulls up the handbrake, but this time, when she looks at me rather than engage in a tête-à-tête, we both just grin.

Thanks to my Toyota, I'm probably going to have to hang around a little longer, and I think I love my car a bit more for it.

Cameron calls Gus, and he drives out to pick us up. He also levers open my trunk with a crowbar so we can collect our luggage. Unfortunately, his retrieval efforts mean I'll also need to pay for a new lock, but with the euphoria I'm feeling, I hardly break into a sweat.

When we arrive at Cameron's home, I hold my bag in front of me like a shield. My feet sink into the luxurious carpet as I follow her down an endless hallway. I take in the high ceilings and huge windows as we pass room after room. There's a lavish lounge area with large white couches and a fireplace bigger than me, the enormous open-plan kitchen with navy blue cabinets and copper pans hanging from a rack in the ceiling. I remember how I used to want to live in there. I think I still might.

When we pad past a library adorned with wall-to-wall books, I imagine little Cameron and her encyclopedia set, but something strikes me straight away about the home – it's stark and modestly furnished with only a splash of abstract art.

"Are you a minimalist or what?" I ask Cameron. "There's barely anything here."

"Commitment-phobe?"

and squeeze my thighs together to stem the annoying throbbing that's happening, but it doesn't help one bit. All of this is so strange, seeing her as a woman years later.

For a few dangerous seconds, I imagine what my life would look like with Cameron in it. I see it in a series of flashes. Cameron squished in on the right side of my pokey bed, Cameron moving in the wrong direction and completely off-beat in my Zumba class, Cameron and I babysitting grumpy Arnold when Lexi's away competing in a triathlon -

"Don't you think, Chloe?" she asks, snapping me out of my dream.

Shit.

Honestly, I love it when she says my name. Something about the way her lips move gets me. Unfortunately, the rest of the conversation appears to be lost on me.

"Uh-huh, definitely," I reply, and Cameron gives me a bemused look that makes my cheeks flush.

Naturally, I'm very distracted by this newfound attraction. It's a powerful thing, feeling like someone understands you without having to explain. For the first time in a long time, I feel alive.

Unfortunately, my car isn't feeling nearly as rejuvenated, and about a mile from home, the car suddenly jerks, and we are thrown forward until it finally splutters to a stop on the country road.

CHAPTER TEN

Chloe

I'm so full of emotions on the drive home, I think I might burst.

Happy that I reconnected with my childhood friend, confused about an adult attraction, and oddly, terrified that all of these overwhelming emotions will soon come to an end when I leave.

Life felt different at the cottage.

Even though it was the same sun in the same sky, everything felt brighter. Perhaps it was the company or being far away from the constraints of the four walls I grew up in. Either way, it was just what I needed.

However, there are only so many times a girl can turn their underwear inside out or go commando, and returning home appears to be the sensible thing to do. We're quiet for most of the ride back but it's hard not to look at her. Discreetly, of course.

How can I not?

Head angled away, out of the corner of my eye. Very stealth-like. Spying in a different, adult way all these years later. Cameron is *gorgeous.* I groan inwardly too tired to talk, yet neither seems compelled to go to bed.

I steal a glance in Cameron's direction. Her eyes are closed, the light and shadow playing across her face. My stomach does an Olympic flip, and I sigh inwardly.

I'm in so much trouble.

Thinking Cameron has drifted to sleep, she surprises me when out of nowhere, she says, "You know, you really pulled off no eyebrows."

Obviously, I didn't really. But it's impossible not to beam at her conviction.

Because Cameron saw me, and still liked me.

All this time, she *actually* liked me.

believe you wanted to be friends with someone like me."

There's a lump in my throat. "Cameron, you're going to make me cry," I start to blubber.

She touches my arm gently. "Please don't."

It'd be so nice to just lever this moment open between us, but I don't quite have the nerve to do that either. Instead, I go with my standard coping mechanism, humor, and sniff. "It's okay. Probably just getting my period."

Cameron chuckles softly. "Oh, come here."

Despite her apparent aversion to public affection, she traps me in a hug, and I completely surrender to it, locked in place by her angles. Eventually, I wrap my own arms around her back, breathing in her signature scent.

"I'm sorry that for all these years, you thought I didn't care. Because I did," Cameron admits, her words resonating deep within me, and I can feel my heart beat against hers. "More than you know," she whispers into my hair.

The wind is still blowing on our faces, but I don't feel it anymore. I feel warm, safe, and like I matter. Something shifts between Cameron and me with that exchange; I'm just unsure as to what.

Later in the night, we find ourselves sprawled out on opposite ends of the couch, legs intertwined, heads nestled against the cushions. The cottage is silent around us, the floor lamps casting shadows. And we're

Chloe

I scoff even though my skin bristles with energy at being so close to her. Smiling, Cameron nudges me, and I nudge her back.

Sometime later, she turns to me and says, "Chloe... For what it's worth, I was also upset when we stopped hanging out. I really liked you. I didn't have many friends, got bullied a bit because I was weird and dorky. You asked me why I was smart. Well, while other kids were hanging with their friends, I made my way through an encyclopedia set in our library. Obviously, the children's edition. Hardly a member of Mensa."

Without wanting to, I blurt out, "So why didn't you come to my party?"

"What party? Your tenth birthday?"

"Uh-huh."

"You didn't invite me -" Cameron surveys my face. "Wait. You did?"

I nod, and see her brain tick over.

There's a flash of anger in her eyes, her voice tightening. "So, my mom."

Rather than respond, I go quiet, then look away.

After what feels like a million years, Cameron grabs hold of my arms. "Chloe, look at me." When I find the courage to meet her gaze, she says, "You know, even though we share DNA, we are not our parents. I'm not my mom, and neither are you. I never thought I was better than you. You probably won't believe me, but I always looked up to you. You were independent, passionate, and always spoke your mind. I couldn't heck knew what 119 times 84 was? Cameron did. She could always do mammoth sums in her head.

Being her friend felt like I knew a secret that nobody else did because she was special, and my life was richer for it.

Cameron smiles. "That's the first time anyone told me they liked my hair."

"Okay, I need to come clean. I didn't really like your hair." She had a humongous eighties-style perm. Is she kidding? "I just wanted to be your friend."

"What?... Fine. Well, I didn't like your shirt. I freaking hated The Muppets. So much singing and dancing. Miss Piggy always karate-ing Kermit -"

"Wait. You said -"

"I wanted you to like me."

"Oh my God. So, we both lied?"

I giggle. "What a pair of liars we are."

"Well, at least we had something in common." Cameron snorts a laugh, and I keep my eyes trained on her. "What?" she asks, patting down her hair. "I know it's a mess."

"Your haircut suits you. Side bangs, too. Since when did you get all trendy?"

"I'm trendy?"

"Uh-huh."

Cameron starts to walk, and her eyes hold mine. "Okay. Well, now I don't believe you. Track record and all."

My heart starts to race, blood pounding in my ears. When it gets too much, I pick up a knife and croak, "Want some cheesecake?"

Cameron smirks. "Sure."

At some point over dessert, her leg brushes mine, and I like even more that she doesn't pull it away. I take a slow breath at the sensation, trying to stay relaxed, but all of this feels like a continuation of what we started on the beach.

When Jenny politely kicks us out and closes the restaurant, we make our way back to the cottage under a dark, star-speckled sky.

Cameron nods her head over to the bickering couple from earlier on. They're making out on a sand dune.

"Oh, how romantic," I coo. "Seemed to have settled their differences."

She cringes, shaking her head. "Get a room." Then she turns to me and says, "Remember when we first met?"

"Uh-huh. We were standing by the fence. I said I like your hair. And you said I like your top," I say it out loud because, for some reason, it's important that Cameron knows that I really *do* remember.

Obviously, not vividly. I can't remember much after that. Cameron was always the one who remembered details because she has a brain the size of Jupiter. I liked that she was smart. She knew the names of bones, stars, and all things wondrous. And who the usually some woman there that she's planted. So, if she's got anything with organizing the event, I try to avoid it."

"But you date, right?" I squirm in my seat. "Like that woman in the bar?"

Cameron ladles some more seafood stew into her bowl. "Oh, that was a business deal."

I narrow my eyes. "Uh-huh."

"Occasionally, lines are crossed, but not that time."

"She was stunning."

"Not my type."

For a moment, we just look at each other and every part of my body is doing a cartwheel. When I don't say anything, Cameron dabs her lips with the napkin. "Obviously, it wasn't a hot and heavy date like you and Max."

My eyes go wide. "*Obviously*. I'm surprised we didn't rip each other's clothes off at the bar."

"Not interested?"

"Not my type."

Cameron pauses. "Touché."

Then we're back to staring. When her tongue flicks her lower lip, I'm taken down a very dark path with thoughts of things I'd like her to do with that mouth.

Oh my fucking God. I don't know what is happening, but something definitely *is*.

She raises an eyebrow. "You want some shrimp?"

"Nice deflection. And yes." I take the dish from her hands and serve myself.

Cameron laughs. "Okay. My last relationship was two years ago with Bec, an engineer from Charleston. She wanted commitment, to move in together."

I gasp. "How awful!"

She gives a small shrug and moves an empty shell to one side, then picks up another oyster. "I didn't want to give her false hope."

My heart sinks a little at this revelation. Cameron *really* doesn't want a happily ever after. Her phone pings, and she says, "Sorry, it's just my assistant, Bianca, but it can wait."

"Assistant?"

"Yes."

"Good looking?"

Cameron rolls her eyes as I attack the seafood stew. "Purely professional these days. Work is busier than ever," she says. "How's the stew?"

"Oh my God. Amazing. So good." I half-moan, and Cameron grins, spooning the spicy tomato mix into her mouth. "Oh, wow. It *is* good," she groans.

Meanwhile, I'm still joining the dots about the assistant. Hmm.

Thankfully, Cameron continues to talk before I can get inside my own head. "You know, my mom meddles too. Loves to send me to these charity events because she knows that I like to support them, but there's

"So, what's your story?" I ask because I'm secretly dying inside to find out.

"Well -"

"Here, we go," says a female voice, cutting Cameron off, and I glance up to a middle-aged woman with wispy coppery wire hair and a harassed expression.

It's Jenny, the server slash cook, and she's holding a ridiculous amount of food. Seeing that we need another table, she yanks one over and wipes her hands down her front. "Enjoy, ladies."

"Thank you. I don't think we ordered enough," says Cameron.

I nod. "Yes, definitely going to starve."

Jenny's face becomes stricken, but she forces a smile. I think she's terrified that we're going to order more and quickly scuttles away.

Cameron and I share a glance. Then together we burst out laughing.

"She couldn't wait to get out of here," Cameron whispers behind her hand.

"I don't think we'll see her again," I reply, and when I peer over Cameron's shoulder, I see Jenny put a sign on the counter. "Oh my God. She just closed the kitchen."

We share another chuckle.

Cameron hands me the platter of oysters. "Thanks," I say, sliding a couple onto my plate. "Now, you were saying about your last relationship?"

Cameron relays the order at the counter and returns with two glasses of sparkling prosecco, handing one to me.

"Thank you." I lift my glass, and Cameron smiles, raising her own in a toast. "Cheers to Alice's cottage by the sea, boat ride adventures, and late-night shenanigans."

I laugh as we both take a sip, the dark waves crashing behind us. "It hasn't been that awful spending time together," I say.

Cameron twirls the stem of her wine glass and then studies me. "Is that a question or statement?"

I shrug. Maybe both.

Her gaze fixes on mine. "No. It hasn't been awful," she says warmly, and I must be imagining it, but is there a different light in her eyes?

Soon, we are lost in conversation. Obviously, wine starts working its way through my veins because any filter I had is quickly disappearing. I even talk about my ex, Erin, and how the relationship slowly crumbled. I also tell her how Lexi saw her smooching her boss in a parking lot. Cameron gasps and rolls her eyes in all the right places.

I take another sip from my glass. "You know, when I confronted her, she denied it at first and then said I'd become boring."

Cameron widens her eyes. "Chloe. You are anything but boring... She sounds like an idiot," she says loyally, and it makes me genuinely smile.

I give up.

ME: *I'm not remotely attracted to her.*

LEXI: *I didn't ask you if you were.*

LEXI: *:) :) I want to know all about your torrid love affair!*

I scoff out loud. She sure has a wild imagination.

The sound of footsteps suddenly has my head jerking upward, and I stash my phone in my bag. Cameron is walking over, but she's not scanning me up and down, she's holding my gaze, and there's another backflip in my stomach. Ugh. This is becoming annoying.

Cameron points to a sign, then hands me a menu. "Looks like they're for sale. Appears Jenny, the server, is also the cook."

I laugh. "Really?"

She nods and takes a seat.

"Guess that would explain the no service," I say.

"Mmm. As much as I want to make her life easy, I'm kind of hungry," Cameron says, browsing the menu.

"Me too." I cover my grumbling stomach with one hand.

We settle on a dozen natural oysters, grilled shrimp skewers, and an Italian seafood stew. Oh, and a slice of freshly baked blueberry cheesecake to share because who knows when we'll get service again.

Her eyes gleam like sapphires. "Yeah. What, like catch your own seafood?"

I roll my eyes. Cameron grins.

She's quite funny, I'm realizing. Under that grumpy demeanor, she is *actually* funny.

Cameron pushes out of her seat. "I'll get some menus, shall I?"

I smile, and my phone buzzes.

LEXI: *Have you two killed each other yet?*

ME: *Alas, not yet. But there is still time.*

I send the photo of us on the beach. Not the spooky ghost one.

LEXI: *Okay, but WHAT THE FUCK ARE YOU WEARING?*

I don't answer. Three dots drum across the bottom of the screen.

LEXI: *Underneath her fancy dress, she's still hot. If I was single, I so would. Look at those eyes!*

ME: *You would not!*

LEXI: *Yes, I would!*

ME: *No –*

At the far end, a wooden jetty protrudes into the sea, hosting a quaint restaurant, and we make our way over. A plastic grapevine hangs across the front counter, and the restaurant is empty, save for a lone couple seated by the window, engaged in curt, hostile whispers.

Cameron throws me a wide-eyed look, motioning outside. I smile because I don't want to be anywhere near that couple either. With no server in sight, we sit at a table under strands of globe lights. Something about the setting feels perfect. Even the sunset is putting on a show, igniting the sky in a powdery pink and bathing us in a rosy light.

Cameron leans forward. "You know when I booked a table -"

"Booked a table?" I begin to giggle. "What to beat the hordes of people?"

Cameron snorts and whispers, "The girl had to check the reservation list and said she could *squeeze* us in."

I collapse into laughter, and Cameron starts chuckling. The not-so-happy couple glances around at us, but this just seems to make it funnier, especially when Cameron's knee hits the table and the cutlery starts to shudder.

When we finally compose ourselves, Cameron swivels her head. "But seriously, does anyone actually work here?"

I shrug. "Might be self-service."

She places her phone down, stretches her arms above her head, gazing vacantly ahead, and her muscles flex in her arms. My own less muscular gut flexes in return as I stare at her. Oh God, and even the way she flicks her hair over her shoulder. I groan inwardly because, suddenly, every movement screams goddess. She looks... what's the word?

Hot, screams my brain. Also gorgeous, dreamy -

Cameron glances over – oh shit – and I move my eyes down to my phone as heat flushes across my cheeks.

Shut up, Chloe. Once you start down that path...

My usually rational brain is being corrupted by my groin area, and the back of my neck starts to sweat. I try to reign in my hormones, but it's not easy.

Either way, the afternoon is a revelation, and it feels amazing to do not much at all. We might even relax and have fun. Playing UNO with a set of battered cards and then several rounds of chess. We demolish the Italian panettone and don't even keep tabs on who's winning. I just feel a strange contentment, like I'm exactly where I need to be.

In the evening, it's almost annoying that we have to leave, but we are both hungry, and the weather app says we are done with the rain, so we decide to venture into town. Because we don't want to draw attention to ourselves, we settle into our clothes from the first night. We also choose to walk via the beach to avoid the bar, Bobbie, and Roger the rabbit.

over our ridiculous photos. There's even one of my yellow hat drifting out to sea.

"You were taking photos while I was rowing?!" I squawk.

"Well, I wasn't very good at rowing. I had to fill in my time somehow."

I punch her in the thigh, and she grins.

We assess and debate whether we should delete each one. She doesn't like her lazy right eye, while I'm convinced that I look like an alien in ninety percent of them. Then she stops at one, where my legs are kicked out on the bicycle, and she's sitting in the basket, knees banging into her chin, and Roger Rabbit's head is popping out of her top.

"This one is my favorite," she announces and flashes me a smile that could turn women inside out.

Not me, I'm immune to her charms. I wriggle uncomfortably in my seat, then look closer at the photo. "Cameron, my cheeks are puffed out. Your eyes are practically closed. Our hair is freaking everywhere... Oh my God. Half your hair is in my mouth! It's awful!"

"Really? I don't see it that way. We just look happy." Cameron smiles at the photo and presses a button on her phone. "Just sent it to you."

And not for the first time today, I'm unable to take my eyes off her. I can't help it. Seeing her so relaxed, happy even, stirs something inside me.

an attractive female has muddled my senses. Would this happen amid a New York snowstorm in cold, dark January? Absolutely not.

Since I can't find a hairdryer, I let my hair dry naturally, soft waves framing my face. Slipping into some sweatpants and a floppy white tee, I emerge from a cloud of steam, only to find Cameron lounging on the couch, annoyingly composed with her hair swept up in a loose ponytail. She's wearing a heather grey t-shirt and hiking up the cuffs of her extra large Batman pajama pants.

I pad across the carpet and settle on the couch, cross-legged.

A moment later, Cameron leans across and sniffs me. "You don't smell like wet dog anymore."

I push her away, growing even more frustrated. "Great. And you don't look like one," I scoff.

This makes Cameron smirk, and I roll my eyes. Next thing I know, she's examining my rash, and I reciprocate by inspecting the wounds on her heels. Unfortunately, her fresh scent and the forced proximity pull me straight out of my safe space and right back into her world.

As rain continues to fall in sheets outside, she grabs her phone, and I study her. It's impossible to get a measure of Cameron. She's at turns standoffish, witty, stern, cheeky. How can she be so many things? She starts flicking through her camera reel, and I shuffle closer. Soon, we're choking with laughter and moaning

Shaking off my reaction, I follow her silly mountaineering boots and leave everything that had and hadn't happened far behind. Soon, a squally wind kicks in, whipping hair around my face. Raindrops start falling like stabby pins on my skin, and it begins to pour. Like really pour.

Grinning, Cameron pulls out an umbrella. Of course, she does. The second she pops it open, it blows inside out. She runs left and then right, with the unruly thing threatening to throw her into the woods.

"Oh my God, Cameron!" I scream when she nearly impales me.

Seems the universe is on my side for once because a second later, the ferocious wind rips the umbrella from her grasp, launching it into the stratosphere. Rain pounds the ground like bullets, and we're soaked to the bone in seconds. Latching onto her backpack, I yank her home. Cameron looks like a drowned rat, and because I'm honest - I tell her that.

Once liberated from our hateful footwear, we both go to shower. Separately, of course.

Squeezing an obscene amount of shampoo into my hands, I lather up my hair as I try to wash away all my unwelcome thoughts. How her eyes lit up at the boat, and perhaps even the tiniest chance that she felt something too?

Frustrated, I place my palms on the glass and try to steady myself before I see her again. I tell myself it's nothing, even though it feels like something. Obviously, the ocean air and being within a few feet of our run of misfortune, I really hope it's rain. I glance skyward to see dark clouds forming, and it starts to sprinkle.

Cameron turns to me with raindrops scattered on her face, and I have the sudden urge to kiss them away. I wonder if she tastes like she smells. Like coconut and flowers.

"Not if you can't find them," she teases.

"I know all your hiding places, Cameron."

Her blue eyes seem to glow. "Even after all this time?"

As if I would ever forget, but I don't say that. "Mmhmm," I reply.

Then, there's a moment when we both realize something is happening. An unsettling feeling buzzing in my frozen toes. Blinking away, I start staring at the foaming waves crashing into the sand, and Cameron fixates on a flock of seagulls squabbling over some skeletal remains.

After a short silence, Cameron exhales loudly, and I swivel around. "Look, Chloe..." she says, her dark hair blown about by the wind. "I know you live for high-octane adventure, but do you mind if we do absolutely nothing for the rest of the weekend? Twenty-four hours in, and I'm worn out."

I burst out a laugh. "More than fine by me."

Cameron helps me to my feet, her fingers tightly curled around mine, and I feel an unwanted flutter in the pit of my stomach. I'm not into her. Hang on, am I?

"Of course not. But sinking would be terrifying."

"Yes, especially if you get attacked by a man-eating jellyfish," I add, catching her eye.

We both collapse into giggles.

After a shaky start, I think I'm starting to enjoy her company.

"Let's take a photo," she says.

I did say *think*.

"No photos for me," I reply, waving her off. I've just fallen head-first into sub-zero temperatures. It can't be a good look.

Predictably, she ignores me and whips out her phone. "One, two..."

"Cam -" I protest, but a flash blinds me mid-squawk, capturing us in a ghostly blur. Of course, I'm the one with my mouth hanging open. "You so did that on purpose!" I snap.

"I did not! Come on, one more," she insists, then whispers out the side of her mouth, "And don't you dare smile."

My God, she is *so* very annoying.

"I mean it. Not even a hint of one." Cameron nudges my shoulder.

Naturally, a smile tugs at my lips, and when she starts to laugh, I give a tiny gurgle.

There's an instantaneous click.

"Just so you know, I'm going to burn any copies," I affirm, and something wet lands on my cheek. Given

"What's wrong?" Cameron asks beside me.

I limp onto the beach, groaning, noting a small red rash on my ankle. "Something bit me."

"Probably a sandfly," she replies nonchalantly.

Is she kidding me?

I scoff at her. "More like a jellyfish."

Cameron glances around. "I don't see one."

"Ow! It really hurts."

Cameron bends over and stares at it, then says, "Mmm. Looks like a sandfly bite to me." She stands, brushing sand from her hands. "But... if it is a jellyfish sting, apparently peeing on it neutralizes toxins -"

"Are you out of your mind?" I snap.

"I'm not offering!"

I slap her away. "Good because I'd pee on it if I was desperate -"

"But that's physically impossible. The sting's on the wrong side -"

"Okay, David."

Cameron laughs. "Well, painkillers should help."

We fall back onto the sand, feet sinking in yellow. I swipe wet tendrils of hair away from my face. "At this rate, we'll run out of painkillers."

When our eyes meet, we start to laugh.

Then there's a lull before Cameron says seriously, "Can you imagine how terrifying it would've been on the Titanic?"

"Cameron! Hardly the Titanic," I almost snort.

And that's when everything goes to hell.

I gasp, my mind working very quickly. "Start paddling with your hands before we get lost out to sea."

Cameron rushes over, and I push her back. "Not on the same side as me. We'll just turn in a circle!"

"Oh my God! We are going to die!" Cameron announces optimistically and plunges half her body into the ocean.

I close my eyes, channel my inner Olympian, and paddle so hard my arms feel like they are going to disconnect from my torso. After a minute of frenetic paddling, we bounce off something hard.

"Huh?" I peel my eyes open.

"Rocks!" Cameron confirms.

Oh, thank God for that. We've made it to the other side.

"Abandon ship!" Cameron declares, leaping into the icy water as though it's a warm bath, and there's an almighty splash.

I take her lead, quelling a shriek, and scrabble into the water almost head first. There's some frantic thrashing before a powerful grip yanks me to the surface.

A voice cuts through my cough. "You okay?"

I nod, teeth chattering, then latch onto the rope, and Cameron helps me heave the boat to shore.

Just as water foams around our ankles, I feel it. It's like I've been branded with an iron. "Oh, shit!"

working the right side with short, slow strokes, but almost immediately, we start pulling to Cameron's side. "Keep rowing," I instruct.

"I am."

"Are you?" I ask because we are most certainly turning.

No response.

"God. This is harder than I expected," I huff with a sideways glance, noting that we're already twenty feet from the shoreline. Why is Cameron so quiet? "What's wrong?" I ask over my shoulder.

"Um, Chloe… Why are my feet suddenly covered in water?"

"What -" I spin around to find Cameron staring at her legs.

Oh, God.

"Just row faster, Cameron. We're starting to drift," I snap, just as a furious gust of wind blows my yellow cap into the water. A second later, it's gobbled up by a white-crested wave, and we collide with a buoy.

I paddle as hard as I can with no result. Why are we going in the wrong direction? A few minutes later, I swing around to Cameron, but she appears to have missed it entirely because now she's staring at her oar.

"Cameron… Why are you just sitting there and doing nothing? Row!"

"I think my oar has a hole in it too." Her head swivels left, then right. "God, where did all these waves suddenly come from?"

It's absolutely freezing, and I know I don't have long until Cameron changes her mind.

Wading into the frigid water, I steady the boat. "Okay. So, jump in," I tell her, and she hoists herself up over the edge, falling forward with her legs in the air like a basted chicken.

"Why does it always look easier in the movies..." she mutters under her breath.

Giggling to myself, I push the boat off the sandy edge and then scrabble over the splinter-riddled exterior but end up straddling the side. So, *so* much worse than a bicycle. Cameron yanks me over, but her hand is smeared in so much sunscreen that she loses grip, and my face practically lands in her crotch.

Shit.

I leap back like a scalded cat, refusing to look her in the eye, and quickly busy myself with an oar. "Here." I shove it into her hand and stumble to a seat right up the front, deliberately facing away from her.

For a moment, we just bob in waves, soft spray on our faces. I tilt my head back to the sky, staring at a tiny puff of a cloud. Taking a deep breath of ocean air, I let it fill my lungs and focus on the push-pull of the sea, the glorious warmth of the sunshine.

"Mmm. Five bucks, it sinks," says Cameron.

Well, that didn't take long.

I roll my eyes and sigh. When a gust of wind jolts us forward, I figure it's time to get moving and pick up my oar. "Let's get going. You paddle on the left," I say,

I shake my head. "Honestly, we're the worst dressed by the ocean."

"On the planet," Cameron replies with a straight face.

Then we double over laughing, and Cameron topples to the ground, trying to remove her monstrous boots, which sets us off again. She is still giggling as she inspects her heels, which are red raw.

I ease the strap of my flip-flop against my skin and wince. The plastic rubbing blisters on the tops of my feet. Appears we have both suffered to get here.

While Cameron sprays every inch of her skin with sunscreen, I kick off my flip-flops and spot a small marine-blue wooden boat on the shore. She hands me the can, and I spray some sunscreen on my fingers, then apply it to my nose.

"Fancy a leisurely paddle across to the rocks on the other side?" I ask more in jest than anything and am surprised by an almost childlike look of excitement on Cameron's face.

She flashes me a grin. "Why not? I've always been a water baby."

Somehow, I doubt it.

Regardless, I shrug off my disbelief and wander to the boat, curling my toes into the sand with every step. The last vestiges of a wave wash over our feet, and we gasp loudly, sharing a smile. My nipples ping in protest because medieval armor couldn't hide how cold I am.

over a swath of glittering blue ocean. The beach, a narrow gold ribbon shaped like a horseshoe.

I step out from behind her, nodding as a strong sea breeze threatens to lift my hat. "Wow, indeed."

We stand there for a while, soaking up the vastness of the sky. It's so quiet that I can just hear the roll of the water. Cameron spreads her hands wide, letting the wind buffet her, and turns around a few times amongst the shaggy beach grass.

"Now, this I love," she beams, then cocks her head over the shoulder. "Come on!"

I grin as wide as the horizon, taking in deep, salty breaths, my flip-flops sinking beneath the warm, golden sand. We settle on a spot in the middle of the beach, and Cameron dumps her bag, grunting at its weight.

"Ow... I can't understand why it's so heavy," she says, rubbing her shoulders, and I roll my eyes.

Sweeping a glance over the beach, I notice a handful of people milling around. A loved-up teenage couple sitting on a towel, laughing and gazing out to the ocean. An elderly man in a red beret walking a child with strawberry-blonde pigtails and a tabby cat. A lone fisherman casting his line from the rocks off to the right.

And then there's us.

Two women that look like they should be anywhere but here.

there like a wobbly flamingo on one leg. When I go to grab it, she pulls it away.

"Give it here," I huff.

"I am not David Attenborough."

"You are too!" I lunge again, almost toppling over, and Cameron jumps back.

"Cameron..." I place my hands on my hips, but she has that infuriating look of smugness, and I flashback to our childhood, where she stubbornly refused to let me out of her treehouse until I gave her ten smarties. Not nine, not eight, but ten. The standoff lasted for three hours. No way I'm winning this battle. "Okay, fine. You're not," I concede.

Cameron grins, then holds out her hand. I snatch the flip-flop from her grasp and slip it on. "You used to do the same thing to me as a kid. Glad to see you haven't grown out of it."

I don't need to look at her to know she is positively beaming.

The trail begins to steepen over a ridge, the ground increasingly uneven, and I'm tripping left and right, pebbles sliding beneath my feet.

"You dare to mock my mountaineering boots," Cameron snips as her long legs power around a bend. I curse, rushing forward only to faceplant into her safari suit. She is the most infuriating person I have ever -

"Wow," Cameron says, and I peer around her body, blinking into the brightness. The sun is a disc of brass

Cameron gives a little snort and then stands, rubbing her forehead. "I don't know, but it's hard to take your fashionista advice seriously. Did you even look in the mirror? You look like a toddler version of Bob the Builder after a year of donuts. And a yellow hat too -" she begins, but I hit her with the closest thing I can find, a crochet cushion with teal blue bobbles.

"Ow," she grunts.

"Says David Attenborough," I snip. "Ready to hit the jungle, are we? Why don't you pull your taupe socks up to your knees?"

"Huh?" Cameron reaches down for her socks. "Oh, good idea."

"Oh my God, Cameron. I'm joking!"

She pulls her socks halfway up her calves. Looks like it's as far as they'll stretch. "I'm not. Bugs like water, and I checked the can of bug spray. It's running low," she says in a serious tone.

I just stare at her in bewilderment. The mind boggles at what she would take on a real hike. No less than ten sherpas to lug around unnecessary crap, I surmise. Fourteen painful minutes later, after watching Cameron pack and re-pack a backpack several times, we hit the road, or the dirt track, at least. Birds sing overhead as we wind through a small, forested area while the sun shines weakly through the trees.

Unfortunately, this lack of sun means that the track soon becomes soft and muddy. My footwear does me no favors, and I lose a flip-flop. Cameron immediately scoops it up in her hand while I stand holding a tan, wide-brimmed hat. "What do you mean?"

"You look like you're going on a cross-country expedition to a faraway land.... Aren't we just going to the beach?"

She waves the thought away with her hat. "Yes, but it's sunny, which might burn my fair skin. Also, I don't think you know the difficult range of clothing I had to work with."

I desperately have to contain my giggle but almost lose it when I clock her footwear. "You're wearing hiking boots!" I gurgle.

"Well, it was boots or purple Crocs, and I flat-out refuse to wear them, Chloe," she vents as though that's the ultimate fashion faux-pax, and I just stare at her incredulously. She then points out the window. "Anyway, it's rocky out there and quite a steep incline. Need something that's going to grip."

"Uh-huh... Exactly like scaling Mount Everest."

Cameron sighs loudly.

A second later, she nods at my green flip-flops, two sizes too large. The front ends savaged by Roger the rabbit. "That there is a disaster waiting to happen." To my surprise, she then starts to laugh. It's not at all subtle. It goes on and on, and irritation begins to surge within me like wildfire.

"Why are you – ... Okay, whatever..." I huff, but the moment she folds over, shaking with laughter, I snap loudly, "What?!"

Then we start to giggle stupidly. Like the type you're only capable of when you're hungover. It's a cross between a groan and uncontrolled laughter.

"Ah, that wasn't even remotely funny," I sigh.

"I know," Cameron replies, wiping suds from her hands. She hangs up the dishtowel. "So, what now?"

"Well, let's get changed. I'll meet you back out here," I say, leaping to my feet, and rush off to find the beachiest clothes I can.

There aren't many options, but I snatch the only hat I see off the rack and slip into an oversized shirt so big that when I stuff it inside my denim overalls, it looks like a small spare tire around my waist.

Ugh. Not ideal.

No doubt Cameron will show me up with some sassy outfit. Unbidden, an image of surf-swept Cameron flipping her long, dark, wavy locks comes into my mind like an unnecessary episode of Baywatch. Go away, I tell it.

Then I open my door, only to have Cameron emerge from the other room at the same time. We both just stand there with a similar look of alarm on our faces.

The image of Baywatch Cameron banishes so abruptly it's like it never existed. "What the hell are you wearing!" I shriek.

Cameron looks down at her khaki long-sleeved button-up shirt and matching baggy cargo shorts. She's

I snort. "Thank God for that. Here." I hand her a plate and some cutlery, and settle next to her on the floor, leaning against the couch.

"Thanks. It smells amazing. A healthy balance?"

I smile back at her grouchy ass. "Something like that. So, what do you want to do today?"

"Not go back to the bar," Cameron replies tersely, stabbing at the bacon.

I roll my eyes, swallowing a mouthful of food. "I didn't ask what you *don't* want to do today, Cameron. Obviously, we're steering clear of that place for eternity."

Cameron gives a grunt, and it's hard not to laugh.

When we finish our breakfast, Cameron refuses my offer to help clean up. Not that I mind, I just fling myself onto the couch instead while she fills the sink with hot water.

"I know! Why don't we go to the beach?" I suggest in an upbeat tone.

"Too many bugs."

"I'll bring the bug spray."

"Too sandy."

"I'll bring a towel?"

"Water will be freezing."

"Oh my God! Cameron!" I clap my hand over my face. "What do you expect? It's the fucking ocean."

CHAPTER NINE

Chloe

"I can't believe you threw the rabbit under the proverbial bus." I wheel around from the fry pan, laughing.

"I wasn't going to say my ass broke it, was I?" Cameron is desperately scrolling through eBay on her phone. She groans, "And I can't believe I can't find a wicker basket that will be delivered out here. Pick up only... Oh wait, I found one." A loud gasp escapes her. "One-hundred-dollar delivery for a twenty-dollar basket! Bobbie didn't even pay for hers. Maybe I should go to a thrift store."

"You should be more careful with your ass next time," I say with mock seriousness, but when I look up, Cameron is giving me a death glare, and I quickly avert my eyes back to the bacon and eggs I'm cooking in the pan.

"Really?" Cameron huffs sometime later, and I switch off the stove, then add enough kale and avocado to make a dietitian proud. She throws her phone away. "There. One stupid basket ordered."

Bobbie's face instantly morphs into a grin. "Oh, that's kind of you. I found that one sitting by the side of the road. Didn't cost me a dime. Ha!"

On that note, I quickly say goodbye and spin Cameron around by the waist before she can open her big, lying mouth.

At least no one can accuse us of not knowing how to make a first impression.

Also, some wine before, but hardly going to chime in now.

Farmer Bill decides to impart his wisdom. "Kids these days have no stamina."

Cameron and I nod in unison.

Bobbie sighs. "Probably my mistake opening up the bar for you girls. But, well, it was your birthday, Chloe, and your odd dance routines seemed to attract a handful of extra customers, so I thought it was the least I could do." Her gaze drifts across to the bike. "Thanks for returning my wheels." She pauses and frowns. "Hang on. Why does my basket look like it exploded?"

I half-laugh. "Oh. Um -"

"Roger!" Cameron blurts out.

"Roger?" Bobbie repeats to her.

"I mean, he had a bit of a nibble. We didn't have any snacks or hay, so you know... understandable," says Cameron, sounding strangled.

Hay?!

God, I cannot risk looking at her right now for fear of laughing.

Bobbie narrows her eyes. "How peculiar.... Well, I suppose he was with strangers."

Cameron claps in an apparent need to end this conversation and hands Roger to Bobbie. "Anyway, I've ordered a shiny new wicker basket on eBay, and it'll be delivered this week."

Bobbie then looks at me. "And what with you being a professional animal acting coach to the stars, I was expecting Roger to spit out some French. Kylie Kardashian being your number one client and all?"

I almost choke. "Me?"

Out of the corner of my eye, I see Cameron's mouth twitch, but her face stays grave.

"Yes, well, that was a few years ago," I mutter quietly. Unfortunately, my mouth keeps moving. It's been a problem my whole life. "Had to move away from Malibu when the paparazzi became too much. I was starting to develop a severe case of agoraphobia."

Cameron coughs to cover up a laugh.

Then there's an unbearable silence, eyes flicking between us.

Bobbie bursts out laughing. "I just asked if you could look after him for the night because I had to lock up early and go on my date with Bill. He just bought the vacant block next to Alice's cottage on eBay. I've been showing him around." Bobbie winks. eBay? Oh my God, is that even legal? Probably not. "He's going to be a farmer!" she adds.

"Congratulations, Bill," I mutter, and Bill gives me a glazed smile. No guesses for what he'll be growing.

Cameron mumbles congratulations, too.

"As for you lot..." Bobbie's eyes dart to Cameron, then me, and I audibly gulp down. "Oh, God. You only had a couple of shots and a tipple of tequila."

"Oh, hello, you two," says a voice, startling us, and Cameron almost launches Roger into the cosmos.

Bobbie steps out from behind a large oak tree through a cloud of smoke, and she stubs something out with her boot. Her eyes big and mildly bloodshot, framed by blue eyeshadow. She's not alone. A skinny, tattooed man of indeterminate age with an explosion of facial hair and sideburns like steel wool skulking behind her.

"Hi, Bobbie," I murmur through my cardboard cut-out smile, and Cameron lifts her hand in a stiff wave.

"Wasn't sure if you would show your faces again." Bobbie folds her arms, and they stop in front of us.

I gulp down, fiddling with the strap of my satchel. "Ha-ha. And why wouldn't we do that?"

Cameron and I share a nervous glance.

"All that carry-on last night. Well, did you teach Roger, my rabbit, any tricks?"

We just look down at Roger, who twitches his nose.

Bobbie points to Cameron. "All those long hours working as a ringmaster in the circus. You said you could train him in next to no time. Leaping through hoops of fire. Using aerial silks to perform a candy cane roll-up. Thought it was a bit far-fetched, but you were so convincing."

Cameron looks baffled, and I start to chuckle. Who knew Cameron had such a creative flair? I might even feel a bit proud.

Cameron picks up his paw, waving back, and says out of the side of her mouth, "Oh my God. Everyone knows him. Did we steal the town mascot?"

"Is that even a thing?" I scratch my head, feeling like we've tumbled into an alternate universe.

"How would I know!" Cameron snaps.

"God. Well, I'm going into the store," I huff and then rest my bike against the wall. "I'll be back in a minute."

"You can't leave me here!"

"You can't come in!" I hiss back. "I won't be long, I swear."

Turning, I push through the door and race through the aisles. True to my word, I'm so fast that I'm actually being watched by the rotund store owner. She definitely thinks I'm shoplifting. No, lady, I just need to get back to my stolen rabbit.

"Quick," says Cameron as soon as I exit the shop. She spins around and starts walking. "Let's get out of here. Some little kid came running over and asked why I had Roger?"

"What?" I rush after her with the bike, hooking my shopping bag over the handlebar. "What did you say?"

"I said his name was Victor, and he was mine."

I stop dead. "Why did you lie!"

"I don't want to get in trouble."

"So, you thought, *oh, well, I better lie some more -*"

Just shut up.

I pull and pull, and finally, I yank it free, then stuff it in my satchel.

"Why couldn't you do that at home?" she grumbles, and I want to throttle her as I emerge from behind the bush.

"I wasn't freaking peeing!" I say in a hushed, angry tone, throwing her an annoyed look. I get one in return. Moments later, I pause as we approach the main street. "Now, the plan is to casually stroll into town and not bring attention to ourselves."

"Oh, real Ocean Eleven's stuff," Cameron whistles.

I scoff.

"No one is going to notice this rabbit. Completely normal," Cameron says, her voice dripping with sarcasm.

I stop, turning to face her. She is beginning to annoy the shit out of me. "Would you just shush -"

"Oh, hello, Roger!"

We spin around to an old man whizzing by on an electric four-wheeler with a fluoro orange flag.

The rabbit's ears prick up.

Roger? Roger Rabbit, I guess it makes sense.

Five seconds later, while we are still standing there reeling from the unwanted attention, a woman in a purple bowler hat waves from across the street. "Hi, Roger! Nice outside today, isn't it?"

Is she seriously asking the rabbit a question?

"Completely fine."

There is *no* way.

Given our state of dishevelment, it takes longer than necessary to get ready, and when I scrutinize my appearance in the mirror, I am not hit by a bombshell but rather the confirmation that we both look as crap as we feel.

"Cameron? Come on, hurry up!" I shout and stumble outside with the bike.

Despite the lurch of my stomach, I'm buoyed by the blue sky that's sharp with sunshine. I smile because it's the kind of day for picnicking and romance -

"I can't see," whines Cameron, shielding her face with one hand.

Of course, she needs to complain.

I roll my eyes. "Just don't drop the rabbit." I do a double-take when I see him chewing on a lone flip-flop.

"What? He wouldn't leave without it."

Okay. Whatever.

We start walking along the dirt road in silence. Interestingly, I spot my shoe when the metallic shimmer from the silver buckle gives it away and lay down the bike, running over behind a small thorny bush.

"What are you doing?" Cameron squints into the sun, and I try to remove my shoe, but it's stuck. "Are you like peeing!" she suddenly yells for all the universe to hear.

Oh my God.

The rabbit looks at Cameron like she is mad and smartly continues to hop away from her before darting under the couch.

"Very original," I mutter and get on my knees, too. I latch onto a flip-flop, waving it at the edge of the couch, hoping to draw out the rabbit.

"Funny. I start hanging with you and begin committing crimes." Cameron shoves her hand under the couch. "Ow! It just bit me!"

"Oh, shut up. I recall someone yelling, *Faster, faster*! as we flew down the hill." I inhale sharply as a memory flashes in my mind. "You had the rabbit tucked in your shirt!"

"Oh my God," Cameron grimaces. "Just when I thought this story couldn't get any worse."

I rub my forehead and give an exhausted laugh. "Look, we need to return bunny and bike to their rightful owners."

Cameron chews the side of her mouth. "But to who?"

A flash of genius strikes me. "Let's mosey down to the bar. Maybe someone will talk to us and fill in the blanks. You know, let's just see what happens."

"See what happens? We'll get arrested!"

I brush off Cameron's paranoia and stand up with a wobble.

Her lips curve into a smirk. "Hungover?"

"No," I lie, even though my mouth feels like a gorilla's armpit. "You?"

Trust her to be logical.

I know it was a fun night, a messy night, and I vaguely recall parking *something*. Little did I know it was a bike. "Wait. I'm starting to remember," I say, slowly kneading my temples.

"What!" Cameron asks impatiently.

"Give it a minute!" I reply, still working my fingers in a circular motion. A vision slowly comes to me. Bar, shots, Bobbie, dancing, laughing like hyenas, swinging around lampposts, riding a bicycle with no hands, wind in my hair, losing my shoe on the road, Cameron squealing –

I stop mid-thought. "Cameron! You were sitting in the basket!"

"Me? I would never, ever -"

We glance at the basket and immediately register broken straw.

I nod. "Oh, you did! We did!"

Cameron blinks, then yells, "My ass did that!"

I nod again.

She cringes. "We went to the bar."

All of a sudden, I gasp, "We took the bike and rabbit!" I sound more shrill than intended.

"We stole them?!" Cameron slaps her hand over her mouth.

"Borrowed sounds better."

"Oh shit..." Cameron drops to the floor. "Here, bunny, bunny."

I sit bolt upright, heart hammering, and gasp loudly. Cameron just standing there like the horrible ogre she is at - I glance at the wall clock - seven in the morning. Her hair is all over the place, and she's sporting pink eyeballs and grey skin.

"God, Cameron!" I shriek, latching onto the bedspread as I sway. My head begins to thump with what appears to be a very, very bad hangover, and I wince. "Why can't you enter like a normal person? You almost gave me a heart attack."

"Chloe," she repeats. "Why the fuck is there a rabbit hopping around the living room?... It's wearing a beaded necklace!"

"What??" Okay, now she's got my attention. Leaping from the bed, I rush after her. I have to rub my eyes. Twice. "What on earth -"

We both just stare at it.

There is indeed a rabbit in our living room. A fat, tawny-colored one with a twitching nose and rainbow necklace. It's also chewing some military-green flip-flops. I pray to the hangover gods that there's some reasonable explanation behind all this.

Cameron turns and points to the kitchen. "Is it somehow linked to the bicycle leaning against the stove?"

"Bi -" My head snaps around. "Cameron... What the hell is going on?"

She throws her hands up in the air. "I don't know. That's why I'm asking you."

Meanwhile, Cameron spins me in and out and then dips me, almost dropping me to a near-certain concussion, but catches me inches from the floor. I immediately yelp. This gives way to mutual snorting and then ridiculous laughter. We are laughing so hard that we do indeed hit the floor, and I don't know how long we stay like this.

Because after this, things become a little hazy.

Sometime in the morning, I tiptoe out into the kitchen in bare feet to get some water when I see a body lifting from the couch underneath a blanket, like the dead rising from their grave.

I startle, flying into the wall.

It's Cameron.

Her eyes are shut. I don't think she's awake. Suddenly, she makes a noise like some rabid wildebeest and slams down into the cushions.

"Jesus. Back to sleep," I mutter more to myself than her and quickly scull a glass of water, then pad to my room. I collapse back onto my bedspread covered in orange flowers like a lazy starfish and immediately fall into a deep slumber.

Sometime later, just as I'm skipping through gorgeous tulip-covered fields under an endless blue sky, the sun warming my entire being, my door slams open.

"Chloe!"

I giggle, hugging each of them.

"Oh, watch your hair!" yells Bobbie and pushes me back, the candle almost setting my hair on fire, but I take it all in my stride.

Doesn't matter that the pretzels are a bit stale, that the ice cream is so icy that it must've been frozen since the turn of the century, or that one slice gives me such vicious brain freeze that I start seeing stars. This arrangement is one of the most beautiful things I've ever had bestowed upon me.

When I finish my cake, I'm overcome with emotion and perhaps one too many shots.

"Don't cry, Chloe," Cameron says with a comforting smile and pats my back as I drip over my plate.

I wipe my tears away. "I'm not. Just poked my eye with some pretzel dust."

Bobbie winks. "Happens to me all the time."

If the cake isn't a revelation, the next part sure is. No sooner have we finished clearing the plates when Cameron shocks me with a sudden urge to dance, spinning me around the dance floor.

I only participate because she calls it a birthday dance, but there's nothing birthday about it. It's completely offbeat, the music is some awful pop remix, and my feet are all but sticking to the laminate floor. It doesn't matter, though, because we can't stop laughing. I don't know where Bobbie is, but I think she is having another funny cigarette.

few rounds now that I'm up." She pulls out a bowl of pretzels from behind the counter and then points to the barstools. "Sit."

So, our night starts with coercion, but it doesn't take long for us to get into the swing of things. A few sambuca shots, swigging tequila from a bottle, and suddenly, we're on a first-name basis with the barwoman.

Turns out Bobbie doesn't mind a drink herself. She even cracks some jokes and tells us a story about her time in Amsterdam when she had a "funny cigarette" (definitely a stoner), then fell off her bike and into a canal.

When I duck off to the bathroom, Bobbie and Cameron appear to conspire against me because, upon my return, they leap up from behind the counter and yell, "Happy Birthday!" almost giving me a freaking heart attack.

Cameron is standing there, plugged into the wall, with colorful fairy lights hanging around her neck, presenting me with what I think is a birthday cake. That is, smashed pretzels in the form of 28 smooshed on top of a large ice-cream sandwich. "Do you like it?" she asks sheepishly, and there's a loud bang as one of her lights blows a fuse. "Um, we only had five minutes."

Hand still clutched to my chest, I say, "I love it!"

I mean it, truly.

"We had to use what we had," Bobbie beams and waves a lit pillar candle around in the air.

the shapes and colors are too perfect. Wait. "They're fake!" I gasp. "What a travesty!"

"Mustn't have much turnover," Cameron says, angling her head to me, light from the streetlamps sweeping over her cheekbones.

Honestly, New York to here is starting to feel like another dimension.

Undeterred by the AR sign, we follow the throb of the music to the bar, but when the door slaps open, we just stand there mutely. The bar is completely empty. Confused, I look down at my watch. It's close to seven in the evening.

"Hello?" I call out tentatively, but there's no response. "That's weird."

Cameron points to an aluminum bell, and we shuffle over to the mahogany counter. Panels of vintage mirrors line the wall, with an assortment of liquor bottles against it. I press the bell, or try to. It sticks a few times, then *ting*!

A woman in her fifties with big round glasses, slightly greasy, jet-black hair, and plum lipstick suddenly appears from behind a wooden door. A dodgy-looking cigarette drooping from her lip.

"Are you open?" asks Cameron.

"No. I just thought I'd interrupt my day, get up from my incredibly comfortable couch, and say hello," she fires back with a tight smile. Her friendliness is so overwhelming that the two of us just gawp at her. "Well... cat got your tongues? You better be ordering a

Suddenly, Cameron comes to a stop, swinging her head around to me. "Chloe, why did you never let me come inside your house? I only saw your room once."

"She was out then..."

"Your mom?"

"Yeah. Sorry, I never knew what to expect when I opened the door. I was embarrassed."

"You didn't need to be. I'm sorry that I was a bad friend. I had no idea what you were going through."

"Why would you? I never told anyone."

Cameron shrugs, and we walk along in silence, but it doesn't feel uncomfortable. It never has been with Cameron. As kids, we never felt compelled to fill the silences, we were happy just to be doodling together in the same space.

"Well, this is the main street as far as I remember," Cameron says, snapping me from my thoughts, and I glance up. She furrows her brow. "Hmm... more quiet than it used to be."

Quiet?

It's deader than a graveyard at midnight.

And town is a stretch. More like a village, a tiny one with the bare essentials – bakery, corner store, and a bar, which has a flashing neon sign but appears to be missing the B, so "AR."

The corner store has a pink post-it note on the door saying *back in ten minutes*, but I have trouble believing that. Instead, I greedily scan the glass case of the bakery. Doughnuts, iced buns, brownies. Hang on,

CHAPTER EIGHT

Chloe

Cameron walks beside me, falling in line with my step. The night above us, a dark blanket of sky and stars.

"Do you remember staring out at the stars from my treehouse? Star-hunting for a supernova?" she asks reminiscently.

It was only my *favorite* thing ever. We spent so much time in there, shoulder-to-shoulder and stargazing, it was like my second home. I was completely obsessed but just say, "Yeah. I remember how we counted and named them."

"Do you still have stars in your bedroom?" she asks.

"Uh-huh. The moon you gave me is still stuck on the ceiling, too. Bit old and floppy around the edges. You know... kinda like you."

A light chuckle falls past her lips, and I smile at my feet, gently kicking stones as we walk.

I lift my eyes to her. "Of course, it's a big deal. I'm so sorry I forgot."

"Cameron, it's been almost twenty years."

My heart twinges. "It has."

But spending time with her feels as though hardly any time has passed at all. She's so easy to talk to. I don't tell her that, of course, but I am determined to make the most of the night.

Even though my legs feel like dead weights, loaded down with cheese, wine has filled me with warmth and made me fuzzy around the edges. I don't want to engage in any more petty point-scoring. I want Chloe to have fun because it's her birthday, and after all she's been through, well, she deserves it.

I jump up from my chair, clapping my hands together. "I think we should wander into town."

Chloe gives me a wary look as though she can't believe I'm suggesting spending more time together. "Okkayy... I'm not sure how much town there is, but I guess I'm game if you are."

I nod and scull the rest of my wine.

Seriously, what could possibly go wrong?

face that was meant to smile. Her smile could light up the darkest of rooms. It doesn't look like she's had many reasons to smile lately, though.

I frown.

"Well, this is the longest break I've had in over six months, so coming here is one for me," Chloe says, adjusting the hem of her sleeve. "Thank you."

"You don't need to thank me," I sigh.

"Why not?"

Because I'm lonely.

Chloe slugs back more of her wine. "I'm sorry. Are you saying you're enjoying my company?"

"Don't push it," I reply with a wry smile and put my glass on the coffee table. "I'm saying that even though I'm surrounded by a lot of people, maybe I don't have as many people close to me as I thought I did."

"So, then that's a firm yes." Chloe grins, and I shake my head, smiling too. Her phone buzzes on the table, and she picks it up, opening a message.

"HAPPY BIRTHDAY BUTTHEAD!" screams a voice.

"Shit. Sorry," she mumbles, hastily muting the sound. "Just a friend from work."

"Wait. It's your birthday?" I glance at my phone screen. 11th March. Of course, it's her birthday. How could I forget?

"Yeah," Chloe says with a small shrug. "It's no big deal."

"No. Just in my mind, you were such a leader. I thought you'd be working at the UN, barking out orders."

"Very funny. What with my Harvard PhD?" Chloe deadpans.

A hint of a smile playing at the corner of my mouth. "Okay. If you could have any job in the world, what would it be?"

"A chef," she replies without taking a breath.

"A chef?"

"What? Not everything I say is a jibe. Cooking has always been therapeutic to me. For me, the kitchen is the heart of any home."

"Your cookies with Alice were always world-class." I flash her a grin, and I'm not sure, but this feels like flirting. "So, why don't you take a chance?"

"Too long in the tooth now to start something new, and I'm a home cook, if anything. Who's into that? Plus, you know, money has obviously been an issue. Between my two jobs, I don't have time to breathe," she sighs, and I feel sad for her. "Sometimes it feels like being in a tunnel. You have no choice but to keep on moving. I have a life. Just not living it..." her voice trails off as I stare at her. Her honesty is such a rare gift these days, especially in the circle I move in, that I've forgotten what it costs.

"Sounds like you need a vacation," I offer softly. My gaze drawn to the small creases at the corners of her eyes, which look like smile lines. Chloe always had a

"Nothing.... I mean, just that we are different. I really want a family someday. I guess because I never had a conventional one. Don't get me wrong, Aunt Marcy was incredible, but yeah... So, why didn't you just sell up?"

"Well, Alice and Gabriel were living in the guesthouse out back. And because I'm stubborn." I laugh, then shrug. "Thought I needed to save our family's honor. What a load of..." Shaking my head, I glance at Chloe, and we both smile.

Chloe pushes off her knees. "Well, sounds like you're very successful in your own right."

"I guess I've done okay in the end. Got my law degree because I wanted to emulate my father's success. He took me under his wing, but then slowly, I started seeing things that I didn't want to see." I stare out the window. She stares at me. "When he passed away, I started my own company, completely non-law related. I look for opportunities to turn businesses around. Sometimes I purchase them, somctimcs I don't. I'm not sure what it is, perhaps beating the odds when the business looks destined to fail, but it's really gratifying. I love what I do. Do you love what you do?"

Chloe snorts. "I work in admin for The Bra Bar, but I do get great deals on lingerie, so there's that..."

"Oh..." I chuckle. Unfortunately, you can't tell someone you sell bras without seeing them in it. Well, that's how my stupid brain works. Not what I need right now.

"You're surprised by my lack of ambition?"

skeletons in his closet to open a cemetery. Mom and I found multiple burner phones. He also left a mountain of debt and a sizeable mortgage on the home. My whole image of my father came crashing down. Who was this person? I felt completely betrayed. I'd blamed my mom for everything, unfairly so. The fights, his death. I can't believe I worshipped him."

"You were a kid, and he was good to you," Chloe says, picking at a bunch of grapes. "Wait. Is that why you pulled the plug on your law career?"

"Huh? Right, Max." I push back my hair. "Yeah, it just felt dirty to practice law. Plus, I found out Max was sending lewd messages to my girlfriend at the time. Didn't think it was wise to start a business with someone I didn't trust."

Her eyes go wide. "Oh, I see..."

Obviously, Max omitted that part.

Chloe collects herself, then changes topic. "How did your mom cope with everything?"

A strained laugh escapes me. "Well, of course, all of this was kept hush-hush, so the family name wasn't torn to shreds. Honestly, I think she was relieved when he died. It was like a weight was lifted from her shoulders. She was free to run off to Paris to live the life she always wanted," I reply without rancor. When her eyes meet mine, I elaborate, "They really didn't like each other, fought like cats and dogs. Hence, why I never want a family of my own. What's the point of all that?"

Chloe makes a weird face, and I ask, "What?"

I roll my eyes. "Chloe, I don't collect gnomes in my downtime."

"Okay, well, now I know!" she beams. "So, they really *are* boyfriend and girlfriend."

"Yeah, but don't call them that. Last time I asked Alice about her boyfriend, she kneecapped me with a dishtowel. Too new age, apparently." We share a glance, and she laughs. "Anyway, Gus used to be in dad's security team. I rehired him when he came looking for some work. He helps out around the house, in the garden."

"What were you two whispering about?" Chloe asks, loading up a cracker with English stilton cheese.

"Oh, just some work stuff that I needed him to do."

Thankfully, she shoves the cracker into her mouth, ending the questions. Surprisingly, we talk easily. She tells me how she never went to college, and I tell her how I hated my law degree but didn't want to disappoint my father, whom I had always looked up to.

"I only found out when he passed away six years ago that he was actually leading a double life. He was a good father to me. I never saw that side of him," I shrug, munching on some prosciutto.

"I'm sorry for your loss. I know how close you were."

"Thanks. We were, but to find out how deeply embedded he was in the criminal underworld, how he defended mobsters in court. Plus, all the Ponzi schemes, mistresses. It was shocking. I mean, there were enough

"Just to survive the night with you." Chloe pretends to throw salt over her shoulder like she is warding off evil.

God help me.

She is grinning now, and I faux-cheerily open a bottle, pouring our glasses to the rim. I hand one to Chloe. Glugging it down takes the edge off. Oddly, we appear to be on the same page. Chloe quickly follows suit, and I refill our glasses. She settles into a shabby-chic armchair on the other side of the coffee table while I plonk down onto the couch, and an odd stare-off ensues as though we're sizing each other up.

Chloe slices into a piece of truffle cheese, and I lean forward, globbing camembert onto a pita chip. "What's the deal with Alice and Gus?" she asks.

"Oh, you noticed. They started dating over a year ago. He even asked for my permission to court her. Not that they need it."

She giggles. "That's so cute."

"Yeah, Gus buys her a new garden gnome every month. Think there are twelve of them now. The last one had an apron. You know, how she likes to wear them -"

Chloe bursts out laughing. Half a cracker almost hits me as it launches from her mouth, but I swerve left, and it lands next to my thigh. "Sorry about that," she says, nodding to the cracker missile. "I thought the gnomes were yours."

after our stay. I swing upright and gasp at a topless calendar hanging off the back of the door. Miss February and her F cups. Did Alice see this?

I groan inwardly. So, so many gripes right now, but I decide to grin and bear it.

Venturing back into the living area, I find Chloe rummaging through Alice's bag of snacks. She looks up with a knowing smirk on her lips. "Like your room?"

"Uh-huh." I fake a broad smile, then give her my back and switch on a couple of lamps, rolling my eyes into the ceiling. "It's perfect."

When I swivel around, she eyes me with suspicion before losing interest and turning back to the snacks. "Prosciutto, cheese, pita chips, crackers, grapes, Hershey chocolate drops, and hmm, one Italian panettone," she says, dropping the items on a coffee table carved out of driftwood, along with a cutting board and knife. Her hand plunges back into the bag. "Oh, and the most important item... wine. Two bottles!" She shakes them in the air.

"Something about Alice's bag doesn't exactly scream snacks for the drive."

Chloe snorts a laugh, unwrapping some items and moving them onto the board. "True. But not bad for plan B."

I head straight to the cupboard, pulling out two wine glasses. "Why? What was the original plan?"

Chloe blasts past me, her eyes lighting up like Christmas at the quaint interior, which is furnished in an unfussy beachy style with coir carpet and the odd seascape on the walls. Simple yet charming. There are mismatched bobble pillows on a corduroy navy couch with a scratchy blanket draped over the back, and a large, worn but plush rug that anchors the space with colors echoing the shades of sand and sea. Aside from a few new furnishings, not much has changed.

While I just stand in the open-plan kitchen and living area like a pot plant, Chloe darts in and out of rooms like the Energizer Bunny. Important announcements follow, such as "Bedroom on the right is definitely yours." "Two bathrooms, thank God!" "Oh, it's *so* cute. I want to move in today!"

When Chloe finally stands still, she turns to me with those big, doe brown eyes that I've always had problems saying no to. "Do you really want to go home, Cameron?"

"I'm fine," I grumble. "I'm not some pampered princess, you know."

Her face says that's exactly what she's thinking, and I don't like it one bit.

Of course, I have second thoughts when I actually *see* my room which obviously is/was Gabriel's. It's no bigger than my walk-in wardrobe, smells like feet, and has Marvel Comic bedcovers.

Frowning, I test the bed, finding myself wedged between The Hulk and Captain America, the mattress so firm that I know I'll need a back straightening device

"Great technique," I say sarcastically. No way she is doing that to my Audi.

Regardless, it's to no avail. The trunk won't open.

"What about the -"

Chloe beats me to it. "The seats don't recline."

I slap my hands on my thighs. "Of course, they don't. This is a relic!"

Chloe scoffs. "I knew you were too rough when you closed it!"

"Rough-... The car is practically held together by rust! What do you expect?" I retort.

"Oh, shut up."

"I can't believe this is happening," I grumble.

It's quiet for a moment, and then Chloe starts to laugh, a slightly hysterical sound that she tries to contain but fails. "You don't have any sheets. How can you possibly sleep?" she gurgles.

I shoot her daggers and turn on my heel, marching to the front door, if you can call it that. It looks like the door is one gust of wind away from being blown off its hinges. I don't even turn the key in the lock, and it swings open.

"Top security. Hopefully, the loan sharks don't follow us here because we are both dead!" I snap.

"Cameron!"

The weekend now seems impossibly long.

I like structure, order, and, yes, my own damn sheets, but I will not let it show.

vacations as a family, but we never did. Not once. Alice spent a lot of time here with her son, Gabriel."

"Where's Gabriel now?" Chloe inquires.

"Married in Florida. Blended family with ten kids. Doesn't visit often."

"Not surprising. He'd need his own plane."

"Funny," I reply, and Chloe smirks.

We eventually pull up to a small iron gate, the car not even at a complete stop when Chloe leaps out and skips over to open and close it. I wish a gate could make me that happy.

Now, I say this in a purely objective, neighborly way, there is just *something* about Chloe. I don't know what exactly, but it's always been there. Like a magnetic pull, it's impossible to draw my eyes away from her.

This could be a problem.

Frowning, I drive the final stretch, stopping outside a small, charming cottage with white-washed walls and faded cornflower-blue roof tiles.

"We're here!" I trill, then pop the trunk and step outside, the cold air waking me up. "That's weird," I mutter as I peer at the still-closed trunk and shuffle toward the back. I try to pry it open with both hands.

Chloe is soon beside me. "What?"

"The trunk won't open."

"Why not? Let me have a go." Chloe jerks the trunk back and forth. She even thumps the top with her fist.

chatting. It's riveting stuff. How she's a lapsed vegetarian but still tries her best. How she buys organic when it's on special. How she doesn't think tin foil hats can stop aliens from reading your mind.

I mean, she is random.

Even when it's increasingly bumpy on the small roads, and I'm convinced it must've shifted my internal organs, she manages to babble along without a care in the world. She also enjoys playing the radio at high volume and treats me to sporadic bursts of singing. Usually, the chorus, perhaps only a solid eight percent of the words correct.

Despite being heavily fixated that the car is going to disintegrate into pieces, there's only one hairy moment around a bend, and that's because an empty soda bottle almost gets snared under the brake pedal. The rest of the drive goes off without a hitch.

An hour or so later with darkness falling rapidly, we turn onto a dirt road and approach a mailbox marked Porter, Alice's surname.

"This is it," I announce, and a strange excitement starts to bubble up inside me. I can't wait to see that view again. To feel the ocean air. My childhood wasn't full of that many happy memories, but I always had fun when we stayed. "I haven't been here since I was a kid."

"Why not? You and Alice are inseparable?"

"That was probably the issue," I say sadly as we jiggle along to limited suspension in a cloud of dust. "Think Mom got jealous and called an end to our weekends away. You'd think that'd mean we'd go on

"Just essentials, Chloe," I say with a large exhale. "You know, clothes, toiletries, books, sheets -"

"Sheets!" she exclaims.

Chloe looks at me like I'm a diva, and I give her my best eye-roll.

With Tetris-like skill, she shuffles around the contents of her trunk and manages to squeeze my behemoth suitcase in beside her small duffel bag. "There!"

"Great," I mutter, placing my hands on the trunk door, the hinges creaking ominously under the weight.

"Now careful -"

Heeding her instruction, I slam it shut without so much as a sideways glance and dart to the driver's seat, tossing Alice's bag of goodies in the back.

"I said careful," Chloe snaps.

Irritating her appears to give me a slither of joy, so naturally, I slam the driver's door, too.

Once I accept that fate has been sealed by my stupid mouth, I try to let go of my frustration and enjoy the drive.

The sky is a deep blue, the sun about to set, and we are soon barrelling down the highway at the car's maximum speed of forty miles per hour.

Keeping my mouth shut.

Chloe is on her best behavior for the first ten minutes, but it doesn't take long until she starts chit-

Chloe slides her sunglasses halfway down her nose, and I immediately tip my head to the garage. "I'll get my car."

"Come on. Live a little," she winks.

My skin prickles, but then I glance at my watch. Mom might turn up any minute. "Fine, but I'm driving," I say, pointing to the flowerbed. "I saw what you did to the Evening Primrose. I also remember when you plowed my go-kart halfway up our century-old birch tree. Still tire tracks on the trunk to this day."

"Sure," she replies nonchalantly, and her calm response immediately arouses suspicion.

Chloe Bentley liked to argue about everything.

I flounder for a moment. That is until she pegs her keys, and I snag them an inch from my nose. I shoot her a level look and instinctively touch the scar above my right brow, which she inflicted during a game of catch all those years ago.

Before I can form a response, Chloe teleports herself to the rear of the car, prompting me to shuffle over. She glances at my suitcase. "You do realize it's just for the weekend?"

I look down. "Huh?"

Now that she mentions it, there does seem to be a significant size differential in our luggage. Hers no larger than a diaper bag.

"How many bodies are in there?" Chloe asks, eyeing my suitcase suspiciously.

Here we go.

CHAPTER SEVEN

Cameron

Standing by the front entry, I hear Chloe's car before I see it. A mix of calamitous rumbling, gear crunching, and high-pitched squeaking.

Tip-top shape, my ass.

I watch as she proceeds to navigate the roundabout by reversing into a flowerbed and driving forward over the foot of a Hellenistic sculpture, I picked up in Kefalonia, Greece, last fall. "Oh, not the..." Twelve hundred Euros! My fists clench tightly at my sides.

Her driving tutorial is then completed with a twenty-point turn, and her dinged Toyota splutters to a stop beside me.

Good God. Her spatial awareness practically non-existent.

I rub my forehead. What is wrong with me? This is undoubtedly one of the stupider things I have agreed to, and it's all come about because I couldn't bear to leave her in a house that looked straight out of The Shining. I'm a careful woman by nature, but Chloe is making me reckless. I need to regain control.

A look of alarm registers on her face. "I'll pack a bag. Meet you out the front in half an hour?"

Huh?

"Sure, okay," I say, confused.

When Cameron leaves, Alice gives me a protracted wink and grins. "Works like a charm every time." Then she flits out the door like a fairy godmother.

It's hard not to laugh.

At least Alice knows how to handle Cameron because I'm not so sure I do.

When I look up, they are both staring at me. Alice covers a snort with her hand.

"God help me," Cameron mutters and then moves to pick up my bag. "Right, this way -"

But Alice steps in front of her, eyes fixed on me. "You know, take Chloe to my cottage by the coast. It's only an hour-ish from here. It's isolated, has basic provisions. And most importantly, no one knows about it. You'll be safe there."

"Alice, this place is like Fort Knox," says Cameron.

"Exactly, she'll be a prisoner in these walls. You two should go tonight." Alice claps and disappears out the door. "I'll prepare some snacks for the drive."

"I'm up for it," I say.

Cameron does a double take, and by the look on her face, she is not. "And I'm not," she confirms.

Told you so.

Unable to resist a dig, my eyes line up with hers, and I say, "I'm sure being papped with me is less than desirable. What would those hoity-toity circles say?"

Cameron scoffs. "What? I don't care what they say."

Suddenly, Alice charges in through the door. "Cameron, your mother just called. She's cutting short her trip to New York and coming this evening. She mentioned something about the McMahon Benefit Gala tomorrow night. She has a ticket for you and Bianca."

"No problem." Gus makes his way back to the door. He turns to Alice and pushes back his fringe. "See you later, then?"

"Uh-huh," Alice blushes, and they share a lingering smile.

Hello, what's going on there?

Alice clears her throat as he leaves. "Gus is the gardener, all-round handyman. Been here for six years. He's a bit hard of hearing, so has these staccato bursts, delivered at volume."

Alice and I share a giggle, but it's impossible not to miss the silhouette of Cameron looming behind her. She's frowning at her phone.

"What's wrong?" I ask, stepping past Alice and dropping my bag on the floor.

Cameron paces over to the sweeping staircase, then wheels around to face me. "Alice mentioned she saw a man loitering around the perimeter of our property today. Just ran my eye over our security footage, and she's right."

"Did he have a limp by any chance?" asks Alice, tugging on her cherry-sprigged apron.

"Limp? No. Yes," I reply, unsure how to answer because he didn't exactly start off with a limp.

Cameron furrows her brow. "Huh? Well, which one is it?"

"Yes. He definitely seemed to have one after I kicked him in the balls," I clarify.

It's out of my mouth before I can retract it.

passes under towering oaks. I pull up outside as an official guest of the Maxwell residence. Well, at least for the night.

I breathe in the freshly cut lawn and shuffle up to the Tuscan-style front door, but before I can knock, it swings open.

"Good evening. How are you?" asks a gruff, manly voice.

"Fine, thanks," I say to his belly button, then lift my head.

He's a seven-foot giant in a plaid shirt with broad shoulders, eyebrows like caterpillars, and a steady gaze. Graying at the temples and with deep grooves etched in his face, I'm guessing he's sixty-something. He's even good-looking, in a lived kind of way.

The giant blinks. "I asked HOW. ARE. YOU?" he repeats.

Alice warmly greets me, then tilts her face skyward. "She said fine, thanks, Gus."

"Oh, okay." He gives her a roguish grin.

"Come in, Chloe," says Alice, and I step inside the foyer onto a pale wood parquet floor. The walls are now a warm stone color, but the crystal chandelier swinging overhead is what really gets my attention. It's bigger than my Toyota.

Cameron waves Gus over, and they have a whispered conversation. A while later, she pats his shoulder. "Thanks, let me know."

stares at it. "Okay, that's it. You're not staying here. You're coming with me."

"No."

"Chloe, I'm not taking no for an answer," Cameron says. I cross my arms defiantly, and she adds, "You just hit me!"

"Because I thought you were that guy!"

"Exactly why you shouldn't stay here! I know there's a lot going on for you in your private life, but I'd prefer you weren't murdered on my watch. You're staying at mine tonight."

"Sorry. What?" I look around. Left, then right. I must be losing my mind. I swear I heard Cameron telling me to stay with her. God, sometimes, these voices in my head are out of control.

"I was asking you if you wanted to -"

Shit.

I gulp down. "Stay at yours? As in, like your house?"

Cameron nods. "Well, I don't live on a boat."

Holy hell, she's not kidding.

I start to smirk, and Cameron rolls her eyes. "I'll retract the offer, Chloe."

"Give me ten minutes," I say, feet already pounding up the stairs.

Not long after, my car rolls through her fancy wrought-iron gates, rattles across a small bridge, and

Cameron exhales loudly and then mumbles thanks. "Chloe... Why are you sneaking in through the back and wielding a bag?" she asks, stepping over a broom. "You tried to gouge out my eyes."

I frown because my reaction was a little extreme. "Some man followed me home the other day and kind of threatened me."

Cameron surges forward. "What! Why?" She narrows her eyes. "Chloe, do you have some sort of... problem?"

"What? No," I reply defensively.

Well, maybe.

I drop my head, staring at my feet for what feels like forever. I swallow the lump in my throat and eventually say, "It's my mom."

"Your mom?"

For some reason, I have a weird compulsion to confide in her, and the story just spills out of me – my mom's life of addiction, the never-ending bailouts, and the recent threats.

"Oh, I see," Cameron says. The pain in her expression seems genuine, and suddenly, I feel naked, exposed, even ashamed. I hate this feeling. She purses her lips. "How much do they want?"

I don't know where to look. "Six thousand."

Cameron simply nods. It silences her briefly, and then she's on the move. She checks the window locks. One tumbles loose and flops onto the floor. "Jesus." She

"Mmm, fine." Her brows draw together. "Do you carry weights in your bag?"

Yes, a ten-pound dumbbell I found under the stairs, but she doesn't need to know that.

I ignore her. "How did you even know I was here?"

Her eyes start darting around the living room.

"I know. It's a little dated and run-down," I say, half-tripping over a bottle of bleach.

Cameron looks down at two dark red stains on the carpet, her eyes widening. "Chloe. I think someone died in here."

"It's wine. Must be," I say unconvincingly because I had visions of a homicide, too.

When I leave the room, I see her frowning. "Uh-huh."

She's definitely *not* seeing the bathroom.

Cameron is still studying the stains when I return with a first aid kit. "Sit," I instruct, and she plonks down on a cracked plastic stool that looks like it's going to snap in half.

A second later, it does.

"Fu-... I'm just going to stand," she huffs, leaping to her feet.

"Okay. Well, this is going to hurt," I say, soaking gauze in antiseptic.

"I'm not a baby, Chloe – Oh, fuck!"

It's hard not to giggle. "You were saying?"

I wrestle with the lock and then shoulder-charge the warped wooden veneer door. I flick on a switch, yellow light pooling out onto the back porch.

Cameron runs her hand over her face. "You're acting weird... Like more than normal."

I roll my eyes and drop my bag on the kitchen counter. "I've just been stressed with all this house business." I take a breath. I'm also vaguely self-conscious about my haggard appearance and start fiddling with my hair which is still up in an elastic. Her beauty intimidates me. There, I've said it. I suck my stomach in, straighten my spine, and then turn to her. "Anyway... sorry for whacking you."

Cameron stays a few feet away outside the door, and I meet her deep, perennially accusing eyes.

"Wh-... It wasn't on purpose, Cameron! Obviously, I didn't know it was you!" I kind of squeak.

Cameron gives a small laugh and holds up her hands. "Okay, then. If you say so... well, sorry if you thought I was an axe murderer." She touches her forehead, wincing.

I rush forward, frowning at some blood. "Oh, God. Is that from me?"

"Well, I don't go around hitting myself in the head... Anyway, it's fine." She moves to cover it.

"Let me see. Must've sliced you with my key." I pull her hand away. "You have a small gash. Come in, and I'll clean it up."

"Wait! Stop!" yells a voice.

Hang on. It's female.

Don't fall for it, Chloe.

I keep smacking them even harder.

"Chloe!" it roars.

I halt mid-whack, breathing hard. "Cameron?"

My voice rockets through the night air in astonishment. I swat away strands of hair from my face, and Cameron steps back into the moonlight. She hunches over, cursing.

Shit.

"Wh-... What are you doing here?" I mumble.

"Oh, I wanted to get hit in the face with a bag and go five rounds with Mike Tyson," Cameron quips, still hunched over.

"Sorry," I reply, feeling embarrassed.

Cameron straightens, then surveys me. "Why are you walking in through the back? In the dark? I thought you were a burglar!"

"What? Do I really have to explain which door I choose to walk through?" I try not to sound agitated, but it's impossible. I don't want to give her the satisfaction of seeing me distressed. "Anyway, I'm fine, as you can see," I mutter.

Last thing I need is Cameron Maxwell to be my knight in shining armor.

CHAPTER SIX

Chloe

It's been two days, and I'm heading back to the house decidedly more ballsy than when I left.

I'm done with hiding and refuse to be scared off by some hairy creepster. I came here to do a job, so that's what I'm going to do.

Even still, I err on the side of caution and return at nightfall, parking my car down the block. I'm grateful to find the house shrouded in darkness and pull out my keys, tiptoeing along the far wall. I breathe a sigh of relief because I don't think I was followed.

Suddenly, I hear footsteps near me and some shuffling.

Oh, please, God.

Not again.

Spinning around, keys still in hand, I hurl my duffel bag at a dark figure as it steps forward, and I scream, charging forward with a battle cry. "Get off me, motherfucker!" I'm slapping their face and poking them in the eyes like they tell you to in those shark documentaries. "Help! Help!"

office. I also rent a small office space locally in Diamond Hill, solely for client meetings. Hardly going to bring strangers into my house.

"I forgot to tell you that Riley O'Hara is coming to New York next week. We should take him out for dinner," Bianca suggests.

My head snaps around. "Did you not just hear my preference to stay local?"

Bianca laughs. "What can I do if he prefers the restaurants in New York over The Flying Wok?"

"Him or you?"

She rolls her eyes. "Do you want the deal or not?"

I groan as she starts waffling on about cuisine options and Michelin stars. Her voice fades into the background because I have more important things to do, like gawk at my neighbor's house like it's prime-time TV.

"I wonder where she is," I muse out loud.

"The neighbor?"

"It's just she was making a lot of noise. Now she's not."

Bianca taps her pen against her lip. "Maybe it's your lucky day, and she's left... Back to being eerily quiet, just the way you like it."

True, but the question remains – where is she?

"I need an invite, really?" Bianca sashays over, kissing me on the cheek, and I'm engulfed in enough Yves Saint Laurent perfume to fumigate a flower shop. She whirls around on her pointed heels, following my gaze next door. "Someone needs to knock that hovel down. Such an eyesore... Oh, the yard's been cleaned up. Well, sort of."

"Mmm. The daughter is back to sell the place."

"Good riddance, I say. You should buy it and build me a condominium," she smirks.

"Ha. Good one."

Bianca pulls a funny face, but I know she's only half-joking; she's as material as they come. However, she is good at her job. She swivels around and adjusts my collar. "Want to grab lunch?"

"What that chicken feed you love so much?" I reply, and she swats my arm. "Cameron. It's quinoa and tabouli with sunflower seeds."

"Exactly, chicken feed. I'll pass. Thanks all the same. What's happening with that small broker in Rochester? What was the name? Ace of Spades?"

Bianca snorts a laugh. "Ace of Trades."

"The fi rst th ing to go when the purchase is finalized is the name."

"Sure thing. Oh, Sandy's expecting you for a three o'clock meeting today in town," Bianca says, jotting down a reminder.

"Good, I hate traveling," I reply. And it's true, I detest the commute to New York and prefer my home months after going through a divorce and being made redundant. Max charmed her way into her pants and her heart before moving onto the next notch in her belt, the messed up eighteen-year-old daughter of a local clergyman, and left me to pick up the pieces of an already fragile Billie. These days, Billie has turned into a bit of a womanizer herself, but she never prays on the vulnerable.

Surely Chloe didn't go home with Max? My stomach churns at the thought of another one of Max's conquests. I dash over to the window, peering at Chloe's house. Binoculars would come in handy. No lights. No signs of life. I tap the wooden frame with my fingers. Something is definitely amiss.

"Cameron. There you are," interrupts a familiar voice, and I turn around to see Bianca, my assistant, trotting over in a white tailored suit and Chanel heels with a Kashmiri scarf looped around her neck. Her long blonde hair wrestled into a severe bun.

"Hey, what are you doing here? You're supposed to be in New York."

Bianca runs our main office in New York, which frees up my time to look for business ventures. I see her more than I should because she grew up in the area, so she visits every other week. My mom thinks I should be with her. Good family, old money, and most importantly, well-connected. I couldn't care less about any of that. Sure, we went on a date or two earlier on, and she occasionally accompanies me on business trips, but that's where it ends.

CHAPTER FIVE

Cameron

Where is she?

My annoying neighbor has been very quiet.

There's been no trespassing, no toting of power tools at the crack of dawn, no flipping the bird at the cameras, no off-key moans of that hideous accordion. Not even a dirty glare across the front yard for days.

Chloe always had an attitude, even when young. Perhaps that's why I was drawn to her. I was as socially awkward as they came, blushing at the drop of a hat. Even at Pastor Brian, who was eighty-two and had a wonky glass eye and a peg leg. Despite my affluent upbringing, it took meeting Chloe to think that someone vaguely alright existed inside.

Last time I saw her was at Cole's Bar, where she was hanging with that vile Max Farrow. My hackles instantly rose, especially when I saw her hand on Chloe's leg, smirking like the asshole she is.

Max has a thin layer of polish that most women fall for, that is, until she chews you up and spits you out. Not me, but I witnessed firsthand what she did to my friend, Billie, when she stayed at my place for a few

I flip over and punch the pillow. So tired. So bone-tired.

After a while, I notice tears running down my cheeks, but I'm too tired to wipe them away. I leave them there. Just when I think I can't take anymore, someone takes what feels like a lump hammer to the wall and shouts, "Shut up, dickhead!"

And I couldn't agree more. Still, it's quite the eclectic taste in music. 90's rave, 80's rock. A trip down memory lane, which happens to coincide with the sky turning from midnight to blue and finally to an orangey pink.

At last, silence.

Unfortunately, the alarm on my phone starts shrieking moments later from under my left shoulder blade, and I pull my pillow over my head, letting out a frustrated scream. Feeling like I've dragged an elephant, I yank my phone free and switch it off. My eyes close instantaneously.

All I know is that I desperately need sleep.

My blood runs cold. "Hello...?" I croak, peering out into the hallway. "Helllooo?"

No response. But then intruders are hardly going to introduce themselves, are they?

Arming myself with a lamp, I eventually scamper down to the kitchen, but there's no one there, and I rush back to my room. No way I'll be sleeping. I just can't shake this feeling, no matter how hard I try. I pace back and forth, back and forth. That's it. I quickly gather my belongings and slip into my sneakers. Even though I can't afford it, I make the hasty decision to stay at the Hacienda Motel for a few nights in the hope that this blows over.

Drizzle mixes in with my tears as I pick up some essentials and walk back to my hotel room, the grocery bag cutting into my wrist. Because am I kidding myself? Is this problem really just going to vanish?

Stumbling inside, I flop down onto the bed and stare at my reflection in the small mirror fixed to the brick wall. My winter white skin looks like cardboard, my hair completely lifeless. It only galvanizes my thoughts – I look as shit as I feel. I shouldn't be in this situation. I just shouldn't.

Lying in the darkness the first night, I don't sleep. Just like at the house, there are too many weird noises - banging pipes, drunken yelling. I think I even hear a rat skittering in the wall. I lie there, still as a statue, and try to remain calm. At some point, it feels like my eyes might just snap shut, but then a party kicks off next door with shrieks of laughter and crashing furniture.

She loses her balance a little, stumbling. "Huh?"

High as a freaking kite.

I roll my eyes. "Some man with a handlebar mustache! He threw me into the wall."

"Oh, that's Roman." She waves her hand as though it's nothing. "He's all bark, no bite."

"You didn't settle that debt from last month, did you? You scored more drugs."

She looks away, scoffing into the phone. "No -"

I don't let her speak. There needs to be an end to this. "Yes. Mom! I'm not stupid. I'm also not some sort of cash cow. Let me be clear. I'm not giving you one more dime -"

She mutters some profanities, then starts again, "Just a few hundred to..."

But I've cracked, and I'm barely holding it together, much like my phone screen. "No! That's it!" I yell, and for the first time ever, I hang up on my mom. Fat, angry tears splash onto my phone. It kills me to feel so hopeless in all of this. I can't help her, but I also can't have her in my life.

The day doesn't improve much after that. I've hardly hit first gear with the clean-up because I'm practically jumping at my shadows. Every unfamiliar noise, every bang of the radiator has me on edge. As night falls, total paranoia sets in, and now I'm convinced someone is lurking in the kitchen.

louder than last time, then strikes her arm with a claw. She flings him away. "Ow! Arnold! Psycho cat!"

I laugh. A moment later, Lexi does.

But then her expression shifts, concern creasing her brow. "Sure you're okay?"

"Yes! Now get back to your burrito," I insist.

We say our goodbyes, and it's as though my mom can hear my thoughts because a minute later, she's Facetiming me, too.

Automatically, I start to tremble. Behind her straggly grey-blonde hair, her dark eyes are sunken, and her cheeks are gaunt. She was using again. She'd been pretty when she was young, but a lifetime of addiction had finally caught up, and I immediately know exactly where the three thousand dollars I gave her went.

Taking a deep, bracing breath, I answer the call. "Mom?"

"Honey." She flashes me her trademark crooked smile, but my eyes are drawn to the shake in her hand and stains down the front of her daisy print dress. "You look beautiful," she says.

Sherie Bentley had worn a lot of labels – cocktail waitress, junkie, stripper, recovering addict, homeless - but never a 'devoted' mother. She needed a shower, rehab, *and* a clue.

My teeth clench, as does my fist. "Mom," I venture cautiously. "Why is some random man following me around, demanding money?"

hard not to compare at times when I'm living on Planet What The Fuck Am I Doing With My Life?

Now, I need to put that in context. No one has the perfect life, do they? You think they do, but everyone undergoes adversity at some point. Some more than others. And some people, you just can't tell because, at least outwardly, they always look like they have their shit together.

That's Lexi.

She tragically lost her sister, Kim, in a hit-and-run when she was seven, but she never talks about it. Still, every morning, she has her coffee in an ugly clay mug that her sister made for her in the second grade.

"Chloe. You don't need to be sorry, okay? You are not your mom," Lexi replies softly. She scoops up Arnold with one hand, and he growls. "I hate that she can affect you from so far away... Anyway, I'm sure Rani will be overjoyed to be graced with my presence for an extended period." I give her a look, and she laughs, stretching on the couch. "What? I would be! Sex on tap."

"You're an idiot."

"Lovable, though, right?"

I nod, smiling. "Very. Thanks, Lexi," I reply, knowing damn well I have the best friend ever. "How are you anyway? Everything okay?"

"Of course. Arnold's having his usual mood swings." Lexi pats his head, and he grumbles again,

I pause as Lexi bends over to pick up a t-shirt on the ground. "Six thousand," I say, and she jerks up, smacking her head on the metal bar.

"Fu- ... Six thousand? Oh my God," Lexi winces, then loops the t-shirt over the frame. "Look, I can lend -"

"No, Lexi. I'm not borrowing any more from you. I'll work out something. I just don't know what."

After some time, she says, "Maybe we could sell something?"

"Like what? A kidney?"

Lexi is one of the best people I know. She's loyal, fierce, and has a heart of gold. Honestly, I'd be lost without her and my aunt. They have helped me, consoled me, more times than I'd like to admit. Of course, she also has a wicked sense of humor.

"Don't be ridiculous. We need both. We drink too much," she says with a big, cheeky grin.

I laugh, instantly more relaxed. You know those people that make you laugh even when there's nothing to laugh about. Lexi is one of them. What I wouldn't give to have her here with me.

"I'm so sorry, Lexi," I say a moment later and groan into my hand.

Lexi has the perfect life. She has a great career, which she loves, a cool, steady girlfriend named Rani, and a grumpy ten-year-old cat called Arnold. She hits the gym five times a week, plays pickleball on the weekend, and regularly competes in triathlons. It's

It must be written all over my face.

I tell her about my run-in with the man.

"Jesus! Chloe!" Lexi blows her blonde bangs away from her heart-shaped face. "This is escalating..."

And it is.

Last month, I received a handwritten letter demanding three thousand dollars for a gambling debt, or there would be "consekwinces." Honestly, I don't know if my mom or these loan sharks were behind the letter, but my mom was always an awful speller. Sadly, I also have no doubt that she would blackmail her own daughter.

I ended up paying after she called me begging. It cost me one month's rent money and depleted my emergency fund. Back in January, I gave her two thousand dollars.

Lexi's face looms large against a backdrop of green Parlor Palms. "Chloe, you need to go to the police."

"I can't," I reply weakly. It's my mom, I say in the subtext. Even though we are FaceTiming, I can't even bring myself to look Lexi in the eye because I know everything about the way I'm handling this is wrong. "I hate to ask, but can you please stay with Rani for a bit? You know, until I can sort this out? I don't want to put you in danger."

Lexi stops in front of the elliptical machine we bought in lockdown but never used. These days, it doubles as a clothes horse. "Sure... How much do they want this time?"

him in the balls. Probably not the best decision, but I'm not one to lead with my head.

"Bitch!" He howls, folding like a bad poker hand.

Heart jackhammering in my ears, I scoop up my phone and rummage through my handbag for my keys. Come on! I fumble with the lock, burst through the door, and then quickly slam it shut, collapsing against the wooden frame.

When will this nightmare ever end?

I rush to the window and, thankfully, see the cretin hobbling away onto the street. With shaky fingers, I pull out my phone, only to find that my screen has cracked. Right now, I couldn't care less. I'll just add that to my list of repairs.

I quickly FaceTime my best friend slash flatmate, Lexi.

Alexis De Marco is a marketing coordinator for a big house fashion brand, but we first met at The Bra Bar when she was one of the Social Media managers. On my first day, Lexi sat next to me and my sad microwaved potatoes in the lunchroom and said with a ready smile, "Fuck, what a day. Is it too early for a gin & tonic?" and I knew she was my kind of person. From that day on, she took me under her wing, and I've remained there ever since.

Lexi's voice crackles through the speaker. "Hey, hey flat-..." She drops a half-mauled burrito on her plate, then squawks through a mouthful of pulled pork, "What the hell's wrong!"

It's him.

Carpet man.

"Get off me!" I growl, coming face to face with chest hair the color of dirty dishwater wrapped around a thick golden chain, and my nails plunge into his arm, clawing at him to let me go. "You can't have my carpet!"

I've always been stubborn as a mule.

"Huh?" He traps me against the wall, looking completely and utterly confused, then shakes his head. "I don't want your carpet, lady. I want your money! You need to settle the debt!"

The debt? A sinking feeling washes over me.

My mom.

"Now, with late fees, it's six grand," he sneers with a venomous grin on red lips, his stale cigarette breath skating over the side of my neck, and all I can produce is a low, pained hiss.

"It's not my debt!" I screech in his face and go for a headbutt, but he dodges me.

Carpet man gives a gruff laugh, then slams me back, pain shooting across my shoulders. "Now, aren't you a live wire? The debt is your mom's. Just think of it as a next of kin kind of thing." He grins like a pointy-toothed monster and shoves his hand into my bag. "Here's my number. You have until the end of the month to pay it, or else."

He releases me, and I drop to the ground. Awash with fight-or-flight adrenaline, I take the chance to kick

Cameron stops but doesn't turn around. I can tell Max's line stung. She's definitely trying to get under Cameron's skin. I'm so rattled that I just blink. I'm also starting to wonder if Max might be a bit of an asshole.

Thankfully, it's almost three, so leaving isn't awkward. But that whole exchange was weird and even though I don't know their history, for some reason, I feel bad for Cameron.

Shaking my head, I walk toward my car. I'm halfway there when I lock eyes with that man from the carpet store.

I stop dead.

The hairs on the back of my neck stand on end, and I swallow a gulp of air. He's casually leaning on a pole across the street, chewing a straw, and staring straight at me. It can't be a coincidence, it can't.

Heart racing, I powerwalk to my car and quickly barricade myself in there. Rear view, side view, rear view again – I can't see any sign of him in my mirrors. I must be losing it.

Get it together, Chloe.

My hands tremble as I twist my key in the ignition, and I tell myself that it's all in my head, but still drive home faster than normal. Pulling up by the curb, I snatch my belongings and bolt up the porch steps when, out of nowhere, someone yanks my handbag, and I'm thrown into the wall with my feet up in the air. My phone clatters to the ground as an arm tightens around my neck, immobilizing me in a chokehold.

I'm not sure why, but Max deliberately leaves her hand on my leg, and Cameron definitely logs it. It throws me off balance. Suddenly, I want to fling Max's hand away, but that would be rude. Instead, I straighten then casually recross my legs, forcing her to remove it.

"Oh, Cameron. Didn't see you there," Max chirps with a fake grin.

She so did.

"Max." Cameron gives her a curt nod. Something tells me that Max annoys the shit out of her.

"And I thought my day couldn't possibly get any better." Max places her empty glass on the counter. "I'm just having a drink and getting acquainted with your charming neighbor, Chloe."

"Hi," I squeak, and Cameron gives me a smile, but it doesn't reach her eyes.

"We were just going to have another round," says Max.

"Oh, I'm not -" I start.

Max interrupts. "Fancy joining us, Cameron?"

"No, thanks. I have better things to do," Cameron replies, handing a fifty-dollar bill to the bartender, and Max snorts a laugh.

God, this is uncomfortable.

When Cameron turns to leave, Max says loud enough for everyone to hear, "You know, we were going to go into business, but then she had a bipolar moment and chucked it all in. Probably the right thing to do, I suppose. She would've been a lousy lawyer."

I laugh. "Yes." Then I pause and say, "You don't want an accordion by any chance?"

Max snorts. "No, I'll pass. My busking days are long gone."

Out of the corner of my eye, I spot the woman with Cameron slipping on a leather jacket. She messes up her long dark hair, then writes something on a piece of paper and hands it to Cameron with a blinding smile. Cameron glances at it, then slides it into her handbag. Well, their meeting doesn't look very business-y to me. Wait, is Cameron gay too?

This time, Max catches my line of sight and turns in her seat. "Oh God, not her." She says to me, "Look, I think we should do this again. Soon."

I nod, still distracted by whatever is happening over there, but Max is good fun, and I guess you can never have too many friends.

Suddenly, she places a hand on my leg. "Now, if you need anything, I mean *anything*... let me know."

My face snaps to hers, and her eyes start twinkling like mischievous fireflies.

Oh my God! She *is* hitting on me! Don't go red, don't go red. Of course, I go red!

Just as my face starts flaming like a bonfire, Cameron strides over in a pair of three-inch heels that make her legs look so long, it's like they have no end. A single shaft of sunlight shines through the window at that exact moment, illuminating her lean frame, and for a second, she looks like a fallen angel.

My God, I just can't escape her. She's cradling a glass and accompanied by a striking brunette with big dark eyes and smooth, golden skin in her early to mid-twenties. But it's Cameron, I can't stop looking at, transfixed by the movement of her hands, her body as she speaks.

Max leans back, throwing a handful of nuts into her mouth. I slump on my stool. Great, now my vision is obscured.

"Ever thought of moving back here?" she asks.

"No," I say quickly and take a slug of beer.

"Oh, I see."

"I just like New York," I counter with a shrug because I don't want to offend her and call this place, I don't know... a shithole.

"Despite appearances, it's changed a lot. I'm sure I could change your mind."

"Mmm," I say distractedly and peek over her shoulder. I wonder who that woman with Cameron is? What are they talking about? Hang on, why do I even care? She's a stranger now. I've survived eighteen years without her in my life, and I'll survive another eighteen without seeing her.

Meanwhile, Max twirls her credit card between her index and middle finger. "Another drink?"

"No, thanks, Max," I smile. "I need to drive and try to make a start on the house."

"Even though procrastination is more fun?"

When I turn around, there's no mistaking the glare on the receptionist's face. She tosses her flaming scarlet hair over her shoulder and rolls her eyes. "Now, will that be cash or card?"

Max may not be a shark, but she sure is.

Max slips onto a stool beside me in the dimly lit bar, clinking her whiskey on the rocks with my Bud Light.

"Hmm, I should be deep cleaning instead of day drinking," I say.

"And I should be working." Max makes a face and leans in, whispering, "But I won't tell anyone if you don't."

A laugh escapes me. "Deal."

"Honestly, all work and no play. Where's the fun in that?" A brief extended eye lock sends my gaydar pinging. Hang on, is she? No, she can't be.

"Something makes me think that you have a very good work-life balance," I say playfully.

Max swills her whiskey and stretches forward to scoop up some mixed nuts. "I certainly try, Chloe. Life's not always a bed of roses, so you need to make the most of your time. I've been a lawyer for almost twelve years, and some of the things I've seen would make your head spin..." Her voice trails off because I spot a familiar mane of hair in the far corner.

Wait, it's Cameron.

Max reclines in her chair, the corners of her mouth inching upward into a smile. "Good girl."

This is getting more interesting by the second, but I came here for a reason. "Is there anything else I need to do?"

"No, that takes care of all the paperwork. The property is yours." Max claps her hands together and rises from her seat. Taking it as my cue to leave, I stand and follow her to the door. "I've already told Bill Waters, the local realtor, that you are interested in selling, so he'll be in touch."

"Oh, great. Thank you."

Max pauses by the door. "In light of your current circumstances, I've also charged you less than normal."

How sweet, and they say lawyers are sharks. Apparently, not all of them. Max must've pitied me after I spilled a bit too much in our email chats.

I flash her a grateful smile. "You've been so lovely, Max. I don't know how to repay you."

Max laughs. "Just join me for a drink down at Cole's Bar? Want to head there now?"

"Oh ha-ha," I chuckle, but she's just staring and smiling. "Wait. You're not joking?"

"No. I have a three o'clock appointment but wouldn't mind getting out of the office for a bit. One of the perks of being my own boss."

"Okay, well, in that case... why not?"

Max slaps the door frame. "Great. I'll see you there shortly. Just need to call a client."

"Thank you. Now... Any questions?" she asks, tenting her fingers in front of her.

"I guess I'm wondering why the place is so run-down if there were tenants? Shouldn't the estate agent be more on top of things?"

Max relaxes and takes a sip from her coffee mug. "Well, it has been vacant for close to a year. And your father rented out privately, not through an agent."

"Oh, right. He was always a penny pincher."

Max gives me a knowing smile. "He moved into care not long after the pandemic hit. A family was renting at the time." She glances over the paperwork, tapping her finger under some print. "The Murphy's. Had a reputation for being a bit out there, playing loud music. If I'm not mistaken, I read something about an accordion they rigged up to an amplifier. Quite a few complaints, mainly from Cameron Maxwell, who'd complain if the wind blew in the wrong direction -" She stops herself and narrows her eyes at me. "Do you know her?"

I shake my head because I think I like where this is heading. "No."

"She is a pain in my... You know, one of *those* people." Her eyes double in size, and wow, she really doesn't like Cameron. "Always sticking her nose in your business, getting in your way. Essentially, enjoys making life difficult, and it shouldn't be, Chloe, now, should it?"

I want to laugh, but I control myself. "It most certainly shouldn't. I'll try my best to avoid her, then."

He grunts. "Follow me if you must."

God, this guy…

I shuffle after him, noticing a burly, unshaven man in a battered leather jacket and lace-up military boots to my left. He has beady black eyes and a handlebar mustache and looks like a heroin dealer. Even though he's milling around in the Persian rug section, his gaze is fixed on me.

Why is he staring? Did I steal his cookie dough carpet?

I take a seat in a worn-out chair, but when I glance around, the man's gone. Weird. Maybe I'm imagining things. After booking an installation date, I pay the cranky assistant and head to my father's attorney's office a few doors down.

Turns out Max Farrow isn't an old man with a hunch but a good-looking female dynamo in her mid-thirties, wearing a navy pantsuit and Converse high-tops. Obviously, not attractive in a Cameron queen-of-the-world way, but there's something about her raven hair cut sharply to her chin, sparkly grey eyes, and demeanor that catches my attention.

Max rattles through all the legalities for close to half an hour, and even though she loses me after about a minute, I think I get the gist of it, scribbling my signature on various documents.

"There you go." I hand her the papers and sink into my seat with a sigh of relief.

I finally snap, "God, get out of my brain!" and fling a roll of carpet to the floor.

Someone clears their throat, and I nearly jump out of my skin. A middle-aged man with salt and pepper hair glares at the discarded sample, pushing his square glasses up his nose.

Blood rushes to my face. "Sorry- It, um... slipped."

He shoots me daggers, not believing me for a second. "Do you need help?" he asks tersely, but nothing about his delivery feels helpful.

I make a snap decision and point. "Yes. I'd like to order some of that style."

Hooray for small miracles! Seems a bit of public humiliation goes a long way.

The retail assistant brightens. "Our solution dyed polyester in cookie dough?"

"Cookie dough?" I parrot. Mmm, I love cookies. Must be a sign from the universe. "Sounds good to me!"

"Do you want matching curtains too? We could re-upholster your ottoman/couch? You can never have too much cookie dough," he says enthusiastically.

Okay, now he's getting carried away.

"Er. No." I shake my head. "Thank you."

"Oh." He kicks the floor with his shoe. Looks like he's sour again. "Well, how much do you need?" he asks grouchily.

"Um..." I look down at my scrap of paper. "Just twenty square meters."

mathematical treatise on chaos theory. Still, as I stand in the shadows of my bedroom like some stalker, I can't help but feel more intrigued than ever. Suddenly, she drops the book and for some idiotic reason, I tumble to the floor.

Shit.

My heart lodges in my throat in a magnificent surge of adrenaline.

Slowly, I lift my head to the windowsill and peer over. She's walking around the bed, hair up in a messy ponytail, wearing nothing but a white tank and dark underwear. Excellent, now I won't only be seeing her smug face in my head. Far easier to ignore if she wasn't so easy on the eye.

I bite my thumbnail and watch her prance around. Left to her dresser, right to the wardrobe, then back to the bed. Whoops, she's changed her mind. Back to the wardrobe. Now, she's dropped something and is bending over, wriggling her butt. I start to gurgle, then cover my mouth. Oh, God, I think I'm enjoying this. This can't bode well for my brain.

And it doesn't.

Twelve hours later, I'm at Carpet World when karma strikes.

All I'm trying to do is replace the downstairs carpet that looks straight out of CSI. Simple task, right?

Not when a scene of Cameron prancing around in her underwear is doing a song and dance in your head. I've perused the same samples at least five times when

CHAPTER FOUR

Chloe

If Cameron Maxwell isn't the most infuriating person in the world, I don't know who is.

Standing there grinning on her balcony over a mug of coffee and giving me the royal wave as I drove past her in the street this morning.

Resisting the urge to strangle her, I plastered on a saintly smile, but I haven't forgotten our last conversation where she wanted me to raze my home to the ground. Still thinking she is better than me after all these years.

Thought I might inflict a little pain of my own with an impromptu gardening session this morning at stupid o'clock, but it didn't seem to elicit the response I wanted. Actually, it may have backfired. Not only am I sleep-deprived, but now I can't seem to wipe her smug face from my mind.

I throw back my sheets and shuffle toward the window, concealing myself behind the curtain's edge. Her room is dark, apart from the soft glow of her bedside lamp. She's in bed, head hidden behind a book, probably reading an exceptionally boring of deep breathing. In through the nose, out through the -

BRRRRRRR!

I nearly jump a mile, coffee splashing over a contract.

FFS.

Leaping up from my chair, I sprint to the window, leaning over the sill. All I can see is a whirlwind of dust and grass on the side perimeter.

Chloe.

My whole body stiffens.

I'm going to bury her under the damn rosebush.

I run to my computer and flick over to the cameras. There she is in goggles, hair everywhere, slashing the air with the weed whacker, looking like she's straight off the set of a very scary horror movie. When I move the camera to the right and hit the zoom button, Chloe startles and looks up. She calmly places the weed whacker on the ground, removes her gloves, then smiles sweetly and gives me the one-finger salute.

I gasp.

The disrespect is staggering.

Naturally, this sets the tone for the rest of the morning, and I get absolutely nothing accomplished.

When I finally call it a night and collapse into bed, I just end up tossing and turning. Chloe's face swims into my mind's eye while I have fantasy arguments with her, thinking about all the clever things I could say.

Unfortunately, my thoughts soon drift to the definition of her features and the dark eyes that seemed dreamier the longer I stared. I think about her petite figure, those surprisingly toned arms, and then I smack my head against my pillow because, dammit, I deserve it!

Is it time to get up yet?!

I twist to the red digital numbers on my alarm clock and feel a horrible lurch. Two o'clock! Are you joking?

Naturally, I spend the next four hours quietly seething and blaming everything on Chloe. My overactive brain, lack of sleep, even her semi-attractiveness. When my alarm starts bleeping, I reach across and slap it quiet. I'm half-asleep and miserable, but I always get up at six, no matter my mood, and today will be no different.

The hours between six and eight are always the most productive for me. No noise, no interruptions. I'm a creature of habit, which means my day kicks off with a glass of warm lemon water, and then I head straight to my home office, where I start up the coffee machine.

Scooping up my double shot latte, I settle into my desk, switch on my computer, and practice one minute

Later that day, I hurry to my car for a meeting with my bank manager. I have one arm in my blazer, with my phone trapped between my shoulder and my ear, when I lock eyes with Chloe in the front yard in a pair of olive-green spandex, brandishing a power tool. She hoists it in the air, giving it a rev.

"Oh, God." I jangle my car keys and mutter, "Is that a chainsaw? She's completely mental."

"Chainsaw?" squawks a voice from the other end of the phone line. Oh, that's right. I'm on a call with Billie, my long-time friend from law school. She now lives interstate in Chicago. "Do I need to call 911?"

Rolling my eyes, I open my car door and slip into my seat. "No, it's just my psychotic neighbor."

"How old?"

I fumble with my seatbelt and click it into place.

"Twenty-eight," I reply. Did she not hear that I called her psychotic?

"Cute?" she asks.

I pause for a millisecond. It's a mistake.

"She is!"

"Don't even think about it. I can hear your thoughts, Billie."

There's laughter down the line.

Billie has bounced back from her setbacks and has been through her fair share of women of late. No chance I'm letting her near my chainsaw-toting neighbor. For her safety, of course.

a closer look, squeezing her by the arms. "You've turned into a beautiful woman, Chloe. Isn't she just beautiful, Cameron?"

I roll my eyes, and Chloe beams at me over Alice's shoulder.

"Alice, how is it possible you still smell like homemade cookies? And you're wearing an apron!" shrieks Chloe.

Alice laughs. "Not the same one, but a leopard doesn't change its spots. You know, I remember how you loved to be my little assistant," she gushes. "Standing on the stool beside me with your big wooden spoon."

"Oh, and don't forget Cameron milling around in the background," Chloe adds helpfully. "She was *so* good at washing up, putting the dishes away, and sweeping up the crumbs."

Yes, cleaning up the disaster you left.

"Not to mention closing the cupboard doors!" Alice chimes in, and they fall about laughing.

Okay, I don't have space in my brain to deal with this now.

"I need to head off," I say hastily and wait for some sort of acknowledgment, but they're too engrossed in catching up. They launch into yet another hug, still squealing about how great it is to see each other.

It appears I have been long forgotten because neither notice me stalking off.

I swing around and spot Alice in her wide-brimmed straw hat and trademark apron milling around the fence, pretending to tend to the apple tree with a pair of pruning shears and looking nosy as ever. We used to joke that she slept in her apron. On occasion, when she forgot to take it off, she actually *did*.

Chloe's appalled expression softens, and she scrunches her forehead. "Alice?"

Alice drops her shears and dashes around the fence at speed, surprisingly nimble for a sixty-five-year-old with an arthritic hip. "Yes, Chloe! I just can't believe it!"

Before I know it, the sun comes out from behind a cloud, and they are rushing toward one another, all sheeny-eyed, like a scene from Gone with The Wind. Chloe even shoulder barges me on the way through, and they embrace in the weedy front yard.

Alice has been in my life ever since I can remember. She started as the help but soon became a fixture as my mom struggled with motherhood. She has always given me unconditional love, patience, and wisdom.

When my dad passed, it was Alice who held me as I cried. Not mom. For days, she stayed with me like a best friend, and I can't imagine my life without her. She has this uncanny sixth sense of knowing whenever I've had a rough day, and when I do, I always find a freshly baked sugary treat on my desk.

"I don't believe it. Where has all the time gone?" Alice kisses Chloe on the cheek and steps back to take

I also like the ten or so light freckles that dot her nose. They're new.

"I had a moment of regret, but it was only fleeting," I reply, and she shoots me a glare that could freeze a volcano. I grin, nodding toward the blue heap by the front curb. "You got your car back? Thought it would be at the wrecking yard."

She lets out an exasperated sigh. "For your information, it was only a loose wire in the undercarriage. Ted said it was in tip-top shape otherwise."

I have to bite my lip not to laugh. She is hot, I'll give her that. "Uh-huh. Lucky you -"

Her lips twist to the side as she cuts me off. "Anything else you wish to pester me about? I have a lot to do. Starting with sleep."

"You could clean up the overgrown garden," I reply, twisting around to assess the yard. "Looks like a snake house, and you know... devalues our property given the unfortunate proximity."

Chloe is practically spitting fire. How do I know? Because her brows bunch together, carving angry little lines into her forehead, just like they always did. "Do you want me to demolish the house too, Your Highness?"

It's not the quip but the courtesy that catches me off guard. "Well -"

"Little Chloe? Is that you?" asks a voice.

punch in the heart. It's also impossible not to register the scratches on her face, nor the dozen or so tracking up her arm.

"Just checking in to see how you are holding up after being chased by a terrifying army of geese," I say. Chloe blinks, prompting me to elaborate, "Yeah, I saw every deft move on our surveillance system. Even Sir Lancelot giving you a love tap on your behind." I point over my shoulder to a state-of-the-art camera fitted to a post inside the fence. "Some sleek maneuvering through the garden, but you'd hardly make a navy SEAL with your big head bobbing over the hedge."

"Big head -" she starts.

I wave my hand in a vague circle. "Please respect property lines and try to adhere to your side of the land." Chloe just scoffs, and I tilt my head to the side, surveying her coolly for a few seconds. "You know, you haven't really changed…"

Chloe sticks her chin out defiantly. "Neither have you. Still annoying as ever."

This earns her a snort, loud enough for it to echo through the yard. "Well, I'm glad your eyebrows grew back."

Her lips all but flatten. "Yeah, thank you so much for letting me be your waxing experiment. You realize I wore my knitted beanie the entire summer? Really enjoyed the hottest heat wave in history."

Firey as ever. I like it.

CHAPTER THREE

Cameron

I think it's time I pay my long-lost neighbor a visit, don't you?

Only just got here a few days ago, and she's brazenly trespassing. It's clear we need to set some boundaries. I steel myself for an interaction and then rush up to the front door, leaning heavily on the brass buzzer until I hear rapid-fire cursing.

I can't help but smile.

A second later, the door swings open.

"Morning, or should I say afternoon?" I beam.

Still in her pajamas and wearing a scowl, Chloe hangs off the door. Her messy honey-blond hair sticking up all over the place. She looks like she wants to beat me with the front doormat. "Oh, to what do I owe this pleasure?" she snips.

This is how she greets me.

I study her face now that I can see her in the light. Sooty lashes framing huge brown eyes, smooth skin, sulky mouth. Sure, the terrain is slightly different, but when I recognized her across the car roof, it felt like a

fry pan). Thankfully, though, I got a yes, and so now, I'm here, but it's hardly a vacation.

Maybe when this is done and dusted, I can treat myself to a *real* one.

damn accordion. I hate you too, I tell it telepathically, but my frown soon morphs into a smile when I pick up my phone. It's Sarah, my co-worker at my day job.

Don't stress. Everything is under control here :)

Then there's a photo of my workstation, computer, and chair buried under an avalanche of bras.

I snort out a laugh.

Sarah and I work in the same cubicle, toiling away for one of the buyers, Chantel. Basically, I'm a glorified data entry clerk processing orders all day like a battery hen. Will Sarah get in trouble for decorating my workstation? Doubt it. I'd bet my life that Gerry, our boss, an Irish rogue, put her up to the prank. Gerry is bald, forty-five, and has a penchant for garish green suspenders and tasseled loafers. I love Gerry. He didn't even blink an eye when I asked for two weeks off.

Total contrast to Guiseppe, the manager at Arrivederci!, who looked at me like I'd just cracked the world's funniest joke. For nine days while he was infuriatingly still *thinking* about it, I did nothing but suck up to him - fetching his dry-cleaning, pouring cream and stevia into his coffee, and even chauffeuring his pet ferret, Aurelio, to the salon.

He's my boss, so I couldn't tell him to hurry the fuck up, but I really wanted to. I had so many murderous thoughts that I almost cracked him over the head with our heaviest *la padella in ghisa* (cast iron

Chloe

Two hours post-geese mishap, I'm in a better place.

I've had yet another shower, and my leggings now share the same fate as my banana peel, but it's the trip to the corner store and a chocolate fudge muffin the size of my head that *really* improves my mood.

Oddly, these geese may have done me a favor because now I'm more resolute than ever to get the hell out of here. I whip open the musty curtains and creaky windows, leaning out for fresh air while praying for a freak gust of wind to clear the stench. But then I spot the goose that bit my ass approaching and quickly retreat inside.

Sighing, I perch myself on the mustard-colored kitchen counter and write a to-do list. However, it soon resembles a dossier, so I whittle it down to a few key tasks: purge clutter, replace downstairs carpet, plug up fist-holes in walls, and make garden semi-presentable. It's all I can afford. I know it needs *everything*, but I'm hoping it's enough to sell the place at a reasonable price.

Rolling up my sleeves, I start clearing out room by room. By early evening, every inch of the living area is taken up with bags of *stuff*, plus random items like an accordion and a rocking horse that no longer rocks.

"So much freaking crap," I groan, glancing around, but I'm nowhere near finished. Now, what's trash and what's goodwill?

Thankfully, my phone pings and it earns me a reprieve. Stumbling over bags, I stub my toe on that sparkling windows, I lose count. Freshly painted white French doors open to expansive, honey-lit gardens, and I immediately get a vision of a young Cameron and me zooming around the manicured green lawns with paper airplanes, high on Coca-Cola and cherry-flavored Twizzlers. Spending sticky summer days eating butterscotch vanilla ice cream and splashing each other in their fountain -

HONK!

What the –

I swivel around and lock eyes with a regal-looking white goose. Out of nowhere, two more geese appear, honking their protest.

My heart stops.

The geese charge toward me, flapping their wings furiously. Awash with adrenaline, I pivot and sprint away. Rose thorns jab at my arms, branches whip my face, and some winged monstrosity the size of my hand goes splat on my forehead. Who knew geese were so damn fast? Or maybe I'm just slow because the regal one nips my behind as I vault over the fence, and I crash down in a messy mix of dirt and concrete, accompanied by a cacophony of honking.

The wind knocked well and truly out of my sails, I fall back in a sweating, shaking heap and stare up to clouds above, rueing this place as much as I ever have.

I knew coming back here was a bad idea.

It doesn't take long until my mind gravitates next door, wondering if it's changed. I rush over to the window but can't see much except Cameron's room, which is the last room on the right. The rest of the façade is blocked out by a fortress of hedges.

Should I have a quick peep?

Of course, I should!

Grinning, I slip on my sneakers one by one as I hop out of my room and rush down the stairs. I creep out the back door, scanning left and right, and then clamber over the wooden fence with all the stealth of a heavy-footed elephant, slightly ripping my leggings in the process, but never mind. Why was this so much easier as a kid?

I zip around an ornamental pond and cut through a rose garden that could put Hallmark to shame, only to meet the judgmental gaze of an owl in the bird bath. What? I glare back defiantly. Unfortunately, I'm not paying attention to the ground and trip over something.

"Oh, shit," I mutter, but then I do a double take and snuffle with laughter. Garden gnomes?! When did Cameron Maxwell get into garden gnomes!

Scrambling to place the gnomes upright, I run through the yard and come to a crouching stop behind a hornbeam hedge. Hmm, not bad, Agent Chloe. Not bad.

Ever so slowly, I peek over the top, taking in the elegant brick exterior cloaked in lush green vines, the imposing square portico entrance, and so many big, escaped from the coop. They're running riot in the kitchen! Elliot, get out of the dishwasher! Better dash, Chloe!"

The screen moves sharply, and a sharp beak fills the frame, then a pair of beady orange eyes.

"Love you!" I yell.

"Argh! Chickens everywhere! Yes, me too. I mean, love you -"

There's a massive squawk and rush of feathers as the line clicks dead.

I laugh and bolt up to my room, unzipping my bag. It doesn't matter what we talk about, I always feel better after chatting with my aunt.

Snagging a towel and some fresh clothes, I shower in the avocado-colored bathroom straight out of the seventies. Feeling refreshed, I call Ted at the local repair shop to organize a tow and try not to keel over when he quotes the job. But even as I munch on a blackened banana from the depths of my bag, memories from my time in this house are never far away.

I sit on the edge of the bed and sigh, then lob my banana peel into the trashcan under my desk. It's only been one night, and I'm already physically aching for my life in New York. I miss the quaint two-bedroom red-brick apartment in Brooklyn that I share with Lexi and her million green plants. I miss the noise, the never-ending hustle. I like that it keeps my mind busy. It's too quiet here to block out all my thoughts.

"After discussing weather patterns for a few awkward minutes, he decided to tell me about the time he was abducted by grey aliens. Apparently, they're the bad ones. Something about purging his childhood from memory. He wears a tin foil hat to bed because that wards off -" She stops mid-sentence, and I don't know who bursts out laughing first. Only that we keep laughing until our sides ache.

Through hiccups of laughter, she wipes away her tears while I try to pull myself together. "Ah... Well, obviously, I didn't hang around for dessert, and when I got home, I was so rattled that I shut down my account for good."

My heart sinks. "But you -"

She raises her hand. "Wait, Chloe. You'll be proud. I made myself a gin gimlet, then set up my profile on that other website you recommended that's only for seniors."

I grin while she attempts to prise open a window. "Oh, good. I don't want you to give up," I reply. "Any likes yet?"

"Yes, a few. Two over eighty years old. Also, a priest from Azerbaijan wanting financial assistance. Wherever the heck that is. And some guy of similar age, and only a stone's throw away in Maine. He sounded promising, but then he told me he belonged to a cult and was looking to add to his polyamorous relationship. As exciting as they were, I had to regrettably decline. Still hopeful, though -" There's a massive shriek. "Oh my God, the chickens have

I scratch my forehead. "Sorry, still processing the trauma."

She chuckles. "Can't be that bad!"

"Ugh, it can. It kind of started on the wrong foot. Mel was late, so I started googling her at the bar, and well, you know how she was a psychologist? Turns out she was delisted. And she was also divorced, right? Nope, according to Google, she was living with her partner."

Her eyes widen. "Oh, dear."

"Probably should've googled her *before* I agreed to a date. Anyway, she eventually turned up three sheets to the wind. You know, wasted, and calling me Carrie. By that stage, I couldn't even be bothered to correct her. Twenty minutes later, she threw up on my shoes."

My aunt snorts, then covers her mouth. "Oh, my... And I thought my date with Boris was bad."

"Boris! You should never trust a man called Boris," I gurgle.

"Oh, gosh. Now you tell me. Well, first of all, he looked nothing like his photo! Ruddy complexion, massive pot belly. I was going to sit at another table because I didn't recognize him. He waved me over. Said something about having a rough year -"

I start laughing.

"It's not funny, Chloe. Anyway, I really needed to sit after all my yard work, so I decided to take a chance." She shakes her head, sighing.

"And?"

She'd say things like, "*Chloe, why are you wearing those awful shoes? They look like they're from Walmart*", and "*I don't want to go to our usual restaurant, Chloe. They never look me in the eye.*"

I remember thinking who is this moron? I tried to make excuses like she's the weather girl now! She has to learn about important things like cumulus clouds, high-pressure systems, and category-five hurricanes! She must be bursting with stress! Seemingly forgetting all of my own.

As much as I saw red flags, I didn't leave. It appears to be a recurring theme of mine, hanging onto relationships when they no longer serve me. For months, I *knew*. Still, it felt like a savage burn when Lexi saw her making out with her boss, Daria, ironically in the parking lot of Walmart. Had she been cheating for a while? Probably. You don't go from running coffee to weather girl just like that.

The two lovebirds were engaged a month later, and honestly, if I had a spare second to scratch myself, I would've totally capitulated.

You see, I've wanted a family for as long as I can remember. Marriage, white picket fence, giggly babies, and definitely a dopey big rescue dog, yet not once in my relationship with Erin did we even broach the subject of marriage or living together. Despite telling myself otherwise, I knew in my gut that we were never going to get there, so why didn't I just leave?

"Chloe, your date? What happened?" My aunt probes.

"Easier said than done. Trust me, I know how hard it is to say no to her, but you need to look after yourself at some point."

"I know."

I also know that it breaks my aunt's heart not to be able to help her sister. She's the kindest woman ever, so when she's at the end of her tether, it means something. It's hard to fathom that they're related when they are such different people.

Aunt Marcy decides to go for a more upbeat angle. Nonetheless still tragic. "So, how did your date go last weekend?"

I groan, and she giggles.

Aunt Marcy and I recently signed up to the eMagic dating site. Her ex-husband, Alf, was a douchebag who had an awful combover and shit ties. A pilot for Budget Air, he left her for a stewardess he met on a transatlantic flight to Frankfurt. Apparently, he just had twins at the spritely age of sixty-six. Good luck with that, Alf.

Obviously, I have zero time for this matchmaking stuff, but I want my aunt to meet someone amazing, and if that means I have to suffer a little, then so be it.

It's been four months since Erin and I broke up. At first, I blamed myself, even for her affair, but she'd been distant for months, making excuses not to see me. I certainly noticed a seismic shift when she was promoted. It's as if she grew a big head overnight.

Collapsing onto my bed, I quickly FaceTime my aunt to let her know I arrived safely. I smile as soon as I see her massive hair and 1960s shirt dress with red rocket ships launch through the screen door.

"Hi, darling! How's it being back?" she asks, pulling off her garden gloves.

"Hey. Interesting, I guess. Hang on, I'll give you a quick tour." I flip the screen and zig-zag through the house.

"Place hasn't changed much," she says of the upper level, but when I scamper downstairs to the living room, she lets out a volume-defying "Good lord!" that echoes off the walls.

I turn my phone back to me, and unsurprisingly, my aunt is wearing a frown. She slumps down on a wooden chair. "Looks like a squatter's den, Chloe. Are you honestly safe there?"

"It'll be okay," I say with a tired but determined smile and try to downplay the level of disrepair because I don't want her stressing about me even more. "Just need to purge, fix a few things, give it a good clean. Won't be too hard."

My aunt wipes her sweaty brow. "Mmm. If you say so... Your mom hasn't called, has she?"

"No. And don't worry, I know. I'm not going to enable her anymore."

"But when she gets wind of your inheritance. Well, you know how she is."

"Please don't worry, I'm fine."

for manipulating each conversation, and even though I knew what she was doing, I caved every time.

My anxiety skyrocketed while my savings tanked.

It also took a toll on my relationship with Erin. We started arguing a lot, so I picked up a second job at Arrivederci! to ease the stress. Around the same time, Erin got promoted to weather girl, and we saw even less of each other. Then, she dumped me. Erin called me boring and weak, and I suppose I was. Who wanted to be with someone who worked day and night? Someone who couldn't say no to being so overtly manipulated? Turns out Erin was also cheating on me, but hey, small details.

Anyway, six months later and barely afloat, I'm still at the restaurant. I say "restaurant" loosely because we're constantly gifted one stars on Google, and last week, we had an outbreak of norovirus. There also isn't a second where I don't want to take a mallet to the looping Tony Bennett CD.

To be honest, selling my father's property and the financial relief it will provide feels like a lifeline. I'm heavily indebted to both my aunt and Lexi and want to repay them ASAP. I'm praying the extra money will also let me quit Arrivederci! because the lack of sleep is starting to make me drop all my figurative plates. For example, last Tuesday at work, I accidentally ordered thirty thousand contour plunge double D bras in lime-green. Thirty thousand! That's a lot when you're supposed to order three hundred.

While college wasn't for me, I managed to graduate from high school, got a job, and tried to save money every paycheck. I stayed with my aunt until I was twenty-two, then traded my comfy shoes for my big girl ones and moved to New York.

I didn't want to leave, but she said that I needed to spread my wings and convinced me that we couldn't be roommates forever (still have my doubts). So, that's what I did. I found some bar work, some friends, and slowly, my own two feet. Meanwhile, my relationship with my mom remained elusive. She never had a fixed address or phone number and only really contacted me when she wanted something. Every interaction left me rattled.

Then, when I was twenty-four, she disappeared completely from my adult life, and funny enough, so did my anxiety. Everything felt easier without her around. I landed a great job at The Bra Bar with an amazing team, moved in with my soon-to-be best friend, Lexi, and even started seeing Erin Brockman, who worked as coffee girl in the newsroom at NPC. It was my first serious relationship.

Things were bliss, stress-free, for a long time. Well, two years and twenty-five days, to be exact, because that's the day my mom walked back into my life. In a warped way, I felt guilty that I was thriving, and she wasn't.

She wanted money, and I gave it to her because she was my mom, whatever that meant. She had a knack

Corey was like most teenagers, grunting through conversation and surgically attached to his phone, so we didn't hang out much, and a year later, he ran off to college in California to study marine biology.

In some way, I think I filled the void left by Corey's absence, and Aunt Marcy, well, she filled every void my mom left painfully bare. She scraped by, working her ass off in low-paid jobs, making sure I could have nice things like my friends – new clothes, even horse-riding lessons until we both admitted in relief that I was too shit at it to continue. Regardless, Aunt Marcy never complained. She just got on with things.

We had Burger Fridays with mince expiring that day and Roma tomatoes from our garden, and watched Family Feud together with our imaginary buzzers. I hardly ever knew any answers, but boy, did I love smacking that buzzer. I was just happy my aunt wanted me by her side.

She braided my hair while I made a bird's nest mess out of hers, attempting to recreate Hollywood-worthy styles. She even read an excerpt from my favorite book every night for a year just because I liked it.

She is my sunshine, my guardian angel. Memories of my mom, on the other hand, are like a revolving door of missed birthdays and holidays. I blanked a lot of them. Growing up, my heart had been littered with broken promises.

I'll change soon.

Everything will be different, you'll see.

forlorn as ever. I was never a great student. Perhaps that had something to do with my mom, but I can't lump her with all my shortcomings.

I think I was eight when I first realized something was off with her. I walked into the kitchen after school, and she was necking a bottle of vodka, watching the microwave spin round and round like it was the greatest show on Earth. Five minutes later, there was an astronomical boom, and the microwave exploded into smithereens. Both of us fortunate not to have suffered the same fate.

Police carted Mom off to a mental health facility while I was temporarily placed with my Aunt Marcy. I don't remember much in between, except that my mom slept a lot.

Then, when I was ten, I found my mom unresponsive and splayed out on the floor with foam trickling from her mouth while a dozen empty pill bottles kept her company. Remembering my aunt's training, I dialed 911, fingers cupping Mom's cheek as I stared into her vacant eyes.

Questions weighted with child confusion ping-ponged in my brain: Did she not even love me? How could she not care?

My parents split; my father didn't want me. Authorities had no choice but to place me permanently with my aunt in Vermont. Her loser husband moved out just as I moved in, and she had to raise two children: her sixteen-year-old son, Corey, and me.

That same year, I was shipped off to my aunt's, but I never forgot the burn of her rejection.

I let out a groan, still struggling to come to terms with the fact that wrench-wielding Aphrodite was her. Gone were the geeky glasses, braces, freaky curls, and in their place, a very formidable and attractive woman.

"Damn you, Cameron," I mutter and kick off my sneakers, falling back on my bed in a plume of dust.

My gaze fixes on the glow-in-the-dark stars and crescent moons on the ceiling, and my eyelids begin to twitch in exhaustion. I used to stare at this same constellation as a child, wishing I could escape to a faraway galaxy.

Funny, all these years later, and I have the exact same wish.

The next thing I know, it's morning.

For a split second, I wake with no idea where I am. My eyes are stubbornly glued together, and my nose is frozen like it hitched a ride on the Polar Express. Slowly, though, my world starts coming back to me in pieces. Not used to the single narrow mattress, when I roll over to check my phone, I flop straight onto the scratchy, office-gray carpet.

Goddammit.

Craning my neck, I notice the greasy blots left by Blu-Tack on the walls, once adorned with posters of bygone pop idols like the legendary Britney. Then there's my study nook at the end, looking as sad and

December, possibly to get some answers, but they never came.

Meanwhile, the Maxwell house looks exactly like it did as a kid, taunting me with its gleam, superiority. And right inside those shiny walls, Cameron Maxwell, who looked nothing like she did when she was twelve. Apparently, they moved in next door a few years before us and promptly bulldozed the existing farmhouse because it wasn't up to their standards.

So, Cameron and I were soon forced together by sheer proximity and lack of other playmates in the street. She was a couple of years older than me, kind of annoying and precocious, yet we still hung out. She would test things on me – makeup, clothes, new hairstyles. I took it all in my stride. Shimmery eyeshadow, bold fluoro headbands, choppy bangs.

I didn't care; I got to escape my mom for a while.

Being with Cameron was like a clandestine cave I could crawl into. But then, as my mom got worse, I saw less and less of her. She stopped hanging out at the fence with me, and I wondered what I did wrong. Too scared to go to her door, I popped a crayon-written invitation to my tenth birthday not long after in her letterbox, but she never replied.

Somehow, though, in my subconscious, I was certain it was because she thought she was better than me. Either way, from then on, I only saw her on rare occasions when she was chauffeured to ballet class or fancy events.

Addiction is an illness, but my father, well, what was his excuse?

Bruce Bentley was the local mechanic who preferred the sanctuary of his garage or the camaraderie down at the sports bar. He had places to hide; I didn't.

When my father was home, which wasn't often, it was like navigating a walking storm cloud. He was tired, grumpy, and about as welcoming as a thorn bush. The last thing he wanted to do was engage with an energetic kid. Sure, he paid the bills, stocked the pantry with staples, and occasionally tackled the unruly lawn, but he didn't take an interest in me, not really. More often than not, he'd say, "Don't annoy me, Chloe. I'm not in the mood."

So, I learned to stay away from him and grew up overnight. Despite limited food options, I always had lunch for school, either a peanut butter and jelly or cream cheese sandwich, and a Ziploc bag full of apple slices.

I also began to cook for Mom and me. I'd stand on a wobbly stool, given my small size, and I'd be there for hours honing my craft, and also, my core muscles. Cooking helped me escape my reality, and I could block everything out with a wooden spoon and a trusty fry pan. It was my secret power. All kids need one, and that was mine.

Suffice it to say, I didn't have much of a relationship with my dad. I did visit him at a senior care facility before he passed away from dementia last that I cough. Gross, this place stinks like ass. Hardly surprising as I glance around and note the sad state of my old home. It's been rented for several years to questionable tenants, and it shows. The last lot evicted for non-payment and noise complaints.

The once-vibrant pink poppy wallpaper is now peeling, while the same orange shag carpet I grew up with is stained and a murky brown. A small flat TV is bolted to the wall, and a box of Carlsberg beer topped with a slab of oak serves as an improvised coffee table. Classy. Looks like someone used the walls as a punching bag, too. One, two, three holes -

Okay, I lose count.

Sighing out loud, I turn off the light and effortlessly weave my way up to my bedroom. Unlike downstairs, it's much the same as I left it. Small, sparse, and uninspiring. There's a single bed, a yellow bedside table, and a rickety set of shelves with a noticeable sag in the middle.

Dropping my bag to the floor, I walk over to the window in a trance-like state and rub a small area on the frosty glass pane with my sleeve, peering out to the landscape and then to the Maxwell residence, twinkling next door like the North Star.

I often stood here wondering why I couldn't have her family. Why did I get the short end of the stick and have a mom who battled with addiction? An absent father who was more focused on working on his prized 1963 Chevrolet Corvette down at the workshop?

CHAPTER TWO

Chloe

Me and my big mouth.

"Dumbass," I mutter, tearing off my nametag and shoving it into my pocket.

Tugging my bag up the uneven steps, I trip a few times in the darkness. Serves me right. She looked nothing like the gawky, pale-faced Cameron I once knew. Still, small town. And hardly going out of her way, the woman lives next door!

Honestly, how I even managed a cordial goodnight at the end is beyond me.

Rifling around my bag, I fish out some keys, and the sensor light snaps on, blinding me in an instant. Argh. Squinting, I unlock the chalky green front door and stumble inside.

Just like that, I'm back. Home. But it's not home anymore.

Standing in the foyer of the house I once grew up in, an ache hits me. More nostalgic than pleasant.

My hand slides around the wall until I find the light switch, and when I flick it on, I inhale so sharply

Apparently, I'm not the only person who could use a driving lesson. I bite my tongue for fear of sounding ungrateful.

"Well... Here we are," she announces, engine still running.

"Oh, right," I murmur, glancing to my right, and there's an instant pit in my stomach.

My small two-story childhood home just sits there in the darkness, looking as unappealing as ever. There's not even a number on the mailbox anymore, just tangled spiderwebs.

How did I think I could actually do this?

The woman clears her throat, and I twist in my seat. "Sorry, I won't hold you up any longer. I really appreciate you going out of your way so late at night. I hope you don't have far to travel."

She offers a tight smile. "No bother."

I extend my hand. "And I'm Chloe, by the way."

"Yes, I know," she replies, pointing to the askew nametag on my t-shirt, and I feel my cheeks burn.

I'm also expecting her to introduce herself, given that I'm holding out my hand like some weirdo, but she just looks at me blankly, so I prompt her. "And you are?"

A nerve flinches in her cheek. "Cameron... Cameron Maxwell."

Not surprisingly, I don't get a handshake in return.

"Huh?" I glance in her direction. "Oh. Well, my dad passed a few months ago. I'll be selling the family home and tying up loose ends. Hopefully, only here for a couple of weeks," I say, fidgeting with my seatbelt.

"Sorry about your dad."

I shrug. "Yeah... You a local?"

She seems to consider this before nodding. "Yes."

I turn back to my window as wooded forest gives way to grassy fields and the odd farmhouse. Soon, I watch Diamond Hill zip past me in all its small-town glory. Diamond Hill, population five hundred and fifty-two, or like I used to say, "too many." The town didn't offer much and seemed to shrink yearly as people moved to bigger cities for work. "It hasn't really changed. Still looks the same almost twenty years later."

"Lots of moose back then, too?" she asks.

"Heaps," I squeak but refuse to make eye contact and watch shadowy streets scroll past my window. I need to change the topic. "Tell me, do the Maxwell family still live next door in their mega mansion?"

"Father had a heart attack six years ago, so the mom moved to Paris, but the daughter is there -"

I slap my hands over my eyes. "Oh, God. Cameron Maxwell... Stuck up, little brat. Probably still as horrible."

"Uh-huh. A total nightmare."

A few minutes later, we come to an abrupt stop, and I jolt forward. Jesus, this woman can't drive.

"Bentley residence. 242 Cotton Way. You know it?"

She stiffens and then nods. "I do."

We slip into the car, fasten our seatbelts, and she starts the ignition while I maintain an iron grip on my bag, still fifty-fifty on whether I'll be murdered tonight. I sniff and assess the surroundings. New car, European leather mixed in with her perfume, which is not too sweet, earthy yet feminine. A far cry from the Sprite slash potato chip aroma in my Toyota. I note the Audi logo on the steering wheel. There's even a real Tissot watch sparkling on her wrist! I only recognize it because my mom recently tried to sell me a knock-off in one of her more creative extortion attempts.

As we roll forward, I steal a proper sideways glance at my mystery savior, now cast in the dim glow of the dashboard. Serious car, serious clothes... seriously bossy – she must be some bigwig professional. I have to wonder what someone like her is doing out here at this hour.

I think she's about my age, twenty-seven, but unlike me, she has flawless olive skin, wavy dark hair, fashionable side bangs, and sharp cheekbones. A small scar above her right brow catches my eye, triggering a vague sense of déjà vu that vanishes before I can try to interpret it because she presses down on the accelerator, hard, and there's a squirt of gravel. My head is thrust back into my buttery seat, and in an instant, the world outside transforms into a hazy blur.

Eyes pinned to the road, she eventually asks, "So, why are you going there?"

"Your hand?"

"A tire wrench."

It's now my turn to narrow my eyes.

"In case *you* were a serial killer!" she quips.

Her explanation seems reasonable.

"Hmm, okay..." I reply slowly, then unclip my seatbelt and pack away my glasses since I won't be driving anymore. I deliberate whether to take my menacing umbrella (I do), along with my duffel bag, and hop out of my car, making sure to lock it.

Just as the potential killer navigates the gravel in her nude heels with the odd slight stumble, I pause and look up to the skies for some divine intervention. *God, I really don't want to end up in a body bag.*

The woman stops mid-stride, glancing over her shoulder. "You know, I'm not standing out here all night while you pray. Don't give me ideas," she says, waving her wrench in swirls of frosty air.

I scoff and shuffle after her, snapping into her skirt-clad rear, "I'm armed, so don't even think about it because I will knock you out in one fell swoop."

Even though I'm a good foot shorter than her and could blow over in a gust of wind, they're fighting words. I hope she takes me seriously. Illuminated by the silvery moonlight, I see her mouth twitch.

Brilliant. She does not.

I stop by the passenger door, and our eyes meet over the car roof. "So, where are you heading?" she asks.

A headline flashes in my mind.

TWENTY-SOMETHING MEETS A GRISLY END AFTER ACCEPTING A LATE-NIGHT RIDE IN THE WOODS

She showed so much promise, laments Gerry, owner of The Bra Bar. She was on track to becoming a buyer in intimate apparel... probably even within the next ten years!

I shake my head, snapping back to the present. "I mean, no," I reiterate. "You might be a serial killer."

An incredulous smile tugs at the corner of her lips. "Ha. I'm wearing heels and a skirt."

"And they're usually the worst!"

This earns me an eye-roll. "Oh, for God's sake. It's late and cold. I'll give you a lift into town. Nobody is going to rescue you tonight. There's no cell service. Do you really want to spend the night in your car perched on top of a pine tree? I mean, you might draw attention to yourself." She waves her hand in the air. "Just saying..."

I remain stock-still.

Her head tilts back, and she lets out a slow exhale. "I'm not going to hurt you."

Says probably every serial killer in the history of serial killers.

"What's in your hand?" I inquire cautiously.

"What?"

God, go away.

Another thump.

Closing my eyes briefly, I crack open the window a mere inch, and that's when I hear it – the sharp, annoyed tones of a woman's voice slicing through the silence.

"Are you freaking insane? I almost crashed into you. This is not a parking lot," she snaps.

I turn to the gap in the window, and the only thing I can make out are piercing cobalt blue eyes.

"I'm hardly parking here!" I hiss back in an equally prickly tone. "I swerved to miss... a moose."

She stares back at me in bewilderment. "A moose?"

I knew it was too much the second it left my lips. The only moose I've seen was on a field trip to the Canadian prairies in junior high, but I can hardly back out now. "Yes," I confirm grimly. "Anyway, I can't seem to steer."

The woman takes a step back and glances down. "Might have something to do with that colossal branch you seem to be impaled on."

Her powers of deduction are outstanding.

She sighs loudly, her shoulders slumping beneath a sweeping dark coat. "Well, get out."

Is she nuts?

"No." I fold my arms in defiance.

She studies me, head tilted to one side. Her eyes narrow slits of deep ocean. "What do you mean no?"

Snatching my phone from the center console, I stare grimly at the moon glow of the screen. "Brilliant. No service either -"

There's an inconsiderate honk, and I startle, my head snapping up so fast my glasses catapult off my face just as someone yells, "Get off the road, moron!"

Are you kidding me?

"Asshole," I growl under my breath and fumble on the floor for my glasses, watching the taillights of the sleek car whoosh past with contempt. Then, out of the blue, the car slams on its brakes, reversing along the gravelly shoulder.

Oh, shit.

I've watched enough crime shows to know that I should lock the doors, but I can't for the life of me remember what to do next. As I mull this over, the driver's door swings open, and a slender figure approaches with something dangling from their hand. I squint into the dark. A weapon?

Fuck me.

My eyes fly around the interior of my banged-up sky-blue Toyota. All I have is a pathetic compact umbrella in an even more pathetic pastel yellow. The button doesn't even work, and I have to force the metal spokes up with my fingers, holding the limp frame in position.

Just as I'm hating on my umbrella, a fist thumps the glass pane, and I nearly jump a mile. Instinctively, I shake my head.

I'm just determined to get there. Flanked by open fields, the windy road begins to narrow, and I feel panicky as the area becomes increasingly familiar, even in the dark.

There's only one thing that can help this dire situation – sugar. Stretching over to the glove box, I dig out a warm bottle of Sprite and unscrew the cap. Bringing it to my lips, I take a large gulp when – bam!

My brakes screech, the car swerves, and I narrowly avoid flattening a tiny rat-like creature, only to skillfully mount a branch the size of a tree trunk. Rattled, I just sit there with half my Sprite down my front as a plethora of warning lights come on. I have no idea what they mean, but one thing's clear – it can't be good.

"Of all the times..." I mutter angrily, then press the accelerator and limp up the road. The tree trapped beneath scrapes the bitumen like nails on a chalkboard. Unable to pull in completely off the road, I grind to a half some fifty yards later.

Smacking my steering wheel with one hand, I slump back in my seat with a defeated yawn. I'm wrecked, and it's no surprise, I'm juggling two jobs to keep afloat. During the day, I work in admin at intimate apparel company, The Bra Bar. After hours, I'm a server at Arrivederci!, a small Italian eatery. I glance down at my uniform – black tee and black jeans – and curse my mom.

I'm in this situation because of *you*.

CHAPTER ONE

Chloe

"Whyyy? Why am I going there?"

It's a desolate one in the morning, the air cloaked in darkness, and I'm heading down the freeway in the wrong direction. I'm also chatting to my steering wheel. Clearly, I'm starting to lose my mind, but not because it's late or because I've been driving for three hours – it's the destination. You see, I've successfully avoided my hometown of Diamond Hill until now.

I'd rather get my teeth pulled by a backyard dentist, or even find myself trapped in the broom closet with smelly "B.O." Bob from the second floor.

Okay, you get my drift. I do *not* want to be here.

It's only come about because my dad passed away a few months ago and bequeathed me, his only child, the family home. My brain was too small to record too many memories from back then, but the ones I had stuck forever. Family? What a joke.

Thoughts of my childhood play out in my head until my knuckles turn ghostly white against the leather of the steering wheel. Condensation gathers on my windows as I finally pull onto a slip road, and now,

Copyright © 2024 Olivia Lucas
All Rights Reserved

FIND ME UNDER THE STARS

Olivia Lucas